'PAYBACK'
WHEN DUTY CALLS

Published by Brolga Publishing Pty Ltd
ABN 46 063 962 443
PO Box 12544
A'Beckett St
Melbourne, VIC, 8006
Australia

email: markzocchi@brolgapublishing.com.au

National Library of Australia Cataloguing-in-Publication entry
       Author: Cleggett, Harvey, author.
       Title: Payback, when duty calls / Harvey Cleggett.
       ISBN: 9781922175250 (paperback)
       Dewey Number: A823.4

Printed in Indonesia
Cover design by Chameleon Print Design
Typeset by Wanissa Somsuphangsri

BE PUBLISHED

Publish Through a Successful Publisher. National Distribution, Macmillan & International Distribution to the United Kingdom, North America. Sales Representation to South East Asia
Email: markzocchi@brolgapublishing.com.au

'PAYBACK'
WHEN DUTY CALLS

Harvey Cleggett

To my wife Leanne who I love and
cherish as my companion for life.

To my son Steven who continues to
exceed my expectations.

CHAPTER
1

Less than twenty-six hours after the brutal execution style slaying in which the victim was found hung, with hands bound and wearing a bullet hole above his right eye, the first golden rays of dawn appeared at 4.50 a.m. as predicted by the TV weatherman. Within minutes warming sunlight washed over the ranch style home, illuminating the slate grey roof. Wide inviting verandas surrounded the homestead with wrought iron bench seats positioned to escape the chill winter winds and scorching summer sun.

Manicured lawns abutted the house on all sides. A tennis court with basketball ring and backboard was located to the east of the homestead. Hidden behind a line of adjoining pine trees were the forest green concrete walls of a squash court.

Continuing north through the property towards the driveway entrance, past the pergola, flying fox, children's swings and sand pit were further landscaped grounds, culminating in a purpose built lake fifty metres across. Complete with jetty, waterfall and island, the lake formed a sanctuary for birdlife and multiple species of frogs. Dark green buffalo grass grew from the water's edge, cascading up over the lake's bank, merging into the lush lawn covering the surrounding expanse of land.

Set on the property line was a brick and bluestone fence, complete with four gate posts, displaying two engraved brass plates with the words 'Ballard Estate'. A bluestone bordered gravel driveway curved in a giant serpentine S one hundred and thirty metres down to the house; the driveway separating the lake on the left from a copse of silver birch, numerous golden Cyprus pine, plus hundreds of native gums on the right. Chelsea Road, which traversed the entire frontage of the property ended in a court.

At 5 a.m., ten minutes after the first glimmer of daylight, the Bose clock radio sprang to life in the master bedroom announcing the 1278 AM news. Detective Inspector Michael Ballard blinked several times to clear his vision, then, glaring at the alarm, stretched his 186 centimetre frame long and hard in the king-size bed. The bedclothes enveloped him in a seductive cocoon of warmth, causing him to flirt with the notion of hitting the snooze button; he resisted the temptation.

The broadcast went on to remind him of the macabre murder of a factory owner, the reason why he had set the alarm so early on what should have been his day off. He felt his pulse quicken as he anticipated the adrenalin charged hunt for the vicious killer or killers, appreciating just how close he had come to losing forever the privilege of participating in these crucial investigations.

He reflected back to his forty-fifth birthday, having spent twenty-five years with the state police, the last fifteen in Homicide. He recalled handing in his resignation, then, within hours, numerous senior management and long time friends challenging him on the wisdom of his decision. In the following days members of his family had questioned his judgement, knowing his intense love for the job.

Recently divorced for a second time and recognising a midlife crisis was a factor in the decision, he had argued that successful property investments throughout his adult life, along with a substantial inheritance meant now was the time to explore other opportunities and experiences. Deep in his heart he feared leaving the force may be a huge mistake; it had become his second family. Once experienced, the camaraderie was intoxicating, almost impossible to walk away from.

During weeks of deliberation in which he had taken leave, the two combatants of reason had raged within him. On the one hand was the powerful allure of peaceful, idyllic days spent on the estate, free to do whatever he chose. Opposing this was the immense satisfaction derived from bringing justice to victims of major crime, while utilising his many investigative talents developed over decades. Throughout this mental conflict he had recognised the day was fast approaching when a younger detective would and should take his place, but that time had not yet arrived.

As a consequence, six years after submitting his resignation he remained in the job, in Homicide, at the same rank. However, there was one significant compromise. He now worked four day weeks unless a challenging case came to light. This was a concession granted in recognition of his years of service, including his ongoing mentoring role to junior members; an activity he enjoyed and excelled at.

The discovery of a factory owner's body in Lalor, strung from a noose inside his own business premises proved to be one of those challenging cases Ballard had jumped at. The news broadcast failed to add anything of significance to the original announcement, however, due to the gruesome circumstances the story was still considered news worthy. He reflected on the sad reality that human suffering contributed more and more to the grist of everyday media coverage.

Tossing aside the bed clothes he stood tall, stretched his lean frame one more time before pulling on shorts and Tshirt. Grabbing a towel from the adjacent en-suite, he padded barefoot along the tiled hallway which ran the centre of the house, noting that despite it being the end of spring there was still a crisp chill in the air, the cold ceramic tiles underfoot reminding him of this fact.

At the far end of the corridor he entered the sports room. This was part of an extension which had an adjoining self-contained Bed and Breakfast and been built soon after he submitted his resignation.

Even though he had made the decision to remain with the police force, the B&B felt like an alternative lifestyle that he would one day pursue as a part-time business. He smiled as he pictured himself greeting his future guests: carrying their suitcases, instructing them in the use of the electronic equipment, how to obtain the best results in the gym and all the while engaging in small talk as he signed them through the register.

Ballard pulled the sports room door shut then flicked on the down lights. The room was large; twelve metres by eight and aptly named. One third of the floor contained a full complement of gymnasium equipment positioned on protective rubber matting.

Against one wall was a Meili massage chair. A forty-two inch flat screen TV was secured on the far wall, viewable from any piece of equipment in the room. Against the right hand wall, located alongside the BodyCraft strength training tower was a

Canadian cedar, infrared heated, three person sauna, complete with radio.

Located in the centre of the room was a three quarter sized pool table with down lights positioned to ensure no area of the table's surface was in shadow. Mounted on the wall nearby were the pool cues, chalks and rack.

The remaining area of the sports room contained a table tennis and air-hockey table. Both used extensively whenever Ballard had family and friends over. It filled him with immense pleasure to see the room hosting up to ten people at a time, alternatively sweating over exercise equipment or in the sauna, enjoying a massage in the chair, playing eight-ball or snooker, pretending to be Olympic standard table tennis players, or shouting as they battled each other at the air-hockey table. The cumulative noise in the room was often deafening, but he enjoyed every moment of it.

Twenty minutes later, lungs heaving with exertion, convinced his daily routine maintained his cardio fitness, he flicked off the lights and strolled back along the hallway, the towel draped around his neck, absorbing the sweat beading on his face and chest.

As he passed the first bedroom to his right he stopped, grasping the door handle to see whether it was locked. Discovering it wasn't he entered, creeping to the side of the bed. Lying under the bedclothes, her blonde hair splayed chaotically over the pillow was a woman in her late thirties; a cream woollen blanket and black satin sheet bunched snugly under her chin. Her rhythmic breathing was peaceful with the faint trace of a whistle as she exhaled.

He stood looking down at the figure, a wry smile touching the corners of his mouth, softening his otherwise stern features.

Taking care not to wake her he reached down, gripping the side of the mattress before jerking upwards in one swift motion.

The sleeping body of Kathryn Ballard, his younger sister, tumbled along with her bedding into an undignified heap onto the floor. He ran for the door before her shriek of disbelief developed into something more physical.

While satisfied his actions were justified as a result of a previous prank in which she had set his alarm clock for 2 a.m., he resigned himself to the fact her retribution would be swift and devious. This was the game they played whenever she came to visit.

On average her stays at 'the farm' as she referred to it, were for several days once or twice a year. However, with the divorce from her husband of three years now final, Ballard noticed the visits were becoming more frequent; this despite having her own two bedroom unit in Ivanhoe and enjoying a successful and financially rewarding career as a physiotherapist.

He made a mental note to sit down and talk over her issues, offering what support he could. He gave thanks there were no children, despite knowing it was her long held desire to be a mother.

After tossing his towel in the laundry he entered the combined kitchen, dining and lounge area. This was the principal living and entertainment hub of the house. It was a large room segregated into the three areas, designed to complement Ballard's need for practicality, while still remaining inviting and comfortable.

A rustic timber eight seat dining table ran lengthways along the middle of the room, an island bench separated the kitchen from the dining area. At the opposite end, cloth covered sofas and armchairs surrounded an open fireplace, complete with a heavy wooden mantel displaying two ornamental kerosene lamps. The lamps a nostalgic reminder of his early years on his parents' farm in South Australia, incredibly without electricity until his tenth birthday. Above the mantel was a large wooden framed mirror; to the left of the fireplace, tucked against the wall, an upright Steinway piano dominated the area.

The perimeter wall was glass to shin height and overlooked the lawn and the one hundred and eighty degree panoramic view across Jackson's gorge. Red Hill to the left, together with Mounts Aitkin and Gisborne, all inactive volcanos, completed the vista. He never tired of the seasonal views, whether they were fog filled winter mornings, dazzling cumulus lightning shows, majestic sunsets or shimmering summer days.

It was this view that had convinced him to build his home here, knowing the Crown land of the gorge would never be developed. It helped that the closest homes on the far side of the gully were over two kilometres away

His stomach rumbled as he shook his favourite breakfast cereal into a bowl, adding ground linseed, almonds and sunflower seeds, a handful of sultanas plus a pinch of cinnamon, topping the concoction with a drizzle of honey. He splashed the lactose and gluten free milk into the bowl before greedily devouring the mixture while standing at the sink.

Half way through breakfast his attention was drawn to a fox strolling across the lawn outside the lounge room window. Oblivious to its surroundings, its large plumed orange and red tail flicked lazily as it continued its graceful movement past the veranda. Ballard was reminded yet again of the proximity of his home to nature and how the rural setting formed an emotional link to his childhood roots.

The two hundred and eighty metre boundary to the left of the property was bordered by a continuous line of mature pine trees, ensuring total privacy from his adjoining neighbour. To the right of the estate a one hundred hectare paddock supported sheep and cattle and was owned by Sam Devlin, now retired.

It was Sam's thirty sheep and new born lambs that were grazing in the lower section of the Ballard's property, saving him the effort of having to mow. Finding a pen, he jotted a note to himself to ring Sam later in the day to warn him of the fox.

After washing the dishes, he shaved and showered, finishing with a burst of ice cold water. As he towelled himself dry, steam evaporated from the mirror, progressively revealing his naked body from the waist up; he noted with satisfaction he was still defying the onslaught of middle age.

Inspecting his face he discovered a drop of blood forming on his upper lip. Muttering under his breath he tore off a piece of tissue and doubling it, moistened it with cold water before pressing it momentarily over the cut.

Stepping into the walk-in robe he selected a white shirt, mauve tie and a grey pinstriped, double breasted Armani silk wool blend suit. He had lost count of the times he had been challenged by his work colleagues for his attire, but he knew there was no malice, despite their often envious glances.

He assumed today would be predominantly spent in the office, bringing himself up to speed with the homicide. Furthermore, tonight was to be a special occasion, one he had been looking forward to for what seemed a lifetime.

After slipping into military polished, black leather lace up brogues, he inspected himself in the full length mirror, noting that while his face resembled that of Sting, his body was taller, more muscled and he hoped, due to his punishing exercise regime, fitter. With a smile he reflected he was fortunate to have more hair than the singer, although much less money in the bank.

Picking up his watch, mobile phone, wallet and police identification from the bedside table, he headed into the hallway. Snatching his briefcase from the study he re-entered the kitchen, collecting his sandwiches from the refrigerator. Scribbling a hasty note for his sister, he flicked on the electric floor heating before striding purposefully to the garage.

His latest acquisition and one that continued to generate immense pleasure was a black 6.1 litre Chrysler 300 SRT8. Activating keyless entry he slid into the black leather bucket seat, pressing the remote for the garage door before firing the motor.

The 425 horsepower monster roared to life. Smiling with satisfaction he allowed the engine to warm before flicking the transmission into 'Drive'. The Chrysler rolled smoothly out of the garage, tyres crunching on the loose gravel. The garage door locked behind him and at the top of the driveway he swung right into Chelsea Road.

Looking back across the lake to the house he felt a warm glow of accomplishment, having transformed the property from a barren, weed infested paddock to its current picturesque state. He now enjoyed a home and lifestyle that rewarded him daily. Despite this there was one vital element still missing; the right partner whom he could love and protect with all the intensity and passion he was capable of.

CHAPTER

2

For the five kilometres to the Calder Freeway he allowed the motor to warm, careful not to exceed 2500 revs. Once on the open highway he booted the 1.8 tonne vehicle up to 110 kph, revelling in the throaty rumble as the Mopar cold air intake drew air effortlessly into the motor.

Using voice commands he activated the Bluetooth; a soft female voice responded. "Please say the name or number."

"Dial Natalie." He was careful to enunciate his words, not wishing the system to revert to German or some other language as sometimes occurred.

"Dial Natalie at home or work?"

"Home."

He shook his head, amazed at how voice recognition was taking over the world. It now selected car temperature, song tracks, navigation destinations. Where would it end? A sleepy female voice brought him back to the moment. "Yes-s, hello."

He glanced at the dashboard clock. "Nat, this is your 6.15 wakeup call."

"6.15! Michael… it's the crack of dawn."

"You wouldn't grumble if I was there with you."

"If you were here you could have your way and I wouldn't even know it."

He reflected for a second, deciding not to take up the challenge.

"Darling, I'm heading into the office. The Lalor murder is going to drag on for some time, how does a non-paying boarder for a few days sound?"

Natalie's voice rose two octaves. "Michael, that's wonderful. Stay as long as you like. What time tonight?"

"Not sure. I'll ring later in the morning when I know more. Sweetheart, the traffic's getting heavier, I'll call you soon. Think of me… I love you."

"Not as much as me." A huskiness had crept into her voice as she drifted back to sleep. Grinning like a teenager, he felt excitement course throughout his body as he looked forward to the evening.

Natalie Somers, forty-five years old, one hundred and sixty-five centimetres, fifty-five kilograms, soft flawless skin despite four children, with an IQ of one hundred and twenty-five. She lived in a large, three bedroom town house in South Yarra; a result of a lifetime of hard work, plus an equitable divorce settlement six years earlier. Her two eldest girls had left home, leaving an eighteen year old daughter and a seventeen year old son still at school.

Natalie worked as a legal secretary for Ericsson & May, a prestigious law firm in Collins street. Prior to that, she had been a theatre sister in a private hospital in Box Hill, graduating from Melbourne University. With the arrival of her third daughter she had made the difficult decision to 'slow down'. This meant a complete career change, exchanging the fatigue of shift work for regular, shorter hours at the law firm. It was at her current workplace three years prior that she had met Ballard. For both it was love at first sight.

Since that time they had been inseparable, with never a night passing they didn't chat by telephone, sharing the day's triumphs and failures, hopes and aspirations. Whenever possible on weekends Natalie would stay at the farm, or Ballard would drive to South Yarra, leaving Monday morning for the short trip to the Crime Department building.

Ballard looked back on his previous relationships, reflecting on two failed marriages; the first resulting in a son Bradley with whom he was awarded custody when he was two years old. As the family home had been in Ivanhoe, Bradley had attended the Boy's Grammar School and at eighteen was fortunate to receive a scholarship to attend the Australian Defence Force Academy.

His move to the army as an officer, while welcomed by Ballard, had been emotionally traumatic as he regarded his son more as a younger brother. Both men were competitive but loving in every way; weekly telephone calls kept the bond between them current and rewarding.

The second marriage ended after four years with Ballard's ex-wife Maureen and their now fifteen year old daughter Laura, living in Bendigo. The most distressing issue of the divorce was the fact that for the past two years Laura had chosen not to visit or contact him. Despite his attempts to reason with her, she and her mother were resolute. Submissions to the Family Court resulted in the formal statement that as Laura was thirteen she had the right to make her own decisions regarding parental visits.

Telephone calls were refused, offers to attend school functions rejected. All he could do was hope time would heal whatever was perpetuating Laura's negative feelings, making it clear in a letter his door would always be open. He regretted she was now too adult for the sand pit and play equipment he had lovingly installed on the farm, hoping instead it would some day be used by future grandchildren.

Meeting Natalie was a new beginning for Ballard. Their personalities and outlook on life were similar, but to his amusement this didn't include their politics. His respect for her ability to raise her family grew daily and her often wicked humour was something he delighted in, plus he didn't find her sharp intellect in any way intimidating. The fact she was attractive, tactile and spontaneous in her approach to their physical relationship was an added bonus.

Just shy of three years later and in no doubt she was the lady he would spend the rest of his life with, he made the decision to marry her. While the request to stay over for several days was under the pretext of work, there was a far more important and pleasurable intent at hand. He prayed his offer would be accepted.

Thoughts of surprising her with an engagement ring were soon dismissed after previous attempts to determine what she liked failed to elicit an answer. This was a lady who was determined to design her own engagement and wedding rings.

He checked the rear vision mirror before manoeuvring to the left lane, feeding off the Keilor exit. The night before a work colleague had rung to ask for a lift into the office, despite having second thoughts when Ballard told him what time he would be calling past.

As he drove into the unit's driveway he sounded the horn twice. Within seconds a tall rambling figure appeared, waving before locking the front door and ambling over to the car. Detective Senior Sergeant John Henderson wound his lanky frame into the front passenger seat with difficulty, despite the Chrysler's ample leg room. Ballard noted he still hadn't cut his unruly mop of light brown hair.

"Thanks Mike. Appreciated."

"Think nothing of it John." Ballard smiled to himself. He knew John loved being driven to work, almost drooling every time Ballard gave the motor a savage boot along the freeway.

John was by far the better driver, having spent years in what was previously known as the Traffic Operations Group. That experience, together with a number of advanced driving courses in both cars and on motor bikes made him the man to be behind the wheel during high speed pursuits.

John looked over his shoulder to the back seat, observing Ballard's briefcase and sandwiches. Raising his eyebrows he stated rather than questioned, "Wholegrain bread, chicken, cheese and salad."

Ballard's expression and expansive shrug preceded his reply. "Were you expecting anything else?"

"Bloody hell Mike. You never change. You're a multi-millionaire yet you make your own sandwiches."

"So?"

"So when are you going to lighten up? I mean for God's sake look at the inside of the car. It's as clean as an operating theatre. Christ, you won't even wear your jacket when you drive because the bloody thing *might* get creased."

Ballard grinned as he looked across at John's food stained, crumpled suit. It looked as though it had been slept in and Ballard was aware of at least two occasions when this proved to be true. "Do you know how much my suits cost me, John?"

"Yeah, point taken. But it still makes you a wanker."

Ballard first met John when they were uniformed officers at

a busy inner suburban police station. John was a newly promoted senior constable who had already made a name for himself as a tireless worker with acute street smarts. What set him apart from the majority of police was the fact he didn't drink or smoke and he hated to socialise after work. This, together with the reality he did everything by the book reserved him from some of his fellow colleagues.

Ballard arrived at the station as a naive constable, eager to learn, also a non-drinker and non-smoker; as a consequence they were destined to work together as partners. Deliberate changes to the station roster by the shift sergeants made this inevitable. Over the next three years their arrest rates became legendary. John was the talented, logical, exacting investigator, while Ballard, although not possessing the same intellect, compensated by working harder, longer and with greater self-discipline.

After leaving St Kilda their careers separated, but every few years they found themselves on the same specialist squad or attending the same course together. It was not until Investigator Training, or what was historically known as Detective Training School that Ballard fully appreciated John's brilliance as a policeman. Not only did he top the internationally renowned course, but he set a final marks record that to Ballard's knowledge had yet to be beaten.

Conversely, Ballard finished mid-point in the squad of twenty-three detectives. Despite this, over the following years their individual arrest rates were similar. Neither Ballard nor John could explain this, even after many philosophical discussions, often late into the night.

John maintained Ballard was 'Just plain lucky'. Ballard put it down to a keener ability to read people's personality, to get inside a criminal's head.

John continued to restrict his promotional prospects by his often brutal confrontations with management. Telling a senior officer he was unfit for the force, justified though it may have been, never placed him favourably when it came to securing advancement. As a consequence, Detective Senior Sergeant was destined to be his highest rank. Maintaining that rank was another thing and on a number of occasions Ballard had pleaded forcefully and at times emotionally with management not to demote him.

John was the first to broach the subject of the Lalor homicide.

"Not good Mike. No real evidence to go on. Just some poor bastard strung up like a piece of meat with the back of his head missing, thanks to a .45 slug found buried in a wooden beam. What sort of shithead does that?"

Ballard didn't attempt an answer. He glanced across at his partner. "As you've the lead, let me know what you want me to do." Despite the rank difference this was how he preferred to work, not always in charge of an investigation but applying his experience as and where required. It was a trait which endeared him to younger Homicide members, allowing him to nurture them into more effective investigators. In this case it was the obvious choice given John's proven ability.

"Mike I want you with me at the scene. You see things others don't. After that we'll tick all the boxes: neighbouring factories, forensics, ballistics, family, acquaintances, the lot.

"My guys, along with Crime Scene and Forensics have done all this but I want you to go in cold. Work your magic. Like you I haven't been to the factory. I wasn't assigned the case until Crime Scene had attended and realised we had something pretty heavy."

Ballard nodded in agreement. "As soon as we clock-on I'll

draw a work car then we'll head out." John settled back in his seat, eyes closed, listening to the rumble of the V8, a contented smile on his face.

CHAPTER
3

The Crime Department building was a nineteen storey, unremarkable structure opposite the Melbourne Grammar School. Moves were afoot by the police executive to relocate all staff to a purpose built complex in the city precinct. Neither Ballard nor John figured they need hold their breath on the building's completion.

Ballard piloted the Chrysler into the underground car park, stopping at the boom gate. "Morning Rob. Any news on the home front?"

The Protective Security Officer shook his head. "Not yet, sir. The doctor will induce tomorrow if nothing happens in the meantime." He raised the boom, throwing a quick salute.

Ballard smiled back. "Give Sophie my best. I'm betting on a boy." Easing around the tight corners he expertly manoeuvred the large car into the bay allocated to him, another condition of his remaining in the job.

Once in the lift, John stabbed the eighth floor button; both men stood looking up at the illuminated numbers. Emerging onto the floor they were confronted with a scene which at first appeared to be confused, almost frenetic activity set in an open plan environment. On closer scrutiny it was in fact professional police officers engaged in very specific tasks.

This was the engine-room of homicide investigations: endless checking of criminal histories in the offender database; preparing statements for briefs of evidence with an exacting eye for detail and accuracy to negate the potential of having the charges declared inadmissible in court; examining photographs of crime scenes or suspects and offenders, comparing them against driver licence photos accessed on-line from VicRoads; endless calls to witnesses or confidential sources; pouring over forensic evidence prepared by the laboratory.

This scene reinforced for Ballard why he was still a policeman and he knew it had the same motivation for John. He shook his head, wondering how he could ever have contemplated walking away.

Officers throughout the floor looked up and waved at the two men, then, in the majority refocussed on their specific tasks, several calling out a morning greeting. While John went to discuss progress with his team, Ballard headed for the superintendent's office. In the process he walked past pinboards containing photos of suspects or known criminals; whyteboards with cryptic messages relating to particular cases; staff rosters and desks scattered with files containing information essential for criminal cases and operational activities. As he neared the office he reflex straightened his tie.

Delwyn Peters, his direct superior, had made Detective Superintendent two years before she was transferred to Homicide. Embracing the male dominated environment she soon proved her effectiveness as an investigator, demonstrating how adept she was at managing strong willed personnel. Any misgivings Ballard felt at the beginning of her tenure soon evaporated, resulting in their working relationship becoming rock solid due to the mutual respect they had for each other.

He gave a cursory tap on the open door. "Top of the morning Delwyn."

Blue eyes crinkling into a smile as she waved him to an empty chair. "Thanks for coming in on such short notice Michael."

He shrugged nonchalantly. "Last time I checked you were still paying my wages."

"Even so, much appreciated."

Ballard noticed she had cut her steel grey hair into a military style short back and sides. It suited her, but he refrained from commenting.

"This one could blow up in our face Mike." Ballard's expression invited clarification. "Some of the reporters are muttering underworld hit. They haven't put pen to paper yet, but it won't be long."

"Could it be?"

"Always possible, but the deceased hasn't any significant record or criminal links we know of. There's no intelligence in our database… nothing. Should the press suggest a hit it would spook the public making our job that much harder. We'd be busting a gut to solve a crime while chewing up resources to prove the rumour was false."

Ballard stroked his chin, reflecting. "How long before this snowballs into a major headline that we're not moving fast enough?"

"You're a better judge of these things than I am. A day. Three days at the most. The Chief's already warned me this needs fixing, one way or the other… and fast."

Ballard leaned forward in his chair. "Delwyn, I'll do everything I can to assist. You know how good John is on these cases. I want him to retain the lead, but if I think we're not adequately resourced, or I see the investigation running out of puff, for whatever reason, he and I will be in here like a shot. We'll sweat this until something gives, but I have to say it doesn't feel good."

He stood to leave then hesitated, smiling ruefully. "Oh, unless the world collapses today, I'd like to be over at Natalie's by 6 tonight. I've an important question to ask her."

Delwyn sprang to her feet, almost climbing over the desk to wrap him in a huge hug. "Best news I've heard all day. I knew you'd get around to it eventually."

Face colouring, Ballard grinned as he extracted himself, concerned as to how lean she felt. "Yes, I'm going to ask her to the pictures on Saturday."

Delwyn, feigning annoyance, stabbed her finger at the door. "Off with you and don't come back until you've popped the question."

Pretending servitude he slunk out of the office, much to the amusement of the younger detectives who didn't know him well.

Heading over to the weapons' safe, he signed out his personal issue 15 shot Smith & Wesson, along with a spare clip. While checking the magazine he silently thanked the department for changing from .38 revolvers, despite shuddering to think what gun battle may ever require fifteen rounds. He prayed he would never have to find out. From there he signed for a police vehicle, then, grabbing his day book headed off to find John.

Spotting him with two of his detectives he strolled over, giving him a playful punch on the shoulder. "Ready? I feel a crime scene coming on."

John looked at the car keys in his hand. "Want to ride shotgun, considering the lift this morning?"

Ballard smiled, aware that returning the favour was not the

real motive; the simple fact being John loved to drive. "Sure thing." He acceded by tossing the keys upwards in front of his partner who plucked them from mid-air, seemingly without looking. One of the detectives whistled in admiration, "Shit hot boss!" What the detectives were unaware of was the number of times John and Ballard had practiced the move until they could do it blindfolded.

Chuckling, John looked across at Ballard, "Good to go Inspector," throwing him a military salute. Ballard reached forward to shake John's hand; when John lowered his to accept, Ballard reverted to a return salute. Both men alternated this routine a number of times in rapid succession, their hands never touching. It came to an end with each doubled over in fits of laughter. The junior detectives looked at one another, shaking their heads in amazement, not understanding the bond that existed between the two older men from years of working together on the brutal streets of St Kilda.

Once in the car Ballard fastened his seatbelt then shut his eyes, knowing the three storey decent to street level would be a white knuckle ride, performed with precision, but terrifying nevertheless. "You do realise I'm getting too old for this kind of death wish." Flicking a sideways glance John chuckled, choosing to misinterpret the statement.

"Bullshit Mike. You wouldn't miss it for the world. The thrill of the moment. Bringing crooks to justice." He lowered his voice to a growl, "It's what keeps us alive." Gunning the motor he accelerated to the first corner.

As Ballard predicted they made the descent with John in total control, as though he were an extension of the car. Once on the street Ballard opened his eyes and felt his breathing return to normal, realising he had been holding it for most of the descent.

John turned the vehicle in the direction of the CityLink tollway; his face that of a man on a mission. Ballard knew murders of this kind were regarded by him as an affront to a civilised society. Failure to find the 'Shithead', as John referred to all criminals, was not an option.

CHAPTER

4

"You know Mike it never ceases to amaze me what human beings are capable of inflicting on each other." It was a rare reflection for John to wax philosophical, underscoring his deep feelings regarding the shooting.

Ballard shrugged. "Human nature at work. A fact of life ever since we crawled out of the swamp."

John glanced over at him. "Thank Christ it's a small percentage of the population. We wouldn't have enough hours in the day otherwise."

Ballard shuffled sideways to face his partner. "I've never mentioned this to you but when I was about eight, my maternal grandfather told me an unbelievable story just before he died. I've never forgotten it. At the time it gave me nightmares for weeks, months in fact. .I know Mum was ropable when she found out."

John's expression made it clear Ballard had his attention. "Grandpa lived in Mundulla in South Australia and it happened when he was about thirty-five," he hesitated, performing mental arithmetic. "I'm guessing that would have been… ah, the mid 1920s. Anyway, he would take Mum on a shopping trip once a fortnight into Bordertown which was about ten kilometres

randfather told you this when you were *eight*?"
He did indeed. And didn't he get a mouthful from my
er."

"So the moral of the story…?"

Ballard took his time before replying. "I guess it all comes ck to the fact human beings are capable of doing astonishing ings. Good as well as bad. It does put *our* homicide into some erspective, though. No excuse of course, just proof the human ace isn't going to change any time soon."

John, still shaking his head, muttered through gritted teeth, "Maybe so, but whoever did the Lalor murder isn't going to get away with it while I have breath in my body."

Ballard's lip curled, reflecting on how many times he had seen John lock onto a case with the determination and skill that made him one of the finest detectives the police force had ever produced.

As if reading his mind John said, "Don't think you're going to get an easy ride on this one Mike. I need your objectivity and political nous to get me through this. The Chief's going to be all over it like a rash, along with the media. You know how that scares the crap out of me."

Ballard acknowledged John's comments with a nod, straightening back in his seat as he stared blankly ahead. "How much longer are you going to keep doing this John? I mean you could retire, put your feet up any time you want."

"Yeah and go bloody mad. It's in our blood and you know it. That's why *you* didn't pull the pin. But it sure baffles the hell out of the young guys." He gave a short braying laugh. "I can see it in their eyes. They can't believe us old buggers can chew gum *and* drive a car at the same time. Unbelievable."

He shook his head, but the grin lighting up his face was one away. They didn't have a car, so grandpa would saddle up the horse and buggy."

John snorted. "Jeez Mike. You're kidding me? A horse and buggy."

Ballard chuckled. "Yep. Remember, this was the twenties. Now here's where it gets interesting. On the way into Bordertown there was a farmhouse that was close to the road. The owner had a reputation for belting his better half. In those days wives had nowhere to go, so she had to put up with it. Anyway, for whatever reason she died.

"Grandpa said her death was never attributed to the husband, but no doubt living in that environment didn't help. From that point on the husband was shunned by the community. No-one would talk to him. He even had trouble buying food and supplies from the shops. For all intents and purposes he had to fend for himself."

Ballard became more animated as the story progressed. "On one of the trips, grandpa noticed the sheep and some of the cows crowding around the farmhouse. This wasn't normal. A fortnight later he saw the same thing again. By the following fortnight grandpa decided to take a look. He dropped Mum home after shopping then back-tracked, knocking on the guy's front door. It was the middle of summer, stinking hot. Grandpa saw the livestock weren't in good shape, water troughs empty, no feed, that sort of thing."

Ballard looked across at John, grinning wickedly. "Then he noticed the smell."

Without taking his eyes off the road John inclined his head sideways so as to be closer. "What smell?"

"Death."

"*Death?*"

"Yep. Grandpa called out for seve[ral] answered, so he forced open the front [door] Said the stench was unbelievable. So much the kitchen sink. But when he opened the d[oor] he did more than throw up." Ballard paused for

"He told me he very nearly soiled his pants."

John was mesmerised, waving his hand im[patiently for] Ballard to continue.

"What grandpa saw was a rope slung over one of t[he beams] with a noose at the end."

"Christ, the bastard hung himself."

"Grandpa said he wasn't hanging from the rope."

John took his eyes off the road and stared at Ballard. "So [he] didn't hang himself?"

Ballard chuckled. "Oh yes he did. Remember… it was the middle of summer and he'd been there for over six weeks."

Realisation dawned on John's face. "*Oh, don't tell me!*"

"Oh yes indeed! The bugger had rotted off the rope. To make matters worse, the idiot had taken a swig of sulphuric acid before he kicked himself off the chair. Grandpa saw the bottle lying on the floor."

John swerved in the lane as he looked across, horrified. "Sulphuric acid! You're kidding me. For Christ's sake, why?"

Ballard gave his reply a degree of simplicity. "Guilt… loneliness… madness. All three. Grandpa then gave me a graphic description of how the body had decomposed. Maggots everywhere. I guess the acid didn't help. When it was all over and the police had attended, along with the local doctor, the body had to be scraped up and shovelled into a box."

John shook his head from side to side, as if blocking out the words and the mental image. "Enough Mike, enough! And

of pure satisfaction. "Just don't go getting yourself killed Mike. The paperwork is a bastard and I couldn't stand being teamed up with some young fool spouting endless drivel while they're in the car with me."

Ballard gave him a wry look. "I'll try not to. Well not any time soon. Besides Natalie would never forgive me."

"*Soooo,* when are you going to pop the question?"

"Ah, you *did* hear the commotion in Delwyn's office."

"Christ Mike, I look up and you're having a knee tremble with her on the desk."

"I think that might be a slight exaggeration John. I trust you're not going to blurt this out when you see Natalie next?"

John gave his best Jack Nicholson leer. "Your secret's safe with me buddy boy."

Ballard shook his head, knowing what the look meant. "That reminds me, I need to ring Nat to let her know what time I'll be over tonight."

John smirked. "Give her my love, plus tell her I can't wait to engage in some juicy gossip."

Glaring at him Ballard dialled Natalie's number, her greeting benefiting from caller ID.

"Hello Michael. I'm wide awake *now*, so you can tell me how much you love me."

"As much as life itself, darling." Ballard thrust out his jaw as he looked across at John who gave an exaggerated roll of his eyes.

"Nat this case may get nasty. Is 6.30 ok by you?"

"Yes darling, besides that gives me more time to prepare after work." Her voice was silken in his ear.

Ballard shook his head, appreciating yet again her wonderful nature to adapt to circumstances and make the most of any situation.

Natalie laughed at his hesitation. "But on one condition. *I* provide the main course while *you* my sweet, provide the dessert." Her voice lowered provocatively, the meaning unmistakable.

Grinning from ear to ear Ballard responded, "Darling, you can be assured I'll bring dessert." He said this while glaring challengingly at John who took one hand off the steering wheel to poke a finger down his throat, pretending to gag.

Giggling and unaware of the exchanges at Ballard's end, Natalie said, "I can't wait," then hung up.

John flicked a quick look at Ballard. "My God, despite only hearing *your* half of that conversation, I was embarrassed. You know, for a couple with a combined age of ninety-five years, you two are worse than hormonal teenagers."

Ballard sighed, looking content. "Guess what John? We're loving it!"

John asked, "And what's with all the daaaarliiiings... darling this, darling that. Christ!"

Ballard smiled, deciding to let the comment slide. Looking down at his mobile he muttered, "One more call. I need to let my neighbour Sam know there's a fox roaming the farm. Some of his ewes and lambs are in the bottom paddock."

Dialling the number he listened as an answering machine cut in. After the beep he said, "Sam, Michael here. I saw a fox wandering past the veranda this morning. Big as one of your cows. You may want to put the Alpacas back to protect the lambs, just in case. Best of luck." He pocketed his mobile before settling back in the seat.

John steered the car to the left lane and onto the exit ramp for the Western Ring Road. Despite the roadworks they made good time. It was 8.15 a.m. when they reached Settlement Road, Lalor, pulling into Ellis Court minutes later.

CHAPTER
5

'Mario's Sculptures' was printed in large black letters across the front of a stand alone, flat roofed concrete structure that was now a crime scene. To the right of the single storey building was a driveway leading to the rear of the property, providing access for concrete and delivery trucks. Police tape extended from each side of the building out to the curb and across the front in a giant rectangle.

Parked alongside the tape was a police car with a fresh-faced uniform officer sitting behind the wheel. On seeing Ballard and John the officer scrambled out, approaching the passenger side of their vehicle. Ballard lowered his window as the policeman leaned down, enthusiastically acknowledging both men.

"Morning. Morning. I'm Constable Downing. I was told over the radio you were on the way."

Ballard smiled up at the constable. "What's your first name Constable Downing?"

"William, sir."

"Well William, this is John and I'm not sir. Michael's my name." He extended his hand as a greeting through the window while John muttered a gruff 'hello'. Ballard scowled at his partner before looking back at the constable. "We're going to poke around inside, then as these factories open up we'll talk to the owners. Do you work in this area?"

"Yes sir... er Michael. I'm stationed at Epping. Been there for two years."

"Do you know the factory owners? Ever needed to attend here for any reason?"

The constable shook his head. "No. Never. We patrol the area of course. Oh well, yes, we have attended here, but that was to speak to the owners so we could update our after hours records should the factories ever get broken into."

John leaned across. "*Have* any of these factories been broken into William?"

Again the constable shook his head. "Not that I know of. I could radio back to the station and have our crime desk analyst search the database if you like?"

John lifted an eyebrow. "Yes William, that would be very helpful. We'll check with you when we've finished inside." His tone implying this was the end of the conversation.

The constable hurried back to the car, pleased with his role in assisting such an important investigation.

John chuckled at Ballard. "Ah, the exuberance of youth. By the time he's finished telling his girlfriend, sister, mother or whoever, he'll believe he solved the bloody case himself."

Ballard grinned. "Now John, don't tell me you weren't eager once."

John sighed, reflecting back to his earlier career. "I guess so. I suppose I still am."

Both men got out of the vehicle and John popped the boot to retrieve the case he took with him to all crime scenes. It contained an assortment of items including protective latex gloves, cloth overshoes, various police forms, plastic evidence bags, adhesive labels, a Pentax 645D digital camera, an Olympus 4G micro voice recorder, a metal tape measure, plus a host of other items foreign to Ballard. John's latest acquisition was a set of Sony 20x digital zoom binoculars, capable of recording up to 13 hours of footage on a 32GB card in both 2 and 3D. When Ballard had asked 'why?' John's answer had been a nonchalant shrug.

Walking up to the building they stripped back the tape; John tossed a set of keys to Ballard who in turn unlocked the front door, swinging it open. Before entering they donned cloth overshoes and latex gloves. While this protection was regarded by some detectives as overkill, considering the Crime Scene Unit had already attended, both men made it a practice to play safe. John armed himself with the Pentax camera before stepping inside.

As always, when at a crime location that had been the scene of a violent murder, Ballard could feel the aura of sinister foreboding. He reasoned it was the body's natural defence mechanism kicking mental capacity to a higher gear. True or not, he always felt his senses were more acute, more perceptive at crime scenes.

The front of the factory was an office consisting of two large desks along with customer sofas backed up to grimy windows. A film of dust covered the desk tops, except for two clean rectangles where computers had been. These were now being analysed by the E-Crimes Squad for every bit and byte of information they contained. Ballard made a note in his day book to check on progress when he returned to the office. Fingerprint dust was everywhere, on the telephone, photo frames, even on the paintings on the wall.

John positioned himself in specific locations throughout the room, taking numerous shots that when laid side by side, would provide a panoramic view of the office. While this would have already been performed by the Crime Scene Unit, together with a full video, John preferred to take his own photos. He would upload them onto his laptop, analysing every detail for hours, often emailing them to Ballard late at night, waking him up to discuss a particular theory. Many a case had been solved by him adopting this practice.

Ballard waited until he had finished then cheekily asked, "Did you get one of the door lock John?"

The resultant look from his partner made it clear he was unimpressed by the question. "Of course. But there was no forced entry as the lock was undamaged… as you bloody well know. This raises the possibility the killer may have been known by the deceased. The time of death has been put around 2 a.m. yesterday. We'll swing by for an autopsy report later on if we get time."

There were a number of dust free rectangles on the floor tiles behind the desks where filing cabinets had been, similar to the areas left by the PCs. The cabinets contents were now being scrutinised by Crime Scene Analysts. Ballard made a second note in his day book. To the rear of the office a door led into the factory showroom.

On entering the first impression Ballard had was of the excavation site of the ancient Terracotta Chinese Warriors. There was row after row of concrete ornaments ranging from pots, animals, garden gnomes to abstract objects. Grey concrete dust covered the floor, accentuating footprints and scuffmarks.

John whistled in awe. "Quite a spectacle, huh? There's something like three hundred and fifty separate pieces here according to the Crime Scene boys."

Ballard muttered a reply, despite his attention being drawn to the chalk marks and extensive blood stains on the one vacant area of floor. "So the chair was here?" He stood looking down at the spot.

"Yeah. It's now with Forensics, same for the rope."

Instinctively both men looked up at the wooden beams running across the room at three metre intervals. The fact that timber had been used instead of steel gave the interior the rustic charm of older, inner suburban factories. Ballard estimated the beams were a little under four metres above the floor. "Forensics have finished photographing the foot prints?"

John confirmed. "Er, yes. There was some thought there might've been more than one shooter, but for the moment they're sticking to the theory of a single guy."

Ballard looked closer at the chalk marks while John took numerous photos. "What was the end of the rope tied to… and I don't mean the end around the guy's neck?"

John hesitated. "Good point. Not sure." Both men looked around but failed to see an anchor point.

Ballard shrugged his shoulders. "My guess is he slung the rope over the beam, pulling it tight so the victim was on tippy-toes, then tossed the free end over again. The gap between the beam and the roof is… say… a metre, so not too hard to chuck the rope over a second time. From there it wouldn't have taken too much effort to hold it taut when the guy went off the chair. Friction on the beam would've taken most of the weight."

John pursed his lips, considering the theory. "I think you're right Mike. I remember Forensics mentioning manila rope fibres were found on all sides of the beam, indicating it may well have been looped several times." He pointed to the spot where the rope had been, highlighted by the chalk marks. "Still, the shooter must have been strong to hang onto the rope with one hand…" he hesitated, holding up his own in mimicry of his suggested action. "I guess he could have stood on the rope while he used his free hand to stop the guy spinning or jerking around before plugging him between the eyes. The dead guy's hands were bound behind his back with plastic ties.

"When our guys found him on the floor, the rope was off the beam and piled on top of him. It makes sense the shooter wasn't going to stand there all day with the rope in his hand, so when he let go the weight of the body pulled it loose and for some reason the killer yanked the rest of it down. Never bothered to take the noose off his neck though, but considering the damage the bullet did to his head I can understand why."

A frown appeared on Ballard's face. "Hmm. I guess so. I have to say it all sounds a bit tricky, looping the rope over the beam while holding a gun at the same time. This makes me think the dead guy had accepted his fate. I mean look around the location of the chair. None of the objects have been kicked over. It appears he didn't make a run for it, even though his hands were tied. Was the chair seat scuffed in any way? Was the guy attempting to twist or turn away from the shooter?"

John glanced about him, musing. "Can't say. We'll check later when we get to Forensics."

Ballard looked upward. "So that's where the bullet lodged after passing through the guy's skull?" He pointed at the wooden beam adjacent to where the rope had been slung. A chalked circle surrounded a single bullet hole with dark blood stains radiating out from where brain and scalp matter had hit the beam and ceiling; all body tissue now collected and forwarded to the medical examiner.

John snorted derisively. "Yep. I'm told the sissy Forensic guy shit himself when he had to climb the ladder to dig out the slug and scrape the poor bugger's brains off the ceiling."

Ballard hitched his pant's leg, propping a foot on one of the garden gnomes before opening his day book. With his pen poised he looked across at John. "Ok. What facts do we have?"

John ticked off the points on his fingers, reciting from memory. "The guy's name is Mario Bivelaqua... can you believe that? No prize for guessing his nationality. Forty-six years old. Lives – or should I say, lived in Templestowe with his wife and two kids. He's owned the factory for ten years, built it himself. Had priors for low level theft when he was a kid, around fifteen or sixteen. One punch up in a pub when he was twenty-five. Received a good behaviour bond and nothing since."

Ballard jotted down the main details before looking up for John to continue.

"He was shot Tuesday morning at around 2 a.m. Crime Scene boys think the slug is a .45 calibre. Despite the damage to it, they believe it's a hollow point."

Ballard winced. John's expression echoed Ballard's feelings. "Mario has two guys who work here part time. Both have been interviewed and given statements. They claim they knocked off the previous evening around 5.30 p.m. We'll interview them again, along with Mario's wife some time tomorrow."

Ballard looked up from his day book. "Do we know for a fact Mario was hung, as opposed to being intimidated for information before he was shot?"

John smiled wryly. "Very astute Mr Ballard. I can tell you this wasn't any run-of-the-mill murder. Yes he *was* hung, no doubt about it. All the tell-tale signs... significant bruising around the neck, swollen protruding tongue. So we have a killer who is physically strong, malicious and a sadistic prick."

Ballard grimaced. "I read somewhere that unless the body drops at least one and a half to two metres the neck doesn't break, as a result death is slow, most likely occurring from asphyxiation. The poor bastard could've been jerking around on the rope for minutes. It's possible that's why the killer shot him to get it over with, not wanting to hold onto the rope any longer."

John massaged his forehead with the tips of his fingers. "Jeez Mike. I've never thought too much about what happens when someone's hung. I guess I've always had the Hollywood version in my head that it's instant."

Ballard shook his head. "Far from it my friend. In many countries years ago, strangulation hangings were common place with the poor buggers taking up to twenty minutes to die, *if* they were lucky. A lot depended on the position of the knot on the noose. If blood flow to the carotid artery was restricted, death in those instances was pretty quick. With this guy, I'm not so sure. The results from the autopsy will clear that up."

John shook his head, his features pained as he looked up at the beam again. Ballard followed his gaze. "I'm sticking with the theory the killer was torturing Mario to get information from him. Then, when he got what he wanted or couldn't get it, he kicked the chair out. Mario jerked around on the rope for a bit before the shooter plugged him. You can see where some of the nearby ornaments have been removed to be tested for blood spatter."

John shrugged. "Anything's possible. I must admit I hadn't figured on the torture angle. Perhaps we should talk to our resident profiler to see what *he* thinks?"

Ballard smirked, knowing John's comment was laced with sarcasm, a result of a long held mistrust of police profilers after receiving bad advice a number of years earlier. An inexperienced profiler had offered a theory on a very nasty homicide that had John pursuing a line of enquiry that wasted three months investigation. As a result he almost lost the case in court and ever since viewed profiler input with great scepticism.

Ballard on the other hand had been fortunate to have had positive assistance from profilers on a number of cases. Despite this, he always regarded their contributions as alternative theories warranting consideration.

Keeping a straight face, he said, "Er, yes John. I think we'll nip over and touch base with Ken after we get back to the office."

John scowled, knowing Ballard was poking fun at him, while at the same time recognising profiler opinions were part of the job. "Yeah. Let's do that."

Ballard grinned, deciding not to push the ribbing any further. "Ok. What else do we have?"

"Nothing of consequence. That's the reason Delwyn's looking over her shoulder to see how close the Chief is and why we're here scratching our heads. All we can do is tick the boxes and keep accumulating facts."

Ballard closed his day book, tucking it under his arm. "Let's go and talk to the other factory owners. I can't wait to hear what the rumour mill has for us."

Both men took one last look around the room before heading back through the office. John led the way out, returning the camera to its case. Ballard followed, pulling the front door shut behind him, locking it before resealing the police tape.

As they peeled off their gloves and overshoes, William hurried towards them, his demeanour one of suppressed excitement. As he flipped open his police issue notebook, John looked up. "Ok William. What've you got for us?"

"Well, nothing for this particular address, but in the street there have been four burglaries and two smashed windows, as well as numerous graffiti reports in the last two years."

"Anyone charged?"

Disappointment flickered across William's face as though the non arrests were his personal responsibility. "Uh… no, 'fraid not."

John remained poker faced. "What! Nobody arrested? No suspects?" William's bottom lip protruded as Ballard gave John a firm kick out of the constable's view. John laughed dryly. "It's ok William. Crime solving isn't something where shitheads throw themselves at you. In most cases it's just plain mind numbing hoof-work with the occasional stroke of luck. In ten years time you'll be saying the same thing to another fresh faced constable when *you're* attending a homicide."

William's face broke into an enormous grin. "I hope so. I've seen you and Mr Ballard, er Michael plenty of times on TV and I can't wait to do Investigator Training."

John clapped his hand on the young man's shoulder. "I'm certain with your enthusiasm you'll top the course. William, we're going to interview some of the other factory owners before heading off to Forensics. Keep up the good work and ensure no-one other than authorised police enter this building. If you have any doubts ring my mobile." He handed William his business card. The policeman thanked both detectives, reluctantly returning to his vehicle.

As John placed the Crime Scene case in the boot, Ballard leaned over and said, "Well, tough guy. Behind that facade you're a big pussy. Thank God… I was beginning to wonder."

John pulled the boot shut, glancing across at William sitting in the police car. "Yep, wet behind the ears, but I guess he has promise, *if* he can overcome his bloody annoying effervescent naivety." Picking up his day book he said, "How do we tackle the factory interviews Mike?"

Ballard looked around the court, counting aloud. "Seven… eight… nine. Nine other factories. I think we'll split up John or it'll take all day. You do the four over there and I'll tackle the four alongside. If we finish up much the same time we can knock over the last one together."

CHAPTER
6

For the next thirty minutes both men introduced themselves to factory owners and staff, asking a series of standard questions that elicited almost identical answers.

After his fourth interview, Ballard waited in the street; five minutes later his partner emerged. As John approached Ballard he shook his head. In his best European accent he drawled, "I saw nothing! I heard nothing! I know nothing!"

Ballard laughed. "Same here. He looked across at the remaining factory located alongside the crime scene building. "Lucky last. Let's see what we can dig up here."

They approached the factory with 'Tony's Custom Designed Kitchens' emblazoned across the front entrance. Both men walked up the steps, entering the small show room.

A short, trim, middle aged man approached them with a worried look on his face, his bald head out of proportion to his body. Reaching forward he extended his hand to Ballard, then John. "I'm Tony Padello. I'm the owner. I've been watching you go into the other factories. I can guess..."

"Yes Tony." Ballard flashed a disarming smile. "I'm Detective Inspector Michael Ballard, this is Detective Senior Sergeant John Henderson. I'm sure you know why we're here and yes I'm aware the police have already taken a statement from you." Both men showed Tony their identification.

Ballard continued. "Unfortunately Tony, witnesses often don't remember all the important details first up. That's not a criticism... more a fact of life. As a consequence we need to ask you a few more questions." He looked squarely at Tony, knowing what the response to his next question would be. "How are you placed for time?"

Tony rubbed the bridge of his nose, hesitating.

John flipped open his day book. "Good. Let's get started then shall we?" Ballard smiled, knowing his polite request was considered by John as pandering. With his pen hovering over a blank page and without looking at Tony, John prompted. "What time do you leave the factory each evening?"

Tony blinked rapidly, looking away before stammering, "Er, that's hard to say, I... er... it varies." He jigged on the spot. "Sometimes it's quite late." Ballard and John glanced at each other, knowing intuitively Tony's discomfort was worth pursuing.

John pointed to at least five plastic bags containing groceries on the floor near the far wall. "A lot of shopping there Tony. Buy them this morning?"

"Yeah. There's a supermarket around the corner."

"Strange that you would buy so much in the morning. Any frozen items?"

A hunted look flashed across Tony's face. "I've a fridge out the back. I put the frozen stuff in there earlier... then I got distracted, watching you guys going into the other factories, but I'm taking everything home tonight."

"Married?"

Tony began to blink rapidly again. "Divorced."

John's questions became more pointed.

"Live alone?"

Tony's agitation increased significantly. "Yeah. Well no. I live with my Mum."

"Your house?"

Further hesitation. "No. It's my Dad's... was his. He died six years ago."

John didn't bother to offer condolences. Rubbing his chin he said, "Strange that you'd buy frozen stuff in the morning when it would mean less chance of loss if you bought it just before you went home. I mean supermarkets are open 'til late."

Noting Tony's distress, John persisted. "Would I be correct in saying this area is zoned business only?"

Tony's eyes widened and his face took on the look of a rabbit startled by car lights.

"Er, yes. That's right..." his voice trailed away, but his large head kept bobbing.

John decided to cut to the chase. "Ever stay overnight when you're backlogged with work? Customers pushing you for their kitchens to be completed?"

Tony shook his head then changed his mind. Looking uncomfortable he admitted, "Yes, sometimes I have to. You've no idea how cut-throat this business can be when you fall behind on orders."

John pretended to look sympathetic. "Mm, must be tough."

Ballard hid a grin, enjoying playing the good cop. "Tony, mate, we've no intention of letting the council know you sleep here overnight. That's of no interest to us. What *is* of concern is whether you were here Monday night, Tuesday morning."

The look on Tony's face answered the question even before he opened his mouth.

"I... yes, I... was."

"Thank you Tony. I understand this is difficult for you. Did you state this fact to the police when you gave your statement earlier?"

"No. I was going to tell them, but I shit myself. I can't afford to be fined. Once the council start sniffing around here there'll be all sorts of problems for me. I *can't* run the risk of losing my business…"

Ballard raised his hand. "Your secret's safe with us Tony. But you'll have to make another statement. Did you hear or see anything during the night that may assist us?"

Tony looked down at his feet. John stepped closer, menacing. "A man was shot Tuesday morning Tony. Fifty feet from where you're standing. Think very carefully before you answer the question. This is a murder investigation." John's sheer bulk and proximity was meant to intimidate; Ballard noted it was working.

The distressed expression on Tony's face increased dramatically. Bobbing his head again he said, "Yeah. I was in bed in the side room and around 1.30 in the morning I heard a loud pop, sort of like a backfire, but muffled."

John scribbled furiously in his notebook. "Did the sound wake you up?"

"No. I was already awake."

"How did you know it was 1.30?"

Tony hung his head even lower, almost to the point where eye contact was lost. "I was awake and looked at the bedside clock."

"Why were you awake at that time of the morning?"

"I uh … I had my girlfriend over."

Ballard clapped Tony on the shoulder. "Tony, it's ok mate. All we want is for you to tell it as it happened, you're not going to get into trouble. You may well have information that helps us solve this crime."

Instead of reassuring him, Ballard's statement appeared to exacerbate Tony's discomfort. In a high pitched voice he said, "I didn't get up or anything, it just *sounded* like a backfire. I didn't think anything of it until I heard the news next morning, that there'd been a shooting. I nearly *did* shit myself. Christ, next door! Mario's a good bloke. I see him all the time.

"Then the cops ... er police officers came in and started asking questions. I told them I'd gone home so I wouldn't be involved. Most nights I *do* go home, but for the last week or so I've been snowed under." He took a deep breath, striking his forehead with closed knuckles, looking despairingly at both detectives. "Sorry... I'm sorry. Am I in trouble? What happens now? I don't want my name on TV or in the papers. I don't want the bastard who did this coming after me." A look of raw panic flashed across his face.

Ballard grabbed his shoulders with both hands. "Jesus... Tony! Take a breath! Your identity isn't going to be made public. This is a *murder* investigation. Believe it or not the press and media know what they can and can't report. But you have to understand, you may well be the one person who can clarify *when* Mario was killed."

Wanting his comments to reassure Tony, Ballard looked at him closely. "Having said that, we'll need to interview your girlfriend. Give me her contact details so my detectives can arrange a time to meet with her."

Tony hesitated, but after seeing John's expression, jotted down two telephone numbers in the folder handed to him. John took back the folder. "Tony we'll arrange for the Crime Scene officers to take some photographs of the room where you were sleeping. In the meantime I want to take some of my own." Grinning he said, "Don't worry if you haven't made the bed. We've seen it all before."

All resistance evaporated from Tony. Almost in a trance, his head still bobbing, he led them into the work area. Walking past the Bosch edge-bander, the Altendorf table-saw, the Hettich hinge inserter then the spray booth, John meticulously noted the brand name and type of each item in his day book.

Younger detectives often viewed this degree of detail as over-the-top. Ballard knew that John's reasoning would be that if the medical examiner discovered an injury on Mario able to be attributed to a specific piece of equipment, then recording the items in the first instance was disciplined investigating. Nothing John ever did in relation to his work could be regarded as less than disciplined.

Kitchen cabinets in various stages of construction were positioned throughout the workshop. Sawdust lay on the floor and in some areas mounds of it were waiting to be bagged. Throughout the room minute dust particles swirled in the air.

Tony ushered the detectives through a closed door into a remarkably clean kitchen that led to a small bedroom. A double bed was situated against the far wall. One side of the room had hanging space for an assortment of clothes and several towels were drying on hangers. To the left of the bed was a side table with an electric clock-radio on top. Ballard and John instinctively cocked their wrists, checking the displayed time against their watches for accuracy.

John made a number of notes in his day book. "Tony, the Crime Scene officers will be here within the hour." Then with an added questioning look. "Has anything changed in the room since Tuesday morning?"

Tony shook his head. "No. As I said, I bunk here when I need to start early, or I've finished late."

Ballard pointed to a closed door leading off the bedroom. "What's through there?"

Opening the door Tony pointed inside. "A shower and toilet. The job's dusty… you have no idea. I scrub up before clients come over to inspect their kitchens."

John and Ballard looked at each other, silently questioning his claim he slept in the factory only occasionally. After glancing in the bathroom, John turned back to Tony. "Don't go anywhere for the next two hours. We'll need another statement from you, along with some photographs of the rooms. As I said, my team will be here within the hour."

Softening his expression he said, "Many thanks for your cooperation Tony. A bit late, but you now know the importance of providing us with all the facts."

Ballard joined in. "Yes Tony. You've been very helpful. Just remember, tell the truth when you're questioned again. You've nothing to hide." He chuckled. "Besides, what red blooded male wouldn't be doing what you were doing at 1.30 in the morning given the chance. Lucky guy."

Tony shook his head, relieved.

Both detectives turned, retracing their steps to the front of the factory. Tony trailed behind them and despite Ballard's comments, asked, "Am I in trouble?"

"No Tony. But cooperate with the police this time when they arrive."

"Do I need protection?"

Ballard stopped and after a quick glance at John, looked reassuringly at Tony. "It's very unlikely the killer knows you were here. You're no different to any of the other owners except for the fact you happened to hear the shot, if in fact what you thought to be a backfire *was* the shot. That's yet to be proven. Now… had you gone outside while he was leaving and he saw you… well that would be a very different matter."

Tony began to tremble again. Once he had calmed down, Ballard and John shook hands with him then exited the showroom, heading to the footpath.

With a measured glance back to the factory, Ballard commented, "Well John, despite what I said to Tony, it'd be a hell of a coincidence if what he heard wasn't the shooter." Smiling, he added, "Who will you pick to re-interview him?"

John favoured him with a scowl. "You know damn well. Bloody Bobby. A fantastic detective, yet every now and then he stuffs things up."

Ballard knew John was referring to one of his most effective detectives, Bobby Georgadinov, Macedonian, young, hyperactive and a workaholic who achieved amazing results but every so often, due to his impetuous nature, missed vital clues.

John shook his head again. "How could he have cocked-up the fact Tony was lying when he said he wasn't in the factory at the time of the shooting?"

Ballard laughed. "I'm sure you'll make him aware of his *faux pas* in your own subtle way. You make the call to get him and the Crime Scene boys here while I nip over and ask William to keep an eye on Tony… make sure he doesn't leave the factory. I'll meet you back at the car."

Five minutes later both men sat contemplating with the motor running. John was the first to speak. "A lot of activity but we haven't achieved much."

Ballard scanned through his notes. "I agree. Random bits of information but we've been around long enough to know they'll fall into place eventually. My worry is it won't be soon enough. Come on, let's do Forensics."

John flicked into 'Drive' and with a brief wave to William, they headed towards the main road.

CHAPTER
7

Forensic Services Department, employing over three hundred staff, was known internationally as one of the largest forensic science services in the world. Nestled in a bushland setting, its unremarkable presence from the outside belied its vital standing in forensic investigation, examining over 27,500 pieces of evidence each year. Those items included glass, paint and fibre material; blood and urine samples; firearms and gunshot residues; vehicle identities; drugs; explosives; fingerprints; biological material such as semen and hair; suspect documents and audio recordings.

Ballard and John often commented how their job was made easier by the fact they had access to such a professional service and over the years, their interaction with the staff had developed to the point where each regarded the other with unquestioning respect.

Twenty minutes after leaving the crime scene, John parked in the 'Police Vehicles' area. Collecting their day books they headed inside.

"Morning Frank." John waved at the stocky middle aged man sitting behind the glass security barrier, surrounded by TV screens monitoring both external and internal areas of the building.

"John... Michael, I guess I know why you guy's are here. Any progress?"

John scribbled his details on the visitor's register before stepping back for Ballard to repeat the process. "Not yet Frank. Early days, but we don't have a lot of time on this one. Let's start with ballistics. Is Robert in?"

Frank nodded. "He is. I'll let him know you're on the way." Hearing the release of the security door they passed through, heading down the long corridor towards the Firearms and Weapons Unit.

Robert Mayne was the senior Firearms Examiner, a police forensics veteran for over twenty years. With an appearance resembling Tom Cruise, but older and much taller, he enjoyed the comparison, having more than a healthy ego.

He had a sharp scientific brain, applying a formidable forensic approach to his work that spilled into his personal life which contributed to his divorce ten years earlier. Over time he had come to accept this and as a consequence had decided not to remarry, content with the worldwide recognition he enjoyed in his area of expertise.

Before Ballard and John were halfway down the corridor, Robert, wearing a white laboratory coat over his electric blue shirt, red bow tie and grey suit trousers, burst through a side door, waving to both men. "Just in time gentlemen. I've the photos of the bullet on the screen." Not one for small talk he spun around and bounded back into the room.

Both men entered, finding him peering at a computer screen displaying an enlarged, high resolution image of a fragmented bullet. Without bothering to look at them as they took up position on either side, Robert began an explanation with great animation.

"What we have here is a left hand twist, .45 calibre ACP bullet." He tapped the screen with his forefinger. "It has a reputation for effectiveness against human targets because its large diameter creates a bloody great hole in the victim, rapidly lowering blood pressure.

"The wounding potential of projectiles such as these are often characterized in terms of their expanded diameter, penetration depth and energy. Bullet energy for .45 ACP loads vary from 350 to 500 foot pounds of propulsion. Proponents of the hydrostatic shock theory contend bullets transferring this much energy in six inches of penetration *can* produce this effect."

As he drew breath, John exclaimed, "Jesus Robert, how do you keep all this stuff in your head?"

Robert ignored him, his expression one of mock humility. "Most ammunition manufacturers market what are termed 'Plus P' loadings in pistol ammunition, including the .45 ACP. This means the cartridge is loaded to a higher maximum pressure level than the original SAAMI cartridge standard. As a consequence higher velocity and more muzzle energy is generated.

"In the case of the .45 ACP, the standard cartridge pressure is 21,000 psi and the SAAMI .45 ACP +P standard is 23,000 psi. This higher grain loading is common practice for updating older cartridges to match the improved quality of materials and workmanship in modern firearms. No shell casing was found at the crime scene, so I'm unable to determine which load was used, therefore this is a moot point."

Both detectives looked at each other, shaking their head, not even pretending to comprehend the finer details. Robert continued. "The full size Glock 37 pistol was introduced by the manufacturer to use the 45 GAP cartridge. After inspecting the few rifling marks remaining on the bullet in question, it's my belief the round was fired from a Glock 37." Pausing, he straightened before turning to face them. "I'm ninety percent certain."

Ballard patted Robert on the back. "Your ninety percent is as good as one hundred percent from the average Firearm Examiner, which you most certainly are not. That's good enough for us Bob."

Robert pretended not to be chuffed by Ballard's comment, but couldn't contain a broad grin. "I saw the Crime Scene photos of the victim and by the powder burns on his forehead the shot was fired from less than a metre. The medical examiner will confirm that. This is simply an off the top of my head observation." With that he broke into an almost maniacal cackle.

Punching both men on the arm he chuckled, "Get it? Off the top of my head... " His voice trailed away as he saw they were less than amused by his crude pun.

He reverted back to business. "What *is* concerning is the fact the bullet was a hollow point." He again tapped a forefinger on the screen. "See the fragmentation around the leading edge? I don't have to draw a picture for either of you what this means. It's clear the shooter wanted his victim to stay dead, first shot."

John agreed. "Thanks Robert. This confirms what the Crime Scene guys suggested earlier. The shooter is a very, very nasty piece of work. When you get a minute, would you email the results through to me, along with the photos. Oh and yes, 'off the top of my head' *was* funny, sort of."

Robert laughed. "Always a pleasure doing business with you guys." He suddenly looked serious. "I just hope you catch the bastard before he knocks over someone else."

Ballard smiled grimly. "We'll do our best Robert. Thanks again."

After shaking hands, Ballard and John headed out into the corridor.

"Jeez Mike. Let's invite Robert to Delwyn's Christmas party. He'd be a real hoot."

Ballard grinned. "I may well do that. I'm sure he and Delwyn would get on like a house on fire... not! Ok, let's check out the chair Mario was standing on before he went off the side."

They headed further along the corridor to the Exhibit Collation Unit. On entering, they were confronted by a secure glassed area behind which sat a very attractive, auburn haired lady in her mid to late thirties. John let out a soft whistle and ignoring Ballard, fronted up to the counter, introducing himself.

Ballard stood back, allowing John his space, knowing that despite the involuntary flirting, he would establish a rapport that may come in useful in the future should a favour be required.

In no time the lady handed John an inventory sheet to sign before disappearing into one of the storage bays. He looked back, flashing a triumphant smile. "Sonia. Thirty-nine, you have to admit she looks younger. Divorced. Plus, as soon as I ask she'll be accompanying me tomorrow night to the steak house I go to in Ivanhoe." He broke into a spontaneous jive.

"You're joking."

"Nup. In the bag my man. Twenty bucks says so."

"You're on."

When Sonia returned, she was holding a very ordinary wooden chair wrapped in protective plastic with an identification tag attached to it. Smiling at John she opened the door and placed the chair in front of both men before returning behind the screen.

Ballard flattened the plastic on the chair's seat to obtain a clearer view of its surface. Within seconds he saw what he was looking for. The white paint covering the entire chair was scuffed in a number of circular patterns consistent with a shoe rotating on the seat's surface under pressure.

"Yep… just as I thought. The poor bastard was strung up to the point where only the balls of his feet were touching the chair, probably while the shooter threatened him repeatedly. I can see at least eight or nine separate rotations where the guy was twisting away from the killer. Christ, who wouldn't, thinking he was about to get his head blown off?"

John stepped in for a closer inspection. "The Crime Scene video has been sent to the office. We'll have a look when we get back. I'll bet Mario's shoes were industrial and we can run tests later to see if the rotation marks match. That of course raises the question, why was he still wearing them at 1.30 a.m. in the morning?"

Ballard rubbed his forehead. "The more we dig, the more I'm convinced the killer was after information or a confession out of Mario, then, when he got what he wanted, or didn't get it, he blew his head off." He picked up the chair and was about to attract Sonia's attention when John snatched it from his grasp.

"Not so fast China. I'll take it from here. Go write up a few notes or something for a minute or two."

Ballard smiled at Sonia as he stepped away from the glass partition. John engaged her in conversation then warmly shook her hand before walking over to Ballard. The grin on his face said it all. As both men stepped into the corridor Ballard took out his wallet, extracting a twenty dollar note. Handing it to John he muttered, "Unbelievable. I hope she knows what she's getting into."

John retorted. "No, but she's about to find out."

This provoked a laugh from Ballard who knew that behind

the cheeky exterior John treated women like goddesses, worshipping the ground they walked on. It was a characteristic that had often left him vulnerable and at times even broken hearted. Ballard hoped it wouldn't be the case this time.

Walking out of the building after waving to Frank at reception, they got into the police car and sat for a minute, each in deep thought. Ballard was the first to break the silence. "We're building a picture of this bastard which keeps getting nastier. What's disturbing is nothing's leading us *to* him, assuming it is a male. Have forensics found DNA on the rope other than Mario's?"

"Too early Mike. I've put a priority on it, but by the same token I don't want the buggers missing anything either. Fingerprints lifted from the crime scene are going through NAFIS for a nationwide match. We *may* get lucky." He didn't sound hopeful. "Anyway, at least we now know a Glock may have been used, so we can start searching the Licensing Services database for everyone registered with one and any that are stolen. Let's hope that allows us to narrow the possibilities from there." Looking glum he added, "Assuming the killer was brain dead and used a registered firearm."

Ballard clipped his seat belt. "Time to get our sugar levels up old son. Full speed to the office kind sir." Despite the obvious perils of suggesting a swift drive back to work, Ballard felt his hunger pains warranted the gamble.

CHAPTER
8

Once in the office, John instructed one of his detectives to prepare the crime scene video for viewing in the conference room. He then told Ballard he would meet him there in five minutes after buying his lunch from the canteen. Ballard collected his sandwiches and a glass of water from the kitchen before walking around with his day book. John breezed in minutes later shutting the door, then, placing his food and drink in front of him, activated the overhead video.

Again both men sensed the foreboding they had experienced at the crime scene, however this time they knew they would be witnessing the brutal outcome of a savage killing. Despite this, they attacked their food with vigour as they watched. There was the initial display of the case file number on a marker card, followed by the obligatory location shots showing the street name. The video then panned to take in all the factories in the court.

The entrance to Mario's premises came into view and both men shuffled attentively as filming progressed to the front office. The additional items such as PCs, filing cabinets and personal objects could be seen, providing them with the details that were missing when they attended the scene earlier. What caught their eye was the pile of empty beer cans on one of the desks; Ballard counted five. In addition there was a half empty bottle of Jonnie Walker. Mario may have been drinking with his two staff, drinking alone, or unwittingly had a drink with the killer; whichever way, it was something that needed to be investigated.

Both men scribbled notes in their day books as the film moved to the factory floor, displaying the rows of concrete statues. Wide shots were taken to give the scale of the room, then the crime scene itself came into view.

As prepared as both men were, John's mouth dropped open, still full of partly masticated food. What they saw was Mario's body slumped on the floor alongside an overturned chair. The noose was still around his neck, the rope lying coiled on top of him. "Jesus Christ. What sort of world are we living in?"

Ballard nodded as he washed down a mouthful of sandwich, staring hard at the screen. "I have to say, I've never got used to the amount of blood that gets splashed around in murders like these."

John stared, his mouth chewing mechanically as he took in the scene unfolding before him. The video showed a close up of the exit wound. Both men placed their sandwiches down on the table, stunned by what they saw.

John gulped down his mouthful before hissing, "My God! Look at the size of the hole in the back of the poor bastard's head." He took the remote, pausing the video before zooming in for a closer view of the grizzly scene.

Neither man was ashamed to admit the images were disturbing, unlike their younger peers who felt such emotional displays were a sign of weakness. They had an 'old school' reputation for toughness which effectively countered their display of humanity.

After switching the video to a wider shot, John got up and walked over to the screen. "Bingo! Your theory about the chair is spot on. Look at his shoes?" As he spoke, he pointed to Mario's footwear. "Definitely heavy duty. My guess steel capped to save his toes from being crushed should one of the statues drop on his tootsies."

Returning to the table he clicked the remote and the video continued its gruesome journey, documenting in excruciating detail every facet of the crime. By the time it had ended, the last image redisplaying the case file number, both men sat in silence, digesting their lunch and the scenes that had played out before them.

Ballard glanced at his partner. "Never gets any easier does it?"

With a clenched jaw John snarled, "I swear to God we'll get the bastard who did this."

To lighten the mood, Ballard collected his lunch scraps and pushed back from the table. "How about we change pace and have a chat with Ken, your favourite profiler."

John grimaced, then laughed humourlessly before collecting the remains of his sandwich and drink, following Ballard to the kitchen. Minutes later they were sitting in a tiny alcove devoting their attention to Ken Straun who performed regular investigations as well as provided the squad with profiler expertise.

Ken wore a perpetual worried expression on his face, even when he was happy. When he was drunk and providing the right music was playing, he transformed into John Travolta. Normally reserved, almost innocent looking with wide rimmed glasses, his appearance contradicted a keen intellect and a disgraceful sense of humour.

Ballard, reading John's body language, arms folded, jaw

jutting aggressively, decided to take the initiative. "I remember reading somewhere Ken that profiling was performed by a police surgeon in 1888 on Jack the Ripper. He in fact documented his suppositions… who would have believed that?"

Ballard maintained a straight face as John scowled at him, then Ken for good measure. The worried look on Ken's face intensified as he glanced between the two men. Taking a huge breath he stared up at the ceiling for at least three seconds before blurting out, "I know you don't believe in profiling John, but I do have a few theories on this case, as fresh as it is."

With Ken still staring at the ceiling, Ballard nudged John with his elbow before saying, "Ken we'll take anything you have, believe me."

"Yes Ken," John grunted, unconvincingly. "Let's hear what you've got."

Ken took another breath, directing his gaze at both men. "Well, if you take the FBI method of profiling, which is used in England, the Netherlands and other European countries, there are five phases. Firstly there's the assimilation phase in which all the evidence or information from the crime scene such as victim photos, witness statements and so forth is examined, as our team is doing now."

He paused to see if there was any reaction from Ballard or John. As there was none, he continued. "Secondly, there's the classification phase. It's here many profilers attempt to classify the murderer as either 'organised' or 'disorganised'."

For the first time John showed a degree of interest. Leaning forward he asked, "Well Ken, which one is *our* guy? In your opinion?"

Ken warmed to his task, pleased he now had John's attention. Ticking off the points on his fingers he said, "Well, it's unlikely this was a random murder, considering the killer was trying to prolong the victim's state of fear by standing him on a chair, threatening to hang him."

Ballard and John looked at each other, nodding in agreement.

"Next, as there was no forced entry, it's possible the killer knew the victim. Following that, fingerprints haven't found a match with anyone with a criminal record so this means the killer either doesn't have one, or he wore gloves. This still has to be proven.

"Now, the victim was shot with what is believed to be a hollow point at close range, I saw the photos of the powder burns on the victim's forehead. Adding to this, the shell wasn't left at the scene."

He leaned back in his chair, now comfortable in his element. "Finally and this is a bit left field, the rope wasn't just tossed onto the body, there was a degree of care taken in how it was placed. All this denotes a man who plans and may even have an obsessive compulsive disorder. I'm imagining him coiling the rope as he dispassionately views his handiwork. In summary, it's very possible this is a highly organised man, assuming it *is* a man."

John looked across at Ballard. "You know Mike, Ken's quite bright. I don't understand why you poke fun at his profiling skills."

It was Ballard's turn to scowl at John. "Ignore him Ken. He hasn't eaten all his lunch and you know what he's like when his sugar level's down."

Ken inspected both men's faces, evaluating their seriousness before continuing. "I have to caution it's in the 'classification' stage where many profilers get it wrong. While it appears the killer is organised, this is only one murder…"

"And let's hope it bloody well stays that way!" snapped John.

"Quite right. All I'm saying is I'm making an assumption on very little evidence. Now, the third stage of profiling involves attempting to reconstruct the behavioural sequence of the crime, that is, the offender's modus operandi." Ken paused to take another deep breath then exhaled. "In my opinion the killer knew the victim, who, for whatever reason let him into the factory, either because he was forced to or he was unaware of the killer's intention. At what time the crook was let in is unknown, but I'm told the shooting was around 2 a.m."

Ballard cut in. "We've a revised time of about 1.30 a.m. It's unlikely the medical examiner will narrow it down any closer, so yes we're looking at 1.30 to 2 a.m."

Ken shrugged. "That being the case, it appears there's a significant elapse time from when the victim would have gone home, say between 5 and 9 p.m. and 1.30 to 2 a.m. in the morning when he was killed." He steepled his fingers while resting his elbows on the desk. "What was the killer doing in all that time? We don't know. Was he playing the cat and mouse capture, release, recapture routine? Was he enjoying his domination over the victim? Remember the deceased posed no threat as his hands were bound behind him with a cable tie. Was the killer trying to get information, or a confession?" Ballard glanced across at John.

Ken leaned forward over his desk. "I don't believe there were any torture marks on the deceased, other than the rope marks and the bullet wound. As such, my thoughts are the killer isn't sadistic." He paused. "In my opinion he isn't capable of what I term in-your-face torture, such as cutting off fingers, bits of flesh, or engage in non fatal stabbing or mutilation wounds. Clearly he *is* capable of... again my terminology, 'decisive' murder. Kicking the victim off the chair then blowing his brains out. In a way that's a far more remote form of killing."

A smile appeared on Ken's face as he looked at John. "Of course there's another theory regarding the shooting which you may not like. Have you considered that the dispatching with a bullet may have been a mercy killing?" Both men looked at Ken, astonished. "By mercy killing I mean as the victim's neck was unlikely to have been broken, he would've been flaying about choking to death. As you know, this can take some time and it isn't a pretty sight. What *may* have occurred is the killer couldn't take it any more, or didn't have the time, so he put the victim out of his misery."

John snorted. "So the killer is really Mother Teresa sporting a .45 calibre?"

Ken smiled politely. "I warned you my theory may be hard to accept."

Ballard stole a look at John, who in turn was looking at Ken with new found respect. Both men remained silent, inviting Ken to continue.

"The final two stages are associated with the killer's signature, in other words, what the offender does to satisfy his psychological needs when committing the crime. This raises the question, has our killer achieved what he set out to do, or is this part of a bigger plan? My belief is if more killings occur, his taste for it will intensify dramatically.

"This murder was controlled rage, perhaps revenge of some kind. He'll relive this over and over in his mind, perhaps even invent an excuse to re-enact it. It may now be an intoxicating feeling he can't resist. Heaven help anyone he plans to kill in the future, should this be his objective. Without doubt he'll drag out the act, extracting maximum psychological pleasure from it."

Ken slumped back in his chair, as though his comments had

physically exhausted him. Again he looked at both men for a reaction. John obliged. "Ken, mate. I'll never doubt your ability to crawl inside a shithead's mind ever again. I'm sorry I ever questioned you." Ballard glanced sideways to see whether John was being sarcastic, surprised to see he wasn't.

Ken's face lit up in a beaming smile. "Always willing to help you guys. You know that."

Ballard stood and shook Ken's hand. "Many thanks, Ken. You've given both of us a lot to think about. I can assure you we'll be calling on you again before this is over."

John grunted his appreciation as he moved from Ken's desk, summing up the meeting. "So what we have is an 'organised' killer who's murdered for revenge in a state of controlled rage, has a penchant for mentally torturing his victim then thinks nothing of dispatching them with a minimum of effort. On top of that, if he's planning to kill again he'll precede the act with some form of extended psychological torment."

Ballard grimaced. "Scary thought John. Ok, where to from here?"

John listed their actions so far. "Well we've checked the crime scene, interviewed neighbouring factory owners, checked with forensics, viewed the crime scene video and had a preliminary profile briefing.

"Sounds a lot but think what's left: catch up on the autopsy; view the interviews with the wife, the family and Mario's two staff; re-interview each of them; see where fingerprints and the DNA take us; check with the eCrime and Crime Scene boys; update the Case Narrative in our offender and intell' databases; write up our reports…"

Ballard threw up his hands. "Enough John, enough. Let's tackle things one at a time."

John ignored him, a devilish grin on his face. "So you're suggesting we eat the elephant by starting with the tail *then* move to its testicles."

Ballard shook his head. "Very classy John, but yes, something along those lines."

As John headed towards his desk, he called over his shoulder, "I'll give the medical examiner a call to see when we can drop around."

Ballard waved a responding hand as he headed for Delwyn's office to provide her with an update. Minutes later, while he was still touching on the key points, John knocked politely on her door. Acknowledging Delwyn with a brief nod he directed his comment to Ballard, "We're in luck. Matthews has finished the autopsy. He can spare us time if we get over there in the next half hour."

Delwyn, looking tired but determined said. "Go guys. Keep up the good work, something's bound to give. I can feel it in my bones."

Handing Ballard his day book, John commented, "I knew there was a reason I didn't finish my lunch. Let's visit the man."

Five minutes later, after surviving another high speed descent in the police car they headed for the Coronial Services Centre, or as John preferred to call it, 'The Morgue'.

CHAPTER 9

'The man', Gerald Matthews, was one of the Institute's most experienced forensic medical examiners, as well as a member of the Royal College of Pathologists. Both men knew that with him performing the autopsy no detail would be missed. Everything would be documented meticulously, photographed from every angle and analysed as it should be; it was a comforting feeling.

John grimaced as he looked reflectively at Ballard. "Remember our first autopsy? If the general public knew what went on they'd do *anything* to ensure they died in their beds of natural causes."

Both men recalled in vivid detail the first all body cavity autopsy they were required to witness as young detectives. The deceased was a middle aged male, believed to have been poisoned by his wife of thirty years. The internal examination had commenced with the medical examiner making a Y shaped incision from shoulder to shoulder, meeting at the breast bone then extending down to the pubic area. The next process involved using a scalpel to peel back skin, muscle and soft tissue. Once this stage was complete, the chest flap was pulled up over the face, exposing the ribcage and neck muscles. Cuts were made to the ribcage on each side, then it was removed from the skeleton after severing the tissue behind it with the scalpel.

Even at this juncture Ballard and John had felt light headed, with a sense of disbelief at what they were witnessing. With the organs exposed, a series of cuts were made that detached the larynx, oesophagus, various arteries and ligaments. Next, the examiner severed where the organs were attached to the spinal cord as well as their connection to the bladder and rectum. Once this was done, the entire organ mass was lifted out to be dissected for further investigation.

It was here the two detectives had excused themselves, rushing over to a wash trough and parting with the lunch they had foolishly eaten prior to the viewing, despite having been warned by more experienced fellow officers.

Embarrassed and very contrite they returned, witnessing the continuing dissection of the organs, including the weighing and sampling of various tissue masses. These samples took the form of slices that could be viewed under a microscope. Major blood vessels were also dissected and studied.

The examiner then opened the stomach, inspecting and weighing the contents. This, he informed both men, who were now as pale as the cadaver itself, was helpful in determining the time of death.

A plastic body block was placed behind the neck of the deceased, like a pillow, raising the head to facilitate the removal of the brain. The examiner then made a cut with a scalpel from behind one ear, across the forehead to the other ear, then around the back of the head, enabling the scalp to be pulled away from the skull in two flaps. Again both men made a hurried journey to the wash trough, repeating their previous actions, this time with much louder, more painful dry retching.

On returning to the scene of their torment they witnessed

an electric saw cutting into the skull, as if by magic not damaging the brain. Following this, the skull was removed and the brain's connection to the spinal cord and tentorium, the membrane that connected and covered the cerebellum and occipital lobes of the cerebrum, was severed and the brain lifted out of the skull for examination.

The examiner, straight faced, despite the obvious discomfort the detectives were experiencing, explained how he would look for evidence of trauma or other causes of death besides poisoning. Toxicology tests on blood and urine would indicate any presence of drugs, including their type and quantity.

At this point the degree of comprehension the two policemen displayed was zero, the sound of blood rushing in their ears almost drowned out the examiner's words. Both men admitted defeat, stating they had to leave or they would pass out and be the laughing stock of their squad if ever word got back.

The examiner took pity, stating they had stood up very well and had they fainted they would have been in illustrious company, including a number of high profile, senior police who had been subjected to the same confronting scenes when they were novices in the job. Grateful for the comments, but feeling no less squeamish, the detectives thanked the examiner, departing as fast as their unsteady legs would carry them.

Ballard and John snorted out loud at the memory. After parking in the 'Police Vehicles Only' restricted area of Coronial Services, both men walked into the multi-storey, light grey building. Approaching the counter they presented their police identification.

Ballard smiled at the receptionist. "Would you please page the medical examiner on duty, Mr Gerald Matthews. He's expecting us." They signed the attendance register then waited by the security door.

Within minutes Gerald Matthews emerged and energetically shook their hands. His white lab coat covered a light pastel green, open necked shirt and faded blue jeans. Piercing hazel eyes matched the colour of his shirt, with greying hair slicked back from his forehead. An educated guess would place him near sixty.

"As you can see by my attire I've finished the autopsy. In fact I was sorting through some of the photographs and X rays while catching up on the forms." He shook his head. "You've no idea the number of reports we have to fill out for each autopsy these days, but I guess I'm not going to receive any sympathy talking to policemen about filling out forms, am I?"

Turning about-face he called over his shoulder, "Follow me gentlemen." Everyone strode along the corridor's continuous yellow line which ran parallel with the left wall, their shoes squeaking on the polished vinyl. "I must say I was glad to hear you were both on the case. Whoever did the shooting is *not* a nice person. The sooner he's behind bars the better. I'm surprised the press haven't made more of it."

Ballard replied. "It won't be long Gerald. A day or two at the most before the story takes on a life of its own."

John joined in. "That's why we're here. So your CSI skills can point us to the single strand of hair the killer left behind on the deceased with the resultant DNA match concluding as we speak."

Gerald stopped, looking closely at both men. "If only life were that simple guys. The shooter was *very* careful not to leave any trace of himself on the victim."

Pushing open a door, he ushered them into a small

conference room with an oval table and six chairs. Pinnéd on the walls were a series of colour photos and X-rays. Sensing the detectives wanted to begin inspecting he pulled back a chair and sat down. "Before we look at the details, I want to give you both some contextual background." John shuffled into a seat alongside Ballard, both registering mild disappointment they would have to endure an informative but complex main meal before they could move onto the dessert.

Ignoring their impatience, Gerald clasped both hands together before continuing. "The victim was in good physical condition. From the internal examination and X-rays there were no injuries on his body other than those caused by the rope around his neck, the nylon ties binding his wrists, plus of course the .45 calibre slug. I've already spoken to Robert at forensics, he's confirmed it was a hollow point."

He gave a shake of his head. "The exit hole was one of the largest I've ever seen, but more on that later. Let's talk about the rope. The victim was swinging for a considerable time before he was shot."

Ballard and John knew from experience Gerald chose not to refer to his subjects by name. Considering what his job entailed, it was understandable a degree of detachment was essential, having to perform the invasive investigations daily.

"The height of the chair was not sufficient for the fall to break his neck, so he was for all intents and purposes choking to death, which may have taken up to…"

John put his hand up like a schoolboy in class, blurting out, "Fifteen minutes or more."

Gerald looked impressed. "Correct." Ballard kicked his partner under the table.

Gerald pressed on. "In this instance, death would have

occurred due to occlusion of the blood vessels rather than asphyxiation. Obstruction of venous drainage of the brain via occlusion of the internal jugular veins leads to cerebral oedema and then cerebral ischemia. The face becomes engorged and cyanotic, that is, it turns blue through lack of oxygen. The victim in this case had the classic signs of strangulation, petechiae, which are little blood marks on the face and in the eyes from burst capillaries. Also his tongue was swollen and protruding."

John shuffled in his seat, looking uncomfortable. "Yeah. We saw that on the video. So you're saying the victim was dead *before* he was shot."

Gerald shook his head. "Not necessarily. The symptoms I've mentioned are accumulative, they would have been evident before death to some degree. That said, the victim *may* have been dead before being shot, or *near* death, then shot. I wish I could be more definitive.

"What I can say is the victim both urinated and defecated which as you know is often a symptom of hanging. However, if I was standing on a chair with a rope around my neck and had someone waving a .45 calibre in *my* face, I'm damn sure I'd have a sphincter malfunction well before I died from hanging."

The detectives chuckled, grinning at the macabre mental image while Gerald smiled at his own joke. "The injury to the victim's neck is consistent with rope, not manual strangulation. Often the hyoid bone is broken when the victim is being choked by someone using their bare hands. It's the single bone in the throat… horseshoe-shaped and situated in the anterior midline of the neck, between the chin and the thyroid. Acts a bit like scaffolding. It wasn't fractured or broken in this instance.

"Now for the damage the bullet caused. I've been in this game for… well never mind, a long time and I've *never* seen an exit wound like it." As if admonishing himself for emotional indulgence, he shrugged before regaining his composure.

"A bullet is a high-velocity missile. The injuries to the victim's head occurred from the initial laceration and crushing of brain tissue by the projectile, as well as the subsequent cavitation. High-velocity objects create rotations, generating shock waves that result in stretch injuries. In many instances the cavity may be three to four times greater in diameter than the missile itself. When the missile is a hollow point, the resultant cavity is *much* larger. Despite the gyroscopic spin of the bullet along its axis being sufficient to stabilize it in the air, the spin is insufficient to keep it on track when it enters the denser medium of body tissue.

"In this instance as soon as the bullet passed into the victim's head, it began to wobble. Its cross-sectional area became larger, the drag force increased and because it was hollow point it rapidly expanded. This all contributed to the damage within the victim's brain. As a consequence, due to the considerable build up of pressure within the skull, brain tissue ejected from both the entrance and exit wounds.

"Robert told me he believes the killer used a Glock." Gerald clasped his hands together, often a sign he was about to wrap up with a summary. "So, what we have here gentlemen is the bullet entering the skull, causing a shitload of damage to the brain tissue on the way through and leaving a barn door cavity on the way out."

Both detectives looked at each other, acknowledging this was the only detail they had come for, but refrained from saying so. Despite the mountain of technical detail, they were grateful for his efforts.

Changing subjects Gerald said, "Now to the victim's blood

alcohol content." Ballard and John sat upright in their chairs. "It was high."

John repeated his impersonation of a schoolboy answering a question by raising and lowering his hand. "We saw in the crime scene video five or so empty cans and a bottle of Johnnie on the office desk. If he'd drunk most of it himself, I'd suggest there's a point three in front of the reading."

Gerald looked impressed. "Zero point three two to be exact John. Stomach contents are yet to be fully analysed, but it was a mixture of beer and spirits with very little food. However, I would suggest he was not a heavy drinker as his liver was in good condition. Either way I'm waiting on the toxicology and serology results."

Ballard decided to challenge his own theory. "Could the victim have been so drunk the only thing holding him up when he was on the chair was the rope around his neck?"

Gerald, unaware of Ballard's theory about Mario twisting away from the killer through fear, looked puzzled.

"Yes. By no means impossible. It would've been very painful, but yes he could have wobbled about on the chair still upright, whereas if not suspended by the rope, he may have fallen down. Having said that I've seen plenty of individuals displaying sobriety with a .32 reading."

Ballard nodded, but was satisfied his psychological torture theory was sound.

Gerald stood up without warning. "Time for the picture show gentlemen. Let's start over here shall we?" He led them to the first series of photographs in which Mario was fully clothed. From there X-rays of the body were taken, as well as a series of photos of the head, with one showing the angle of the bullet as it travelled through the skull.

Gerald depicted this by inserting a thin piece of plastic, similar to a long knitting needle, through the entry point above the right eye, extending it out the cavity at the back of the skull. The subsequent profile photos showed the bullet's trajectory; simple but effective, a signature of Gerald's work.

Both men commented on this fact; Gerald suppressed a satisfied smile. "All part of the service. You'll also note the powder burns on the victim's forehead. The shooter was up close and personal. Now do either of you have any questions before I go?"

Ballard placed a hand on Gerald's shoulder. "No. You've provided us with everything except the identity of the killer. If you come up with that any time soon, be sure to give us a call."

This time Gerald did smile, but without real humour. "Make sure you get him as soon as you can. None of us like animals like that roaming loose in our streets."

Both detectives agreed as they led him out of the room and back along the corridor. At the security door they turned and shook his hand. With that Gerald hurried away to what would be another complex autopsy and for the relatives and victims involved, a traumatic chapter in their lives.

CHAPTER
10

Arriving back at the office, both men found Delwyn in the conference room viewing the crime scene video, her expression indicating she was troubled by what she saw. For the next fifteen minutes they gave her an update on the day's progress, including the salient points associated with Gerald's autopsy report. Following that they suggested further actions that needed to be taken, including reinterviewing Mario's family along with his two workers. Ballard emphasised it was here the breakthrough, if one existed, would occur.

Delwyn agreed, then checking her watch, muttered she had to attend a media briefing with the Assistant Commissioner. Gathering her folder and bottle of water, she bolted out the door, calling out encouragement over her shoulder. John looked at Ballard, shaking his head. "You wouldn't catch me doing that job for all the money in the world. She earns every dollar I'm telling you."

Ballard stood up. "Wait here John. I want to assign some background research to Susan, see what magic she can come up with."

Senior Constable Susan Deakin was the newest member of John's unit and one of the most intuitive detectives Ballard had ever worked with. Fresh out of Investigator Training, she displayed an almost Sherlock Holmes ability to accumulate and analyse facts. With a capacity to rapidly absorb information from a brief of evidence, or dig into background evidence applicable to a case, she was a rising star with a great future as a member of Homicide.

At first Ballard and John were concerned her attractiveness and single status may pose problems in the squad. What they didn't count on was her unshakable determination to prove herself, a trait often associated with red heads, of which she was a proud member. A number of squad mates found out the hard way she could mix it with the men while still maintaining her obvious femininity. Further to that, it wasn't long before word got out she was in a committed relationship with a uniformed officer. From that point on she was just another member of the unit, albeit one who at times wore short dresses, oblivious to the glances from other members.

Ballard ushered her into the conference room as John raised a hand in greeting.

"Hello Susan. We need a lead. *Anything* to get momentum on this case." Over the next five minutes he gave a concise briefing of the actions undertaken so far.

Susan wrote copious notes in her day book, asking probing questions at pertinent points, including one from left field. "Could this be a relationship gone sour, say Mario bedding the shooter's girlfriend?"

Ballard and John hesitated, not having considered the crime could be the result of a romantic liaison gone wrong.

Susan shrugged. "Cleopatra? Look at the havoc she caused? Failed romances will do it every time. Crimes of passion over women can be incredible motivators in the wrong minds."

The two senior detectives sat shaking their heads, not wanting to concede such base motivation could result in this brutal act, but mutually agreeing it had to be considered.

Ballard was the first to respond. "Susan, sometimes these investigations need a woman's perspective. I want you to do what you do best. Check Mario's bank accounts for unusual withdrawals, mobile phone records for any patterns. Include his wife in this. I wouldn't think she had the strength to do the actual deed, but she may have arranged for someone else to do it for her. See if she's taken out any insurance policies on Mario. Sweat the two workers with Bobby, see what comes up there. Check on recent customers. Did any of them owe Mario large sums of money. Was he into drugs or gambling? Cast the net as wide as you can justify."

Susan flashed an anticipatory smile at both men. "While it's horrible such a crime's been committed, I love getting my teeth into investigations like this. It's why I joined the job." Collecting her folder she hurried off to begin work.

John called out as she was about to leave. "Don't forget to go home at some point."

Ballard ran his fingers through his hair. "I think we've unleashed a bloodhound." Jotting down several notes he said, "I'll update the Case Narrative if you knock over some of the forms. Half an hour should see me out."

John paused. "Yep. We knew today would be fact finding. I'll pull a police car and head home as soon as I'm done." Grinning wickedly he added, "Oh, don't forget to say hello to Nat for me."

Ballard waved a dismissive hand in mock disgust.

Both men went to their desks, logging onto their respective systems, ensuring every pertinent fact collected during the day was recorded for the intelligence of the detectives working the case. A briefing would be conducted in the morning to bring them up to speed.

John left thirty minutes later with Ballard finishing shortly after. Picking up the telephone he dialled Natalie's mobile. "Hello Nat. I'll be there in twenty minutes, say around 6.45. Did you miss me?"

"Darling, every minute of every day I miss you. You've turned my ultra simple life upside down and I love it."

"Me too. See you soon."

He sat for a moment looking at the photos of his son, daughter and Natalie on his desk. He reached forward, briefly touching all three, feeling yet again the stab of pain caused by the separation from his daughter, Laura. He gazed out of the window and down into the grounds of the Melbourne Grammar school, watching several boys playing cricket on the oval. He wondered which one of them may be Australia's next Prime Minister; the school having produced three since 1858.

Breaking from his reverie he crossed to his locker, grabbing a fresh towel and his toiletries before heading for the wash room. Five minutes later, face rinsed, teeth cleaned and hair combed along with a splash of aftershave, he was ready to meet his future wife.

Just as he was about to head downstairs he hesitated, returning to his desk to ring his sister. "Hi Sis. Recover from this morning?" He held the phone away from his ear as she responded. Grinning he said, "Glad to hear it. Now the reason I'm calling... things are looking a bit grim here so I won't be home for a day or two. Are you staying over?" Kathryn confirmed she was as she loved having the farm to herself, which included long sessions of strength training in the gym.

"Well young farmer girl, would you ring Alan D and ask

him to bring his ride-on over for five or six hours mowing. Get him to put the bill on my tab? I'll be at Natalie's tonight, tomorrow night and perhaps even the next. Take care and yes, before you remind me, I'll give Nat your love."

Waving goodbye to the remaining detectives, he headed to his car.

CHAPTER
11

Traffic along Toorak Road was light. After passing Punt Road, Ballard turned left into Caroline Street, then half a kilometre further on made a second left into Windsor Court. Natalie had commented on the fact they both lived in a court the first time she visited his home. Unlike the farm however, Natalie's property was compact, her Federation style double clinker brick town house dominating the block.

A high pitched slate roof added to the picture postcard aspect of the building, along with large bay windows festooned by white lace curtains. An immaculate cottage garden dotted with colourful flower beds, bordered by rows of neatly trimmed English box hedge greeted visitors.

Ballard pulled into the driveway leading to the double garage on the left of the house. He remembered the first time she had shown him through her home, eager for his opinion. An ornate but tasteful front door opened onto a small entry hallway. On the left a timber staircase with polished handrails led to the upstairs bedrooms; to the right a double doorway opened into the lounge.

Every item in the room complemented the atmosphere of elegance and femininity, in sharp contrast to Ballard's home where the furnishings were practical, minimalist and masculine. Plush, cloth covered sofas and comfortable arm chairs were positioned in front of an open fireplace, complete with a marble mantle-piece. Polished Tasmanian oak floor boards added to the luxurious ambience, complete with a ten foot ceiling, intricate cornices, a ceiling-rose and ornate brass light fittings.

Moving along the hallway, Natalie had shown off the timber kitchen, the benches, including the preparation area, topped in white granite. The kitchen table was positioned to allow meals to be eaten on the run, a must for her children. For more formal occasions a small dining room led off the kitchen; the mirrored finish of an antique, French polished, myrtle dining suite complementing a matching glass fronted crystal cabinet.

Foregoing the laundry and downstairs powder room, Natalie had taken Ballard by the hand up the staircase, their footsteps muffled by the central carpet runner in Florentine burgundy. He noted each step was fitted with a brass, heritage tipped rod to ensure the carpet remained anchored in position. Radiating out from the upstairs landing were three bedrooms and a bathroom. Opening her son's room she displayed with pride how Josh kept it in immaculate condition. In direct contrast she allowed Ballard a millisecond's view of daughter Kayla's room, the opposite in tidiness. Eyes twinkling she then ushered him into the master bedroom.

Taking pride of place and dominating the room was a king size, four poster bed, complete with white netting curtains. Ballard remembered standing open mouthed, speechless that a petite lady would require such a large bed. He also remembered the wicked unapologetic reason she had given him, her candour refreshing as she seductively whispered her excuse in his ear. Adjacent to the bedroom was the ensuite, complete with double shower, double vanity and high backed, cast iron claw bath. He had refrained from enquiring the motivation for the opulence of these items.

The double garage door began to lift, dragging him back to the moment. Natalie appeared and quickly struck a provocative pose to the left of her dark sapphire blue, BMW. Dressed in a rose pink raw silk negligee and embroidered silk slippers, the sight of her took his breath away. Dimming his lights he drove into the garage, flushed with excitement, her clothing heralding the children must be staying over with friends. As soon as he stepped from the car she flung her arms around his neck, kissing him passionately. "I've missed you *so* much today, I couldn't think of anything else." Her voice was low and husky as Ballard hugged her with equal intensity.

"You look stunning. Sometimes I forget *how* beautiful you are, so when I see you again it all comes flooding back."

Natalie smiled contentedly. "Thank you Michael... I think." The smile turned into a mischievous grin.

After taking his coat from behind the driver's seat and draping it over her arm, she clasped his hand in both of hers and led him inside. The inviting aroma of roast lamb and herbs engulfed him. His digestive juices rumbled and he realised how long it had been since his midday sandwiches. Natalie placed a hand on his stomach in sympathy. "I left work an hour early to cook you something special."

Ballard kissed the side of her head in appreciation, asking if he had time to take a shower before dinner.

"Yes, the roast won't be ready for at least twenty minutes. You go and freshen up while I finish off down here."

Five minutes later he stood in the shower feeling the stinging jets of hot water soothe away the day's tension. As he rinsed the soap from his eyes he heard the shower door open then felt Natalie's body press hard against his from behind, her hands exploring him deliciously.

"Who says we can't have dessert *before* the main meal?" She kissed his ear as she pressed against him even harder. Passion rippled through his body. Turning he wrapped her in his arms, kissing her on the lips. "For a lady who's so demure in public, you sure have everyone fooled."

"But not you darling."

Five minutes later, breathless and laughing like children, they dried each other with over sized towels before slipping into white, corded velvet robes and padded slippers. Arm in arm they strolled downstairs, Ballard helping Natalie serve up the dinner.

After sitting down to eat they discussed everything except work; how the two youngest were doing at school, did the eldest daughters Emma and Tricia have boyfriends, was there anything he could do to help in the garden? It was an unwritten law they explore family matters before touching on work.

Natalie chatted about office gossip and where the law firm was heading in terms of its merger. Ballard gave a sanitised version of the day's events and how the investigation was devoid of any specific leads, with the probability the press would ratchet up the pressure by attempting to force an outcome in the coming days. Throughout this, Natalie absorbed the information, asking specific questions that demonstrated her understanding of the seriousness of the crime, plus her intuitive appreciation of Ballard's frustration.

On hearing of Susan's involvement, she squeezed his hand. "She's like the daughter you feel you don't have." Ballard gave a single negative shake of his head, having heard the comment before.

"No darling. She already has two fathers. A natural father and a step-father. I think two is enough, don't you?"

Natalie smiled. "No doubt, but you look out for her like a father. I think that's a good thing. Especially for you. As I've said, your daughter *will* come back some day, but it may take years before it happens. I just hope the ruthless aspect of your character doesn't take control over your tender loving side… which you'll need to show if you want to have a relationship with her."

She leaned across, kissing him on the forehead. "Such a complex man. I don't buy your 'I'm a simple country boy' routine. But I wouldn't have you any other way."

Ballard sensed he had just been analysed, but felt no resentment as he knew Natalie could read him like a book, at the same time supporting him without question. He squeezed her hand.

After they washed and dried the dishes, Natalie poured herself a glass of vintage port and snuggled alongside him on the sofa. "This is as good as it gets darling."

Feeling excited yet uncharacteristically nervous he took her glass, placing it on the table beside him. Holding both her hands he looked into her eyes. "Natalie you know how I feel about you."

She blinked, alarm flickering across her face. "Yes… is anything wrong?"

He smiled, shaking his head. "Quite the opposite. Ever since I met you I've known how lucky I am, how suited we are for each other. I can't image not being with you, always… so… I desperately want to marry you. *Will* you marry me?"

Natalie's face lit up in the broadest of smiles, then began to crumble into joyous tears as she flung her arms around his neck.

"Yes and yes again!" She pulled back, wiping her eyes with the sleeve of her dressing gown. "And about time, Michael Ballard. I was beginning to wonder if you would *ever* say the words I longed to hear. I love you more than I ever thought possible and that's the reason I'm so certain about this. We both know when something's right and this is just *so* perfect."

Ballard smiled with relief, unable to think of anything to say, feeling the sting of tears in his eyes. Despite his attempt to conceal the fact, Natalie kissed both in turn, indicating nothing escaped her, not when it came to his emotions.

For the next hour they discussed wedding plans, what the future would hold for them, the impact of their decision on her youngest children, what they could look forward to as husband and wife. All the while they sat side by side, knowing all their previous life experiences, both good and bad, had contributed to their understanding of how fortunate they were to have each other; this together with the health, wisdom and financial stability to enjoy it.

Natalie noted how tired Ballard was. She took his hand, then, switching off the lounge room lights, led him upstairs. Together they brushed their teeth after which she playfully applied moisturiser to his face. "You're very fortunate to have had parents and grandparents with such good genes. You do know that?"

He smiled, scooping her into his arms before taking her into the bedroom, placing her tenderly on the bed. Removing her robe, he slipped out of his while gently kissing her breasts. Cuddling alongside her he felt the warmth of her firm body, aware that tonight would be the beginning of the rest of their lives. Within minutes they were sound asleep.

CHAPTER
12

"Mike – mate. Wake up!"

"John I *am* awake – *now*. I'm talking to you on the phone aren't I?" Ballard was irritable at having been so rudely disturbed from a deep sleep. Natalie snuggled closer alongside him, warm and inviting. He scowled at the clock radio, surprised it showed 7.00 a.m.

"Bobby came through. Too complicated to explain now. Get in here as quick as you can. Delwyn's with me." He hung up.

Ballard knew that as enticing as Natalie's presence was, the anticipation of being able to progress the case was impossible to ignore. Crawling out of bed he slipped on his robe.

Natalie stirred. "I'll get your breakfast."

He sat on the edge of the bed, stroking her hair. "No need darling, I'm a big boy…"

Her lips curled. "You certainly are."

Smiling, he ignored the comment. "Stay here, I'll be fine." He shuffled into his slippers before trudging downstairs.

No sooner had he begun preparing his regular breakfast than Natalie appeared, yawning, looking dishevelled yet beautiful at the same time. He smiled, knowing her old fashioned values prevented her from ignoring her man. He splashed milk into the bowl then began gulping it down.

"Michael, you'll make yourself sick."

He winked at her, but continued devouring at the same pace. Natalie went to the fridge, taking out the remaining roast lamb to make two sandwiches, topping each with lettuce and tomato.

Twenty minutes later, shaved, showered and wearing one of the numerous suits he kept at Natalie's, he was ready to leave. Just before he stepped into the Chrysler he gave her a lingering kiss. "Don't work too hard today Mrs Ballard." She shivered with delight, kissing him back.

As he drove out of the garage, she assumed seductive poses then finished with a brief flash of her breasts, almost causing him to back over a line of box hedge. With a wicked grin she pressed the button to close the garage door and was gone. Ballard shook his head, wishing he could stay but already feeling his pulse quicken as he anticipated the task ahead.

Twenty minutes later he was sitting listening to his animated partner in Delwyn's office.

"Well, after I gave Bobby a verbal whack yesterday he reinterviewed Tony along with Mario's two workers, in case they were holding out on anything. Guess what old son, they bloody well were." John's expression was dynamic. "Self preservation is a wonderful thing Mike. I'll explain.

"About a week before the shooting, the two workers were guiding one of the cement trucks down the driveway at the factory when a guy came storming out of the showroom and got into a Mitsubishi Pajero. The workers remembered this because the driver had to wait while the concrete truck was reversing in. He must've been in a hurry because he blasted the horn several times causing one of the workers to give him the finger.

"Bobby asked if either of them remembered the number plate. Bugger me, one of them *did*. Well, the three alpha characters that is." He broke off, letting out a cackle. "Sorry, I'm on an adrenalin rush here. The letters were the same as the nickname he's given his daughter… 'TES'. Can you believe it?"

Ballard continued to be mystified as to why John was so upbeat. "Anyway, the worker had no idea what the three *numbers* of the plate were. This backs your theory of witnesses remembering only facts that interest them, but as luck would have it the other worker did. Well the first *two* numbers anyway… he wasn't certain of the third. So Bobby ran the remaining ten combinations through VicRoads and *voila*, out popped the Mitsubishi. From there it was simply a matter of showing the workers the driver licence photo of the registered owner."

He paused for breath. "Hasn't it been great for investigators since the techos' gave us online access to VicRoads photos?" Not waiting for an answer he pressed on, his excitement infectious. "Both workers confirmed the guy who came out of the showroom matched the licence photo."

He paused long enough for Ballard to ask, "So John, what's the significance of all this?"

"Glad you asked. The significance my friend is that when the workers went back inside the showroom they found Mario staring blankly at a wall in the office, drinking beer. Something he's *never* done before… well not at that time of day. When they asked what was wrong, he bit their head off. They said from that point on he wasn't the same guy, right up to the shooting. Withdrawn one minute, snapping at them for no reason the next… often just staring into space."

Ballard decided to fill in some of the blanks. "So the workers put two and two together and like Tony, didn't mention this when they were first interviewed because they thought if they didn't get involved as witnesses there was a chance they wouldn't finish up like Mario."

"Correctamundo! Between you and me as they're both married with a young family, it's understandable. However," he leaned forward, his index finger pointing skyward for emphasis, "thank Christ Bobby did extract that information from them… now for the *big* surprise as to who the Mitsubishi driver is."

Ballard shook his head, still perplexed. Opening his day book, John slid an A4 sized photo across the table. Ballard reached over and picked it up, his mouth dropping open in disbelief.

"That's…" he broke off, looking at John then Delwyn before studying the photo again. "That's Richard Parnell's brother, Eric!"

"Spot on. It is indeed. Small world, huh?" Having delivered the bombshell John sat back with a smug look on his face, hands folded across his stomach.

Ballard's mind flashed back to the events leading him to charge Richard Parnell with murder in the Supreme Court eleven years earlier. A security van had pulled up alongside a NAB bank in the Southland Shopping Centre. Two security guards, each armed with a Smith & Wesson .38 and carrying a metal money box entered the bank, emerging five minutes later with the payroll for a trucking company.

Within seconds they were confronted by two men wearing stocking masks each holding an eight shot, M30 Bentley pump action shotgun. Both guards were forced onto their knees as terrified shoppers fled into shops or hid behind protective cover. The two guards were then struck on the back of the head with the butt of the shotguns, fracturing one guard's skull and knocking the other unconscious.

The thieves then picked up the metal box containing the money and after firing a shot at the security van's windscreen to ensure the third guard remained inside, they began walking nonchalantly from the shopping centre.

Their arrogance cost them dearly because the guard they thought was unconscious managed to draw his weapon and fire two shots, hitting one of the thieves in the shoulder and thigh, dropping him to the ground. Despite his injuries the thief returned fire, striking the security guard in the head and chest. The second accomplice, showing no concern for his wounded partner, hefted the box and ran to a black sedan parked in a disabled zone.

As he drove off he fired several shots into the air, guaranteeing witness statements varied hopelessly as to the car's number plate, the make of vehicle and the direction it took off in. The car was later found abandoned in a side street, burnt-out, the fire accelerated by additional petrol contained in a charred metal can located nearby.

While all this was occurring, the thief who had been shot was tackled by a retired army officer and subdued. Still bleeding profusely, his life was saved by his captor applying direct pressure to the wounds. Police and ambulance arrived and the injured offender was rushed to hospital under heavy police guard.

Initially the Serious Crime Task Force took responsibility for investigating the incident. Two days later, when the guard with the fractured skull and gunshot wounds died of complications, it became a Homicide matter.

Ballard spoke with the guard's wife and was so stricken by her grief he contributed $2,000 to a fund established for her and the family. When John found out he reprimanded him... not for contributing the money, but for becoming too emotionally involved.

Ballard interviewed the offender a number of times while preparing a brief of evidence for the murder trial; this included secondary charges of manslaughter and armed robbery. Those witnesses brave or foolhardy enough to have watched the proceedings at the bank identified him as the man who had struck the savage blow on the guard before shooting him.

His name was Richard Parnell, a thirty-five year old career criminal whose record stretched back twenty years. Ballard discovered over the course of the investigation he had a twin brother, Eric, a complete contradiction in character. This brother had no criminal record, was married with a two year old daughter, had a mortgage on his home in Northcote and worked a full time job as a brick layer.

Eric was soon eliminated as the other accomplice, his alibi placing him on holiday with his family in Italy; his flight itinerary, overseas accommodation and passport verifying this.

From day one Richard Parnell refused to divulge who his partner in crime was. Throughout the committal hearing and finally in the Supreme Court he continued to ignore demands to name his accomplice. Ballard's gut feeling then, as now, was a threat was hanging over Richard, extending to his ill mother, his brother Eric and Eric's family. Fear prevented Richard from making a statement, or entering a plea on his own behalf. The threat was real and current because even after receiving his sentence of fourteen years, with a non-parole period of eleven, this still failed to shake his stubborn silence. Ballard appealed the sentence but lost his request to have it increased, further devastating the dead guard's wife and to a lesser degree Ballard himself.

He brought himself back to the present. "You're both aware six months ago I gave evidence at Parnell's parole hearing and managed to have his request for early release denied?" Delwyn and John nodded.

Delwyn produced a printed note from her folder. "I've got here that four months later Corrections Victoria notified you of Parnell being bludgeoned to death in the gym at Barwon prison."

Ballard drew in a Ken like lungful of air. "Yes, I went to his funeral and remember standing back from the mourners watching Eric, the brother, help his frail mother to one of the waiting cars. As they shuffled past, the look of sheer fury on his face when he saw me was bloody disconcerting. I don't mind admitting it shook me up a bit."

He relived the event. "It was over ten years since I'd seen him. The change in the man was unbelievable. He was much stockier, his head clean shaven and the rage in his eyes nothing short of fanatical."

Ballard remembered updating the Case Narrative in the offender and intelligence databases, then pushing the incident from his mind, albeit without success for a number of days.

John leaned forward. "So here are the facts as we know them, Mike. Mario is blown away in his factory Tuesday morning. A week before Eric Parnell is seen coming out of the show room in a bit of a tizz." He glanced across at Delwyn. "That's copper terminology for 'really pissed off.'"

Delwyn laughed. "Is that so John"

"We know Eric's brother Richard was involved in an armed robbery over eleven years ago. Never dobbed in his side-kick, but I have to say Mario's fast assuming first choice on that score. Six months ago Michael prevents Richard from getting back onto the street, then four months later he has his head caved in at Barwon. The funeral takes place with the brother a very unhappy camper. This is where Susan comes in."

Ballard looked questioningly at John who continued. "When Bobby returned to the office around 7 p.m. yesterday, right after we'd left to go home, he called Susan asking her to come back to work. He certainly wanted to make amends for the other day." He laughed humourlessly. "Anyway, they've been digging up facts all night. You won't believe what they've come up with.

"After entering Parnell's name in the database it came back that you'd charged the brother with murder. Susan got hold of one of the public servants who manages the Archives & Storage Centre at Laverton. She had him picked up by a police car then taken to his work in the bloody middle of the night mind you so he could unearth your brief of evidence on the armed robbery. She sugared it with overtime and he accepted."

Ballard looked across at Delwyn who shrugged noncommittally. "That's right Michael, above and beyond."

John snorted. "Rubbish. Exactly what they should've done considering Bobby's screw up in the first place. Anyway, Susan went through the file with Bobby for background information. They came across Eric's address, 14 Allison Street, Northcote. This matched the VicRoads record on the licence photo that Bobby showed Mario's workers." He tapped the photo of Eric on the table in front of him. "Can you believe he hasn't moved in over fifteen years?"

Ballard smiled. As John had always rented, never owning property, living fifteen years in one location seemed an eternity. Ballard thought of his parents' stone farm house in Bordertown where he grew up, built in 1881, now owned by his brother and still standing.

John frowned as he said, "It was at this point Bobby and Susan went overboard in initiative, but it's turned out for the best. They drew a car then went around and sat off his house." John looked at the wall clock. "They reckon it was around 5 a.m. when they got there. Straight off they saw the Mitsubishi in the driveway. The plate matched the VicRoads record so they knew they had the right location.

"That's when they rang me. After I bawled them out for getting me up so early, they gave me the story I've just given you. I told them to do nothing and stay where they were and I'd be there as soon as I could. I also arranged for several plain clothes units to back up Bobby and Susan."

John took a sip of water from the glass in front of him. "About thirty minutes after they rang me they saw Eric come out of the house carrying a box of some sort under his arm and get into the Mitsubishi. Guess where he went?" He looked at Ballard as if testing his powers of deduction.

Ballard smirked, taking a punt. "My dear Watson he drove past Mario's factory, elementary I would have thought."

John's mouth dropped open. "Jesus! I have to say for an old guy you're good. You should've been a detective…"

Delwyn chipped in, grinning. "Get on with it you two."

John scratched his head. "Things got a bit messy from there on… they lost Eric. Yep, got caught at the Epping railway crossing and he disappeared in the traffic. Poof… gone! Anyway, knowing I was coming over to Eric's place they drove back and waited, well sort of. Bobby couldn't help himself and deciding to do a bit of door knocking either side of Eric's house."

Ballard erupted. "You're kidding me. Why not bloody well park three uniform cars outside Eric's address for good measure? Jesus John!" Anger flashed across his face.

John held up a calming hand. "Believe it or not he did it rather well. Starting a few doors back he worked his way along the street towards Parnell's house. At the house two doors down he told the old guy who answered the door, in his pyjamas mind you, that a dog had been found wandering the street and was being held in one of the cells back at the station. Bobby explained the dog had a tag listing Allison Street, Northcote, but the number was unclear. The guy's house number was ten.

"Bobby said the dog was going berserk so the police at the station thought it best to find the owner as soon as possible."

Ballard looked sceptical. "The guy bought the story?"

John laughed dryly. "Yep. Bring a lost puppy into the mix and you can convince the public of almost anything. Anyway the guy said the dog wasn't his. Bobby asked if the next door neighbour had a dog… the guy said no. When Bobby asked about Eric's house, number fourteen, the guy said no because the elderly lady who used to live there with the 'nice couple and their daughter' didn't like dogs."

"Used to live there?"

"Yeah. The guy said the old lady, Roma, died two months ago. Her husband had passed away ten years before. Your arrest brief had Eric's mother's name in one of the statements, Susan and Bobby remembered it being Roma. Now, two months ago…" He looked up at the ceiling in reflective thought. "That would have been right after Richard's funeral. Anyway, the neighbour didn't stop there. Said the young daughter had been hit by a car only days after her grandmother died. Hit-run. Broke her leg, banged about a bit but she was ok, healed up in time for her and her mother to go overseas."

"Are you for real? How does the guy know all this?"

John tapped the notes in his day book before answering.

"He's a bit of a good Samaritan, brings the bins in for all his close neighbours. Loves to gossip, so I'll leave the rest to your imagination."

"So Bobby stumbled on the one neighbour who knows everybody's business?"

"Yes sir. Luck of the brave." John shuffled into a more comfortable position on his chair. "Now get this, the wife and daughter, her leg still in plaster, left for an overseas holiday in Italy the day before…"

Ballard felt his pulse quicken. "Don't tell me, the day *before* Mario was shot."

John's head bobbed vigorously. "Bobby and Susan rang the airlines and got lucky. Susan has a contact there who did some digging."

"Has Eric got a ticket to join them?"

"Don't know. The airlines are a bit more sensitive about giving out information for impending flights, so Delwyn's working on that aspect."

Delwyn looked at both men in turn. "Yes, I'm waiting on a call." She paused. "Well done guys. With a healthy mix of experience and luck, together with youthful endeavour, we may have a suspect. The trouble is we haven't a clue where this guy is right now. I've already requested Special Ops to sit off his house until further notice, around the clock if necessary. I'm arranging for an arrest warrant to be issued, along with a warning for members not to approach but to track him and notify us.

"Neighbours for four or five houses on either side of his house have been told not to go anywhere near it, or him. We're also trying to determine where he works. No luck on that front which is frustrating. We checked with the nosy Good Samaritan… even *he* didn't know. We've notified the airport of course, should he try to leave the country. I've sent Bobby and Susan home as they were running on adrenalin and not much else."

She gave both men the steely look she was renowned for. "It's vital none of this information gets out. No-one other than your immediate squad members need know the details until we have something concrete. I shudder to think if the press get hold of this."

She stood up, pushing her chair under the desk. "This is all circumstantial at this point, but by God it feels right. Keep digging and make sure this doesn't leak out. I'm off to let the brass know where we're at." Smiling she said, "It's true. Nothing beats experience mixed with youthful energy." Grabbing her folder she hurried from the office.

CHAPTER
13

Both men sat grinning at each other before John declared, "We've just been complemented... I think."

Ballard let out a soft whistle. "Christ, I leave work for *one* night to propose marriage to a beautiful woman and you and your crew move mountains."

John reached over, shaking his hand energetically. "Congratulations. She's a wonderful lady, I'm as jealous as hell. Make this one work."

Ballard winced. "Er, yes John. I intend to."

Getting back to business, Ballard asked, "If it *was* Eric doing the shooting, why so blatant? Why not pick some quiet location to blow Mario away? Had he done that, this case would have remained open forever. I'm assuming the need to know who the hit-man was has everything to do with it. Ok, let's get Ken. I want to run a theory by him."

John rolled his eyes as he followed Ballard out of Delwyn's office.

They found Ken in the kitchen. Grabbing him by the arm they ushered him back to his desk; the worried look on his face intensifying. For the next five minutes they detailed what had happened since they had last seen him.

"So Ken, what do you think?"

"It's obvious, assuming Eric *is* the shooter and all you've told me is correct, that he's gone over the edge. The question still remains though, has the threat that prevented him from knocking Mario off before this been removed? Looking at it logically, the intimidation directed at his family as well as himself for over ten years is enough to screw with anyone's mind. So... we now know the brother's dead, along with the mother. Further to this, the wife and daughter are safely out of the country."

Taking one of his famous breaths he continued. "This leads to several possibilities. If Mario had someone else doing the intimidation to Eric or his family, why is Eric still in the country? Why not fly out to join his wife and daughter after doing the deed to Mario? By sending his family out *before* he killed Mario he was ensuring their safety, should he fail.

"Perhaps he *did* find out the hit–man's identity and is going to knock him off when he finds him. On the other hand, if Eric didn't find out the guy's identity, then the fact he's still here after Mario was shot, well it's clear..." He stopped, looking at both men like a school teacher having asked his pupils an elementary question. Ballard and John sat in silence, realisation suddenly dawning on their faces.

John responded first. "Of course. Unfinished business."

Ken slapped his hand on the desk. "Correct. And with Eric's current state of mind it won't be pleasant. It's possible he isn't even planning to leave the country. His wife may have found out the hit–run was Mario's doing to let Eric know he still had a hold over the family, even though the brother and mother are dead. She could've panicked and decided to opt out with the daughter, leaving the husband to sort out the mess.

"So who does Eric still want to target? Other than the hit–

man, who would he hate so much he's contemplating killing again, all the while running the substantial risk of being caught … perhaps not even *caring* if he's nabbed or killed."

Both Ken and John looked across at Ballard who shrugged noncommittally.

"Maybe so guys, but this wouldn't be the first time I've been threatened by a crook."

Ken then added the final piece to the puzzle, hitting Ballard like a sledge hammer.

"And if he can't hurt that person directly, or it's not sufficient revenge for his current demented state, what about that person's family?"

Ballard sat bolt upright before blurting out, "Jesus… Natalie or the kids, perhaps my sister…" An edge of panic entered his voice.

John grasped his partner's shoulder. "Mike, we'll make sure nothing happens, I promise. We'll find a safe location and have a uniform escort the kids from school and Natalie from her work. The same for your sister, I'm not sure how to tackle the issue with your daughter though?"

Ballard snapped out of his momentary funk. "It's ok John, I'll handle things with Laura. Give me five minutes, I need to ring Natalie. You work out the location details."

He took his mobile knowing caller id would ensure a prompt reply. When she came on the line her voice was upbeat. "Hello Michael. Wish you'd stayed a bit longer…"

"Natalie!" The urgency in his voice shocked her into silence. "*Where are you right now?*"

"About to… to get in the car for work." Fear caused her voice to waver. "Michael, what is it?"

"Nat, listen carefully, *please*, you and the kids *may* be in danger because of this case I'm on. It's possible I'm under some sort of physical threat. We can't rule out our suspect knows about you, where you live or where Kayla and Josh go to school."

Ballard glanced at his watch. "The kids won't be there yet. Call them on their mobile, *insist* you pick them up. Tell them it's urgent. Once you've got them go to the Prahran Police Station and ask for the senior sergeant. Arrangements are being made right now and you'll be taken somewhere safe." His eyes narrowed, thinking fast. "What about Emma and Tricia? Where are they?"

"Interstate. Emma's on holidays this week in Queensland. Tricia's in South Australia for work until at least tomorrow…"

"*Ok*. Once you have the kids at Prahran and *only* then, contact Emma and Tricia. Make sure they stay away for at least forty-eight hours. Things should be clearer later today. I can't explain any more, there's no time. Just get out of there *now*! I promise I'll be in touch some time later this morning. I love you darling."

With an aching heart he hung up as she pleaded with him to be careful. He took a steadying breath, waving John over. "I've spoken with Nat, she's picking up the kids. Give the senior sergeant a call at Prahran. Minimum details and have her met by the escort. I'll sort out the issue with Laura then ring Kathryn."

Ballard rang his ex-wife's mobile, surprised and relieved when she answered instead of adopting her usual practice of screening the call. He wasted no time. "Maureen. Listen very carefully." He gave the same rapid explanation he had with Natalie. "It's possible the suspect knows I have a daughter, but as I haven't been in touch for so long the probability of that is low, however we can't take the risk. Do you want Laura taken to a safe location here in Melbourne?"

He sensed reluctance by her hesitation. "Ok then. Take Laura somewhere that isn't one of her girlfriends, or your friends, nowhere obvious. Book a motel if you have to. I'll pick up the bill. This will only be for twenty-four, perhaps forty-eight hours. Don't tell *anyone* where you are, not your mother, not even the school. Maureen... I'm so sorry to drop this on you but the less people who know the safer you and Laura will be. Keep your mobile on and ring me if you have any issues."

She began a string of questions but Ballard hung up, needing to make a final call to his sister.

John tapped him on the shoulder. "Prahran's been notified, they'll be ready for Natalie and the kids as soon as they arrive. We contacted the AC for verbal authorisation and he agreed, saying, 'whatever it takes'. Mate, everything's going to be alright." John's face was intense but controlled as he attempted to reassure his partner. "You're doing the right thing by not taking any chances."

Ballard met his gaze. "I've one more call to make. Kathryn's staying over at my place for a few days. I need to get her out of there. Let's put her up with Natalie and the kids so we're not chasing family on too many fronts."

Punching in her speed dial number her phone rang three times before switching to her recorded message. He waited for the beep, anxiety etched on his face.

"Kathryn. Ring me back *straight away*. I need to talk to you urgently." As soon as he had completed the message he rang his home number. The call went to message bank. Frustrated he delivered the same request, hanging up with a growing sense of unease. He considered the necessity of ringing his son Bradley but assessed the likelihood of any danger occurring at the Military Academy as minimal.

John could see the tension on his partner's face. "Mike I'll get the Gisborne police to drop around and have Kathryn call you while they're with her. Once you've explained the situation she can follow them back to the station. Then we can work out the logistics of putting her with Nat and the kids."

For the first time in ten minutes Ballard forced a weak smile. "Thanks John. There's nothing like having your family threatened to highlight what's really important in life." He rolled his head from side to side, massaging the back of his neck to ease the tension.

As he headed to the kitchen for a glass of water his mobile signalled the delivery of a message. He scanned the screen, relieved to see Kathryn's name on the display. His relief instantly turned to gut wrenching horror as an image of Kathryn appeared, distraught, dressed in a blue track suit, squatting awkwardly on the lounge room floor with both wrists shackled by cable ties to the leg of the piano. The frozen image of her face was pure terror. His senses screamed denial as blood pounded in his ears, his legs buckling.

John saw the colour drain from his partner's face and rushed over to inspect the image on the screen. "Jesus Michael. Christ Almighty! Ok, take a breath. Let's work this out."

As Ballard collapsed onto a chair, his back to the wall, a second message was delivered. Sick with fear he pressed the view key. The image was from another angle in the lounge, still showing Kathryn but this time with the addition of an innocuous brown box alongside her, its purpose evident by the digital clock taped to it.

Ballard leaned forward, emitting a protracted moan as though in immense pain. Aware of John gesticulating and shouting instructions above him, he rubbed his hands over his face, distraught.

"The bastard! God knows what's in the box, but we *have* to assume the worst."

John inhaled deeply, leaving his hand on Ballard's shoulder for support. "That'll be the box Bobby and Susan saw Eric with this morning. He's gone by Mario's to check out what was happening there, saw it was being guarded by police then decided to head out to your place instead."

Ballard slumped further forward, willing his brain to act logically. "John, the potential of a bomb means…" Again his mobile signalled a message. This time the image was of Eric Parnell holding a device in his right hand. The photo was distorted as he was taking the picture using Kathryn's mobile in his outstretched left hand. "God! He's got a detonator switch of some kind, or *pretending* to have one. It's his way of controlling the situation, he's basically saying, 'Kill me copper and your sister dies.'"

With an effort Ballard got to his feet, years of training and experience cutting in. "John, get two of your guys in the conference room to take instructions. We'll use it as a control centre before we head off to Gisborne."

John let out a shrill whistle, stabbing a finger at two of his team who had been watching from a distance, waving them over. He barked orders and they bolted away, returning to the conference room within seconds, their day books open, waiting for orders.

John gave a rapid summary of the situation and Ballard saw both men glance at him, their faces registering alarm; despite this they continued to focus on the flow of information. Ballard began by asking the two officers to write down the required actions as he detailed them.

"We have to assume the box is a bomb, despite the probability it's a ploy to control the situation. Have the Bomb Response

Unit put on standby to move when we give the order. As they're part of Special Ops they can pass on the details to mobilise the tactical team as well."

One of the detectives, Phil, who had been scribbling furiously rushed from the room to make the call while the other, Adam, looked at Ballard and John, his pen poised.

Ballard continued. "There's only one way out by car from my house, Chelsea Road intersects at right angles with Peters. My place is at the end of Chelsea Road, number 77. That's a rural number which means my driveway is seven hundred and seventy metres from the intersection with Peters. We need to set up a checkpoint at the intersection to stop cars entering the area. The quickest response will be from the Gisborne Police, but I stress they mustn't engage with Parnell."

John took the licence photo out of his day book, pushing it across the table towards the detective. "Contact Communications, plus Gisborne direct and have the local cops move as soon as possible to the check point. Get Gisborne's sergeant or senior sergeant to coordinate until the duty officer arrives to assume area command. The SOG will take over when they get there. Have the Gisborne boys seal off the location. Allow no one in. If a silver Mitsubishi Pajero is driven out by this man," John pointed to the photo which included the registration number of the vehicle, "tell the police *not* to engage. If he has a female on board, follow him at all costs, but at a safe distance. At this point we *think* he may have a bomb. Tell the local guys to run a licence check to bring up his photo and print off a number of copies before they attend. It's vital everyone at the checkpoint know what he looks like."

Ballard sat bolt upright. "I've just realised, Parnell may be driving Kathryn's car, so if the police see a blue Honda Civic…

Jesus, I can't remember her reg' number. Have one of the guys out there run a check on Kathryn Elizabeth Ballard, she's the only one under that name on the VicRoads' database. If Parnell's in the vehicle, then the same instructions apply. There's to be *no* shooting as he may have my sister down on the floor, or even in the boot."

John glanced momentarily at Ballard. "To emphasise Michael's point, whether Parnell is or isn't alone in the Mitsubishi or Honda, have whoever's in charge at the time make a decision how they'll follow the vehicle without losing him. They're *not* to engage, I stress this man will shoot to kill or perhaps explode the bomb. They're to follow him any way they can, radioing for backup.

"Communications will drop the chopper up there unless it's involved somewhere else in the state. At the very least have them send a couple of highway patrol cars to the intersection, they're better equipped to handle the higher speeds if Parnell makes a run for it. We'll also need the dog squad there should he finish up on foot at some point. Get the ambulance, fire brigade and SES to the location on standby. Finally, have a radio channel assigned we can use exclusively when we get on the road."

The detective finished his frantic note taking then looked up, hesitating. John snapped at him. "Adam, go!" The young man rushed from the room, colliding with Phil who was returning. The detective dropped into his chair, stating the Special Operations and Bomb Response Units would be ready to move within minutes.

John half smiled for the first time. "Thanks mate." Turning to Ballard he said, "We need to contact Delwyn and let her know what's happening as soon as we've got this under control. What's next Mike?"

Ballard ticked off the issues. "Let's pray the local police get there in time to seal off Peters road. The SOG will have their specialist negotiator as this is a hostage situation. John, not a word to Natalie about this until it's over. She's worried enough. God I hope the chopper's free to track Parnell if he makes a move."

Looking at Phil, Ballard asked, "What've we missed?" The detective responded immediately. "We need to send the SOG and the Bomb Unit up there now sir. I'll give them a call to move out if you agree."

Ballard forced a smile. "Make it happen. Push the point with the SOG they're to stay at the intersection until *we* get there."

Phil turned to leave but Ballard stopped him. "One more thing Phil, have one of the local police change into casual clothes and warn the neighbours in the street to evacuate. I'm pretty sure most of the residents work so they may not be home. There's eleven properties in the street, not counting mine. I know it's unlikely the bomb, if it is one, would be powerful enough to affect anyone else because of the distances involved, but again we have to play safe. Get the copper to go in on foot as this'll attract less attention. Tell Gisborne police to inform whoever the officer is *not* to go anywhere near my place." Phil rushed off.

John looked across at Ballard. "Parnell will demand to speak to you, you know that."

"Yes John, but when? When it's too late?"

John stepped to the door and bellowed Ken's name. Seconds later Ken rushed in, standing awkwardly in front of them. John waved him to a chair. Again he gave a succinct summary of the events.

Ballard leaned towards Ken. "Do I ring Parnell *before* we go up there?"

Ken's response was immediate. "You need to take the initiative. At the moment he's controlling everything. The photos are his way of thumbing his nose – that he's taken charge. My belief is after so many years of feeling helpless due to the threats, he's now obsessed with the need to control every aspect of this situation."

John snorted in disgust. "Yeah… and I'd say he's doing a bloody good job of it!"

"Maybe so John, but let's regain some authority. Kathryn can't be left in this state for much longer."

Ballard slumped further in his chair as images of his sister flooded through his head, threatening to overwhelm him. Had she been physically or sexually assaulted? Up to this point his professional instincts and actions had shielded him from succumbing to the brutal reality this may have occurred.

Against his will he began visualising the sheer terror his sister must be experiencing.

Ken's voice jolted him back to the moment. "The SOG are powerless because Parnell has a detonator with his finger on the button. Negotiation is the one thing that may lessen his current dominance. Somehow we have to determine what his real motives are." Ken stared hard at Ballard. "I don't want to alarm you any more than I already have, but my belief is he wants to get you in the house with your sister and…" he hesitated, "I *think* he sees himself going out in a blaze of glory, taking you and Kathryn with him. Death by cop."

Ballard stared blankly as John said, "You're right Ken. But thanks to you we're at least getting some way into the crazy bastard's demented mind."

Ballard snatched up his mobile. "Let's see if he's willing to talk." He dialled Kathryn's number and within seconds signalled

that Parnell was on the line. After identifying himself he began
to speak but stopped as though struck, his eyes flicking towards
John and Ken. For the next three minutes he stood rooted,
listening, his face ashen.

Hanging up he looked ten years older. "Pure naked rage.
And yes Ken, he's about to tip over the edge, certain he'll be
dead within the next few hours. He started by shouting that if
I said *one* word he'd let the bomb off. I was to listen and say
nothing. He's fanatical about having absolute control. He then
went on a rambling monologue, come confession.

"He blamed *me* for his brother's death because I convinced
the parole board to extend his gaol time. He was actually
sobbing, raving about his mother dying prematurely from the
grief caused by her son being bashed to death in prison. He then
flew into a screaming rage, babbling his brother had confessed
Mario was the other accomplice in the armed robbery eleven
years ago and how Mario avoided being caught by threatening
the whole family. It seems immediately after the robbery Mario
warned that if *anything* should happen to him he'd make sure
Parnell's entire family were wiped out, with him last, death
coming slowly and painfully.

"But it was when he described his daughter being run
down to ensure Mario's involvement in the robbery remained a
secret… Christ I thought he was going to lose it then and there,
he was almost hysterical. He said that after he told his wife the
full story she made a snap decision to take their daughter to Italy
to live with relatives, for good.

"He also believed it was only a matter of time before Mario
put a hit on him so he decided to get in first. He even confirmed
stringing Mario up to find out who he'd hired to do his dirty
work, posing an ongoing threat…"

John interrupted. "And did he find out?"

Ballard shook his head. "Apparently not, but I can't be certain. So now he assumes he's a dead man walking. He claimed he's been in hiding ever since he fronted Mario at the factory and has only been back to his house two or three times, including this morning. He's convinced that either by the hit-man or the police, he'll die at some point today and he's desperate to take me with him, hence the rambling confession. In his demented state, killing me as well as Kathryn is payback for his brother and mother's deaths. He's demanding I be there alone and unarmed within the hour." Ballard looked at both men, seeking direction, but he knew the decision had to be his.

John ran his fingers through his hair, attempting to look calm but not succeeding. Without waiting for a response Ballard decided the next move. "Time we got up there John, we'll assess our options as we go." He turned to Ken. "Have the guys ring me with the radio channel. Get Bobby and Susan back here in case they've got some information that may help. Check with Prahran that Natalie and the kids are safe. Not one word of this to her. Get Delwyn on her mobile and brief her as soon as possible."

Ken ran from the room.

CHAPTER
14

Ballard and John bolted to the lift. For the first time the descent to the street was not fast enough. Minutes into the trip the office rang with the number for the radio channel. Reaching forward Ballard flicked the selector, adjusting the volume so the transmissions could be heard, but not loud enough to distract either of them from planning the next move.

John looked across. "How are you holding up?"

Ballard shook his head, his eyes shut. "I can't believe I didn't see this coming. Am I losing it John?"

"Bullshit Mike! Nobody could've guessed this. How a robbery eleven years ago threw together each of the players – then surfaced as it did. No. Nobody could have guessed this." He struck the steering wheel with the heel of his hand. "You know the SOG will want to take over the hostage situation and stop you from going into your house?"

Ballard looked resigned. John continued. "They'll assume they're running the show. Under normal circumstances that'd be the right thing. In this case, as dangerous as it'll be for you, it's *not* what should happen. You're going to have to get in the ear of the Area Commander as soon as we arrive."

He swerved to avoid a motorist travelling erratically in the right lane. "Now Mike, we have to come up with a plan. I hate bringing this up mate, but you need to think through the possibility you may only have a split second to make a decision that could cost you or your sister's life.

"You *have* to think it through. If asked to choose *right now*, which way will you go? Are you prepared to risk dying to save your sister?" There was a look of anguish on his face as he posed the question.

Ballard rubbed the palms of his hands hard against his eyes, attempting to clear his thoughts. "Jesus John, *I just don't know*! I can't imagine losing Kathryn *or* putting Natalie and Laura through the pain of me dying." Both men lapsed into silence as the enormity of the decision sank in.

A voice on the radio had Ballard snatching the hand piece. "Ballard."

"Michael, it's Inspector Tim Robbins. I'm with the SOG and I've assumed command here at the intersection of… Chelsea and Peters roads. We have the local police in attendance, also my units are here with the Bomb Squad. The Dog Squad are heading over and shouldn't be long. What's your ETA?"

Ballard glanced across at John. "Fifteen minutes, tops."

"Good. One of the local highway patrol cars has just pulled up. Fire, ambulance and SES are almost on site. One of my guys is notifying neighbours to evacuate the area. Some residents have already left, don't worry, we checked the vehicles, including the back seat and the boot before we let them through. We've copies of Parnell's photo for reference. Oh, and your gardener Alan Dempsey turned up with his ride-on, but we sent him home so he's out of harm's way."

Ballard felt a sense of relief as he listened to the crisp, decisive statements. "Thank you, Tim."

"I want you to know we'll do everything we can to get your sister out of there safely. See you when you get here."

"Again, thank you."

Ballard knew the Inspector's last statement was encouragement for encouragement's sake, but despite that it felt good.

John chipped in, "He's right. No bloody shithead's going to mess up our day."

Ballard smiled weakly.

Less than a minute later his mobile rang. With dread he stared at the screen. Relief coursed through him when he saw it was Susan calling.

"Michael, I'm heading back to the office. A couple of minutes ago my contact at the airport called… unofficially. Parnell *does* have a flight out of Melbourne today, 1600 hours, booked on Qantas for Rome."

Ballard jotted down the details. "Well done. Do you know when he booked the tickets?"

"Yes. An on-line booking yesterday afternoon." She hesitated. "I… I know how much you love Kathryn, we all do, but *please* be careful."

Ballard nodded as though she could see him. "Have you ever known me to be anything else? Don't worry. John and I are going to sort this out. Thanks again and oh… thank Bobby for me." He hung up, not feeling anywhere near as poised as his words implied.

John guessed the context of the conversation. "So Parnell *does* have a ticket?"

"Yeah, purchased yesterday afternoon. Direct Rome flight out of Melbourne, 1600 hours…"

"So as of yesterday afternoon he was confident he was going to leave the country. But was it his intent to kill you or Kathryn before he left?"

Ballard hunched sideways in his seat. "From the conversation I… well… *attempted* to have with him, I'm certain he's been planning this for some time. I'd be kidding myself if I thought he'd have any difficulty finding my home address. I guess it's not hard knowing where Homicide operates from and that I drive a black Chrysler. Following it all the way from work to my house would be a walk in the park."

John almost choked with exasperation. "It'd be like following the bloody Star of David."

Ballard's mind raced. "What if he came up yesterday and waited until after dark, then snuck around to the lounge room windows and stood out of the light, watching to see who was home? The trouble with country people is we don't take our privacy seriously enough. Perhaps he was observing Kathryn for several hours. When I didn't show up he assumed I wasn't coming home."

John joined in the speculation. "Knowing it was highly likely there was a hit on him, plus his flight departure left him little room to move, he had to force the situation. Hence he cobbled together the bomb, or supposed bomb to gain the control he knew it would give him. I mean where would he *get* the explosives? The more I think about it, the more I'm certain the bomb is nothing more than a ploy. For example the digital clock strapped to it – it's all… bloody amateurish." He hesitated. "But Jesus, we're taking a major gamble assuming it's *not* a bomb because any idiot can download the damn instructions from the internet."

John continued to weave with precision through the traffic while he progressed his theory. "Parnell would've also assumed that if he got back to your place early enough this morning

Kathryn would still be there." He thought out loud. "Parnell left his house around 5.30 a.m. and got over to the factory about 5.40. From there he took the Ring Road to the Calder, then up to the farm. He'd have been at your place by 6.30. Knowing your sister I can guarantee she wouldn't have been up at that hour."

Ballard agreed. "At that point he rings the front door bell, spinning Kathryn a line. Assuming that didn't get her to open up, he shoulders through the door. The way he's built that wouldn't have been a problem. Minutes later he has a hostage and things unfold from there. So something has dramatically changed in his thinking for him to give up on getting out of the country once he's killed me."

He drew a deep breath. "Jesus, John. Can you imagine how Kathryn must be feeling?"

"Mike... mate! Don't go there. We're professionals. We're going to get her out. There may be ten alternative scenarios to the one we've just run through, but I'm betting we're not far off the mark." He attempted a half smile but it appeared more as a grimace. "And you're right, it does show he's moved from thinking yesterday he had a chance of getting away after killing you. Blind revenge is now consuming him and he doesn't give a stuff that knocking you and Kathryn off will mean him dying. Unless..." He broke off.

"Unless *what*?"

"Well, he must know you wouldn't be coming up here alone. Perhaps he's hoping to kill you and Kathryn then take his chance that he'll be arrested *after* the event, copping his time in prison rather than be on the run forever from some unknown hit-man."

Ballard tentatively agreed. "Either way we'll soon know.

The trouble is we're applying common sense to a man who is running on native cunning, but not thinking logically and getting less logical by the minute."

John muttered as he put his foot down, concentrating on the job at hand.

CHAPTER
15

As predicted, fifteen minutes after the radio conversation with the Area Commander, they pulled up at the intersection. The view greeting Ballard was surreal compared to the sleepy country road he normally drove along. Now it was anything but. Police vehicles were parked everywhere, but despite the appearance of chaos they were angled on the nature strip facing the road should they need to be driven out at a moment's notice.

In one group were the emergency services: fire, ambulance and SES. Closest to the intersection were two menacing, gunmetal grey SOG vans. One of them had its rear doors open exposing the bomb disposal vehicle with an officer finalising its preparation.

SOG officers grouped alongside one of the vans, their black uniforms bristling with weapons in every conceivable position. They all wore radio mikes and were carrying Heckler & Koch rifles fitted with scopes.

John parked the car. As he and Ballard climbed out a stocky inspector in uniform hurried over to greet them. "Tim Robbins." All three shook hands.

"As you can see we're good to go. Generally in situations like this we'd take control but your involvement makes this quite unique. Can you tell me what you know that may be relevant?"

Ballard spent the next few minutes informing the inspector of Parnell's background, his family history and potential motives. He showed the photos on his mobile, giving details of Parnell's current state of mind, including the conversation he had just had with him.

The inspector asked for the phone, instructing one of his officers to download the images to a PC so they could be analysed by the bomb experts. He indicated to Ballard the enlarged images may provide vital information as to the type of detonator being used.

Ballard continued. "Tim, Parnell's a control freak. He's told me in no uncertain terms he won't accept any communication other than me ringing Kathryn's mobile. He's given me an hour to get to the house. That time's up in the next few minutes.

"John and I believe the bomb threat is just that, an empty threat, but hell…" Ballard looked around him. "It's a very effective threat. Because he's killed so recently and his state of mind is deteriorating rapidly, I *have* to go in. Kathryn's been under enormous emotional trauma for hours now. That's going to impact on her ability to react when I need her to. Every minute I wait it'll get worse."

Tim, looking grim, agreed. "I understand. As it's your house and your sister being held hostage and given your years of experience, I respect the fact you can do what's required. My job is to mitigate the risk of either you or your sister being killed or injured. How close can I position my guys for them to be of any value?"

Ballard gave details regarding the row of pines on the left boundary of the property, fifty metres from the house. "The best you can do is spread the men along the trees on the east boundary so they cover the north and south sides of the house. As far as I know from Parnell's photos, Kathryn is still in the lounge room at the far end of the house.

"There's no effective cover on that side for a line of sight without being seen… and we *can't* take that risk." He looked fiercely at the inspector as he emphasised the point.

A SOG member ran up to return Ballard's phone, informing the inspector the images were not sufficiently clear to determine the type of switch. This meant it could either be pressure or toggle, so pressure switch had to be assumed. Taking the inspector's day book Ballard drew the outline of the house and the respective rooms with their internal and external access doors and the direction they opened. "This is the best I can do."

The inspector hurried over to the grouped SOG members, issuing rapid instructions. Almost immediately they moved out, using the cover of the properties leading to Ballard's house to position themselves amongst the pines. The inspector returned and informed Ballard his men would need five minutes to set up.

Turning to John, Ballard held out his hand. "Car keys."

John handed them over reluctantly. "Mike, are you taking a weapon in?"

"I can't. Parnell said the first thing he'll do is search me. If I have one, or wear a wire, that'll be it.

"I'll drive down the driveway with the radio mike taped open so I can give updates until I get out of the vehicle. After that, well…" He shrugged. A steely determination formed on his face. "I can only hope my knowledge of my house gives me an edge." He grinned weakly. "Who knows, my negotiation skills *may* save the day."

John exploded. "Bullshit Michael, the man's a bloody lunatic! What about a vest at least?"

Ballard made a feeble attempt at humour. "John, not much use against flying debris if it *is* a bomb, bloody Kevlar all over the shop."

John's expression remained bleak. Ballard extended his hand. "If anything *does* happen you need to support Natalie and the kids as we've discussed. My son will handle the financial stuff."

John's bottom lip quivered. "Piss off Ballard! Just get in there and do what you have to do."

Ballard smiled briefly and after taking the roll of electrical tape handed to him, ran to the police car. Taping the radio button to continuous transmit he placed the handpiece on the seat alongside him and waited for the signal that the SOG had moved into position. Once given, he began driving down Chelsea Road towards his house. As he did so he dialled Kathryn's number.

"*Yes!*" The word was hissed.

"I'm two minutes away."

CHAPTER
16

Ballard felt the acrid taste of fear rise in his throat. Over the years he had learned to embrace it as nature's way of sharpening his reflexes and focussing his senses. He confirmed in his mind his only objective was to save his sister and it was at that moment he knew he would do whatever it took to secure her freedom. No matter the cost.

As he passed the line of pines he slowed. Despite looking intently to the left, he couldn't see any of the SOG officers he knew must be positioned amongst the trees. Satisfied they were not visible, he continued.

Reaching the driveway he began providing frontline commentary for the police back at the intersection and the SOG members monitoring his channel. "Entering my driveway now. Parnell's Mitsubishi is parked in front of the garage. It's facing towards the road. No sign of him or my sister. Half way down the driveway. Still no movement. Ten yards from the concrete apron. Still no – *shit!*"

The windscreen of the police car shattered. He ducked, slamming on the brakes. The vehicle slewed sideways as it skidded across the gravel surface. Ears ringing he forced himself to continue. "Single shot fired. Windscreen gone. Not hit. Can't locate the shooter. Maintain your positions." At that moment he saw peripheral movement in the shrubs to the right of the garage.

"Get out! Walk towards me. Hands away from your body." Parnell's voice was strained, high pitched.

Ballard stepped from the car and stood motionless. "Get over here." The words were snarled, thick with fury. Ballard obeyed.

Within feet of the shrubs Parnell appeared, unshaven, his stubble flecked with grey. Ballard noted the rage in his eyes; his expression that of a caged animal. In his left hand he held a small metal box with a toggle switch partly obscured by his thumb, in his right hand was a Glock.

It occurred to Ballard the bomb threat may well be real. Perhaps he had been planning to blow up Mario's factory after he killed him; payback for the possibility Mario used the money from the robbery to finance the business. The realism of the device with its flashing LED light caused Ballard's senses to race. He fought to remain calm.

Attempting to assert some authority he asked, "Where's my sister?"

Parnell motioned for him to turn around and thrusting the barrel of the Glock hard against the nape of his neck, he hissed, "Let's find out."

Shuffling along the west wall of the house, out of view of the SOG, Parnell directed Ballard through the side entrance into the corridor. Locking the door behind him he thrust Ballard savagely in front of him. As they reached the double sliding doors leading into the lounge, Parnell struck Ballard on the back of the head with the butt of the Glock. Pain exploded in Ballard's head as he slumped to his knees, lights bursting in front of his eyes. Parnell quickly frisked him.

"*Crawl* into the room you prick or I'll blow your brains out!" As dazed as he was, Ballard realised the order was a display of power to emphasise who was in charge.

He did as he was told and saw Kathryn slumped on the floor near the piano, both her wrists raw from the plastic ties securing her. Her mouth was covered by grey duct tape. On seeing her brother her eyes widened. She shook her head from side to side, attempting to dislodge the tape. On top of the piano was the bomb.

Ballard crawled over to his sister, holding her in his arms, rocking her back and forth, trying to comfort her. Kathryn's nostrils flared as she fought to breathe, tears streaming down her flushed cheeks. Despite Ballard peeling the tape from her mouth as gently as he could, she moaned in pain. Once removed she breathed deeply.

Stepping forward Parnell struck Ballard viciously above the right ear, causing him to slump onto his sister. Sobbing, she cried out her brother's name.

Looking at the tape lying on the floor, Parnell snarled in Ballard's face. "I'll tell you what you can do and *when* you can do it!"

Ballard put a hand to his throbbing head, feeling blood ooze through his fingers and down his neck onto his shirt collar. Parnell grabbed a handful of Ballard's hair, dragging him across the tiled floor. Scrambling, Ballard tried to regain his feet but couldn't.

Parnell kicked him hard in the chest, dropping him onto the floor. Ballard gasped for breath. Parnell leaned down, hissing, "When I saw you at the funeral, gloating, I could've killed you then and there you arsehole." Ballard knew reasoning was pointless. As he struggled to stand he was kicked again, collapsing him face down onto the tiled floor. Witnessed the brutality being inflicted, Kathryn screamed for the savagery to stop, sobbing uncontrollably.

Parnell continued his mindless tirade, spittle spraying from his lips. "You bastard! My brother would be alive if it weren't for you." He emphasised this with another kick to Ballard's head, causing blood to flow freely from a gash to his lips. Ballard ran his tongue around his mouth, surprised his teeth were still intact. Parnell grabbed another handful of hair, then kneeling down, spat in Ballard's face. "My *mother* would still be alive!"

Sensing another blow was about to be delivered, Ballard attempted to protect himself with crossed arms. Parnell's foot crashed into him. From the searing pain in his left hand Ballard knew several fingers were broken. Parnell continued his verbal tirade "You prick! Now, because of you I've lost my wife and kid."

Rage switched to retching sobs as Parnell renewed his physical assault. Again Kathryn screamed. Ballard could see her straining against the plastic ties, her wrists bleeding.

He knew he couldn't continue absorbing this punishment if he was to overpower his attacker. He recalled Ken's profiling comments; it was obvious Parnell was dropping into a mindless abyss of uncontrolled rage. It was also evident the helpless frustration Parnell had endured over the past eleven years was erupting.

Sneering, he sensed Ballard was about to engage him in negotiation. "It's over. I'll be dead within the hour. One way or another. Why do you think I spilled my guts to you earlier? I know you've got police crawling all over this place. And if *they* don't get me, there's some bastard out there who will. I couldn't give a stuff anymore. Both of you are coming with me." The venom in his voice caused Kathryn to curl into an even tighter ball, her eyes darting between her brother and Parnell.

Ballard spoke for the first time since entering the room. "You've got *me* now, let my sister go. There's nothing to gain…"

Parnell stepped forward kicking Ballard viciously in the head. Stars burst in front of Ballard's eyes.

"Shut up!" Placing the detonator on the dining table behind him, Parnell reached into his trouser pocket, producing a pair of metal handcuffs. He threw them to Ballard.

"Put one on *your* right wrist and the other on *her* right wrist." Ballard knew instinctively this would restrict their movement should they be required to walk side by side. One of them would have to hold their right arm either behind their back or across the front of their body; an effective technique to reduce their ability to move freely.

He hesitated. Parnell sprang forward, thrusting the barrel of the Glock hard against Kathryn's head. She cried out in pain, shrinking away from him in terror.

"Do it!" Parnell hissed, his head bobbing snakelike towards Ballard.

Despite the threat Ballard delayed, knowing this was a major decision that once complied with would reduce his chances of tackling Parnell. Ripping her head back by the hair, Parnell struck Kathryn across the face with the barrel of the Glock, drawing blood and a sobbing whimper.

Rage erupted inside Ballard. He fought to control it. Crawling over to Kathryn he snapped the handcuffs onto her right wrist then his own. Parnell reached down, squeezing Kathryn's cuff tighter, causing her to cry out in pain. He did the same to Ballard, ensuring neither could slip their hand free.

Ballard sensed his chance and struck upwards at Parnell's

groin with his left fist. Parnell twisted sideways, the blow glancing off his thigh. Intense pain shot along Ballard's arm, his broken fingers searing agony. Enraged Parnell kicked Ballard twice more in the stomach, causing him to double over, fighting for breath as he dry retched.

Agitated, Parnell strode the length of the room, slapping his thigh with his open hand. With a brief grunt he withdrew a black handled vegetable knife from the block located on the kitchen bench. Returning, he waved it menacingly. Kathryn shrank back in terror and Ballard had no doubt he was about to stab them both. He lashed out with his foot but missed. Parnell kicked the side of Ballard's head, causing him to collapse onto the floor, passing in and out of consciousness.

Leaning down, Parnell sliced through the plastic ties securing Kathryn to the piano. "Get up. Both of you." Ballard, still recovering from the last blow, took several seconds to comprehend the command. Struggling, he attempted to help Kathryn to her feet. Repeatedly she made the effort but collapsed, moaning in pain as blood circulated to her legs, numb from being trapped against the piano.

Eventually she staggered to her feet. Ballard encircled her waist with his left arm. The right side of her face was coated in blood; she looked up at him, her eyes swollen but filled with defiance. "I'm sorry, Michael." He squeezed her harder, kissing her forehead. "Stay strong."

Parnell retrieved the bomb from the piano, threading his left arm through the looped cord that was attached. After snatching up the detonator he fired two shots at the largest window in the room. The noise in the confined space was deafening. Ballard and Kathryn ducked instinctively. The safety glass of the double glazed window shattered into a thousand pieces, scattering across the floor and out onto the veranda.

Ballard wondered if this was the moment the SOG would put a bullet in Parnell's head, despite the possibility of detonating the bomb. Nothing happened; he reasoned they must not have a clear shot.

Parnell gestured with the Glock. "Get out. *Move!*" With his right arm held across his waist, manacled to Kathryn's right wrist, Ballard placed his left arm around her shoulders for support. Shuffling forward they crunched through the scattered glass. Reaching the window Ballard had to kick out a large section still suspended by the frame. Together they stepped over the window ledge onto the veranda as further pieces of glass broke free.

Parnell instructed Kathryn to back up against the window. Reaching forward he snatched a handful of her hair, twisting it tightly around his right hand which held the Glock. She cried out. He pressed the weapon hard against the base of her skull. Stepping over the ledge onto the veranda he held the detonator in his left hand in full view, his thumb on the switch.

Ballard knew the snipers would be receiving instructions via their ear piece to hold fire until given the order. He also knew the one thing preventing Parnell's head from exploding from multiple high velocity bullets was half a kilogram of pressure on the respective SOG officers' triggers.

Parnell motioned towards the small gate that led into the paddock sloping down to Jackson's creek. At the bottom was the gorge, carved ten thousand years before by molten lava flowing from the now dormant volcanos several kilometres away.

Ballard had taken Natalie to the edge numerous times, amused at her nervousness as he showed her the vertical drop onto the rocks forty metres below. With pride he had pointed out the natural waterfall that flowed throughout the year, adding to the area's charm.

At the bottom of the paddock he was ordered to release the catch on a second gate and all three stepped through. Fifty metres separated them from the gorge's precipitous edge. At this point the ground sloped away at an ever increasing angle. A number of scrub trees grew on the extreme edge of the gorge and at irregular intervals rocks protruded from the ground. Ballard looked across at the pines to his left. He estimated they were sixty metres away, close enough for an easy head-shot.

Still gripping Kathryn's hair, Parnell thrust both his victims towards the edge. Five metres short of the vertical drop he stopped. Releasing his grip on Kathryn he pushed her in front of him, ordering both to face him. Images of Mario's fatal head wound flashed through Ballard's mind.

He took a large breath knowing they were probably seconds from being executed. Raising the Glock Parnell snarled, "Two choices. Jump or be shot. If I have to shoot you Ballard your body will drag her over, either way she'll be alive when she goes down."

The next ten seconds were a blur of movement.

Ballard thrust Kathryn sideways with his body, at the same time kicking at Parnell's right hand holding the Glock. Parnell lunged backwards to avoid Ballard's foot at the very instant a volley of bullets whistled overhead.

Losing his footing, Parnell landed on his back, sliding across the damp grass towards Ballard. A deafening shot from the Glock rang out as Parnell involuntarily squeezed the trigger; the bullet passing harmlessly across the gorge. As he slid closer he dropped the detonator but managed to hold onto the Glock. Frantically wrapping his arms around Ballard's right leg he attempted to halt his slide as the detonator bounced and rolled into the gorge.

The momentum of Parnell's body dragged Ballard and Kathryn to the ground, all three beginning a terrifying slide towards the edge. Kathryn screamed as Ballard snatched unsuccessfully at a rock.

Seconds before plunging over the side, Ballard's handcuff bit savagely into his flesh, halting his progression despite Parnell clinging desperately to his right leg, the bottom half of his body dangling in mid air.

Hearing Kathryn cry out in agony, Ballard looked up and saw her left arm crooked around a tree stump; her right arm, handcuffed to his, outstretched out at an impossible angle. He knew her shoulder must be dislocated; somehow she clung on tenaciously. Grasping a tuft of grass he attempted to relieve the pressure on her arm.

Looking down he saw Parnell's face contorted in rage as he lifted the Glock for a shot. Ballard reacted. Drawing up his left foot he smashed the heel of his shoe into Parnell's face. Three times he did this before Parnell lost his grip, crying out briefly before slipping over the edge, tumbling once then smashing onto the rocks below.

Moans of pain continued from Kathryn. Ballard did his best to minimise the strain on her shoulder while SOG members scrambled to assist. Moments later the pressure was released as he and Kathryn were lifted to their feet.

A call for bolt cutters was given and within minutes they were free. They clung to each other for what seemed an eternity, Kathryn sobbing. After kissed her brother on the cheek she allowed herself to be placed on a stretcher. A pain killer was injected before she was carried gently to a waiting ambulance.

Ballard was offered a stretcher but refused, choosing instead to slump down onto the grass to gather his thoughts.

"Michael!" The booming voice of John echoed across the gorge. Within seconds he scrambled down to where Ballard was resting.

Dropping to his knees John wrapped Ballard in a giant bear hug, the first he had ever given him. "Jesus Christ Mike. You left that to the bloody last second. What were you *thinking*? And so much for your damn Armani suit."

Ballard smiled. "Not like in the movies John, especially when your nuts are on the line."

John stepped closer to the drop and peered over. "When Ken said Parnell was going 'over the edge' I didn't think he meant it literally."

Ballard laughed, despite being weak with exhaustion, appreciating John's attempt at humour. He stood up, shaking. John put his arm around him for support. Together they looked down at Parnell's broken body; his left arm concealed beneath him, his right twisted awkwardly behind his back. Blood pooled out from his head in a crimson halo.

John spat over the edge. "Shithead!"

Shivering, Ballard turned, allowing John to help him stagger up the slope towards the house. Halfway up they saw Tim Robbins who asked if Ballard wanted a stretcher. John waved him away. "No thanks Tim, street hardened copper here... old school." He beamed with pride.

Drawing level with the house Ballard saw several SES men placing a canvas tarpaulin over the shattered window, sealing it until it could be boarded up. Limping around to the front he slumped onto a veranda seat, feeling the warmth of the sun against his skin.

Police moved in and out of the damaged front door, the

result of being forced open by Parnell earlier that morning.

Kathryn was nowhere to be seen, by now well on her way to hospital. A second ambulance appeared down the driveway; once parked, a medical officer rushed over with a black case. He opened it and began cleaning Ballard's cuts and bruises with a solution that caused him to wince.

John chuckled. "Pussy." Ballard contemplated giving him the finger but the pain in his hands prevented him. The medical officer splinted his broken fingers, offering to assist him to the ambulance. He refused; no way was he going to desert his home with so many strangers occupying it.

Tim appeared just as John stepped away to answer a call on his mobile. Sitting on the seat alongside Ballard he said, "My guys rappelled down and confirmed the box *did* contain explosives. Considering the damage to it there's no way of knowing whether it would have detonated. We believe the clock was there for show to get your attention… but everything else was real."

He hesitated before continuing. "I don't have to tell you how this will pan out. Your home is now a crime scene and will be for some time. Ethical Standards will need to interview you, but under the circumstances that can wait. Leave that to me."

He placed a hand on Ballard's shoulder. "It took a lot of guts doing what you did. I'm very, *very* relieved you and your sister came out of it ok." Ballard smiled but didn't reply.

Both men knew the physical injuries to Kathryn would heal over time; the psychological scars were another thing and at this point, unknown. Despite this Ballard was aware of the incredible resilience his sister possessed, praying it would be sufficient to help her tackle the mental hardship she was about to face.

John snapped his phone shut. "That was Susan. She and

Bobby went out to Parnell's house and found a suicide note. He confessed to everything and it's clear he was going to take you with him old son. Backed it up by saying he wanted a 'death by copper' finale. Ken was right, Parnell planned for you to suffer by seeing your sister go over the edge. What a prick."

He kneeled down in front of his partner. "Delwyn's on the way. Now for some good news, Natalie's been told you're in one piece, so as you can imagine she's cut loose, demanding to be brought here. She'll be coming down the driveway in fifteen to twenty minutes. Give me Maureen's number and I'll let her know everything's over."

Ballard complied, almost in a daze, at the same time experiencing a surge of love for Natalie stronger than he had ever felt before. It was tempered however, with concern that considering what had just taken place she may not feel safe living here after they were married. He was grateful Parnell hadn't died in the house as that would have been a harder image to repress.

Thirty minutes later, after receiving hugs and kisses that threatened more injury to his aching body than his confrontation with Parnell, he heard Natalie utter the words he had been hoping to hear.

"Of course, Michael. This is *your* home… our home. Nothing will prevent me from living here with you for as long as you'll have me."

Ballard hugged her as hard as his injured limbs would allow while John stood to the side, smiling contentedly.

Ballard took Natalie by the hand and they walked inside the house, heading for the lounge. He felt the need to defy the terror that had been enacted there less than an hour before. Despite the flurry of activity as officers gathered crime scene evidence, nobody prevented their entry.

Standing alongside Natalie in front of the windows he looked across the gorge, detailing the dramatic events that had just unfolded. Natalie gazed up at him with ever increasing compassion as she began to fully appreciate the horror that had been inflicted on both him and Kathryn. He also told her that he would be required to complete a debriefing as soon as he was well enough. After that he would take a month's sick leave followed by four weeks long service.

Natalie hugged him in delight. He kissed her on the cheek. "Is that enough time for us to prepare for our wedding?"

She turned, looking up at him, her face beaming. "More than enough time my darling. I'll make sure of that."

He kissed her softly on the lips. "Welcome home, Mrs Ballard."

CHAPTER
17

"Michael... darling. It's my turn to give *you* a wake-up call and guess what, it's not the crack of dawn."

Ballard's heavy eyes and sluggish limbs refused to respond to mental commands. He squinted into what appeared to be a thick fog swirling above him; his mouth was unbearably dry and he felt lethargic. By contrast, he experienced a soothing sensation as a cool, gentle hand stroked his brow.

Gradually he made sense of his surroundings. The pervasive scent of disinfectant engulfed him as light flooded his senses. Vision clearing, Natalie's concerned face came into focus.

Waiting until she was sure he was conscious, she leaned across, pressing her lips against his forehead. She looked reassuringly into his eyes. "Hello handsome. I spoke with the doctor. Everything went well, you'll be up and pretending to be twenty again in no time."

He struggled to stay focused on her face. His lips, swollen from the beating he had received from Parnell, slurred his words. "I love you."

"Hmm... What's that darling?"

"I said, I love you."

Natalie's eyes crinkled. "I'm so sorry, but I still didn't catch what you said."

Frustrated, he shuffled into a more upright position. "I said I love…"

She burst out laughing. "I know what you said sweetheart. I just wanted to hear you say it one more time."

Forgetting the injury to his mouth he attempted a smile, instantly wishing he hadn't. Natalie stopped laughing, concern on her face. "Oh my poor baby, I'm *so* sorry. Is it very painful?"

He nodded, inviting an even deeper look of sympathy as she hugged him, kissing him on the cheek. He whispered in her ear. "Yes, but what I really wanted was for you to kiss me again."

She chuckled. "Ok smarty. So you're a quick healer – well I intend to help that along by taking you home and after slipping into my nurse's uniform, I'll be looking after you for the next week."

Moving closer, her lips brushing his cheek as she whispered seductively in his ear. Pretending to be shocked he looked about him, checking no-one in the recovery room had overheard. Natalie fluttered her eyelashes and he knew it wouldn't be long before he was on the road to recovery.

Despite the pain in his left hand from minor surgery and the stitches in his scalp, he felt almost normal. Breathing was painful due to his bruised ribs, but bearable. He sipped from the glass of water Natalie held for him, accepting a glucose lolly to suck on as she plumped additional pillows behind his back.

"How's Kathryn?"

Natalie resumed stroking his hair. "She's fine. They've reset her shoulder and she's…"

"What about the scar where Parnell belted her with the Glock?" Agitation was etched across his face.

Natalie held his hand in both of hers. "Michael, you've arranged the best surgeon money can buy. They can't operate until the swelling in her face goes down, I checked before I came in to see you. The charge nurse said that within twelve months there'll be hardly any scarring at all. But I dare say she won't feel too attractive for the first few weeks post op. You must accept that."

He slumped back on the bed exhausted, closing his eyes.

Fifteen minutes later he was roused by the deep voice of Alan Proctor, the surgeon who had operated on his hand. Taking the clipboard from the end of the bed he pretended to study it. "You're a lucky man Michael."

Ballard shrugged. "It takes a lot more than a midday punch up to stop me…"

Alan dipped his chin as he stared at him over his reading glasses. "No, I mean I wish it was me being looked after by Natalie for the week."

Ballard began to smile but stopped, remembering the previous painful experience. "It's a tough job Alan, I just hope I can cope."

"Lucky sod." Alan replaced the clipboard, his face serious. "Now to business. Your anaesthetic was light, we call it twilight, so you won't feel drowsy for too long. You did however, suffer a hairline fracture of the skull. I had the trainee doctor super-glue it together and…"

"He what?" Ballard struggled upright in the bed.

Natalie placed a firm hand against his shoulder while Alan rocked about in fits of laughter.

"I'm kidding. No, we just stitched you up." With an effort he brought himself under control. "Considering the beating you received we put you through a full body MRI, thankfully it came back clear. Amazing under the circumstances.

"I can't say the same for your fingers though, the middle and index were broken. Not a big deal to align the bones as the break on each finger was, using our terminology, a simple fracture."

Ballard inspected the metal guard on his left hand. "When can this come off?"

Alan shrugged. "You're in good shape so your fingers should mend within four to five weeks. Within two to three months you'll have full strength. *If* you look after yourself and providing you don't do anything silly."

Ballard winced, but not from the pain. "When can I start fooling around with my fiancée, doc?" Natalie punched him on the shoulder.

Alan looked at both of them. "You're as bad as each other. Remember Michael, fail to take proper care of your hand now and Mr Arthritis will be your companion for life." Ballard pursed his lips, understanding the seriousness of the statement.

As soon as Alan left the room Ballard struggled upright.

Natalie attempted to hold him down. "Michael, what on earth are you doing?"

"I've got to see Kathryn."

"You've just come out of surgery."

"You heard the man, the anaesthetic was twilight. I'm fine."

He was in fact feeling anything but fine, however he refused to remain in bed. He had insisted Kathryn have a private room, free from prying eyes and endless questions from other patients. The downside was the extended periods she would be alone. For this reason he was determined to visit her as soon as possible.

"Natalie. Help me with the drip. You push the damn thing while I walk. Some exercise will do me the world of good."

Knowing he had made up his mind, Natalie put her right arm around his waist and with her left hand, pushed the stand supporting the drip in front of her.

"My God Michael. Have I got forty years of this, you putting me in an impossible position?"

"Darling, if I *ever* put you in an impossible position, be sure to let me know."

She spluttered, laughing like a school girl. "What am I going to say when the nurses see us?"

"Tell them we're heading off to consummate our marriage."

"But we've only just got engaged."

"They don't know that."

"I'll tell them."

"I'll say you're kidnapping me… slowly."

"You're ranting, the anaesthetic can't have worn off yet."

He continued his sluggish progress past the nurses' station and despite his swollen lips, flashed them a high voltage smile. Much to Natalie's amusement they waved back, asking if they could assist.

"No. But thank you for asking. I have an ex-nurse here who's assisting me very nicely. I'm off to see my injured sister." The nurses smiled in unison, impressed by his determination.

Natalie stood on tiptoe, whispering in his ear. "Be sure Mr Ballard the only nurse you get your hands on is the one currently holding the back of your gown together."

The smile disappeared from his face as he realised the only thing preserving his modesty was Natalie's strategically placed right hand as they shuffled down the corridor. "Aaagh, it's true, I really am at your mercy."

After what seemed an eternity, exacerbated by the fact he dare not admit how tired he felt, they came to Kathryn's ward.

Conferring with one of the nurses they entered her room.

Natalie whispered as they stood by her bed, "Don't be alarmed. The bruising and swelling on her face is temporary. It'll go down… in time. The operation on her shoulder was a total success, but that won't stop her being a sore puppy for a week or two."

Despite the warning Ballard's knees buckled when he saw his sister. She was deathly pale with numerous sensors attached, the constant beep of a heart monitor caused him to turn back to Natalie.

"Why's she hooked up to the monitor?"

Natalie took his hand. "She complained of minor chest pains earlier…"

"But she's as strong as a horse!"

"Not *everyone* is made of steel like you my sweet; she had a slight panic attack, quite understandable under the circumstances. The monitor is precautionary."

He shook his head, realising the mental and physical ordeal Kathryn had endured. He and John had often discussed the fragility of the human body. They shared mutual disquiet that films with their graphic fight scenes and seemingly invincible heroes had conditioned the public into a dangerous and unrealistic belief as to what the body could endure from physical trauma.

Kathryn was in a deep sleep with her head turned to one side. Ballard winced when he saw how much the right side of her face had swollen. The contact point where the Glock had struck her was covered in gauze; he forced himself not to imagine the torn flesh that lay beneath the dressing.

Without thinking he began stroking her hair, as Natalie had for him. Placing a chair behind him, Natalie helped him shuffle onto it. Checking Kathryn's medical sheet on the clipboard she said, "They've given her a hefty sleeping pill so she can get a good night's rest. Before you know it she'll be back playing all sorts of practical jokes on you again. As I said, the cut on her face will heal. You *must* be patient though."

He drew her to his side, placing his arm around her waist. "We'll do whatever it takes darling. After the operation she'll need counselling." He looked up. "It's amazing how I've changed my tune on that front." She kissed the top of his head but didn't reply, knowing he had to release the tension he was feeling, along with the undeserved guilt. "John and I have always scoffed at therapy, now here I am planning sessions for my sister. I guess blood *is* thicker than water."

He stopped stroking Kathryn's hair and struggled to his feet. "When do you think they'll operate?"

Natalie shrugged. "It could be up to a week. The swelling won't go down for at least three to four days. They'll hold her overnight and tomorrow I'll pick her up mid morning. Having her stay at the town house means I can regularly change her dressing. The kids rang their father and he volunteered to take them for a week. While I couldn't stay married to the man, in his favour he does have his good points. I'll toss a coin as to which room I free up for your sister, but I'm guessing it'll be Josh's, considering the state of Kayla's."

Ballard grinned as the mental image of Kayla's room flashed to mind.

Natalie continued. "As soon as the swelling goes down they'll operate, unless she gets an infection or a cold. That's the other reason the kids are staying with their dad, so they don't pass on their school germs." She peered at Kathryn again, inspecting the right side of her face, noting the dark bruising around her eyes.

"It's always best to do this type of surgery as soon as possible. Once that's over she'll stay in hospital for a day or two, then more recuperation with us." She turned back. "That way I'll get to keep an eye on two Ballard's for the price of one."

He reached forward drawing her to him, hugging her with all the passion his painful body would allow. "Thank you darling. This means a lot to me and I know it will to Kathryn. She's very lucky to have you as a future sister-in-law."

Natalie laughed. "I'm glad to have an ally who isn't afraid to take it up to you when necessary. You know how stubborn you can be, wanting to get your own way, despite disguising it with ultra politeness."

His expression conveyed a silent 'who me', but he knew he wasn't fooling her.

Taking his hand Natalie said, "Time for the return trip. Shall I get you a wheelchair?" The look on his face was his response.

Kissing Kathryn on the forehead he turned, allowing Natalie to guide him back to his room. Relieved, he collapsed back onto his bed. Gazing up at the ceiling he was certain it was revolving, but decided not to mention this anomaly.

Smiling, Natalie said, "I'll check with the nurses to see if it's ok for you to leave. You won't need the drip any more and the anaesthetic should be mostly out of your system by now. But you'll feel weak for a few days as you recover from what even you must admit was a horrible ordeal."

He shrugged as though it was nothing, but surprised himself by saying, "Nat, Delwyn will insist on therapy for me and I'm going to accept. I don't think I need it, but what have I got to lose… perhaps I'll get some ribbing from John, but I can live with that."

Natalie put her hand to her mouth. "Michael I'm sorry, I

forgot to mention, John was here when you were coming out of surgery. As soon as he heard you were ok he took off. I don't think he's very big on the emotional stuff." Ballard nodded but didn't say anything. Natalie continued. "Another thing, Delwyn sent me a text while you were coming out of the anaesthetic, checking on your progress. I let her know you were fine."

He struggled to keep his eyes open. "I'll see her and the rest of the guys tomorrow after some TLC from you and a good night's sleep."

Natalie accepted it was pointless arguing, knowing he needed to tie up loose ends as soon as possible. "I'll drive you to work in the morning."

He mumbled his thanks. "I think I'll have a quick shut eye before getting dressed."

"Good idea. While you're cat-napping I'll be with the nurses and sign the paperwork." Within seconds he was fast asleep.

After what seemed like a few minutes he felt Natalie's soft hand stroking his face once more. She leaned down. "How do you feel?"

He sat up in the bed. "Ten minutes already?"

"Er … more like forty-five."

He groaned, rubbing his stubbled jaw. "No way."

"Afraid so, but I put it to good use planning for the wedding."

His eyebrows rose as she continued. "You know the lovely old mansion in Sunbury, Rupertswood? I thought it might be the perfect venue. When you're up to it, we'll take a look."

He took her hand and in a voice gravelly from sleep, said, "I'd get married in a cardboard box as long as it's to you. If you want Rupertswood then that's where it'll be." Natalie kissed him on the cheek, her eyes glistening with tears of joy.

"Now Mrs Ballard. Pull the curtain across and help me get dressed. And no funny business."

CHAPTER
18

Thirty minutes after leaving St Vincent's, Natalie turned the BMW into her driveway. Ballard hated to admit even to himself that the effort of walking into the town house was a complete drain on his remaining energy.

Natalie placed a hand on his shoulder. "Some warm soup and perhaps a scoop of ice cream if you're a good boy, then off to bed with you." He didn't argue as he knew one of the reasons he enjoyed excellent health was his ability to fall asleep under any conditions.

When he woke the next morning he looked across at the clock radio, amazed to see it was 8.30. He couldn't remember how he had got into bed, but seeing Natalie with her back to him, proved he wasn't dreaming. Kissing her neck he cuddled into her warm body.

"Hi sweetheart," he whispered.

"Hello darling. What time are you getting up?"

"As soon as I can tear myself away from you."

"Take all the time you need. I'm off work for the week, remember?"

"I wish I could, but I need to put in a statement for the brief and arrange for an interview with Ethical Standards."

Natalie turned to him, concern on her face.

He waved a dismissive hand. "Don't worry, it's routine procedure, it's not every day you kick someone to their death down a gorge. I suppose I should feel some pity for Parnell, but I'm afraid I don't have it in me. Not under the circumstances. I guess the shrink will explore that angle. Besides, I need to get to work to thank everyone who was involved."

Crawling out of bed felt like he had gone ten rounds with a heavyweight boxer. After shaving he hobbled downstairs and ate a light breakfast before showering. In considerable pain and hampered by the guard on his left hand, he dressed in a white shirt, burgundy tie and navy blue suit. Tying his shoe laces was an ordeal but he persevered, knowing he wouldn't always have Natalie close at hand. Inspecting himself in the mirror he was amazed at how normal he looked other than the facial bruising and swollen lips.

Natalie emerged minutes later looking stunning in a knee length burgundy suit over a cream silk blouse. "Do I pass inspection Mr Ballard?"

He nodded appreciatively. "Just drop me off *near* work. I don't want the guys seeing you and being distracted for the rest of the day."

She pretended not to be flattered. "I've made you some lunch. Your briefcase is still at work so I've put some sandwiches and a little treat in a hamper for you." He kissed her on the forehead.

Twenty minutes later Natalie pulled alongside the Crime department building. Looking across she said, "I can't believe less than three days after such a horrible ordeal you're back at work. Are you sure this is the right thing to do?"

He reached over and took her hand. "Natalie, I've got a

cut on my head that's been stitched and two of my fingers were broken and they're now healing. I agree I was given a belting in the ribs and face, but again I was lucky, no fractures or teeth missing. That just leaves the mental issues." He shrugged expansively as though attempting to shake a load from his shoulders. "The most effective way I know to overcome any psychological trauma is to get right back on the horse."

Natalie leaned over, kissing him warmly. "I *think* you've reassured me." She looked at him, analysing. "Ok, I'm convinced. Get in there and knock their socks off."

Ballard glanced at his watch. "It's 10.15. I won't be late tonight. I'll drive back and yes... before you ask, I *can* drive with my hand like this. Another reason I won't be late is I want to get home to see how Kathryn's recovering. Ring me if you have any concerns when you pick her up."

He kissed her before extracting himself from the BMW, wincing in pain. Once he had retrieved his suit coat and lunch hamper from the rear seat, he tapped the car roof twice before striding into the building.

Riding up in the lift he felt a jolt of nervousness. Today was going to be a test of his ability to overcome conflicting emotions. Despite what he had said to Natalie he admitted to himself that such a dramatic event, together with the ongoing issues his sister would be facing, was going to take all his experience and maturity to reconcile.

CHAPTER
19

The lift door opened and Ballard stepped onto the homicide floor. The moment the detectives saw him they broke into spontaneous applause. Holding up a hand in greeting he was besieged with colleagues wanting to clap him on the back and pump his hand. He thanked his luck it was his left and not his right hand that was injured.

"About bloody time you got here old son." John's voice boomed across the room as he strode over and gave Ballard a playful punch on the shoulder, causing him to wince.

"For heaven's sake John, damaged goods remember." Delwyn rushed up to Ballard, planting a kiss on his cheek. "It's good to see you in one piece. Come to my office when you're free."

Susan struggled to get near him, her exasperation showing as she pushed the other detectives out of the way. "You *promised* me you'd be careful Michael, then you go and…"

"Susan I'm here aren't I?" He winked at her, accepting another kiss on the cheek.

Ken also muscled his way close, surprising everyone. "Yes Michael. We're all glad you came out of it ok. I hear Kathryn's doing well too."

Ballard nodded. Fifteen minutes later he extracted himself from the group and entered Delwyn's office, dropping onto a chair.

"Are you sure you should be back at work?"

"Natalie's already quizzed me on that score. I told her work and planning for the wedding would be good for me."

Delwyn agreed enthusiastically. "No doubt about it, but you do realise I want you to have some counselling. Today if possible. Even if it's only a short session."

"How many sessions were you planning?"

"I'll leave that to the counsellor, but as many as it takes." Her expression was business like.

Ballard held up a hand in acceptance. "I've no problems with that. And you'll be happy to know I'm not going to do a John and say street hardened coppers don't need counselling."

"Thank goodness. I wasn't sure how you'd take it."

He leaned forward in his chair. "What I would like though is to have my ESD interview as soon as possible. Can you arrange it for this morning?"

"Yes. I've been holding them back, but they said they'd fit in with your recovery. Go and make yourself a cup of tea while I put in the call."

He thanked her and headed for the kitchen, bumping into Ken along the way.

"Well Ken, I owe you a huge debt. Thanks to you, Kathryn's alive and well. It could have been very different."

Ken glanced down with embarrassment then almost jumped off the ground, startled by John who had approached him from behind, clapping him on the shoulder.

"Yes mate. You saved the day. As I said before, you got inside that shithead's warped mind and it helped us no end in formulating a plan. Couldn't have done it without you."

Placing an arm around Ballard's shoulder John steered him away to a quiet corner of the squad room. "Mike I've done all the paperwork, except of course your statement and Kathryn's. No rush but the sooner the better."

Ballard nodded. "I've just spoken with Delwyn. The first thing I want to square away is the ESD interview. I don't see any issues, but I'd like to get it over with."

John agreed. "Yep. Good idea. I'm glad everything was done by the book. No doubt they'll want to know why you went in instead of the SOG, but with a bomb strapped to Parnell's arse and your sister alongside it, I think we've ample justification. Tell 'em to get stuffed if they think otherwise. I know I will if I have to give a statement."

"Yes, no problem John, I'll be sure to do that." Ballard's half grinned at his partner's dubious words of wisdom. "By the way, where's Bobby? I want to thank him for everything he did."

"Out doing what he does best." John chuckled. "You've no idea the number of times he's apologised to me for not interviewing Tony properly the first time. I let him sweat for a couple of days before telling him how I'd made the same mistake twenty years ago. How it taught me a very valuable lesson, the hard way. It still didn't stop him from constantly apologising. In the end I had to tell him to piss-off."

Susan walked up to both men, excitement registering on her face. "Guess what?" Without waiting she continued. "I've been through Mario's financials and I've found a pattern of withdrawals dating back to just after the robbery down at Southland."

John responded first. "Great work Susan."

"Would you believe there's been quarterly withdrawals for over ten years from the same account? Susan flicked over several sheets of bank statements. "Initially the amounts were ten thousand dollars… in the last few years this increased to fifteen."

Ballard took the statements, scanning them before looking at John, then back to Susan. "No wonder you're excited. Quite possibly it's the account used to finance Mario's muscle. Not a bad little earner on the side considering the guy didn't have to do anything all those years…"

John snorted in disgust. "Yeah right! Anything except do a hit-and-run on a young girl as an in-your-face warning to her father that the family were still within reach."

Ballard and Susan glanced at each other, surprised at John's passion.

Handing back the statements Ballard said, "Susan, keep digging. Are there any witnesses to the hit-run?

John answered. "No, but we're going to canvas the street again. It'd help our cause if someone put their hand up. Back on the money issue though, it was withdrawn as cash so I'm assuming it was handed over by Mario direct to the guy. If it had gone to another account we may have got somewhere."

Ballard massaged his left hand to relieve the throbbing. "Do we know if the daughter saw the vehicle that struck her?"

Susan shook her head. "Her statement indicates she didn't."

Ballard was not convinced. "I'll bet the father stopped her from talking for fear of reprisal. We need to question her again as well as her mother, when or if they return for the funeral. If they don't come back we'll have the Italian police track them down and question them over there."

John agreed. "Yeah, we're on it. We've put in a request for the local cops to follow up on the mother's relatives. Separate to that you would think the funeral should bring them back. The danger for them back here is over I would suggest. The money supply from Mario will have stopped and his muscle hasn't anything to gain by killing them. Quite the opposite."

Susan turned to Ballard. "You're right about the daughter. We spoke with the officer who took her statement in hospital and he said that apart from being very distressed as you'd expect, she clammed up after speaking with her father."

Shrugging she continued. "John has asked Bobby and I to check with owners of any vehicles reported stolen before the hit-run that were later recovered and had unexplained damage. We'll re-interview the owners and see if we get lucky."

Ballard chuckled. "Quite a lot of 'ifs' and 'assumes' in there Susan, but keep at it. The pieces *will* fall into place, I've no doubt about that. Either way the details need to be investigated and placed on record for the future, no matter what unfolds."

She agreed. "Just following your motto, 'whatever it takes.'" She turned and headed back to her desk.

John commented as she walked away. "Never gets discouraged. A pretty handy trait for a detective, especially in Homicide."

Delwyn walked up, placing a hand on Ballard's shoulder. "ESD's coming over in the next fifteen minutes or so. Do you want me to sit in?"

He shook his head. "No. I'm fine. This isn't my first interview, albeit the others were for different reasons."

John snorted. "Yeah, goody-two-shoes here *has* had the odd question and answer session with the boys over the years. He's quite a pro at it now."

Delwyn hesitated. "Ok. But if you change your mind, stop the interview and call me. Oh, by the way, the Police Psychology Unit is sending over a clinician this afternoon to have a brief chat with you."

Ballard offered his thanks, refusing to look at John, knowing his thoughts on the matter.

Twenty minutes later he was sitting in the conference room with two ESD detectives; a sleek police recorder on the table in front of him. After checking with Ballard, the taller detective activated the machine before speaking into the mike.

"It's Tuesday, November 28 at 1150 a.m. This record of interview is being conducted by myself, Detective Senior Sergeant Walter Jamieson and Detective Sergeant Thomas Sadler. The interview will record all relevant facts associated with an incident between Detective Inspector Michael Ballard of the Homicide Squad and Eric Edward Parnell, deceased, on November 25 at a property located at 77 Leslie Road, Gisborne."

Walter looked across at Ballard. "Michael, during this interview we'll record all the events as they occurred on the day. Should you wish to stop the interview at any time, please let me know. Do you agree to continue?"

Ballard responded without hesitation. "Yes."

"For the record, please state your full name, rank and current duties."

"My name is Michael Bradley Ballard. I'm a Detective Inspector attached to the Homicide Squad and have held this position for fifteen years. I've been employed by the force for thirty one years."

For the next twenty-five minutes both ESD detectives questioned the events leading up to his and John's arrival at the check-point. After the initial round of questioning the younger detective, Sergeant Sadler shuffled forward in his seat with purpose, assuming the lead role. Ballard smiled to himself knowing the detective had drawn the short straw, having to address the more direct, hard hitting issues.

"When you arrived at the check-point what did you say to the Area Commander, Inspector Tim Robbins as to how the situation should be handled."

Ballard chose his words with care. "Thomas, I was forced into a situation where my sister was being held captive in my home with a known killer. Parnell had in his possession what we all believed at the time was a bomb. Special Operations have now confirmed it *was* a bomb. In addition, Parnell had confessed to me less than forty-five minutes earlier that he'd murdered Mario Bivelaqua in Lalor several days before. I was therefore dealing with a brutal killer. I informed Inspector Robbins that Parnell had made it clear to me I was to enter my home alone. Parnell stated if anyone else fronted he'd detonate the bomb, killing both himself and my sister. I took the threat seriously."

For the next fifteen minutes he gave a detailed account of every action from the moment he drove down the driveway to the point when he kicked Parnell over the cliff to his death.

Thomas finished writing on his notepad before looking up. "What would you say if I put to you it was your intention to enter the house alone because your sister was being held captive and you wanted to kill Parnell? That his death would be justified payback for the physical and mental anguish he had put her through?"

Ballard felt a flash of anger, picturing how John would erupt in a volcano of vitriol; instead he took a deep breath, realising the job the detectives had to perform included assuaging public perception.

"I wasn't contemplating any course of action other than preventing further harm being inflicted on my sister. Certainly

Parnell's well being was not a consideration for me at any time. My sister was my focus and I was prepared to risk anything to achieve her safety. End of story."

Both detectives looked at each other, nodding collectively. The senior sergeant laced his fingers before speaking. "I'd like to say on behalf of Ethical Standards that you acted appropriately and displayed considerable bravery. That's what I'll be stating in my report." He then concluded the interview by repeating the date and time. Standing, he offered Ballard his hand, the sergeant following.

Ballard felt relief flood over him as he said, "I understand this whole episode needed scrutiny so it wouldn't be perceived as a revenge killing by an out-of-control cop. Thanks for being so professional about this. I'm assuming you've interviewed Tim Robbins?" They confirmed they had. "I want to say on record he was a brilliant Area Commander, did everything by the book and at the appropriate time. He gave me considerable confidence throughout the crisis. Very professional."

Both men thanked him, indicating they would be updating Delwyn before they left. Ballard slumped back in his chair, running over what had just transpired. Despite knowing he was legally and morally in the right, he was relieved the interview was over.

John burst into the room. "Did you tell them to get stuffed as I suggested?"

Ballard laughed with relief. "Yes John, I sent them packing, they won't be coming back. Well, I guess they'll have to if they want to interview you at some point."

John clapped him on the back, again causing him to wince. "I *do* understand they have a job to do. Can't wait for my turn if it's needed."

Ballard looked at him seriously. "John, *do not* lose it with these guys. Ok?"

John chuckled. "You can depend on me buddy boy. I'll be putty in their hands." Ballard wasn't convinced.

Delwyn came in minutes later, sitting opposite Ballard. "ESD have told me how they're going to write up the report. Well done. It's always nice to get these things out of the way without either side blowing up." She looked pointedly at John as she made the comment. "You've satisfied their requirements. I'll let headquarters know all's well." Smiling at Ballard she stood and left the room.

Ballard punched John playfully on the shoulder. "I'm going to spend the next half hour or so thanking everyone for what they did." He went to his desk and began ringing the key members involved. Those he couldn't contact he forwarded an email promising to get in touch. For each of them he extended an invitation to attend a BBQ at his farm once he had recovered from his injuries.

Following that he had lunch with John, Ken and Susan, chatting about everything other than the case. The light hearted mood and good natured banter the best therapy he could have wished for.

Twenty minutes later he was tapped on the arm by a tall lady with prominent front teeth, jet black hair and dressed in a tailored navy pants suit.

"Michael Ballard?"

He looked up, realising this must be the psychologist. "Yes, may I help you?"

"Marjorie Otterman. I'm from the Psychology Unit. I believe you were expecting me?"

"Yes I was. Thank you for coming over at such short notice."

He stood and shook hands, introducing her to the group.

Looking confident she said, "This is a preliminary discussion today and shouldn't take more than thirty minutes. Is now a good time?"

"Yes it is." Pointing to the conference room, he said. "If you'd like to set up in there, I'll be with you in a minute. May I get you something to drink?"

Marjorie shook her head. "No, thank you, I'm fine. I'll see you when you're ready." Turning, she headed off to prepare.

Ballard looked across at John. "Ok, let's get this over with."

John smirked. "Whatever do you mean Mike?"

Unconvinced, Ballard turned to leave just as John mouthed 'pussy' to the others. Ballard washed his cup then winked at the group as he strode to the conference room.

On entering Marjorie looked up, flashing a warm smile. "Michael, from the outset I'd like to say I'm aware of your background and experience. As such you may be wondering how a woman who's never seen active duty could help a seasoned veteran like yourself, especially under these circumstances?"

Ballard appreciated her honesty and said so.

Marjorie continued. "I can't begin to imagine what you went through, or relate to how a policeman with your experience thinks. My role and expertise is limited to diagnosing whether or not you may be suffering from any form of post traumatic stress. Would I be correct in assuming your partner John isn't a great believer in counselling?"

"You picked that up in thirty seconds?"

"Body language is a great revealer and I'm very good at what I do." This was said without arrogance. "It's important I know what peer pressure you may be subjected to, considering

Homicide is such a 'blokey' environment. If I don't evaluate this then any good I may do today or in the future could well be negated."

Ballard chuckled. "Don't worry, John and I go back a long way. He supports me in everything I do, even if he pretends not to. He's fine."

Marjorie scribbled in her folder. "Good. I'm glad we can cross that off the list."

Producing a sheet of paper she pushed it across the table.

"As I said, my role is to determine whether you show any symptoms of stress as a result of the incident. Five main categories where stress materializes are listed on that sheet: physical; anxiety; general lack of interest; behavioural changes and mentally recreating the event."

Seeing him nod she continued. "Let's take the physical category first. Have you experienced any recent symptoms such as headaches, fatigue, sweating, nausea or similar?"

He held up his left hand, then pointed to his face and the side of his head. "I've got the obvious physical injuries resulting from a pretty intense beating. Apart from some bruised ribs that make sleeping a bit uncomfortable, I feel fine."

Marjorie looked intently at him for an extended period. He held her gaze, smiling but saying nothing, having conducted too many interviews using lengthy periods of silence to entice offenders into confessing to not know what she was doing.

Marjorie nodding knowingly. "Silly me. No doubt you were using this technique when I was still in primary school."

Ballard paused. "Er, try when you were still in nappies." They both laughed.

"Ok Michael. I won't labour this: anxiety symptoms, mood swings, general agitation, panic attacks?"

"I'm fine on that front Marjorie, but I do confess to feeling considerable guilt."

"Guilt?"

"Yes. Think about it, my sister visits me in my home and as a result she comes within a hair's breadth of losing her life."

"But that was something you couldn't have foreseen. The moment you were made aware of her danger you came galloping in like a white knight. You actually saved her life."

"Yes, but the end result is Kathryn has a scar on her face that may be permanent, *plus* the mental issues still need to be determined."

"Am I right in believing you've already begun actions to mitigate your sister's physical injuries?" She looked at him, her expression expectant.

"As a matter of fact I have. I've engaged a top plastic surgeon who'll operate on Kathryn within days. My fiancée used to be a nurse and she tells me within twelve months there should be little to no scarring…"

"Well then?"

Ballard shrugged. "That's on the outside – but what about the inside?"

"On the physical front there's nothing more you can do, so put that to rest. Now, her emotional issues, what form if any do you think they'll take?"

Ballard hesitated before replying. "I've always known her to be mentally tough. She's recently gone through a divorce but appears to be handling it ok." He hesitated, deciding not to mention the fact Kathryn was visiting the farm more often since the break-up.

"Was she attacked sexually?" It was obvious Marjorie wanted to explore the unspoken subject Ballard was alluding to.

He shut his eyes, as though blocking out the image. "I've already asked that question and she assures me there wasn't even an attempt – medically she's been given the all clear... "His voice trailed away as he fought his emotions, his eyes moistening.

Marjorie continued as if nothing had happened. Ballard admired her professionalism. "So what I'm hearing is *you* believe Kathryn may have psychological issues, but by your own admission she appears to be a pretty resolute young lady. Nothing you've said so far contradicts that."

Ballard fought to regain his composure, still not trusting his voice.

"What have you done to lessen her mental trauma?"

Ballard recovered. "Well, er ... I'm going to make sure she sees a psychologist of her own choosing and see where that leads."

"What if she doesn't want to?"

Ballard smiled grimly. "I can be very persuasive when I need to be."

Marjorie chuckled. "She's one lucky lady to have you as a brother. My advice is take things slowly – something I've a feeling you're not very comfortable with."

"Yes, I've been told that over the years."

This time Marjorie laughed out loud. "Well, other than predicting the future and wrapping her in cotton wool, I don't see how you could have done anything differently. Again I stress the guilt you're feeling is natural, but you've been around long enough to know it'll fade. A lot will depend on how well she comes out of this physically and psychologically, but I'm guessing the person who's beating themselves up on this whole issue is you."

"Hmm, you might be right Marjorie... you just might be

right." He ran his fingers through his hair, careful not to dislodge the stitches. "There's no doubt about it, the residual impact of crime, it's like ripples on a pond." They both reflected on the statement.

Marjorie shuffled into a more upright position in her chair. "I'm going to skip the remaining three categories. You seem as balanced and 'normal' as any person I know considering your ordeal. But I need to ask what your plans are regarding some leave."

Ballard responded immediately. "Well, I've asked my fiancée to marry me and…"

Marjorie's eyes lit up. "That's wonderful news, in more ways than one."

He understood what she meant. "As soon as I've finish here, I'm putting in for a month's sick leave…" He hesitated. "At last count I have over four hundred days owing. On top of that I'll take a month's long service leave, but that doesn't mean I won't pop into work every now and then."

Marjorie smirked. "Yes, I'm sure you will. You wouldn't be surprised if I told you I did some homework on you before I came here today. You've quite a reputation in the force." Ballard shrugged.

Continuing Marjorie said, "Well, I'm done. I won't be requesting any more sessions unless you need them, or I'm directed to do a follow up. Do you have any questions you'd like to ask me, or anything you want to talk about?"

"Not that I can think of, other than to say our chat today has been excellent and yes, I'll keep in touch and let you know how I'm travelling."

He stood and shook her hand. "I guess you'll want to brief Delwyn so I'll get out of your hair. Thank you again."

"No, thank *you* Michael. I wish you the very best for the future and your wife to be. What's her name?"

"Natalie."

"Lucky lady."

"I tell her that every day."

Marjorie laughed again and after handing Ballard her business card, headed for Delwyn's office. Relieved, Ballard walked out of the conference room.

"Boss!"

He spun around, seeing Bobby rush towards him. They shook hands and for a split second Ballard thought he was going to hug him.

"Jesus boss, am I glad everything worked out. I shit myself when I thought I might have stuffed up and put you and your sister in danger."

"Bobby, nothing could be further from the truth. If it wasn't for some of your work and what Susan did, things may have been very, very different."

Bobby's expression relaxed as he shook hands again. "Good to have you back." He turned and headed in Susan's direction.

Ballard went to his desk and sat down, reflecting on what had transpired since he stepped onto the floor. As tiring as it had been, he felt he was getting his life back together and apart from being directed to take sick leave, he knew Delwyn would understand him applying for a month's long service leave.

He logged onto his computer and after accessing the HR system, completed the necessary forms, forwarding them to Delwyn for approval. That done he began typing his statement, concentrating so as to ensure every detail was included. He estimated it would take over an hour due to the restriction of his left hand. Looking at his watch he saw it was 2.50 p.m. With any luck he figured he would be finished by 4.30 at the latest. From the way he was feeling he knew this would be his limit for the day.

The thought of two months away from work, other than the odd day or two back at the office was both exhilarating and unnerving. For over thirty years he had never been off work for any extended period, so this was unfamiliar territory. As a compromise he made a mental note to sign out a laptop so he could remain in touch and clear his never ending stream of emails.

Picking up his phone he dialled Natalie's mobile. When she answered he forced his voice to be upbeat, hiding the tiredness he was feeling.

"Hello darling. How's your day been?"

"Michael… you sound exhausted. Are you alright? How did the interview with ESD go?"

He shook his head, amazed at her ability to read his every mood. He decided honesty was his best option.

"Actually I feel like I've been run over by a truck, but despite that, everything went well. I'll explain tonight. I need to finish off my statement before heading home. I should be there by 5… 5.30 at the latest. Now, enough about me, how's Kathryn?"

"You'll be amazed. Her wrists are bandaged and there's a small steri-strip and gauze pad covering the wound on her face. Other than the obvious swelling, she looks fabulous. She's been joking all day."

"You're kidding?"

"No. She's one resilient lady. Her shoulder's still very sore, but she's not complaining."

Ballard felt relief course through him. "Great news darling, all my love. I'll see you both later."

"Be careful driving."

"Always."

Turning back to his statement he worked without interruption for thirty minutes before John returned and stood behind him, reading what was on the screen. Ballard printed a hard copy which John took to his desk to edit; Ballard continued typing. Ten minutes later John came back with a number of suggestions and after modifying the document, Ballard printed the entire statement. Both men rechecked the facts and after final amendments, the report was ready for inclusion onto the brief.

"Mike you looked knackered. I'll finish off the last reports tomorrow. Right now I'm going to drive you home, you're staying at Natalie's, right?"

Ballard shrugged. "I'd argue, but I don't have the energy."

"Think nothing of it. You know how I liked driving the 'beast', despite it being just the *once*."

Ballard noted the emphasis on the word 'once'. "Well you were hooning around as though it was a hotted up Ferrari. I didn't know a car that size could do the things you were making it do."

John chuckled. "Don't worry. Considering the state you're in I'll make like the chauffeur in 'Driving Miss Daisy'. Bobby can follow me in the police car and drop me back here."

Ballard signed three original copies of his statement, handing them to John. "Give me a minute. I need to see Delwyn before I leave." He turned and headed for her office.

As he knocked on the door she looked up. "So it took something as serious as this to drag you away from work for an extended period?"

"I have to admit it's a strange feeling Delwyn. It'll take some getting used to."

"Forget work just for once Michael. I think you've earned it, besides, you'll have your hands full over the coming months. To begin with you have to get yourself physically better. You've taken some terrible punishment which I must say adds to your reputation. Then there's your wedding plans, I'm so pleased for you. Natalie will make a wonderful bride and wife. Make every day count.

"Without Marjorie admitting it I get the sense you blame yourself for your sister's injuries. While I don't agree, I understand your feelings which you'll have to work through as well. So all in all, what you're doing for the next two months is stopping work to carry bricks."

Ballard snorted. "The last time I heard that phrase it came from my mother."

Delwyn grimaced. "Thank you Michael. That's made my day." She checked her PC screen. "I've approved your leave, so that's out of the way. Is your statement finished?"

"Yes, John has three copies all signed. He'll complete the other reports later. I'm assuming the inquest will be scheduled in the next month or so. Give me some early notice on that front. If I'm needed for anything at work I'll pop in… just send me an email, I'm taking a laptop home."

Delwyn shook her head. "No, I can't imagine we'll have to. As Marjorie said, you need to recover, don't underestimate the impact this has had on your physical and mental health. And talk to her any time you feel it's necessary, or anyone here for that matter. We all care about you very much Michael, I don't need to remind you of that."   Standing, she came around her desk and gave him a warm hug. "Take care and come back refreshed."

"Yes ma'am."

He headed out of the office and over to where John was

sitting. "Feel like driving a real car?"

John looked up then glanced over at Bobby. "Georgadinov, let's go!"

Bobby sprang to his feet, shrugging into his coat before rushing over. Ballard did a quick round of the office, shaking hands and kissing cheeks before joining John and Bobby at the lift.

"Thanks for this guys. I have to admit I'm starting to flag a bit and the last thing I need is to dent my wheels."

CHAPTER
20

Minutes later, having experienced a very tame descent to street level, Ballard leaned back in the passenger seat, watching John weave his magic through the traffic. True to his word he drove without risk and despite feeling out of place not being behind the wheel, Ballard felt himself dozing off. John looked across at him, opening his mouth to speak then changed his mind.

After turning into Natalie's driveway, Ballard shuffled into a more upright position and reached for the remote to open the garage door.

"Home sweet home." John hesitated then blurted out. "Jesus I'm glad you're ok. When I said the other day 'don't go getting yourself killed', I never thought it may happen!"

Ballard grimaced. "We had a job to do John and we damn well did it. That'll give the young'uns something to think about." John appeared choked for words.

Bobby walked up to the side of the car as Natalie opened the garage door leading from the hallway. A mini reunion ensued and despite being invited inside, John and Bobby declined with thanks. Natalie and Ballard stood arm in arm, waving as the two detectives drove off.

Natalie looked up at Ballard, concern on her face. "Come

and sit down, you look exhausted. Kathryn's in the lounge room dozing on and off. And yes she's fine. You're the one I'm worried about." With her arm around him she escorted him inside.

Entering the lounge he saw Kathryn lying back in the armchair, relaxing. On seeing her brother she leapt up, despite his protest for her to stay.

"Nonsense Michael. I'm fine, *but you look awful*."

"Thanks for those words of encouragement."

"No really. I think I'll have to take time off with Natalie to look after you, a sort of tag team effort."

"Very funny." He avoided looking at her face which was still swollen and bruised where she had been struck. "How do you feel?"

"I'm fine… I *am*! Now let's get this over with." She took his hand and led him towards the window where there was more light. "Look at my face so you don't have to go on pretending there isn't a melon where I was hit. I spoke with the surgeon you arranged and he's given me all the details I need and more." She paused for breath. "The hardest thing for me will be waiting for the scar to heal after the operation. He said the cut's quite clean and he has every hope it will fade over time."

Natalie slipped alongside Ballard, giving him a hug. "See darling, I told you everything was going to work out. You have a wonderful, resilient sister."

Ballard felt tears swell in his eyes. He blinked hard, unable to speak; both women gave him a hug and all three stood clinging together.

Kathryn was the first to break from the group. "Enough of this soppy stuff. Get in the kitchen and let your wife-to-be serve up a home cooked meal. I had mine earlier so I'm going upstairs for a little lie down after all this excitement." Turning she headed for her bedroom.

Ballard stared at Natalie in amazement. She smirked in return. "Perhaps we're *not* the weaker sex."

"It would appear so… now what culinary delight have you rustled up for me?"

She led him into the kitchen, pointing at an egg and bacon pie with scalloped potatoes. His tastebuds watered and twenty minutes later he knew why. Wiping his mouth with his napkin he leaned back in his chair.

"Unbelievable. Beautiful *and* multi talented. How clever was I to find you?"

Natalie beamed.

Ballard looked over his shoulder, checking to see if his sister had returned, "So, how much of that was an act?"

Natalie knew what he was referring to. "Look, I've no doubt she's going to have some low days, but I'm certain she'll come through this with flying colours."

"I still want her to see a counsellor."

"I agree, but you may have difficulty getting her to one. My advice is to take it one day at a time. Please don't drag her anywhere by the scruff of the neck."

The look on Ballard's face had Natalie persisting. "Don't give me that 'who me' look Michael, you know how relentless you can be. I don't think that will help her at this point. No doubt you'll get your way, you always do, but you may not get it in your time frame, which for you is yesterday."

Ballard opened his mouth to reply but refrained, instead nodding reflectively.

Natalie began clearing the dishes and Ballard stood to help.

"Not tonight big guy. For once you're going to sit in the lounge and rest. I'll be there in a flash. I want you to tell me what happened at work, then upstairs to bed with you."

He began to protest but Natalie took his arm, dragging him into the lounge.

"Now stay!"

He did as he was told.

Minutes later she reappeared and cuddled alongside him. He commenced by detailing the interview with ESD; a look of relief flooded across her face when he informed her of the detective's finding.

"I'm glad that's over. I knew everything would work out, even though that little voice kept saying 'but what if…?'"

He chuckled. "You heard it too?" He then went on to describe the meeting with the psychologist and how it had clarified a number of issues he had not thought through.

Natalie put her hand on his arm. "She's right. Look how Kathryn's taking this. To her you're the big hero brother who saved the day."

"Yeah, right."

"It's true. I had a long chat with her in the car on the way back from the hospital. She thinks you can walk on water. Come to think of it, so do I."

Ballard shook his head, but didn't say anything; Natalie allowed him time to consider what she had said. He cupped her face, kissing her forehead.

"Hmm. I'm going to have to mull that over for a bit, but I'll get there."

Turning fully towards her he said, "Now for some very important news. I've had my month's long service leave and four weeks sick leave approved, so that should…"

His remaining words were smothered by Natalie crushing her lips against his. "Thank you so much Michael. I was worried we wouldn't have enough time to prepare everything for the wedding. Having you for two months will make all the difference." Smiling mischievously she continued. "While you were at work today I rang Rupertswood and spoke with Margaret the manager. We discussed possible wedding dates. While Saturdays seem to be taken for the next twelve months, there are plenty of Sundays we can choose from."

"Then a Sunday it will be."

Natalie smiled contentedly. "Simple, but elegant."

Ballard knew what she meant. "I can't imagine anything you do being simple – elegant yes, but not simple. How many people do you plan to invite to this elegant wedding?"

Natalie pretended to perform arithmetic in her head before blurting out, "I've taken into account your family and friends, so together with mine I'm thinking seventy to eighty."

Ballard sighed with relief. "Thank God, I was expecting a much larger number. I agree, let's keep this intimate and of course *no* presents."

Natalie agreed. "Depending on when you take Kathryn to counselling, or should I say *if,* can we drive out to Rupertswood in the next day or so?"

"The sooner the better."

"You're not just saying that to please me?" A look of concern crossed her face.

Ballard laughed. "I proposed to *you*, remember? I want this to be the happiest day of your life and every day after that happier than the one before."

Natalie hugged him so fiercely he had to loosen her grip for fear of choking.

Smiling he said. "Come to think of it, that's a good line for my speech." He shrugged. "Besides, planning for the wedding is going to be the best therapy money can buy. You've no idea how much I'm looking forward to it. I've even started preparing what I'll say at the reception."

Natalie placed her hands on his shoulders, observing him at arm's length. "Why am I not surprised." After kissing him one more time she said, "Now off to bed with you. I need you mended as soon as possible, we have a lot to do in the next four to six weeks."

Ballard arched his eyebrows. "Never has a truer word been said. I also need to throw in a BBQ for everyone who helped save Kathryn. But let's not swamp ourselves. There's nothing we can't do, providing we plan and throw money at it."

"I'll be contributing my share financially."

He began to protest but she cut him off.

"Trust me, by the time I've designed the engagement ring you won't mind me paying *some* of the cost of the reception. I need to do this. I want to have some degree of independence in this marriage... so it's fair I chip in. By the way, I have some rough sketches of the ring already."

Ballard's mouth dropped open as she rushed out of the lounge, returning seconds later with three pieces of paper. On each was a detailed drawing of an engagement ring.

"You know how artistic Kathryn is – well I got her to put those skills to work as I thought it might take her mind off things."

"How altruistic of you darling." He chuckled as he spoke.

"I've always wanted a marquise as the centre stone, set at a forty-five degree angle with a split band sweeping in an arc on either side. As you can see I've inset baguettes in each arm to complement the marquise." The concentration on her face was so intense it was all Ballard could do not to burst out laughing.

She continued, oblivious to his amusement. "Now on each side of the engagement ring will be a separate wedding band crafted so all three fit together as one. Kathryn suggested these should have a line of round diamonds to soften the amount of gold that will be showing. What do you think?"

Ballard studied each drawing; after deliberation he pointed to the second sheet. "If your finger is big enough to accommodate all this bling, then that's the one. I know a jeweller in Camberwell who's excellent. We can pop down there tomorrow for a quote. After that we'll swing over to Rupertswood."

Natalie looked cautiously at him before blurting out, "This jeweller... you haven't had him make any *other* engagement rings have you?"

He shook his head. "No. I promise you're the first... and the last."

Relief flooded her face. "Thank you darling. I know that sounded petty but I had to ask."

He stood up. "I think I'll take your advice and have a quick shower then hop into bed. While I'm happy with what I've achieved today, I can't deny I'm bushed."

Thirty minutes later he and Natalie were lying together, their bodies moulded as one; in no time they were sound asleep.

CHAPTER
21

Repeating the previous morning, Ballard woke and looked at the bedside clock, this time it showed 8 a.m. Again Natalie had her back to him, sleeping peacefully. He stroked her hair and she began to stir, stretching before rolling over and kissing him on the lips.

"Good morning my wonderful man. How do your fingers feel?"

He held up his left hand, inspecting it. "Sore, but considering the alternative I can't complain. The waterproof covers they gave me for the shower do the trick... I just have to remember to put them on. The protective guard's a bit restricting but I guess the doc' knows his stuff, so I won't do anything foolish."

A dubious expression appeared on Natalie's face.

He attempted to look serious. "No, honestly, I won't. Like he said, Mr Arthritis isn't a fun guy and it is only for four weeks."

Natalie's expression softened. "Good. My job is to keep you to your word. I'll check your stitches later to see there's no infection."

He adopted a compliant expression. "Yes boss."

Putting on dressing gowns they headed down to the kitchen to find Kathryn tucking into a bowl of cereal and yoghurt, along with a cup of steaming coffee. Alongside her was an open magazine advertising holidays on a luxury liner.

Looking up she smiled as best she could, the swelling on her face distorting the result. "Good morning, how are the two love-birds?"

Natalie responded. "We slept like babies." She went over and inspected Kathryn's face. "Hmm, the dressing will need changing." Turning to Ballard she asked, "Would you mind if I take five minutes to patch up your sister?"

"Go ahead. I'll make breakfast. The usual?"

She nodded as she switched on the kettle to boil water before collecting an array of bandages, swabs and creams and a small plastic bowl. She then began removing Kathryn's gauze pad covering the steri-strip, soaking it first with moist cotton wool. Kathryn pretended to read the magazine but Ballard saw her flinch.

Once the scar was revealed Kathryn asked to see the wound in the mirror. Natalie remained resolute, stating she wanted to clean away the dried blood that had congealed over the scar line. Kathryn looked agitated but stayed seated; once the area had been prepared she rushed into the hallway and stood in front of the mirror.

Both Natalie and Ballard heard an audible drawing of breath. Moments later she returned, her mood sombre but determined. "The bastard! I wish it'd been me who'd kicked him over the edge."

Natalie placed a reassuring arm around her shoulder. "Time Kathryn, time. It *will* heal, so too will your emotions." Kathryn sat on the chair in front of Natalie, nodding but remaining silent.

After re-cleansing the area, Natalie applied another steri-strip, followed by a patch of gauze wadding. "To you the swelling looks the same, but I can assure you it's going down. My guess is four to five days. Today's Wednesday, so that'll make the operation Monday morning with any luck. I'll keep the doctor updated on your progress."

Kathryn took Natalie's hand. "I can't tell you how grateful I am for all your help." Natalie shook her head but Kathryn persisted. "No Natalie, this is healing me physically *and* mentally and having Michael here, well that's icing on the cake."

Ballard sensed the mood needed lifting. "Speaking of cake Nat, what have you decided regarding the wedding?"

Natalie's reply was instant. "I'm making it myself."

"You're what!" Ballard and Kathryn spoke as one.

"I'm baking the cake. It'll make the reception more personal."

Kathryn shook her head. "Brave girl. Are you sure you need that much pressure before the big day?"

Natalie appeared relaxed. "In a way it'll be therapeutic. I'll make it early enough so if something goes wrong I can start again."

All three sat at the table with Ballard and Natalie tucking into their breakfast while Kathryn read her magazine. The discussion between them was light-hearted and centred around wedding plans. Natalie showed Kathryn the engagement ring they had decided on.

"Michael knows an excellent jeweller in Camberwell who can make the ring."

Kathryn looked at her brother, her expression dubious. Natalie chuckled. "Don't worry, I've already asked the question. And no, this jeweller hasn't made any others for him." Ballard shook his head, pretending bewilderment at the cognitive processes of the female mind.

Natalie placed her hand on his arm. "Let's invite Kathryn

along. Girls love looking at diamonds."

Kathryn shook her head. "No thanks Natalie, I'm going to chill out on the hammock in the sunshine and read… a lazy day for me. Besides, three's a crowd when it comes to hunting for engagement rings." She saw Natalie begin to protest. "Go! I'll be fine. I need time alone and depending on when you get back, I'll cook dinner. It'll be good for me." Although uncertain, Natalie agreed.

Thirty minutes later, animated as she discussed every aspect of the wedding, Natalie drove Ballard to the jewellers. He watched as she skilfully negotiated the late morning traffic. Taking his mobile he rang, pre-warning the jeweller of their arrival.

Minutes later, after easing into the tiny parking area, they entered the shop, passing under the business name 'John Simmonds Jeweller'. Beaming at each other they glanced up at the old fashioned bell that heralded their entrance. A small man approached them, no taller than Natalie, his weathered face having seen more sun than was healthy; his smile exposed perfect teeth that would have been ideal in a toothpaste commercial.

Despite looking hard at Ballard's bruised features, he refrained from asking the obvious question. Ballard shook his head. "Morning John. Just one of the perils of the job. It's a long story. Sorry about dropping in like this. I'd like you to meet my fiancée, Natalie."

John smiled, shaking Natalie's hand by grasping it in both of his. Ballard shrugged as he said, "I guess I jumped the gun a bit, proposing before I had the engagement ring. Nonetheless, when you see Natalie's design you'll see why I didn't even try."

Natalie produced the drawing, handing it to John. Putting on glasses suspended around his neck by a fine gold chain, he began making noises of approval. Looking up he said, "This is one of the most beautiful and unusual designs I've ever seen. With the right stone, the finished product will be magnificent and very unique." Natalie shivered on the spot, her excitement palpable.

Turning, he told his two assistants he needed to keep the next thirty minutes free. After leading Ballard and Natalie into a small viewing room, he ensured they were both comfortable before rushing out, returning with a small tray of diamonds.

He placed them on the table. "For some reason Marquise aren't as popular now as they were a number of years ago. Do you know how they came by their name?" Both Ballard and Natalie shook their head. "The name's derived from the design chosen by the French king, Louis XIV for his lover the Marquise de Pompadour. He wanted the shape to match her smile."

Natalie squeezed Ballard's arm. "How romantic."

John continued. "With the popularity of this cut waning, there aren't many on the market." A look of concern crossed Natalie's face. "Fear not my dear, all's not lost. I've several small and as luck would have it, a number of larger Marquise that have excellent quality, clarity and are free of colour." He held up a warning hand. "Having said that Michael, the larger Marquise *are* expensive."

Ballard shrugged. "Let's pick the diamond we want, then worry about the price."

Taking fine pointed tweezers John picked up a diamond, holding it out for Ballard and Natalie to inspect. "This is a beautiful diamond and would sit nicely on Natalie's finger." He took her hand, positioning the diamond at a forty-five degree angle across her ring finger. She drew in a large breath.

Ballard leaned across to inspect, immediately shaking his

head. "No John, too small."

"Yes, I agree. As Natalie wants a fitted wedding band on either side of the engagement ring, this size Marquise would be swamped by the wedding bands. But I wanted *you* to come to that conclusion, not hear it from me." Turning to Natalie he said, "Because of the design you've created, the centre diamond needs to be substantial to ensure it remains the focal point." Natalie looked across at Ballard, uncertainty on her face; he held her gaze reassuringly.

John returned the diamond to the tray, selecting another. This time, as he held it across Natalie's finger she gasped in amazement. "My God! It's beautiful and *huge*. Look at it sparkle Michael." Ballard checked it out, agreeing it dramatically captured the light.

John placed the diamond on a black cloth in front of them. "This is an exquisite diamond., 2.4 carats, E colour, which is one level down from the best. It's also VS2 in clarity and an Ideal Cut which is what gives it such lustre and life. I recommend the claws securing the stone be white gold as this accentuates the diamond, making it appear even larger. Do you want the band to be yellow gold?"

Natalie blurted her agreement before looking across at Ballard. "It's beautiful – but the cost?" Again he shrugged. John took a pen and wrote a figure on a notepad; tearing off the page he handed it to Ballard. Glancing down Ballard pretended to slip sideways off his chair as he dropped the paper,. The look of concern intensified on Natalie's face.

Ballard grinned. "Lock it in John. How long will it take to make?"

Natalie flung her arms around Ballard's neck.

John hesitated. "Three to four weeks, which will include

you both coming back several times to check on its progress. That way we can discuss every aspect before I commit to the next phase. It saves me time and you the anxiety that I may not produce exactly what you want."

For the next twenty minutes Natalie and John discussed in excruciating detail how the engagement ring and wedding bands would look. John suggested the wedding band's gallery at either end of the Marquise could be softened by including some filigree, allowing additional light to shine under the stone to add to its already significant lustre. Natalie agreed, choosing an elegant design. John then meticulously documented all her instructions before turning to Ballard.

"Now Michael, will you be wearing a wedding band?" Ballard didn't hesitate.

"Yes John and my request *is* simple. Nine millimetres wide with a half round face."

Natalie took his hand. "Are you sure you don't want some detail on it sweetheart?"

He shook his head. "No. Just eighteen carat, plain yellow gold."

John looked at Ballard's injured left hand, suggesting he measure his right ring finger instead. "We can always adjust the size later if required." Ballard agreed, holding out his right hand while John slipped on a number of measurement rings until he was satisfied with the fit. John then sized Natalie's ring finger succeeding on the third attempt.

He wrote copious notes before sitting back, looking content. "If all my customers were as well prepared and decisive as you both are it would save me so much time and effort. It's been a pleasure. I promise you Natalie the finished product will be stunning. I do have one word of caution. The green eye is going to appear with some of your friends and you may be quite surprised as to who they'll be. I know this is a generalisation as I don't know them, however, something as spectacular as this *will* generate considerable discussion.

"Every time I say this to a lady who's chosen an impressive ring she says 'no way', then when I see her years later she agrees that jealousy *did* raise its ugly head." Natalie shrugged, not fully convinced.

John wrote out an invoice with full details, including the final price. Placing it in an envelope he handed it to Ballard who slipped it in his pocket.

"Thank you John and yes, I suspect you're right regarding the jealousy thing, but that's something we'll have to address when it happens. Much appreciated."

Standing he shook John's hand while Natalie gave him a warm kiss on the cheek, causing him to look somewhat flustered. Saying their goodbyes they left the shop.

Once in the car Natalie turned to Ballard, overwhelmed with joy. Several pedestrians stopped and looked at her, startled by her squeals of delight; seeing them she waved a reassuring hand. "Darling, in my wildest dreams I never thought I'd be wearing an engagement ring so beautiful. How can I ever thank you?"

Ballard leered wickedly. "Oh, I'll think of something – don't you worry about that."

"So I win on both counts?"

Ballard pretended ignorance. "Whatever do you mean Mrs Ballard?"

She beamed. "I don't know about you, but after all this excitement I'm famished. There's a fantastic gourmet sandwich bar down the road." She looked expectantly at him and was rewarded with a nod of agreement.

CHAPTER
22

Thirty minutes later, hunger pangs satisfied, Natalie headed the BMW along Bell Street towards the Tullamarine freeway and Sunbury. "Darling, in my handbag you'll find several printouts that give the history of Rupertswood. I glanced through them earlier... it's *very* interesting."

Ballard retrieved the sheets and began reading. Within seconds he laughed out-loud. "Well I'll be... Rupertswood was built in 1876. That's two years after my parents' farm was established in Bordertown and five years before the house I grew up in was built."

Natalie beamed at him. "I love history – I just can't get enough of it, yet the funny thing is at school I wasn't interested at all."

Ballard continued. "My God, the original property around Rupertswood was thirty two thousand acres." He looked up, his lips moving as he performed mental arithmetic. "If a hectare is point four of an acre, then that's just under thirteen thousand hectares... thirty two times the size of Dad's property at home. That's some farm."

Natalie glanced sideways, observing how he was warming to the task. He went on.

"'Rupertswood was the residence of Sir William John Clarke who happened to be an Australian born Baronet.'" He turned to Natalie. "So where does a Baronet sit in the hierarchy of the English aristocracy?"

Natalie tooted politely at a driver weaving between lanes and travelling twenty kilometres an hour below the speed limit. "A Baronet is below a Baron and above a Knight, it's a title for commoners who have lots of money. They're referred to as sir. I think it's a hereditary title. Apart from that I'm at a loss, plus they're no longer bestowed here in Australia."

"Hmm, interesting. Now, 'Rupertswood itself was built in the Italianate style, with a whopping thirty metre tower overlooking a circular driveway at the front. The grand entrance has Victorian tessellated tiles…'" He looked across at Natalie.

Her reply was instant. "They're tiles laid in distinct patterns without grout lines."

Ballard shook his head. "I should have known that gem would be on the tip of your tongue. It says here 'Rupertswood boasts six stained glass panels which are considered to be some of the finest examples in the world.'" He continued reading before exclaiming, "I don't believe it… 'the Duke and Duchess of York, who later became King George V and Queen Mary visited Rupertswood, along with Dame Nellie Melba.' I have to say darling, when you choose a location to get married, you do it in style."

Natalie failed to hide her satisfaction. "Nothing you don't deserve my sweet."

"Now, for the sporting enthusiasts, 'it was on the oval at Rupertswood the cricket match between the visiting English team and an Australian team consisting mostly of Rupertswood staff was played. We lost and as a result a cricket bail was burnt by Lady Clarke with the ashes placed in a small pottery urn – hence the tradition of the Ashes has perpetuated via this tiny trophy.'" He rested the sheets on his lap, sitting back in deep thought.

Natalie swung onto the Tullamarine freeway. "So, I chose wisely selecting Rupertswood?"

He touched her arm. "Very much so."

They drove in reflective silence until they passed Tullamarine airport. Ballard looked to his right, observing a Qantas A380 swing in low over Bulla road, wheels and flaps down as it made its final approach.

"Amazing."

"What's amazing sweetheart?"

"That something so heavy can hang in the sky like that."

"Perhaps one day we can go on a holiday overseas in one – maybe on our second honeymoon."

"And where do you plan to go on this one?"

She glanced at him before negotiating the first roundabout after leaving the freeway. "I've always dreamed about going on a cruise. Not a long one, maybe a week – lazing about doing whatever we want or nothing at all, maybe catching up on some sleep…" The wicked expression on her face left Ballard in no doubt as to her real meaning.

"I agree, that's a distinct possibility."

She slowed down as she negotiated the bridge over Deep Creek which was north of the Bulla township. Accelerating, she booted the BMW up the steep climb out of the gorge onto Sunbury road.

Ten minutes later she turned into the Rupertswood driveway, passing the majestic bluestone gateposts and the impressive Gatehouse building as large as a medium sized house.

The driveway continued past the famous cricket ground, then the lake where ladies from a bygone era idled away the hours in wooden boats rowed by smartly dressed suitors, on through the landscaped grounds and up to the stunning mansion.

After parking on the circular driveway, they got out and gazed up, admiring the building's majestic tower and intricate lacework verandas. Natalie squeezed Ballard's arm. "Just perfect."

Walking up the bluestone steps they pushed open the solid front door and stepped back in time. Their senses embracing the old world charm; from the intricate tiled floor to the six metre high ceilings, the ornate cornices and elaborate brass lights. A magnificent staircase with a polished walnut handrail led to the upstairs bedrooms and what used to be the servants' quarters. At the far end of the foyer the famous stained glass panels were illuminated by natural light, creating a kaleidoscope of colour that was breathtaking.

Ballard kissed Natalie on the forehead. "I hope my wedding speech is worthy of these surroundings."

"Nonsense. Yours will be perfect. It's *my* speech I'm worried about. I'm hopeless in front of a crowd."

"Don't worry, I'll be with you all the way."

Looking unconvinced she picked up the reception bell, ringing it several times. Within seconds a lady in her forties appeared and hurried towards them. Her blonde hair was styled in a bob and although taller than Natalie, she was still petite. A cream blouse and tan skirt was matched by practical, light brown flat shoes.

"You must be Natalie." Without hesitation she gave her a kiss on the cheek. Looking up at Ballard's bruised features she smirked at Natalie. "I thought ladies waited until *after* they were married before showing their husband who's boss?" Smiling, she shook Ballard's hand. "I'm Margaret, the manager of this humble abode."

Ballard responded. "Michael – and there's nothing humble about this grand old mansion. I've driven past it countless times, but never been inside. It's quite magnificent."

Natalie joined in. "Yes Margaret. Everything's so beautifully maintained."

Margaret winced. "It should be. I've spent a fortune renovating the place, but I'm pleased to say everything I intend to repair will be finalised well before your big day." She inclined her head towards double doors on the right of the foyer. "Let me show you the Drawing Room where we host the receptions."

Ballard followed Natalie who gasped as she entered the room. Over twenty metres long by ten wide, the room was nothing short of stunning. Margaret pointed to the bay window on the far side. "That'll be where we locate the bridal table, it's a great spot to overlook all your guests."

From that point on Ballard was a mere observer as both women discussed where the ceremony would be conducted, its format, the number of tables required for the reception, what floral decorations would be best, the menus and every other aspect down to the finest detail. He reflected how police operations were seldom planned with more care and he knew of many that weren't.

One and a half hours later, after touring the building, Natalie turned to Ballard, holding his hand, a sympathetic expression on her face. "My poor darling, you must be at wits end. But at least Margaret and I have touched on the basics."

"*The basics!*" Ballard blurted the words before he could stop himself. "My God, General Eisenhower didn't do this much planning for D-Day in World War Two."

Natalie glanced at Margaret, seeking confirmation. "Brides want their wedding day to be perfect Michael, this takes preparation."

Twenty minutes later, after exchanging mobile and email details with Margaret, Ballard and Natalie said their good-byes. Once in the BMW Natalie sat for a few seconds to compose herself. "The wedding's going to be perfect. Venues are so important, but the one factor that will make it magical is *you* my precious." She leaned across and kissed him.

He grinned in appreciation. "On a practical note, having the option for the ceremony to be either in the gardens or in the foyer in front of the stained glass panels is reassuring. That way guests won't be inconvenienced if it rains which will reduce *our* stress on the day. Well planned my dear."

Natalie started the motor, easing away from the building. She looked at the clock on the dashboard. "Hmm. Just after 4… we should be home by 5.30. I can give Kathryn a hand preparing dinner."

Ballard took his mobile and began making calls. The first was to the office to see if a court date had been set for the Coroner's inquest. He spoke with John for several minutes before hanging up. "No date yet and nothing of any substance happening on the case. The Italian police still haven't located Parnell's wife and daughter, I'm not sure how hard they're trying."

The next call was to Alan D to inform him his mowing services would be required on the farm until Ballard's hand had fully healed. He also asked Alan to inspect the replacement window in the lounge to confirm it had been fitted correctly, along with the repairs to the front door. The fact that Alan was a master builder added credence to his inspection. Finally he placed a call to Vera, the lady he employed to clean the house whenever he was away for extended periods. As she had provided this service for over ten years she was now regarded as a member of the family. Ballard trusted her without question and as a consequence she had the remotes to activate and deactivate the garage door and house alarms. This enabled her to come and go as she pleased. Leaving out the graphic details, he explained why there was fingerprint dust throughout the house, and a new window in the lounge.

Finishing the call he leaned back and placed his hand on Natalie's thigh, feeling her firm flesh under his fingers; his hand began to move upwards. She glanced across at him. "I'm glad to see you've recovering from your ordeal Michael. In all honesty I wasn't sure how well you were going to come out of it." Without taking her eyes off the road she took his hand and kissed it before returning it to her thigh, a tad lower than from where she had taken it. "Let's try and make it home in one piece shall we?" Ballard chuckled as he relaxed back in his seat.

CHAPTER
23

As the traffic proved to be lighter than anticipated, Natalie pulled into the garage twenty minutes earlier than her prediction. Stepping into the hallway Ballard was reminded of his childhood on his parents' farm as the aroma of lamb and vegetable pie wafted over him. Kathryn turned to them as they entered the kitchen, a tea-towel in one hand, an oven mitt in the other. "Thirty minutes more by my reckoning. TV dinners are *so* much easier at my place."

Natalie peeped through the oven door. "You beat me to it Kathryn. I was going to lend a hand, but I see you're on top of things. I could get used to this."

Ballard looked across at his sister. "Mum's recipe?"

Kathryn nodded. "It is. I memorised it years ago, but I've been too lazy to make it for myself. This is a small thank you for everything you've done for me."

Ballard was impressed. "Keep this up Sis and you won't be going home... ever."

For the next ten minutes Natalie described the events of the day and Ballard felt a glow of satisfaction as he observed both women engrossed in discussion about diamond rings, wedding ceremonies, receptions and honeymoons. His initial concern that the excitement associated with Natalie's personal plans might remind Kathryn of her divorce dissipated as he saw his sister genuinely engaged in Natalie's affairs.

After dinner, which included a second helping, Ballard washed and dried the dishes while Natalie changed Kathryn's dressing. Following that Natalie checked the stitches in Ballard's scalp, confirming they were healing without any sign of infection.

Once they were seated in the lounge, Ballard broached the subject of counselling. Kathryn rejected the proposal outright but he persisted. "Sis, I don't think anyone would regard me as anything other than an 'old school' copper. Despite that I was instructed by my boss to take counselling, which I did. That was yesterday and to my surprise, I found the experience positive."

The look on Kathryn's face indicated she was not convinced, but he pressed on. "My issue wasn't the fact I kicked Parnell over the edge. That was a necessity – life or death. No, my problem is the feeling of guilt I have for putting you in harm's way."

Kathryn spluttered, refuting the statement, but he shook his head. "Logic doesn't come into this. Deep down I know I couldn't have foreseen what happened to you. That doesn't lessen the fact I *do* feel guilty, but as the counsellor stated, this is a natural reaction and will lessen as time goes by."

He placed his hand on her arm. "I'm not asking you to have counselling for counselling's sake. It's just that I've spoken to many victims in my career and often they've told me it was years later when the cold sweats began. Kathryn please don't be a tough guy on this issue. Come with me tomorrow and talk to a psychologist I know very well – one I've referred other victims to with considerable success. Just once, then after that if you still feel the same way… well I'll bow to your wishes."

Natalie took his hand in hers; looking at her Ballard hesitated before adding, "We *both* want to help you Sis in any way we can."

Kathryn looked between her brother and Natalie. "What can I say that won't sound ungrateful? Yes Michael, count me in. I'll treat this as a positive experience. Now, for a confession. When I was down the street today buying the meat for the pie, apart from feeling self conscious with this damn bandage on my face, I couldn't stop looking behind me to see if anyone was following." She held up a hand. "I know, I know, this whole episode is over, but yes, as much as I want to forget it, it's going to take time. Thankfully I *can* talk about it with you both and I do see the wisdom in getting some professional advice."

Ballard leaned over and squeezed her arm. "Thank you. You won't regret it."

"On one proviso."

He looked puzzled. "What's that?"

"I want you in the room with me, along with Natalie, *if* she agrees."

"I'm not sure that's how this guy operates…"

"I don't care. That's the deal. I'm not worried I'll break down or make a fool of myself. For God's sake, you saved my life and Natalie's nursing me back to health. We're in this together."

Natalie agreed.

After a moment's deliberation Ballard consented. "Bill… the psychologist's name is William Sykes, he knows me from way back, I'm sure he'll understand. Ok Kathryn, we'll do this your way. He's aware of the circumstances because I've already spoken with him, filling him in on the main points." Taking his mobile he rang the psychologist's office; as there was no pick-up he left a message indicating that if possible he would like an appointment tomorrow. He also gave a short explanation regarding Kathryn's wishes.

Hanging up he sat back and noted the expression on Natalie's face. It consisted of fifty percent approval along with a 'so you got your own way again' look. He gave the faintest of shrugs, followed by an even fainter smile.

For the next half hour they watched the evening news, talking, joking and passing the time away, grateful for all the good things in their lives. Ballard's mobile rang mid commercial and looking at the clock he saw it was 7 p.m.

"Bill, you're working late." He got up and walked casually into the kitchen.

Kathryn glanced at Natalie. "I know he *thinks* he's being subtle, but he doesn't fool me. I'll bet the psychologist is getting his instructions how this should play out as we speak. Michael really cares about me doesn't he?"

Natalie paused. "Enough to risk his life for you Kathryn."

Minutes later Ballard returned, grinning from ear to ear. "All done! William can see us if we get to his office by 8 a.m. in the morning." Kathryn let out a protracted groan.

"Come on Sis, it'll be good for you. His office is in Collins Street, a couple of blocks up from Natalie's work. I suggest we catch the tram in, fresh air, the hustle and bustle of a modern city. My guess is we'll have to get up – oh, say around six."

Kathryn groaned even louder.

Ballard laughed at his sister's anguish. "That being the case I'm calling it quits for the night." Winking at Natalie he kissed the top of Kathryn's head then headed upstairs.

CHAPTER
24

What seemed like only a few short hours after going to bed, all three found themselves sitting on a city bound tram watching morning joggers circle the Royal Botanical Gardens. Dodging peak hour pedestrians they got off at Collins Street and after walking two blocks, entered the multi storey building in which William the psychologist practised. They took the lift to the twenty-seventh floor. An attractive receptionist in her mid forties escorted them to an office along the corridor. Knocking twice she stood politely to one side while they filed into the room.

Sitting behind a large mahogany desk was a grey haired man in his mid fifties. He was dressed in a dazzling white shirt and mauve tie. His grey hair was slicked back behind his ears and his face was tanned. Springing to his feet the moment his guests entered he crossed to where they stood, a genuine smile lighting up his face. As tall as Ballard, he exuded quiet confidence.

"Michael, it's good to see you again... well perhaps the circumstances could be better." He peered for several seconds at Ballard's bruised features. "And so too your face."

Ballard shrugged before shaking his hand. "Thanks for seeing us on such short notice Bill. May I introduce my fiancée

Natalie and my sister Kathryn?"

William shook Natalie's hand first. "At long last we meet, now I have a face to put with your name." Glancing back at Michael he said, "I can see you weren't exaggerating." Turning to Kathryn he beamed a warm smile. "Ah, the famous sister I've heard your brother talk so much about and with such pride." He took her hand in both of his, holding onto it. "Please everyone, take a seat. Coffee, tea?"

They thanked him but declined.

Kathryn looked around her. "What, no couch to lie on?"

William shook his head. "Er, no Kathryn. While many psychologists still believe in this technique, I've found it a barrier to getting clients to relax. When you think about it, asking a patient to lie down in a stranger's office, encouraging them to pour out their heart, well it's quite unnatural." He patted the side of his comfortable cloth covered armchair. "I find cosy chairs much more inviting."

Facing each of them in turn he said, "I've agreed to see Kathryn, along with you Michael and Natalie, despite the fact this isn't how I normally practice. By way of explanation, having you both here while I chat with Kathryn has the positive aspect of making her feel more relaxed and supported than if she were on her own. However Kathryn, I must highlight the disadvantage of this arrangement is you may temper your answers consciously or unconsciously because your brother is in the room. Even at this point I can see the bond you have with him and it's very understandable, but because you may not want to worry or disappoint him, that *could* alter your answers and restrict the value of this session. Do you have any questions regarding what I've said so far?"

Kathryn shuffled in her seat. "I hadn't thought of that aspect

Mr Sykes, I must admit…"

"Please… William."

"Thank you… William. No, I haven't any questions, although I *can* see having Michael in the room may be an issue, but he'll agree I'm very independent. Having said that, I'll keep your advice in mind."

William continued. "Thank you Kathryn. I wanted to make sure everyone was aware of some of the dynamics that may come into play during the session. Now despite what you might have seen on TV or films, I allow my clients to conduct the proceedings. I do this by finding out what's most comfortable for them in terms of how they want the discussion to unfold. We're here because you've been subjected to a stressful incident and there are a number of ways to proceed.

"I could explain how trauma affects people. Alternatively, you could start by telling me how you feel, or you may want to describe the events as they took place on the day. These are *your* choices."

Kathryn glanced across at Ballard for guidance and blushed when she realised what she had done. She shrugged and looked self consciously at William. "Caught me. Strike one, William."

William's features remained positive.

She resumed. "Ok, perhaps if you list the signs of stress, trauma, grief or whatever it is you think I may be experiencing, then I can confirm or deny I have the symptoms. After that I'll describe what happened and I'm guessing from there you'll diagnose my condition. Is that a plan?"

William leaned forward. "I can see you're a very brave woman. Your suggestion is most practical.

"To begin, trauma and stress reactions can be broken into four main groups: emotional, cognitive, physical and behavioural.

Taking emotional first, have you been experiencing feelings of anger, mood swings, denial or fear since the incident?"

Kathryn didn't hesitate. "Yes, all of the above."

Ballard and Natalie glanced at each other, failing to hide their surprise.

William noted their reaction. "Which ones in particular Kathryn?"

"They alternate and I can say in all honesty they're pretty balanced in intensity." She turned to Ballard and Natalie. "I'm sorry I haven't admitted this to you... but I didn't want to worry you and I figured the feelings would pass. Unfortunately they haven't, well not yet."

Natalie glanced at William before turning back to Kathryn, "Well you fooled me, you certainly know how to hide your emotions. I thought I was an expert in sensing people's moods, I'm embarrassed for not picking up on this."

Kathryn shook her head. "Nonsense Natalie. You've *both* supported me every every step of the way and it's working."

William agreed. "Quite right Natalie. Michael's told me what you've been doing for Kathryn and I applaud your actions. Now Kathryn, on the cognitive front, how often do you relive the experience?"

Kathryn responded immediately. "I don't run over the events in my mind from start to finish – rather key bits pop into my head and over the course of a day I seem to relive most of everything. None of the images are better or worse in intensity – but they're all pretty graphic when they surface."

"Do they keep you awake at night?"

"They did at first, but not so much now. Must be a good sign, right?"

"A very good sign indeed and being able to sleep now

indicates your sub conscious is beginning to cope… in turn this is going to ensure your physical health returns to normal. Have you noticed any behavioural changes such as increased or decreased appetite?"

Kathryn grinned, embarrassed. "I've been hitting the fridge a bit, so I'll have to watch out for that because I can't do my normal exercises at the moment…" she pointed to her face. "I don't want to finish up like the side of a house."

Ballard snorted. "With your metabolism it would take months before that happened… but I take your point. Natalie, put a lock on the fridge and give *me* the combination."

Kathryn attempted to look concerned. "Do that and I'll go the take-away route."

William held up a hand. "I'll let you two work through that. Ok Kathryn, now for the tough part of the session. Do you want to detail what happened on the day or talk more generally?"

Kathryn grimaced. "I know talking about this *has* to be good for me. Michael and Natalie have been very kind and not asked questions, but I realise I haven't been all that brave… denying to myself it even happened, weird as that sounds. It's time I bit the bullet, figuratively speaking." She gave a wry smile.

William nodded encouragement. "At your own pace Kathryn. Say as much or as little as you want."

She drew a deep breath, pausing before relaying the events. "Well, to put everything into context I need to start the morning before, when my brother tossed me out of bed onto the floor while I was sound asleep."

William shot Ballard a long look, a startled expression on his face. Ballard shrugged without explaining; Kathryn continued.

"We play practical jokes on each other and it was my turn to be on the receiving end. This was around 5.30 in the morning.

I was staying at Michael's and as I was on holiday, I wasn't going to get up at that crazy hour. I'd had quite a few late nights before, so I guess I was asleep again within ten to fifteen minutes. I crawled out of bed around 10.30 and lazed around the farm all day, other than some gym work.

"I went back to bed around eleven that night. I knew Michael wasn't coming home because he'd rung me earlier. I think I was asleep within minutes. The next thing I know I'm woken by the front doorbell ringing, I mean *really* ringing. I looked at the clock and it was just after 6.45."

She glanced at her brother. "I couldn't believe it – for some reason I thought you must have come home and decided to play a practical joke, so I ignored it, but the ringing kept going… on and on. I knew then it had to be someone else, so I slipped on my track suit and runners and went to the front door and looked through the peep-hole."

She wrapped her arms around herself, shrinking down in her chair.

"As soon as I saw Parnell standing there…" She paused, looking across at William. "Michael's explained to you who he is, or was?" William nodded.

"Well as soon as I saw him at the door, unshaven, mad eyed, I knew something was very wrong." She hugged her arms even tighter as Natalie placed a comforting hand on her shoulder. "I didn't know which way to go, whether to answer through the door or pretend I wasn't there, so I chose the latter.

"I didn't have my mobile with me so I ran back to my bedroom to ring 000 and then hopefully Michael. When I heard him crash against the front door I knew he was trying to break in. At that point I thought he was someone robbing the house.

"I grabbed the mobile and thought if I could get into the

gym at the end of the corridor I'd be able to hide there long enough to make the call. I knew that because Michael had sound-proofed the room with double solid timber doors, Parnell would have had difficulty breaking through. I thought I'd made it, but he burst into the corridor just as I opened the gym door and he saw me. If I'd been *five* seconds quicker I could have locked the doors and made the call, everything would have been different." Kathryn's eyes were wide and staring.

Ballard leaned forward. "Kathryn, on the contrary, not making the 000 call saved your life." Everyone in the room stared at him as though he were mad. He continued. "Parnell was set on killing both of us, we know this from his confession note. Had you made the call and he found out he would have realised he had limited time to get away, so he would have killed you before he fled. No doubt in my mind whatsoever. His need for revenge was all consuming.

"Even if you'd managed to lock both doors, it may have given you *some* breathing space, but I can say with complete certainty the strength of the man was such he would have broken through without much effort. As absurd as this sounds, his getting to you was the best thing that could have happened; he wanted you as bait so he could draw me up there. This meant keeping you alive. A successful 000 call would have taken that option away and therefore, in his mind, he'd have had no choice but to kill you before taking off."

Kathryn shook her head, not in disagreement but more as an act of digesting the facts. William cleared his throat. "As you can see Kathryn, talking these issues through often throws up different perspectives. Now you don't have to go on if you don't want to. Getting this far is very courageous and there isn't…"

"*No!* No, damn it." She stopped, her face flushed, embarrassed.

"I'm sorry William, I didn't mean to snap at you. No I *need* to go on. As I said I panicked and instead of locking the doors, I tried to get one of the sports room hand weights so I could at least have something to smash him on the head with." Her voice began to tremble as she relived the ordeal. "I *did* manage to pick one up, but he grabbed me from behind and knocked it out of my hand like it was a toy… like Michael said, he was so *strong*! I screamed, but of course no-one could hear me."

Ballard, his head bowed, muttered. "Even if I'd been home the night before instead of at Natalie's, I would have left for work at least forty minutes earlier – probably passing the bastard on the freeway, not knowing." William turned back to Kathryn, his expression encouraging her to continue.

"Parnell then dragged me by the hair along the corridor back to the lounge and threw me on the floor near the piano. It was then he pulled out a gun and I thought he was going to shoot me. He also had a box with a clock taped to it. I realised it was a bomb and almost passed out in fear."

Natalie, although determined to be a silent observer, let out an involuntary gasp and leaned over, hugging her. "My God – what you've been through, you're so brave."

Tears began to form in Kathryn's eyes. "If only this were true Natalie." She looked at William and then Ballard before blurting, "I was *so* terrified I actually wet myself…" She hung her head, too ashamed to make eye contact.

Everyone in the room reacted. Natalie hugged her even harder and stroked her hair while Ballard took her hand, looking helpless. William assumed control by stating very emphatically, "Kathryn, this is a completely normal physiological reaction and as it's understandably distressing you, I'm going to detail *why* it occurred.

"Urination is a biological process controlled by sphincters. Speaking in common language, sphincters act like gates by contracting muscles around an opening. Whenever you feel like urinating, as a result of pressure exerted by a full bladder, your brain sends a signal to the sphincter to relax and allow the urine to flow.

"Under extreme circumstances of fear and anxiety the sphincter does just that, it relaxes. In this instance the act is completely involuntary, totally normal and in fact, considering the fear you were experiencing, it would have been abnormal if you *hadn't* urinated. Let's not forget you thought you were going to die."

Kathryn shrugged weakly, not looking convinced. "I guess we're getting down to the nitty-gritty?" Everyone in the room agreed. Looking exhausted but determined, she pressed on. "I tried to engage him in conversation, but he kept shouting at me to 'shut up', something about this being 'payback'. I had no idea what he was on about.

"He then used those plastic strips to tie my wrists to the piano leg." She extended her arms towards William, bandaged wrists uppermost. He looked at them briefly, his expression one of professional concern. Kathryn continued. "After that he began pacing up and down like a madman. Watching him scared me to the point my brain shut down, I just couldn't think."

William sat forward. "Again, a very natural reaction Kathryn. Your senses were on overload and as a consequence your brain went into survival mode. This is where only the essential functions in your body are being serviced. Understandable and normal."

Kathryn took a tissue from her pocket and blew her nose. "At one point he went out of the room and I didn't see him for over an hour, in fact I thought he'd left. I prayed he had. Then I heard the door open and shut and he came back in just as my mobile rang which was in his pocket. It went to voice mail and of course it was Michael asking me to ring back. Parnell pointed the gun at me, demanding the PIN to access the stored message and when he heard Michael's voice he went berserk – kicking chairs over, generally going nuts.

"After a while he got himself under control and started taking photos with my phone of me and the bomb, he then sent them to Michael. Ten minutes later, after taping my mouth, he received the call from Michael. That set him off again, ranting for what seemed like ages. When he said he'd killed someone I just went numb."

Ballard flexed his shoulders to ease the tension. "Yes, that's when I first spoke to Parnell and he confessed to everything, the murder in Lalor, issues with his brother, mother, wife and daughter, the lot. It was a ranting, rambling confession. The longer I listened, the more I was convinced he was a madman who was going to kill Kathryn and myself, then finish it off with a bullet to his own head."

William addressed Kathryn. "As obvious as this question may seem, what emotions were you feeling?"

"I was terrified Michael was going to attempt to rescue me. I knew that's what he would do and it had me imagining all sorts of horrible scenarios. I wanted to call out and warn him, but I couldn't because of the tape on my mouth. A bit over an hour later, when Michael *did* come into the room… well, was shoved in by Parnell holding a gun to his head, everything went crazy." She began to weep. "The beating you took Michael – I mean *you* were feeling the physical pain, but every kick, every punch, I felt them too. The guy was an animal, out of control. I don't know how you stayed conscious."

Ballard shrugged, the look on his face one of understanding and compassion. "You're my sister and I was going to do whatever it took to keep you safe." He grinned to lighten the tension in the room. "I didn't do much of a job of it for the first thirty minutes though did I?"

Kathryn laughed for the first time. "I have to admit it was eight rounds to Parnell and zero to you at one point, but I knew you'd come through." Natalie kissed Ballard on the cheek, the distraught expression on her face indicating she was near to tears herself. She fought to maintain composure, determined not to add to the emotion-charged situation.

Kathryn took a huge breath and collected herself. "William, I think I'll stop here. It's amazing how this has made me feel so... tired. The rest of what happened Michael knows about, but I do have one question. When Parnell hit me with the gun," she pointed again to the bandage on her face, "I felt the pain but was too concerned about Michael for it to register. Now I feel very very angry at what he did. I'm glad he's dead and I said so several days ago. My concern is I don't feel guilty for thinking this and that *does* worry me. Have I turned into some sort of vicious monster?"

"Kathryn. Considering what you've experienced I'm astounded at your composure."

"Yeah, right. I bet you say that to all the ladies."

William shook his head emphatically. "I can assure you I don't and I've counselled hundreds of victims of crime over the years. Believe me, you're exceptional in how you've managed to describe everything in such detail. Don't read too much into how you feel towards Parnell just for the moment – your emotions are still raw."

He massaged the side of his face with his fingertips, contemplating what to say next. "Kathryn, I've one or two more questions I'd like to ask. However, if you don't feel up to it, feel free to tell me."

Kathryn shook her head. "No, no I'm fine, well not really, but go for it."

"Firstly, have you thought about how you'll feel returning to Michael's house?"

She paused, surprised by the question. "Not in any detail, but I'd be fooling myself if I thought it won't be tough, at least at first."

"If I may make a suggestion, it'll be a lot easier for you to go back when there's a number of people there you know and you're able to blend in as one of the crowd."

Ballard held up a hand. "I'm having a BBQ in the next week or so to thank everyone involved in helping Kathryn and myself, along with some neighbours. Perhaps Kathryn could invite a couple of her friends up as well?"

Looking nervous she replied, "It sounds like a great idea, yes I guess I'll have to face the situation at some point and having friends around me *will* make it easier." It was clear she was forcing herself to believe her own words.

William agreed. "Exactly Kathryn. Without question it'll be difficult, but I believe you can do it and do it well. Remember, each visit will get easier. The fact of the matter is *you* control your feelings, not Parnell, especially now he's dead. Never forget that."

He turned to Natalie. "Now, a question for you without notice. How will *you* feel living in the house in the coming days, weeks, or not too distant future as Mrs Ballard?"

Momentarily taken aback, Natalie regrouped. "I'd say

216

you've provided me with the answer William. I'll be living with Michael and that's all that matters. Wherever he goes, I go, no question."

William smiled at Michael. "I can't argue with that." Chuckling, Ballard agreed.

William indicated the session was at an end. "We've all made good progress here today. Kathryn, this session hasn't healed your mental wounds, but we *have*, metaphorically speaking, cleaned out the infection, applied some antiseptic and reapplied a fresh dressing. Now, depending on how you want to proceed you can, again metaphorically speaking, apply your own dressing, or myself or another psychologist can help with more sessions. You've an excellent support team around you in Michael and Natalie and I dare say your friends will prove to be invaluable as well. Don't rush into an answer right now. One thing's for certain, it'll take some time before you put this horrible incident in its rightful place, where it no longer impacts on your life."

Kathryn appeared delighted. "William what a beautiful analogy of what we've done here this morning. Be assured I'll be slopping on the antiseptic and changing the dressing every day. However, in a few weeks I'd like to come back for an update on my progress. I'm very grateful for everything you've done for me, well, I guess for *all* of us this morning."

Everyone stood and William took Kathryn's hand in both of his, as he had when they first met. "You're a brave lady with a fantastic future in front of you, make the most of it."

She stood on tip toe and kissed him on the cheek. Natalie followed suit and Ballard was sure he saw the faintest of blushes on William's face, despite his tan. "You're going to dip out with me William. All I'm giving you is a firm handshake."

"Thank God. After the dizzying perfection of these two

beautiful ladies I don't want to be dumped back to earth too unceremoniously." He led the way from the office, escorting them to the lift. On entering they turned and acknowledged him as the lift doors closed.

Natalie put an arm around Kathryn. "He's right you know. You were very brave in there and it's given me another perspective of what you *both* went through." She shuddered. "It must have been terrifying."

Ballard also gave his sister a hug. "Yes Sis. Now the best thing we can do is get on with our lives. Having said that, whenever you want to talk about this, don't hold back — raise it as often as you want. Promise?"

"Promise."

CHAPTER
25

As they climbed onto the tram to head back to Natalie's, Ballard turned and asked, "How long since either of you have visited the Shrine of Remembrance?"

Natalie replied first. "I'm ashamed to say not since my eldest two were children."

Kathryn chuckled. "Twenty years for me. Isn't it terrible when you think we drive past it all the time, but never make the effort to stop and go inside?"

"Well ladies, this is your lucky day. I'm going to pop into work to catch up on some things, so why don't you both play tourist for an hour?" Out of Kathryn's line of sight he winked meaningfully at Natalie. "I'll give you a call on the mobile when I'm finished." He got up and checked the timetable on the tram wall. "It's coming up to 10.15 now. There's a Toorak road tram due past the Shrine around 11.45 so that should give us time to do our thing and still catch it. I'll meet you back at the stop where we get off."

Sitting back they watched the view change from bustling city streets to the serenity of the Yarra river. As they crossed Princes Bridge, Ballard leaned forward, pointing down at the water. "Can I interest you both in some historical facts?"

Natalie tilted her head to one side, smiling. "Michael, I've been travelling up and down St Kilda Road all my life."

"Ah yes, but did you know the first bridge to span the Yarra was built in 1840 and prior to that, traffic crossings over the river were by private punts?" Natalie and Kathryn shook their head while looking at each other, amused at Ballard's enthusiasm.

"And I'll bet you don't know why Princes Bridge is so wide?" Again there was much head shaking. "As you can imagine this isn't the original bridge; the one we're on now was built in 1888, still well before motor cars. The reason they made it so massive was to allow a stage coach with a team of horses, or a bullock team, to turn around on the bridge if required.

"At the time of construction it was the largest single span bridge in the world. Prior to it being built the clay they excavated out of the Yarra to prevent it flooding was used to landscape the garden areas throughout the Domain."

A simultaneous "Really!" was expressed by both women.

Now on a roll, Ballard continued by pointing at the Concert Hall to the right. "In 1901 that site used to be the location of a permanent circus and remained so until 1950." Grinning as Kathryn and Natalie shook their head in amazement, he launched into full throttle tour-guide mode. "Back in the 1850s, a bit further down St Kilda Road, bushrangers often stole from travellers as they rode along what was then a dirt track. The bandits were known as the St Kilda Road robbers.

"The trees near the footpath on each side are Elms and those on the median reserve are called London Plane." He scratched his head. "Not sure what all that means, but anyway, taking the maturity of the trees into account, the road's overall width, the extensive parkland and garden settings on the eastern side, along with the numerous mansions and business offices along its length, St Kilda Road is regarded as one of the premier boulevards in the world."

Kathryn laughed out loud. "How do you *know* all this?"

"I work four day weeks Sis, what else am I going to do?"

Looking at Natalie, Kathryn quipped, "Get yourself a life Michael, but I admit it *is* fascinating to hear all this history. Isn't it amazing we're on a tram at the very spot bushrangers terrorized the locals all those years ago."

Natalie placed a hand on Kathryn's knee. "Please don't humour him any more… he'll be insufferable for the rest of the day."

Five minutes later they stepped off the tram. After giving Natalie and Kathryn a kiss on the cheek, Ballard walked to the Crime Department building located opposite the Melbourne Grammar School.

Flashing his identification at reception he activated the electronic security barrier. Stepping onto the Homicide floor he felt like a stranger for the first time in his working career, realising that once he left the job the feeling would be permanent. He thrust the thought from his mind.

Walking over to where John was sitting he tapped him on the shoulder. His partner spun around. "Well if it isn't the holiday boy. Need a map to find the place?"

While the comment was meant to be light hearted, it bit deeper than Ballard cared to admit. "If this is the greeting I get after less than a week, what'll it be like after two months?"

"Don't worry Mike, you and I have skills that'll take these buggers decades to master. How's the head and fingers?"

Ballard inspected his left hand as though for the first

time. "Bloody sore, but I'll live." For the next five minutes he summarised what he had been doing on his sick leave with Natalie and Kathryn, concluding with the session just completed with the psychologist.

Looking concerned John asked, "Is she up to giving a statement yet? I know we need it to finalise the paperwork for the inquest – but I don't want to push the issue until you give the ok."

Ballard hesitated. "The swelling in her face is going down. My guess is she'll go in for surgery either Monday or Tuesday next week. Natalie said she'd need a day to digest what she went through this morning, so I'd say either the day after tomorrow or the next for her statement. How does that suit?"

"Mike, you give the word and we'll slip over to Natalie's whenever it's convenient. We can take the statement in the backyard over a cool drink, then pop back to the office and print off three copies before swinging by again for verification and signing. Smooth as a Vaseline coated finger." He hesitated, realising what he had just said, a sheepish look creeping across his face. "You know what I mean."

Ballard lifted an eyebrow. "Yes John. We all know your mastery of the English language." Taking a chair he sat down near his partner. "How long do you think it'll be before the inquest? I'm hoping to take Natalie over to Bordertown for a few days to show her where I grew up."

John rubbed his chin. "Can't see it being less than two, perhaps three weeks. Not by the time we finalise Kathryn's statement and file the paperwork. The date will depend on what happens in Italy while we're hunting for the wife and kid. I'd prefer to have their statement on the brief if possible."

Ballard opened his mouth but John beat him to it. "Have

the Italian police had any luck? No is the short answer, but for reasons I can't fathom they're very upbeat they'll locate them. It must have something to do with how their mother's treat them like gods when they're young. Eternal optimists."

Ballard shrugged. "Let's hope their optimism's justified. It'll fill in a few blanks if we can get them back here for an interview. Ok John, time for me to do my rounds and oh, by the way…" He hesitated. "Any progress on the withdrawals out of Mario's account?"

Frustration flickered across John's face. "Nup, zip, zero. Absolute dead end. As I said before, once he withdrew the money as cash we had nowhere to go and it's highly unlikely he shared this arrangement with anyone else. I guess we can run it past Mario's wife, but again what are the chances?"

Ballard clapped him on the shoulder. "Hang in there. I'm assuming Susan and Bobby are out solving crime?" John nodded, looking disconsolate. Ballard pondered how to lift his partner's spirits and took a gamble. "Say hello to them for me and before I forget, how's Sonia?"

The transformation on John's face was instant. Grinning from ear to ear he gushed. "Mate, I've struck gold. She's funny, beautiful, intelligent and that body. What she sees in me I have no idea…" He lapsed into silence, shaking his head.

Ballard looked relieved. "Good to hear and don't sell yourself short. She could do a lot worse."

"Thanks, I think."

"Ok. I'm done here. I'll circulate for a bit then be off."

Fifteen minutes later, having caught up on the news with the other squad members, including repeating his activities over the last week to various detectives, he was informed Delwyn was in a meeting at headquarters. He rummaged around for a memo pad and left a note on her desk. Checking his watch he saw he had ten minutes to saunter back to the tram stop. He gave Natalie a quick call as he headed out of the building.

Watching her and Kathryn stroll down the hill from the Shrine over the freshly cut grass, he thanked God he had managed to overcome his fear and enter his house to rescue his sister. He waved a greeting as they approached. "Ah, the intrepid tourists return."

Both women had a healthy glow from their walk. Kathryn was bursting to speak. "Fascinating. You don't appreciate the history of the place when you visit it as a schoolgirl."

Natalie nodded in agreement. "Now it's our turn to play information guide. Tell me darling, when was the Shrine built?"

Ballard pursed his lips in concentration. "I know it was originally a memorial to the men and women who served in World War I, so my guess is around nineteen thirty, it would have taken quite a while to choose a design, raise the funds then build it."

Natalie confirmed his supposition. "It was dedicated on the eleventh of November, nineteen thirty-four to be exact."

Kathryn joined in the tag team quizzing. "And how much did it cost?"

Ballard looked up, as though praying for guidance. "Half a million pounds?"

"No way, José. Believe it or not it was half that, two hundred and fifty thousand. According to the guide, that's about seven million dollars today."

Natalie, not to be outdone, chipped in with a two pronged question. "The marble Stone of Remembrance is illuminated by direct sunlight at 11 a.m. on the eleventh day of November each year. Now that we have daylight saving, how do they get the sunlight to shine on the stone at the right time and what's the word that's illuminated?"

Ballard chuckled. "This is punishment for my little episode earlier this morning isn't it?" Both ladies nodded. "Ok, the first part I *do* know. They use a mirror to reflect the light onto the stone at the precise moment. Now, the word that's illuminated..." After pondering for a moment he shrugged in defeat. "I *should* know."

Natalie chuckled. "Don't beat yourself up sweetheart. We didn't know either. It's 'Love', short for 'Greater love hath no man.'"

Ballard struck his forehead with the palm of his hand, regretting it instantly. "Of course, from the Bible. Ok, my turn. Did your guide tell you what design the Shrine was based on?"

Both women looked at each other as though the question had stumped them, then as Ballard was about to triumphantly inform them, Kathryn blurted, "The Parthenon."

Ballard closed his mouth then changed his mind. "Ok, one last question and I'm done. This has multiple answers. Who protects the Shrine and what does the uniform they wear represent?"

This time, despite concentrated looks on their faces, the answers were less than decisive.

"Well the guys had on what looked like World War I uniforms."

"Ex army guys...?"

"The uniforms represent the, um, the army...?" Their voices trailed away.

Ballard smirked. "A little vague ladies. I'm pleased to announce the police have taken over responsibility for the

Shrine's security and the Protective Services Unit provides the officers. When the Shrine is open to the public, or during a ceremony, they wear a uniform representing the Australian Light Horsemen of World War I with the police force insignia."

The rumble of the number eight tram caused them to turn in its direction, stepping back as it pulled to a halt, brakes squealing. Climbing on board, Kathryn held out her hand to her brother. "Game over. I think it was ladies three and gentleman one."

Ballard agreed, shaking her hand before sitting back, pressing his leg comfortably against Natalie's.

She looked across at him, sadness etched in her eyes. "Such a waste. All those young lives, both men and women… and not only the ones who died. What about the injured, physically as well as mentally? We can be thankful the children of today are taking up the cause and marching, realising the stupidity of war in all its forms."

Ballard remained silent, knowing there was nothing to add.

Kathryn shrugged before inhaling deeply. "Puts my issue into perspective doesn't it." She looked meaningfully at Ballard. "But of course that was the plan wasn't it dear Brother?"

He feigned ignorance, but she persisted. "Don't give me that. *Everything* you do is analysed and assessed before you do it. We just *happened* to come into the city by tram. You just *happened* to need to go to work and the Shrine just *happened* to be near where we had to get off. Coincidence Michael?"

Natalie, pretending ignorance of Ballard's wink earlier in the morning, turned to him. "Well, I'll be…"

"Ok, perhaps the thought *did* cross my mind. However, the tram trip was a pleasant interlude you must admit and I did have to go to work. It's convenient when the planets align, don't you agree?" Ballard attempted to look innocent.

Concern crossed Kathryn's face. She leaned forward in her seat, placing a hand on his arm. "I wasn't criticising Michael, far from it. In fact I'm thanking you for yet again thinking of ways to help me. I realise its time I got on my own two feet and started helping myself. Time I did something with my life which… thanks to you, I still have. When I think what may have happened, it's a bit childish for me to go around as though I need to be treated with kid gloves."

"Good for you Sis, but don't overdo the bravado bit. Ease into it slowly."

Natalie nuzzled up against him, kissing him on the cheek. "Feels good to be in charge, huh?" He pretended not to hear, returning her kiss.

"Oooh! Boy germs." Kathryn's voice mimicked that of a teenager. "Please, get a room you two."

Ballard pressed the button to signal for the next stop. "Are we going home or eating out?"

Kathryn shook her head. "Save your money. There's some left over pie in the fridge and other bits and pieces. I'll prepare while you two spend some time together, you look as though you need it."

Natalie looked at Ballard, grinning. "Thank you Kathryn. I'll take you up on the offer." After a fifteen minute walk they arrived home and had their leftovers lunch, spending the remainder of the afternoon chilling out in the backyard.

Later that evening, after dinner, with the dishes washed, they sat in the lounge, each in deep thought. Natalie was the first to break the silence. "Kathryn, how would you like to come with me tomorrow afternoon to help choose a wedding dress? I've some tentative bookings with a number of dress shops."

Ballard beat Kathryn to a reply. "I'll come."

Natalie pulled a face. "You most certainly will not."

Kathryn chipped in. "It's bad luck for the groom to see the wedding dress before the day – you *know* that."

Ballard held up both hands defensively, wincing as his injured fingers reminded him of their delicate condition. "Just joking. Besides, I'd faint if I saw the price tag."

Natalie chuckled. "You very well may."

Kathryn wriggled in her chair. "Natalie I'd love to – in fact, try keeping me away."

Ballard shook his head, bewildered that the selecting of a wedding dress could transform two intelligent women into giggling, self indulgent teenagers. He shrugged before turning to Kathryn. "On a more serious note Sis, while I was at work today I spoke with John who asked when you'd be well enough to give your statement. Sorry to ruin the mood, but I need to give him some idea when you might feel up to it."

Kathryn didn't hesitate. "Whenever he needs me I'll do it. I wasn't joking before… I need to step up."

Ballard was momentarily stumped. "Well… ok, it can be taken here and then printed off at the office; the lads will bring back copies for your signature. We thought it might be easier for you if Natalie and I were nearby."

"How about tomorrow morning?"

"Tomorrow morning?"

"Tomorrow morning, before I head off with Natalie. That'll let me finish the day on a positive note."

He shook his head, still recovering from her reply. "You're sure about this?"

"*Yes* Michael, I'm sure. Now make the call, any time after nine. My new resolution is not to sleep in as much as I used to.

I have a life to live."

Ballard pretended to take his pulse. "Just making sure I'm not dreaming." Kathryn poked her tongue out.

Ballard reached for his mobile. "Ok Sis. I'll see if John's good for tomorrow" He dialed the number.

"Michael my man. Missing me already?"

"Actually I've an early morning witness statement for you."

"Really? Kathryn?"

"Yes indeed, the lady by the same name."

"How early?"

Ballard mouthed 9 a.m. to Kathryn to confirm; she nodded in reply. "How does 9 a.m. grab you."

"Are you kidding me?" John's voice rose in disbelief. "Kathryn up at nine when she's not working?"

"*You're* surprised. How about me? I've watched her sleep in until midday all her life."

"Are you two quite finished?" Kathryn feigned wounded indignation.

John overheard the comment. "Tell Kathryn I'll be there with Susan at nine sharp. My guess is we'll wrap this up in less than two hours."

"Sounds good to me."

Natalie motioned for the mobile. "John, would you like me to make you some breakfast?"

"Natalie, you know the answer to that. Ok if Susan joins in?"

"More the merrier. See you in the morning." She handed the phone back to Ballard.

"Thanks John. It'll be nice to get this behind us. I'll catch you tomorrow."

"Mate, think nothing of it." He hung up.

Ballard looked across at Kathryn and Natalie. "Thank you…

both of you." They shrugged as though they hadn't a care in the world.

Seconds later a frown appeared on Kathryn's face. "I've just had a thought. Will I have to give evidence at the inquest?"

Ballard hesitated. "There's always the chance the Coroner will request verbal evidence from you, however, as I was present I can make a strong case that your written statement is enough. I'll be pushing hard for you not to attend and I'm certain this will be the outcome." Kathryn didn't look convinced. Half an hour later with everyone yawning, they nodded at each other in silent agreement that an early night was in order.

After showering, Natalie and Ballard lay in bed, gazing up at the ceiling. Natalie turned onto her side, combing the hair on his chest with her fingers, the light from the bedside lamp silhouetting her face. "Will Kathryn be ok tomorrow?"

"Darling, she'll be fine. Despite his craggy exterior John can show considerable empathy when he needs to. Especially with women... even more so when they're attractive."

Natalie punched him on the shoulder. "That's your sister you're talking about."

He rolled over and whispered in her ear. "Enough of that. It's time we ignored the rest of the world for a while." Reaching forward he began kissing her forehead before lingering on her lips and neck, then ever so slowly moved to her breasts. Natalie wrapped her arms around him as he continued along her body. "It's good to see you're back to your old self." She caressed him, then gasped. "Ooh, you *definitely* are back to your old self!"

Ballard chuckled as he renewed his exploration, eliciting a soft gasp as he nuzzled against the sensitive area on her stomach. As he persisted she writhed in alternate ecstasy and ticklishness, one second pushing his head away, then pulling it back in earnest.

Continuing on his journey her sighs transformed into heavy breathing, followed by progressively louder moans. At one point he took a pillow and placed it over her mouth, both of them collapsing in fits of laughter. Thirty minutes later they lay back in each other's arms, content in the pleasure they had just shared. Ballard looked across. "I don't know how you do it, but it keeps getting better and better."

Natalie cuddled closer, kissing him. "It takes two, darling, but we do seem to have a winning formula." She switched off the bedside light and within minutes they were fast asleep.

CHAPTER
26

By 9.30 a.m. the next morning, with breakfast dishes washed and stacked away, Ballard and Natalie stood side by side at the sink, looking out the kitchen window into the backyard. Sitting at the wrought iron table and chairs were Kathryn, John and Susan. They had moved the furniture under the silver birch trees for shade so that Susan could read the screen of her laptop. She had informed Ballard at breakfast she was the designated typist after losing a single game of rock-paper-scissors on the way over. Her suggestion of 'best out of three' had been dismissed outright by John. Resting on the table in front of Kathryn was John's Olympus recorder.

Ballard reflected how policing had changed with the introduction of technology, be it ever so slowly. He thought back to when he used to take statements in triplicate with an old fashioned Olivetti typewriter; his eyes smiled.

Natalie looked up at him. "What's so funny?"

He explained.

She laughed at the mental image. "I spoke with the kids before and they appear to be enjoying themselves at their father's, so my conscience is clear on that score. They're coming home Monday night after school. Also I caught up with Emma and

Tricia and they send their love. They're going to pop over in the next few days."

Ballard continued looking through the window. "Say hello for me. We'll have them up for the BBQ. So, when do you think Kathryn will have her operation?"

"I rang the surgeon yesterday and based on my assessment of the swelling, everything is set for Monday. She'll be held overnight and all being well, discharged the next day." She shook her head. "It would seem you need to have open heart surgery before they'll keep you in for more than a day. Kathryn's insisting on going straight to her place after the operation – she said her girlfriends will be staying over."

"She'll be able to change her own dressing?"

"Uh-huh, the chance of any post-op infection is low, so she only has to keep it covered and clean, but she may be asked to attend weekly check-ups for a while. Then it's just a matter of time for the scar to fade." She took Michael by the shoulders and shook him forcefully. "*Then you can relax and stop worrying!*"

"Who me?"

"Yes *you,* Mr Control Freak."

"That's a bit harsh."

"Well, it's a fact."

"At my age I can hardly change who I am."

"I know. It used to worry me, but now I find it quite comforting, it's somehow… predictable *and* protective." She went to the fridge, taking out a bottle of apple juice. "I'll go and top-up their glasses." Ballard opened his mouth but Natalie stopped him. "I know, I know, police business in progress. But that doesn't mean they can't be comfortable. I'll be as quiet as a church mouse."

An hour later John, Susan and Kathryn walked inside.

Kathryn looking tired but relieved. "It was much easier than I thought it would be. John isn't the grouch you say he is Michael." There was a twinkle in her eye.

Susan joined in. "Oh no? Today's Friday, you should see what he's like on Mondays – unbearable, we make sure to keep out of his way. But come to think of it, for the last few weeks he's seemed almost human." Ballard and Natalie glanced at each other, acknowledging their mutual secret.

John gulped the last of his apple juice. "Thank you ladies. Natalie, care to join in with your contribution?"

Natalie put an arm around him, kissing him on the cheek. "Just a big Teddy Bear." Ballard snorted, but Natalie insisted. "No, I've known him as long as I've known you Michael and I'm telling you, he's a push-over."

John smirked. "Thank you Natalie. I'll leave the money on the hall table." His face grew serious. "Kathryn, that was an excellent statement. Even *I* didn't know the full extent of what you went through. Very gutsy."

Turning to Ballard he said, "Must run in the family. I wish I'd met your mum and dad. They would have been *some* parents."

Ballard agreed. "Yep. I'd soil my pants whenever Dad got mad but…"

"Michael!" Natalie pretended indignation.

"Mum was the peace maker. Always the voice of reason. I guess the combination was good for us. But when Kathryn was born they changed overnight. Because she was so much younger than my brother and I, it was as though they regarded her more as a grand daughter than a daughter."

Kathryn looked indignant. "So you're saying I got a free ride?"

"Damn right, Sis … they were like putty in your hands.

You've no idea how jealous I was. I should've known butting heads with my father was never going to get me anywhere. My brother was smarter than me and knew when to keep out of Dad's way."

John picked up the laptop. "Kathryn – we'll print off some copies and bring them back in the next hour for you to check and if they're ok, get your signature." He turned to Natalie. "Does that still fit in with your plans to shop for wedding dresses?"

Natalie looked at the clock. "As long as we're out of here by 12.30 that'll be fine."

"Easy. Well Susan, time to hit the road." Everyone said their goodbyes.

Kathryn sat at the kitchen table. "Despite what I said before, I'm glad that's over. John confirmed what you said Michael, *very* unlikely I'll have to give evidence at the inquest. That's a load off my mind."

Ballard pulled out a chair, rubbing his ribs in pain as he sat down. He carefully drew Natalie onto his lap as he addressed Kathryn. "Nat tells me your operation may be Monday."

Kathryn instinctively touched her face. "Uh huh, appears so. Another challenge that'll be good to get out of the way. Thanks to Natalie's pre-op routine the swelling has almost gone and the wound doesn't look anywhere near as angry as it first did. Even I'm convinced there won't be any long term scarring. How lucky will that be?"

Natalie twisted on Ballard's lap. "See Michael. You just have to have faith in my diagnosis."

"I do, I do. But it's nice to see it for real. Now ladies, I'm going to leave you for a day or two." Natalie spun further on his lap, her face registering disappointment.

"I need to do some maintenance up at the farm, but I'll be

back here Sunday to drive you both to the hospital Monday morning." Natalie's lip protruded. Ballard hugged her tighter. "I promise I'll make it up to you when I get back."

Kathryn grimaced. "Too much information. Besides, if I stay here any longer I swear I'm going to have to buy ear muffs."

Natalie let out an involuntary gasp before quickly controlling herself. Looking at Ballard who was gobsmacked she asked, "When are you heading off darling?"

"I'll have a quick bite to eat then hit the road."

CHAPTER
27

Thirty minutes later he looked to his right across the city from the apex of the Westgate Bridge, noting the smoggy haze hanging heavier than usual amongst the tall buildings. Once on the Ring Road he slipped the transmission into manual mode and dropped back to second. The revs shot up to 4,000 without the car exceeding the speed limit.

As he had been instructed by his mechanic, he needed to give the Hemi motor a 'kick in the guts' every now and then to clean the 'crap' out of the engine and 'wake up' the on-board computer. This he was assured restored full performance. Several minutes later he dropped the transmission back into automatic and noted the car was indeed more responsive.

While he had been factual in telling Natalie he had numerous chores to complete, the primary reason for returning to the farm was to come to terms with what had taken place there. As such, throwing himself into his work was the best way he knew to achieve this.

The moment he turned into the driveway a wave of apprehension washed over him. Forcing himself to breath normally he activated the remote for the garage door and drove in. For the next twenty minutes he moved from room to room, deliberately leaving the lounge until last. Vera had excelled herself; the house was spotless, with fresh flowers arranged in all the vases.

Walking into the lounge he instinctively looked at the piano leg to which Kathryn had been held captive. Reaching down he attempted to lift the leg off the floor; despite exerting full strength the best he could manage was to raise it a few millimeters. Shaking his head he concluded she never had a chance of freeing herself. The foreboding he experienced at all crime scenes began to engulf him as he realised his own house had just been one; despite this he knew from experience the apprehension would lessen over time.

Next he inspected the new window and noted Vera had cleaned it inside and out. He saw several glass chips on the veranda and made a mental note to sweep them away, not for tidiness, but to remove any reminder of the incident. He turned and crossed the hallway to the front door. Opening it he was pleased to find the wood panelling undamaged. He noted the door jamb had been replaced and reflected that with several coats of Estapol, all signs of forced entry would be removed.

Changing into his work clothes he caught sight of himself in the hallway mirror. Smiling he wondered what his collegues would say now, comparing his tattered attire to his Armani suits. Returning with a drop-cloth he positioned it under the door and began sanding the jamb. Once he had achieved a finish to his satisfaction, he wiped the wood clean with a dry rag before applying a thin coat of Estapol. Chocking the door open he returned to the garage and drove the Chrysler onto the concrete apron. He began by spraying off the road grime and half an hour later the car gleamed as though it had rolled off the showroom floor.

Following that he topped up the John Deere ride-on with petrol and despite it not being necessary, started cutting the lawns around the house, careful not to strain his damaged and still throbbing fingers. He knew this burst of activity was the quickest way for him to return to normality. As he mowed alongside the tennis court he wondered how long he should wait before venturing to the gorge. It took him several seconds to decide this final test wouldn't be happening today.

Once back in the house he inspected the front door and despite the Estapol being touch dry, he knew he would have to prop the door open overnight. Slipping on the safety chain he thumbed his nose at any foreboding he may experience once nightfall arrived. In spite of this he reminded himself to set the perimeter alarm enabling him to move freely within the house. He rationalised he wouldn't be negligent about security, but was determined not to compromise his laid-back life style.

Checking the fridge he was delighted to find Vera had stocked it with all the basics, along with an egg and bacon quiche which she knew he loved. He silently thanked her and decided on the spot to increase her weekly allowance.

To ensure he didn't forget this and a host of other tasks, he stuck a Post-it note on the bench and wrote out a list for the next day. He started with Vera's allowance: sweeping the glass off the veranda; visiting the neighbors to apologise and explain what had happened; applying another coat of Estapol to the front door; sweeping the tennis court and checking the electric pumps that operated the pop-up sprinklers. He jotted down new tasks as he thought of them.

Swapping his farm clothes for a pair of shorts, a Tshirt and old runners he headed out through the garage to the front veranda, striding its full length to the squash court. Flicking on the internal lights he snibbed the door behind him. Taking one of the racquets propped in the corner and the double yellow dot squash ball, he began thirty minutes of punishing drills that left him heaving with exertion and dripping with sweat. Smiling he promised himself he would give his son a run for his money the next time he visited, despite the twenty-four year age gap.

Deep down he knew this was wishful thinking as Bradley was a natural athlete who adapted effortlessly to whatever challenges he faced. He toyed with the idea of playing him under a handicap, already imagining the good natured banter this would elicit, 'Feeling your age, old man', or similar. He knew Bradley respected his level of fitness but would never admit it, his own competitive streak even more evident than Ballard's.

After switching off the lights and returning inside, he showered while the quiche and a bowl of vegetables were heating in the microwave. After eating and washing the dishes, he armed the house security and slumped onto the lounge room sofa with the cordless phone. He punched in Natalie's number and lay back, hoping she was free to talk.

"Hello sweetheart, is this a good time?"

"Michael, you know better than that. I'll always make time for you. So what have you been up to at the matrimonial home?"

He laughed. "I've never heard you refer to it that way before. It has a nice ring to it." He went on to explain everything he had done.

Natalie understood the psychology of his actions. "Feeling more relaxed are we, now that you've worked yourself to the bone?"

"Well I wouldn't classify what I've done..."

"Nonsense, you couldn't wait to get up there and take

control. You forget I know you almost as well as you know yourself."

"Sometimes I think you know me *better.*"

"I hope so darling. We all need a helping hand at times, even you. What have you planned for tomorrow?"

"Oh this and that, but enough about me, how did your dress hunting go?"

Natalie's voice rose an octave. "*Very* well. I think I've narrowed it down to a possible ten."

He chuckled. "Really! So few?"

She continued, ignoring his light hearted dig. "Kathryn has an excellent eye for style and she isn't afraid to express her opinion. You've no idea how it helped me, plus I think she enjoyed herself."

"I tell you what Nat, send me photos of the possibilities and I'll reduce the number even further."

"No way buster. I want you to be surprised on the day and until then you're not going to have a clue."

"You forget I'm a trained detective, skilled in surveillance, shadowing bad guys… all that stuff."

Hesitation crept into Natalie's voice. "You wouldn't, promise me you won't try to find out? I know how you like to control things, but this is *my* special project and a very important one at that…"

"Relax darling, I promise I won't do anything to spoil your crowning moment."

Natalie's tone indicated she was far from convinced. "Michael, you mentioned the other day you'd like to go to South Australia to visit your family. How long will we be away?

"It'll be a lightning visit. Over Friday and back Sunday."

"That being the case I was thinking of having Mum and

Dad drop in on the kids once or twice while we're away. So, how about we call in on my folks this Monday after we've taken Kathryn to the hospital? We can then pop back to the hospital in the afternoon to check how the op' went."

He swallowed hard. "Good idea. I haven't spoken with Barbara and Robert for some time – yes, let's do that." He was sure his micro-second hesitation had not been detected by Natalie. He chatted with her for the next ten minutes, then after reminding her how much he loved her, he hung up.

Sitting in the lounge staring blankly, concern developed on his face. He hesitated before ringing John.

"You really *are* missing work Mike, I can tell…"

"John I need some advice. The more I think about the Parnell case, the more I'm convinced it isn't over."

John paused before replying. "Go on."

"Don't tell me you haven't thought it too. The guy that ran down Parnell's daughter, assuming it *was* a guy and I think we can agree on that, what if he thinks we know his identity?"

"Mike if he thought…"

"No John, hear me out. Mario's strung up in the factory by Parnell to extract the identity of the guy who knocked down his daughter and would take out his family should anything happen to Mario. Let's call him the hit-man. I then kick Parnell into the gorge and every newspaper and TV channel across the country, *Christ the world*, runs the story. It's gone viral! I'd be amazed if Parnell's wife and kid aren't aware of it. So how does the hit-man know I *don't* have his identity, that Mario told Parnell and *I* got it out of Parnell before he died?

"The truth of the matter is…"

"The truth of the matter is he *doesn't* know John."

In a very controlled voice John said, "Why do you think I

was so frustrated when we found out the regular withdrawals out of Mario's bank account were cash? As I said when you came into work the other day, the transactions left us nowhere to go. It's also the reason I've had surveillance sit off Natalie's town house for the last week…"

"*You what?*"

"Mike, after what happened anything was possible. We figured it was a long shot, but couldn't be ignored, so I got Delwyn to pull some strings and draw a budget for some short term surveillance. We reasoned your 'hit-man' would presume that if he wasn't fingered within the first few days then his identity wasn't compromised. I believe given this amount of time this is the situation. Simple as that."

Ballard drew a deep breath. "So I was kept in the dark because…"

"Because it was such a tenuous possibility. We didn't figure worrying you and more to the point, worrying Natalie and Kathryn was going to help the situation. Natalie's kids were away. Kathryn was either in the hospital or with you guys, so it was easy to keep you all protected while not spooking anyone. I made it my call and I can tell you for the first few days I was part of the surveillance and shitting myself every minute I was there. Then when nothing happened the threat had diminished as far as I could tell."

"Jesus John. I don't know what to say. What about now, is Nat's place still under surveillance?"

"No. You know how this works. We can't chase shadows for the rest of our lives, the budget won't allow it… Christ, I'm sorry mate, but that's how it goes."

"John I'm *very* grateful for what you did and yes, you're right. Whoever the guy is, he's either out of the country by now or sitting at home thanking his lucky stars he hasn't been fingered. So what do I do regarding Natalie and Kathryn?"

"Tell them nothing."

"Nothing?"

"Considering the circumstances, this guy isn't going to run the risk of exposing himself now, not after this length of time. Telling *anyone* is only going to unduly worry them. It sure as hell will impact on Kathryn's recovery. No, this is something that has to stay in-house, it goes with the territory."

"Ripples on a pond. That's how I described it John, the impact of crime." Ballard's tone was philosophical, bordering on bitter.

"True Mike, but we can't live our lives dodging shadows. Besides this isn't over yet. Finding this prick will never be a cold case for me, I promise you."

Ballard nodded his appreciation, then realised what he had done. "Thank you John. If anyone's going to track this bastard down, it'll be you."

"Bet your tidy fortune on it Michael."

"Ok, let's keep this between us. Thanks again."

"What are mates for?" John chuckled before hanging up.

Ballard sat for the next few minutes reflecting. Glancing at the clock in the kitchen he saw it was approaching 10 p.m. and decided an early night was in order. Twenty minutes later he was sound asleep, to all appearances without a care in the world.

CHAPTER
28

Despite being on sick leave and not setting the alarm, Ballard woke at 5 a.m. He lay in bed wondering whether his old habits would change once he stopped working; again feeling the apprehension of retirement engulf him. He rolled out of bed and headed for the gym, looking forward to a savage twenty minute session. Following breakfast he added five more chores to his list, including pruning the thirty rose bushes along the front veranda.

Four hours later, tired, but very satisfied with his efforts, he tossed his work clothes into the laundry, showered, then had a light lunch of leftover quiche and vegetables. He chuckled to himself knowing Natalie would be aghast at the thought of him having identical consecutive main meals. She would gently admonish him with a 'you have to *enjoy* your food Michael, not just shovel it down.'"

The final task he set for the day was to provide his neighbours with details of the incident that had taken place the week before. He knew they would have a general idea as a result of the TV and press coverage, but he felt it his duty to fill in the gaps. House by house he knocked on doors and in the majority was invited inside with the offer of a cuppa and a sympathetic ear.

Two of his neighbours however, were not as understanding and stood stoically at their front door, arms folded. Their body language indicating in no uncertain terms their displeasure at the risk they had been exposed to, despite neither of them having been home at the time. All Ballard could do was explain calmly what had happened. He stated the incident couldn't have been foreseen and the police had done everything possible to minimise potential harm to the street's occupants.

He finished by attempting to reassure them there was no likelihood of a repeat occurrence. He knew he hadn't convinced them and was certain from their demeanour they would be doubtful attendees for the planned BBQ.

Returning home he slumped into a lounge chair, mulling over their reactions. He called Natalie and made every effort to be upbeat.

"Is everything ok?" Natalie voiced her concern. "You sound a bit down... missing me?"

"Damn right I miss you, but no, that's not the reason." He shook his head, both frustrated and amazed she could so effortlessly read his moods from what appeared to be another galaxy. "I've just visited the neighbours to explain what happened."

"Not happy campers?"

"Well, two out of the eleven aren't overjoyed. They'll get over it, but the annoying thing is I can't blame them. I mean, they buy a property in the country for a quiet lifestyle, so the last thing they want is a madman with a bomb on their doorstep waving a Glock around."

"You did your best Michael. In the end that's all you can do."

"Yeah." He sighed, unconvinced. "On a positive note though, I've made good progress on everything I need to do here. I might head over your way around eleven tomorrow morning.

As its Sunday is that too early for you?"

"Never. Now, guess what, I'm winning with my design for the invitations. This wedding preparation caper is a breeze."

He continued. "I was also thinking my sweet, why don't we see your parents tomorrow and take Kathryn with us. She isn't going to feel crash hot *after* the surgery, so let's do the visit before she goes into hospital."

"Darling, that's a wonderful idea. Mum and Dad haven't seen her for ages. They'll love it. I'll ring now and let them know."

"Ok, it's a date. Now, I'm going to be rude and run. I'm feeling a bit guilty for not ringing my son this week. When he called after the incident I promised I'd keep him up to date. He sent a text yesterday asking what was going on. Oh, before I forget, as we're going to Bordertown next weekend I've booked the BBQ for the weekend after. I'll check with the caterers tomorrow morning."

"Fine by me. I'll make some desserts the day before." She paused. "I can't wait to see you tomorrow. Ring me when you head out. All my love. Good night my future husband."

Ballard responded with a long, audible kiss.

Grinning, he dialed his son's mobile and was surprised when Bradley answered on the second ring. "G'day Dad. Jeez' I can't believe how many times I've seen you on TV over the last week. They keep repeating the same interview. At this rate you'll be joining Actor's Equity."

Ballard shook his head, surprised how someone Bradley's age even knew about the organisation. "Yesterday's news I can assure you. As soon as something else takes the public's fancy I'll be fish 'n chip wrapping."

Bradley chuckled. "I have to say you looked a bit knocked

about. I'm glad you got the bastard. How's Aunty Kath doing?"

"Pretty good, considering." He explained what happened with her visit to the psychologist, the statement she gave John and Susan and her involvement in choosing the wedding dress with Natalie.

"Awsome. Sounds like she doesn't have time for the operation. Hey Dad, do I get to give a speech at the wedding?"

"If you want."

"Are you kidding? And miss out on telling everyone what a ruthless bugger you were as a father, even though you've mellowed in your old age?" He laughed. "Looking back though, I'm glad you put me through my paces when I needed it. Because of that army life has turned out to be a breeze."

"Yes, thank you for that little gem Brad. I'm sure the guests will be riveted. Now tell me, what's happening at the Academy that my tax dollars are funding?"

Bradley launched into an account of the events at the Military Academy and everything that was happening in his life, including a new girlfriend. Ballard felt a warm glow as he heard the enthusiasm in his son's voice.

"Well it sounds like you made the right decision in sixth grade when you told me you were going to join up. Congratulations young man. Knock 'em dead, but keep safe. I'll ring next week."

"You too Dad… *especially* you." There was a click and he was gone.

Feeling blessed and proud for his son's future prospects in life, Ballard decided two early nights in a row would be a good thing. Again, within minutes of his head touching the pillow he was sound asleep.

CHAPTER
29

Ballard slept until 8 a.m. the next morning. Feeling guilty and not sure why, he did a short workout in the gym, followed by breakfast and a shower. Realising there wouldn't be time to do anything meaningful around the house, he powered up the laptop and logged onto his work emails. For the next thirty minutes, despite being hampered by the finger guard, he wound through the endless list, replying as necessary and forwarding invitations for the BBQ where appropriate.

First timers had a map attached to the email to make the trip to the farm less of an adventure. He then rang the caterer's mobile and confirmed the date and menu for the BBQ.

Thirty minutes later he was on the freeway, enjoying the light traffic of a Sunday morning. He rang Natalie to inform her he was on the way before settling down to concentrate on the drive. As he did so he thought back to the first time he met her parents.

To say it was unsuccessful would be an understatement. Both had lucrative careers: Robert as a high-end-of-town financier and Barbara a real estate advocate. Robert was now semi retired, save for the odd favour for a former client or friends but Barbara continued to work as hard as ever. She loved real estate and over the years both she and Robert had been astute with their finances, now living in Hawthorn in a house three times larger than they needed. Ballard was careful never to mention this fact, even to Natalie, besides, who was he to judge considering the size of his home.

On meeting them for the first time, despite them showing every kindness, he sensed from the outset his work as a policeman was in their eyes, a social step down for Natalie, their only child. Despite this he couldn't fault their interaction with him, always down to earth and very funny; Barbara more so than Robert.

Robert was old school military, a Vietnam veteran, having served in the army for thirty years and as such assumed the role of family patriarch. Barbara accepted this but very much held her own, aided by a sharp intellect and an even sharper sense of mischief which she had passed on to Natalie.

Robert verbalised his significant concerns that police work might expose his daughter to criminal elements and unnecessary danger. Ballard recalled reassuring him that he would always keep his professional and private lives separate, thus protecting Natalie. He winced as he thought of having to confront her parents in less than two hours to explain what had gone wrong, rationalising it was a meeting that needed to take place sooner rather than later.

He was counting on Kathryn being a steadfast ally, along with Natalie should he need them. He admitting to himself that defending his actions to Natalie's parents was going to be difficult, considering his own remorse at having placed her in such danger.

Shortly after midday he pulled into the garage and was welcomed by a warm embrace.

"Darling, you've no idea how much I've missed you.

Whenever we're apart now, well, it's *torture*." He hugged Natalie in return, deciding this wasn't the most opportune moment to remind her that even after they were married she would need to remain living at the town house until Josh finished high school. That was a conversation that could wait.

Natalie leaned back while holding both his hands, studying him, her head to one side. "Everything ok? You look a bit tense. In fact you usually *are* when we visit my parents. I promise they won't bite."

He decided truth was the best option. "I know, but Robert's bark is often quite brutal. And I'm just a little anxious about what they'll say considering you and Kathryn were embroiled in what was *my* police case."

Natalie squeezed his hand. "No point in pretending they won't be concerned. I can only advise you tell them the facts and they'll just have to deal with it. Kathryn and I will defend you to the death and they know that, so I doubt they'll make too big a thing of it."

Ballard shrugged, far from convinced. "I hope you're right." Kathryn appeared and rushed over to kiss him on the cheek. He inspected her face. "Coming along in leaps and bounds Sis. Ready for tomorrow?"

"As much as I'll ever be. I'm not so much worried about the surgery as having to start all over again with another swollen face."

"All in a good cause, you'll be fine. Now, before we head off, there *may* be some concern expressed by Natalie's parents as to how you and Nat were placed in harm's way." Kathryn began to protest but Ballard held up a cautionary hand. "I know, I know, but they're wonderful parents to Natalie and have both of your interests at heart, I can't fault that. All I can do is take Natalie's advice and tell it as it is. From there they'll have to cope with the reality the best way they can."

Natalie agreed. "I'm sure they will. Don't worry, everything's going to be ok… I rang them before and they're looking forward to the visit. I said we'd be over in the next half hour." Ballard held the passenger doors open and after both women were seated, slipped behind the wheel, chuckling to himself.

Natalie glanced across at him. "What's so funny?"

"Oh nothing, just looking forward to entering the lion's den." She ruffled his hair, smiling knowingly.

Twenty minutes later, having made good time due to the light Sunday traffic, they parked in Robert and Barbara's lavender bordered, cobblestone circular driveway. Sunlight splashed onto the ochre coloured bricks not yet covered by the variegated ivy that cascaded down the north facing wall of the federation style home. Robert was halfway up a ladder, wielding an electric hedge trimmer like a battle sword in a failed attempt to tame the ivy encroaching on the lounge room bay window.

Even before stepping from the Chrysler Natalie called out. "Dad! Are you out of your mind?"

Robert looked over his shoulder, smiling at his daughter. "You see, there's still life in the old dog yet."

"Yes, I regret to say," Ballard muttered the words under his breath as he joined Natalie's side. She elbowed him in the ribs.

Climbing down, Robert arched his lean frame backwards to ease his aching muscles, then hugged Natalie and Kathryn. After taking off his leather gloves he shook Ballard's hand. "Good to see you Michael."

"You too Robert. I see the garden's as immaculate as ever."

Robert shrugged. "Yes, but for some reason it takes me twice as long these days. Isn't old age a bugger?"

Kathryn chipped in. "I wouldn't call seventy-five *old*."

Robert chuckled. "You always say the nicest things, Kathryn. Now go inside and see what Barbara's up to." As Ballard moved to open the front door, Robert called out. "Michael, would you give me a hand with the ladder?"

Ballard winked at Natalie, knowing full well moving the ladder was just an excuse for him to remain behind. Natalie hesitated but Ballard held the door open for both women, stating, "We won't be long. Say hello to Barbara for me."

Robert took his arm as he led him along the driveway. "I'll come straight to the point Michael."

Ballard remained poker faced. "You always do Robert."

Robert paused before continuing. "I've seen the TV reports and read in the papers what you did to rescue Kathryn, also Natalie's told me how you arranged for her and the children to be taken somewhere safe when the incident began. Your actions were prompt and professional and I might add, very brave... for that Barbara and I thank you."

Ballard smiled wryly, knowing this was the preamble for what was to come.

"The concerns we've discussed before regarding Natalie's safety and by default, the safety of her children..." his brow furrowed as he recalled the conversation, "I guess that's getting on to two years ago – well my fears have now come to pass."

Robert put a conciliatory arm around Ballard's shoulders as they strolled in step to the end of the driveway, then across the front of the property via the footpath before returning down the opposite side. "Natalie's our only child and it would destroy Barbara and I if anything were to happen to her, or her children.

"You've displayed your love for all concerned and risked your life proving it – I appreciate that more than I can say.

However, I'm also aware that Natalie idolises you and I can see why, but the potential of her being placed in danger still remains high as a result of your line of work. Now that you're planning to marry, the danger will be ongoing."

He stopped, then said in a voice edged with steel, "Unless you were to resign from your job, or take a non operational role within the police force. Your financial situation is sound, so you have no monetary necessity to continue in Homicide."

Ballard drew a deep breath. There it was, blunt and to the point; just what he had expected. Robert remained silent, allowing Ballard time to collect his thoughts.

"Robert, you and Barbara have always treated me with the greatest of courtesy. You're also aware of my love for Natalie and her children. As you said, I've done everything in my power to ensure my professional life doesn't encroach on their personal safety and wellbeing, as much as humanly possible."

He stepped in front of his future father-in-law, looking him in the eye, their faces level. "What you're asking me to do is to leave a job that protects the public and keeps people like yourself and Barbara safe at night when you're asleep in your bed. All this might sound dramatic, even clichéd, but I don't have to remind you what happens in society when law and order breaks down. The trouble is, the provision of that law and order is achieved by ordinary men and women just like myself."

Robert nodded slowly, taking in Ballard's words. "So Robert, the fact of the matter is, while my job can be performed by someone else, that's the conundrum, it still has to be undertaken by someone who has loved ones.

"I'm good at the job I do, I'm proud to protect the public and I'll continue to do just that for some years to come." His features remained firm. "Unless of course management tap me on the shoulder first. I'd give anything to say to you and Barbara that my family will never be impacted by my work, but I can't. I don't need to tell you how difficult that is to confess, but as I wish with all my heart to take Natalie as my wife, this is the challenge I'm confronted with."

Robert remained silent and Ballard braced himself for round two.

"Well Michael, you didn't get to where you are in either your professional or personal life by being a wallflower. You've made your position very clear and I respect that." Robert's jaw muscles clenched. "Besides, all my huffing and puffing isn't going to change your decision."

Ballard agreed.

Robert continued, resigned to Ballard's stance. "Natalie will back you one hundred percent and I respect that. So I'm not left with a lot of room to move, well none at all come to think of it. And you know what, if I were in your shoes, I'd say the same thing."

For a moment Ballard thought he had misheard the comment. Robert sensed this and continued. "Yes Michael. I would have said the same thing. In many ways we're very similar you and I. And a man *has* to do what he thinks is right… plus life *is* full of risks. Most can be mitigated, however some we can only react to when they occur. I want you to understand that as a father and on behalf of Natalie's mother I *had* to put the proposition to you. I hope you accept it as the request of a concerned father, concerned parents, nothing more. No hard feelings?"

Ballard hesitated before replying. "Robert, of course not. You know the respect I have for you and Barbara and I wish I could give you a cast iron guarantee. The only guarantee I *can* give you is I'll risk my life to protect Natalie and the kids." He smiled wryly "After all, it's my job."

Robert held out his hand and both men shook before turning and heading inside. As they entered the lounge room, Barbara looked up from where she was sitting with Natalie and Kathryn. "Well, have you two finished spraying testosterone all over the front yard?"

"Mother!" Natalie looked shocked while Kathryn laughed as much as her injury would allow.

"Well I can assure you Natalie, that's *exactly* what they were doing."

Robert responded. "As a matter of fact sweetheart, Michael and I had a very productive discussion." Looking across to his daughter he said, "I suggest you book the wedding as soon as possible and make sure he doesn't get away."

Natalie's jaw dropped in amazement. "Are you feeling alright Dad? You didn't fall off the ladder and crack your head?"

"No and I can assure you your mother feels the same way."

Barbara agreed. "The only difference Natalie and I'll include you in this too Kathryn, the only difference is I knew from day one. Robert just took a bit longer, men are like that, but they *do* get there eventually." She leaned over and kissed her husband on the cheek.

For the next hour everyone devoured generous servings of piping hot, home made fruit scones topped with obscene dollops of cream and jam, all washed down with copious cups of tea and coffee. The conversations ranging from the disappearance of the grandfather clock from the hallway for much needed repairs, Kathryn's impending operation, the design of the engagement and wedding rings, guest invitations, before moving onto reception dates and the honeymoon.

Ballard readily joined in, relieved and also chuffed that for the first time he felt like a fully fledged member of Natalie's family. Robert caught his eye, his expression acknowledging what Ballard was now experiencing; each man respecting the other with a new and unbreakable bond. The interaction was not lost on Barbara.

While driving back to the town house, Kathryn put into words what Ballard was thinking. "Natalie, I'm really glad you're marrying Michael and that I'll be your sister-in-law, as well as part of your mum and dad's life." Natalie reached back and both women clasped hands, savouring the ever growing bond between them.

After parking in the garage they trooped into the kitchen. Kathryn went to open the fridge but Natalie placed a hand on her arm. "I hate to be the bearer of bad tidings sister dearest, but you've had your last supper. Your surgery is tomorrow morning, remember?"

Kathryn clapped her hand to her mouth. "Oh my God, I clean forgot I had to fast."

Natalie paused knowingly. "I thought you had. That's why I didn't say anything when you were scoffing down the scones. I figured if you didn't eat anything after we left you'd *just* make the curfew."

Kathryn quipped. "I feel like a condemned prisoner heading to the guillotine."

Ballard chipped in. "Perhaps a little melodramatic Sis, but yes there are similarities. However, in your case you'll only be knocked out for an hour or so and afterwards you can go home with your head still attached to your shoulders."

Kathryn snorted. "Yeah... apart from the fact it'll be twice its normal size." She gave an exaggerated shrug. "Well if this is my lot for the evening and considering we have to be at the hospital by 7 a.m., I'll bid you both good night and go and read for a while."

She gripped Natalie and Ballard's hands. "Thank you both for *everything* you've done for me. Looking back now I don't think I would have coped very well on my own. I'll never forget this."

Natalie waved her hand dismissively. "Nonsense, you're a Ballard, tough as nails. You'd have been fine."

Smiling Kathryn shook her head as she headed upstairs. "I have my doubts. I'll see you both bright and early, goodnight."

Natalie and Ballard sat side by side on the couch without speaking, enjoying the simple pleasure of each other's company. Natalie broke the silence.

"Mum's extremely happy you and Dad are now on better terms. It makes life so much easier for all concerned."

"You're not kidding. How do you think I feel? As your father said, 'I'm not a wall flower…'"

"Really! He said that?"

"He certainly did. And despite the fact I'm not, he has a presence about him that scares the hell out of me and reminds me so much of *my* father. You don't mess with guys like that. Natural born leaders."

Natalie snuggled closer. "He sees a lot of you in him when he was younger – he's spoken to Mum about it. He respects you Michael and what you did for Kathryn proved him right."

Ballard wrapped her in a protective hug. "Well everything seems to be ok now and I can tell you that after today, future visits will be a breeze. I just pray his fears never eventuate, I promise you darling, I'll do everything in my power to protect you and the kids."

Natalie pressed her lips against his, reassuring him. "I know that darling, I know that."

CHAPTER
30

At 6.45 the next morning Ballard pulled into the St Vincent's Private Hospital car park. Carrying Kathryn's overnight bag and holding Natalie's hand, he led the way to reception. Kathryn gave them both a lingering hug and Natalie responded by kissing her on the cheek. "We'll be back this afternoon. Don't worry, the operation will be a success – you have a wonderful surgeon."

Ballard winked. "Yes Sis. Everything will be fine and you'll have men flinging themselves at your feet before you know it."

Kathryn embraced them a second time, then after an unconvincing wave, headed off along the corridor with the admission's nurse.

Ballard and Natalie thanked the staff at the reception desk before walking outside. Glancing up at the sapphire blue sky scattered with post card white clouds, Ballard asked, "Fancy a stroll in the city?"

Natalie squeezed his arm enthusiastically. "Yes please. Let's do the arcades and window shop. Kathryn's operation isn't until nine so she won't be out of recovery until at least 12.30 this afternoon. We can have lunch, then come back and check how it all went."

Catching a tram they gazed up at St Patrick's Cathedral along with its surrounding gardens, then, on turning into Collins Street they were taken back in time by the architecturally romantic buildings, squeezed between modern steel and glass monoliths.

Stopping off at Swanston street they strolled charming arcades and fashionable shops throughout the central business district. Lunch in one of the boutique restaurants found them discussing wedding plans and future aspirations. Ballard reached across and held Natalie's hand. "My only regret is we're too old to have children." Natalie gazed into his eyes, not speaking, her expression that of silent longing.

By one o'clock they had returned to the hospital and were standing alongside Kathryn's bed. Kathryn looked up at them, groggy from the anaesthetic but smiling nonetheless.

Minutes earlier the theatre nurse had confirmed the surgeon was happy with the operation, indicating the scar would fade into Kathryn's natural expression lines. Natalie and Ballard were ecstatic they could pass on the positive news.

"You're not just saying that, it really went well?" Kathryn's brow was furrowed with concern.

Natalie looked down at her, nodding reassurance. "Even better than any of us could have hoped for. Now do your bit and allow it to heal. The swelling will take a week or so to go down. Take your tablets for infection and change the dressings as often as advised and this horrible incident will be a distant memory before you know it." A single tear of relief trickled down Kathryn's cheek.

Natalie took a tissue and wiped it away. "Are you sure you want to go back to your place when you're discharged?"

"Yes Natalie. My girlfriends will be in later and they'll stay with me for at least three or four days. I'll be fine, thank you again, both of you."

"Shh, it was nothing, was it Michael?" Natalie looked at Ballard for confirmation but received a wicked grin in return.

"Are you kidding me? She's eaten all your food, used your electricity, drained all the hot water, then put us through hell with the psychologist and finished up by lazing about every day. Thank God she's only been with us a week."

Natalie reached over, pretending to choke him. Kathryn smiled weakly, waving a reluctant goodbye as they left the room.

Sitting in the car with the motor idling, Ballard asked, "Where to my lady?"

"To the castle kind prince. I've children being dropped off after school by their father and I need to fix Josh's room before they get back."

"Your command is my desire... er, your wish is my request, aah... your demand is my pleasure."

Natalie laughed.

Later that evening they sat in the lounge with Kayla and Josh, having decided now was the appropriate time to provide them with at least some of the answers to the inevitable questions they would ask.

Josh led off with the obvious. "We saw you on TV Mike, were you scared when you were down at the gorge?"

Ballard answered immediately. "No doubt about it, Josh. The Parnell guy had already killed a man, so anything was possible. That was the scary part. But I was more concerned for my sister."

Natalie and Ballard had decided they would use direct and factual language as both children were mature for their age and would expect honest answers.

Kayla, looking concerned, asked her mother, "Is Kathryn going to be ok? Will she always have a scar on her face?"

Natalie held Kayla's hand. "She'll be fine sweetheart. She had her surgery this morning and the doctors have told us she'll heal completely, but it'll take up to a year for the scar to fade. When you see her next act normally, it's quite ok to inspect her face, there's no point pretending she hasn't had an injury. Kathryn told me she's ok with this." Kayla digested her mother's advice.

Josh suddenly smirked. "Any chance of a few autographs Mike? I could make heaps at school, even upgrade my iPad."

"Josh, you'll do no such thing!" Natalie's response was immediate and forceful, realising his request was genuine.

Josh shrugged. "Worth a try. Do you still have stitches in your head Mike?"

Ballard answered by leaning forward and parting his hair. Both Josh and Kayla were wide eyed as they observed first hand what serious injuries a brutal physical assault could inflict. Ballard sensed their concern. "Not like in the movies is it?" They shook their head, unaware of the valuable lesson they were learning.

"Have all the criminals been caught? Is the investigation over?" This time Kayla directed her question to Ballard who responded without hesitation, smiling at her formal terminology.

"Yes Kayla – it's all over." Despite John's earlier advice, Ballard had discussed with Natalie the ramifications of the hitman still being at large. Both agreed nothing could be gained by informing the family.

Josh looked first at his mother then at Ballard, a thoughtful expression on his face. "Well, if I can't sell autographs, perhaps

I could hold info' sessions with the other kids in class, charge an entrance fee."

"No Josh!" Natalie and Ballard's response was in unison.

"How about time off from school for post traumatic stress?" Natalie and Ballard burst out laughing. "Not a chance."

Kayla squeezed her mother's hand. "What date have you set for the wedding Mum?"

The sudden change of topic took Natalie by surprise. "The first Sunday in January, at Rupertswood in Sunbury." The conversation then continued on a wedding theme between Kayla and Natalie while Josh fired questions at Ballard about the Special Operations officers and their weapons. Ballard responded with as much detail as he was permitted to impart.

Twenty minutes later the discussions came to an end, with Kayla and Josh's need for information satisfied, at least for now. Natalie opened her mouth but Josh beat her to it. "Yes I know Mum, homework, we're on it." Turning to Kayla he said, "Come on, let's go upstairs and pretend we're studying."

Before they left they took photographs of themselves with Ballard, despite Natalie's suspicion as to the photo's purpose.

Natalie and Ballard sat together on the sofa, half dozing, half watching TV for the next hour. Nodding at each other as to how tired they were, they headed upstairs. Thirty minutes later, after bidding the children goodnight, they lay cuddled together before drifting into a deep sleep.

CHAPTER
31

The next morning, with breakfast over, five minutes of frantic activity ensued with Kayla and Josh rushing about as they packed lunches into school bags before bolting out the door for the bus. This was followed by Natalie showering and dressing for work, having stated earlier she would put in three days at the firm before driving up to the farm Thursday night. From there she and Ballard would head over to Bordertown Friday morning.

Backing out of the garage, Ballard sat with the engine idling, waiting for Natalie to emerge in the BMW. Once she was clear of the garage, they mouthed their mutual love then with a wave, drove their separate ways.

On the trip to the farm Ballard experienced the emptiness he felt every time he parted from Natalie; he knew the next three days would seem like an eternity. He saw this as a positive sign as his feelings had deepened to the point he hated being away from her, even for the shortest of periods; but he also accepted he would make good use of this time on the property.

The moment he parked he changed into his work clothes, deciding it was time to finally face his demons. Opening the farm gate he headed towards the gorge and minutes later stood at the point where he and Kathryn had almost died. Taking care, he traversed the path leading down to the rock ledge, smiling wryly to himself as he reflected on the irony that should he slip he could possibly injure or kill himself at the very spot where Parnell had tried to achieve that end.

On reaching the ledge Ballard observed the blood stains and chalk marks outlining where the body had landed. To his surprise the feelings he predicted he would experience didn't materialise; in fact he felt no discernable sensation at all. He rationalised that he had suppressed his raw emotions so effectively he was now unable to release them. He was about to discover how wrong he was.

Looking up he was stunned by the height of the ridge, shuddering he comprehended for the first time how the drop was sufficient for he and Kathryn to have experienced several seconds of terror before dashing onto the rocks. It was this realisation that triggered a flood of mixed emotions which seconds before had been suppressed.

He forced himself to stand and allow the tide of panic, anger, frustration and helplessness wash over him in ever decreasing waves.

He was also surprised that although the discussion with the psychologist had helped clear his mind, it was only now, standing at this fateful site that his current feelings were so dramatically released. He reminded himself that throughout his career nothing ever matched real life experience.

Turning he made the slow climb back up to the ridge and after one final glance over the edge, walked back to the house. Slumping onto the sofa he was glad he had made the journey, despite feeling exhausted; he knew time would eventually draw a line through the traumatic event.

Reverting back to the certain remedy to soothe his battered frame of mind, he took his list of chores and began adding tasks.

He commenced with a final coat of Estapol on the front door, then added some of the annual jobs such as cleaning gutters, finishing with a reminder to revisit the two neighbours who had justifiably expressed negative feelings several days prior.

Taking his mobile he accessed the number of the hotel he and Natalie would be staying at while in Bordertown, making a booking for two nights. Following that he gulped down a glass of apple juice before beginning work.

The next three days were lonely without Natalie to wake up beside. Despite this he managed to complete his tasks and even succeeded in moderating the opinion of one of the neighbours as to how the police had handled the incident; he failed to change the conviction of the second.

Thursday evening saw him standing on the concrete apron in front of the open garage, waiting impatiently for the first sighting of Natalie's BMW. Walking up to one of the rose bushes he broke off a bud; seconds later he heard the twin toot of Natalie's car as it wound its way down the driveway. The instant she stopped he drew her out of the driver's seat, wrapping her in a welcoming hug.

She pressed up against him. "Would it be fair to say you're *very* pleased to see me darling? I know it's been horrible without you these last few days." She paused. "That sounds terrible doesn't it – of course I had a great time with the kids, but nowadays they seem to have their own lives and I swear I'm nothing more than a landlord to them." Smelling the rose she snuggled up against him. "Well now you can reciprocate and put me up in *your* lodgings."

He kissed her. "I'll even turn down the bed and make your breakfast in the morning. Does that please m'lady?"

"It pleases her very much." She popped the boot and took out a small suitcase. "Leave the big one there, we'll put it in the Chrysler in the morning."

His eyes widened. "Er Nat…we're going for three days not thirty. It isn't the honeymoon yet."

A whatever-do-you-mean smile flitted across her face. "A girl has to look her best, even in Bordertown. What would your old school chums think if I looked dowdy?"

"Now there's an old fashioned word I haven't heard for years. Besides I don't think you would ever qualify as 'dowdy' my sweet."

"Hmm. Well I'm not taking any chances. Remember, this is my first trip over and I want to make a *good* impression with your friends."

She pointed to a blue bag. "Could you take that darling? I thought I'd bring dinner as you've been living on quiche and leftovers for the last few days. I'll make sandwiches in the morning for us to have when we stop at a park on the way. I hate paying for takeaway food that tastes like plastic."

He shook his head, smiling at the attention to detail she applied to everything she did. He knew it would drive him crazy, but nonetheless, it was a craziness he was looking forward to. Fifty minutes later, with dinner over, they both lay back in the claw bath, Natalie's head resting against his chest as excess bubbles oozed over the side each time they moved.

She chuckled. "Is it safe to sit in so much water immediately after we've eaten?"

He gently cupped her breasts. "Probably not, but I promise to keep you afloat."

"Ooh, you're so kind." She sighed and he was convinced he could hear her purring like a contented feline.

CHAPTER
32

By 9.30 a.m., with cruise-control set, they observed pine plantations and rolling farmland as they bypassed Ballarat. Natalie snapped photos and commented on the scenery which Ballard considered the most picturesque of the whole journey.

Thirty kilometres on he directed her attention to a line of giant wind turbines on a ridge to the right, their blades rotating in what appeared to be slow motion. She positioned her camera and clicked away.

As they crossed the Adelaide-Melbourne railway line in Ararat he pointed out the park and swings where he had often stopped for a picnic with Bradley when he was little. Natalie touched his arm.

"In a few more years he'll be doing the same thing on a trip somewhere with his own children – the cycle of life Michael."

"Just the thought of it makes me feel old."

"You'll never be *old*."

"Some days I feel it."

"I can assure you that *wasn't* the case last night."

He chuckled. "You say the nicest things."

"Let's have our picnic here to relive the times you had with your son." He agreed and swung over to the left, parking in the shade. Selecting a wooden table they set up their food and watched as a dozen children rampaged amongst the play equipment, their doting parents looking on.

An hour later the majestic sight of the Grampians came into view; the rock formations over four hundred million years old.

Natalie clicked away. "Just spectacular. When you told me our next trip may involve a night or two in one of the holiday cabins, I did some homework." She placed the camera on her lap and faced him. "Now, imagine a time fourteen thousand years before the pyramids were even thought of."

He glanced at her, curious. "Go on."

"Around then, in one of the caves an aboriginal mixed ochre and water in his mouth and placing his hand on the cave wall, sprayed out the solution leaving the outline of his hand. It's still there today."

Ballard shook his head. "Unbelievable. And here we are, white settlement… what, less than two hundred and fifty years old. In terms of history, there's no comparison is there?"

He placed a hand on her thigh. "I created a monster when I gave the tourist lecture on the tram the other day, didn't I?"

"Not really. As I said, I just love history. You've simply reignited my passion for it."

They drove on with Natalie pointing out landmarks and commenting on how charming some of the small towns were. As they entered Nhill, Ballard lowered the driver's window. "Time for another break. There's a park in the main street we can stop at."

Minutes later, unable to find a free table they spread their food on a park bench. Ballard pointed to a shop on the opposite side of the street. "That's where my mother bought my second three-wheel trike."

"*Second* trike?"

"Yep. Somehow I demolished the first one and kept nagging my parents for another. I was three and can still remember being in the shop with Mum when she bought it. It was on the top shelf and the lady had to climb on a ladder to get it." He looked wistfully at the shop. "A long time ago Nat, a long time ago."

Natalie placed an arm around his shoulders, hugging him. "Good times?"

He hesitated. "Yes – for the most part. Dad was a hard task master, but I coped and I'm sure he thought he was doing the right thing. I guess he was of the generation that didn't know how to relate to children." He looked directly at Natalie.

"I've never told you the reason why I don't drink alcohol, or anyone else in my family for that matter, not even Bradley, despite him being in the army with all its temptations." Natalie said nothing, holding him tighter. He continued, grim faced. "It's ok darling, I'm *not* a reformed drunk." Natalie eased the pressure on his arm. "However my grandfather on my Dad's side *was* and a pretty bad one at that." He hesitated, unsure how to continue.

Natalie placed the back of her hand on his cheek. "There's no need to go on if you don't want to. I love you for who you are, not for what happened in your family before you were even born."

He shook his head. "No, I want you to know everything about me and my past, not just the good bits." He swallowed hard and took a deep breath. "My grandfather was quite brutal in his treatment of my Dad and often Dad would sleep outside in the haystack." Natalie looked startled, despite her effort to remain unemotional.

Ballard pressed on. "Not a pretty image is it? Dad was

fourteen, his brother thirteen and his sister nine. My grandmother was thirty-seven and my grandfather forty-two.

"By all accounts my grandfather used to verbally and physically abuse my grandmother in his drunken rages and this wasn't over a short period, apparently it went on for years." Natalie rewrapped the uneaten sandwiches as she listened, her appetite lost.

"I've subsequently found out my grandfather was treated over a number of years by the Bordertown doctor for what was termed in those days as 'delirium tremors and alcohol poisoning.'"

He hesitated as a young couple strolled past, arm in arm. "Backtracking and this is a bit left field but relevant, my grandfather's dad, my great grandfather, died when my grandfather was forty-one. As a consequence my grandfather inherited the entire farm. All his brothers and sisters had left or married, going their own way in the world with a cash settlement at the time. So my grandfather scooped the pool; I guess this strengthens the theory that receiving wealth too soon often results in it not being appreciated by the recipient. Whether this caused him to be an alcoholic – nobody knows." He smiled grimly as he brushed Natalie's hair back from her forehead. "Hanging in there so far darling?"

Natalie kissed him on the lips. "I'm here to stay and don't you forget it."

"So there we are, a wealthy farm property with three young children and a drunken father, giving mum regular biffo, along with verbal abuse. Then one day she snaps."

"Snaps?"

"Snaps big time. Two days after Christmas, it was a Saturday morning, she shot him."

Natalie's hands flew to her mouth. "She... she... *what?*"

Ballard's reply was brutal. "Yep. Blasted him twice with a shotgun. But to make matters worse, before she did it she asked my uncle, her son, remember he was thirteen, to load the gun. She shot my grandfather the first time, but only clipped him in the arm. She demanded uncle reload the gun then she shot grandpa in the chest at close range."

"My God..." Natalie's voice trailed away.

"Even the second shot didn't kill him outright and get this – my grandmother left him on the ground and went inside to change her clothes and make the bed. Can you believe it? *Then* she went out with my dad and rolled grandpa onto his back and said, 'Yes, he's dead now.'"

Natalie's hands slid from her face. "How do you *know* all this? Did your parents tell you?"

He shook his head. "No way. My mother hinted as I was growing up there'd been a family tragedy, but she didn't know the details because Dad never said a word to her about what happened."

"So how did you find out?"

"A work colleague was on Google and put in my surname, up popped the newspaper article detailing the Coroner's inquest of my grandfather's death. After he picked himself up off the floor he emailed it to me. It's public knowledge for God's sake. Of course there wasn't Google when I was young and no-one in the district ever spoke to me about it. The older residents would have known the circumstances, but nothing was said, I guess everyone was too uncomfortable to bring the subject up."

Natalie shook her head to clear her thoughts. "So what happened to your grandmother? I mean you've told me stories of how after Sunday school you'd ride your bike up to her house and she'd give you lemonade and fruitcake. Didn't she go to jail?"

"After the inquest she was formally charged with manslaughter then released on bail while waiting for the trial at the Circuit Court in Mount Gambier. It turns out there was sufficient evidence of bruising on her body, along with the doctor's account of his treatment of my grandfather for alcoholism to have my grandmother acquitted on 'extreme provocation'. So that's my confession, end of story. From that day on my grandmother banned alcohol in the house and years later, Dad adopted the same principle.

"Now none of us drink. On reflection, it's a wonder we aren't all alcoholics. But anyway, I figured it wasn't worth tempting fate, just in case I *did* have the faulty gene scientists now suspect exists in alcoholics. I've never regretted the decision, despite the fact I'm not always accepted by some of my work colleagues because of it."

Natalie placed a hand on his cheek. "I never knew... you poor darling, so much violence in your past and even now. How do you remain *normal*?"

He attempted a smile, but his eyes were hard. "You know, the sad thing about this whole episode is *everyone* lost something. My grandmother had a rough marriage and lived an unhappy life. So too my grandfather and as a result his stay on this earth was cut short, as I said only forty-two. He could have lived to twice that age.

"Then there was my Dad, uncle and aunt growing up without a father and my brother, myself and Kathryn without a grandfather. *Again* the ripple effect of provoked violence." He looked ruefully at Natalie. "Well this turned out to be more emotional than I'd planned. I feel I need to apologise."

"Nonsense. You won't do any such thing. It's an incident in the past you had no control over. I'm just glad it hasn't had a negative impact on *your* life, because for many it would."

Reaching across the table he scooped up the sandwiches. "After all this confessing I'm starving." He offered one to Natalie who shook her head in disbelief that he could move so rapidly from the circumstances he had just shared.

She muttered to herself, "It's a man thing, I'm convinced."

He grinned at her as he wolfed down two sandwiches in quick succession.

Back in the Chrysler they settled down for the final leg of the trip, with Ballard booting the car up to the speed limit. "Kaniva is the next main town and it happens to be where I was born."

Natalie wiped her hands with a moist towellete, offering one to Ballard.

"I remember you telling me once you were born in Victoria, but not the reason why."

"Pretty simple really, the only doctor in the Bordertown hospital at the time was a drunk. He'd often disappear for days on end because of his binges. As a consequence my parents decided to play it safe and chose the Kaniva Hospital in case he went walkabout at the crucial moment."

Natalie shook her head. "So that's why you joined the police in Victoria instead of South Australia, because Kaniva was in Victoria?"

Ballard pursed his lips. "Being a Victorian *was* one of the deciding factors." He grimaced. "I know I wasn't too popular with my parents, especially my Dad because Kathryn decided to follow me and come to Melbourne after she finished her physiotherapy degree in Adelaide.

"My folks believed I was a 'rebel' influence, even though Kathryn's clientele base in Melbourne was twice what it would have been in Adelaide."

Natalie laughed out loud. "You have no idea how weird that sounds Michael, that anyone would refer to you as a rebel."

As they drove through the main street, Ballard pointed to the hospital, indicating where his mother had endured twenty-four hours of excruciating labour, something she had often reminded him of throughout his youth.

Natalie nodded knowingly. "So you've been causing angst from day one."

Crossing the Victorian, South Australian border, Ballard informed Natalie they were now nineteen kilometres from Bordertown. She shuffled in her seat with excitement. "I can't wait to see where you lived for your first twenty years. You have no idea how much I'm looking forward to this."

He shrugged expansively. "I hate to disappoint you, but there isn't much to tell. Just an ordinary, shy country kid growing up on a farm who realised early in his youth that life on the land was never going to be his vocation, much to the disgust of my father. He even cut me out of the will for ten years because of it."

"You're kidding."

"Cross my heart. I didn't know about it until my mother told me I was back *in* the will."

Natalie shook her head. "There's no denying it, the Ballard family are a volatile lot, in more ways than one." She reached across, placing a reassuring hand on his arm.

CHAPTER
33

By early afternoon they were booked into their room at the Woolshed Inn, lying back on the bed, shoes kicked off and reflecting on their trip. Ballard brushed Natalie's hair back from her ear and kissed her on the cheek. "Want to head out and discover the delights of our downtown metropolis?

She nodded enthusiastically.

After two hours they had explored the majority of Bordertown's main streets with Ballard reminiscing on childhood memories: the cinema he had attended every Saturday evening with his brother and parents; his primary and high school where he had won athletics events; the railway station to which he had ridden his bike to collect his mail order archery set and twelve months later, the Bullworker exerciser; the same station where he had taken his BSA motorbike to be railed to Adelaide and sold before moving to Melbourne.

Natalie absorbed each story, fascinated as she held onto his arm. She was most interested in the house where his maternal grandfather had lived for the last fifteen years of his life, inspecting the creek at the rear that had flooded the property all those years ago.

"It's sad there aren't many of your school friends left in the district."

He agreed. "Too right, they've all gone their own way. Unless they inherited large farms there wasn't enough work here to make a reasonable living, well not for a family. I guess that's the sorry state of affairs for many country towns, wherever they are. The young just up and leave."

He pointed to the Bordertown Hotel across the street, surrounded on all sides by an intricate lattice decorated veranda. "The reason we're not staying there is because they don't have private en-suites, but they do serve great meals." Natalie hugged his arm as they headed inside.

After a stomach expanding three course meal and a chat with a number of locals, they strolled arm in arm through the remainder of the streets, walking off their dinner before finishing back at their room. Following a quick shower they lay in bed, listening to the street sounds and the public passing outside their bedroom window.

"Not as quiet as on the farm."

Natalie sighed contentedly. "Yes, but I don't mind. I can't sleep right now, my head's spinning from everything you've told me today. I think I've learned more about you in one day than I have in the past year."

Ballard pretended indignation. "And what does *that* say about our relationship?"

"It says we're going to grow old together, loving every minute, that's what, because I adore everything about you my wonderful man."

"Why thank you my sweet. If I may be so presumptuous, you've provided the perfect answer." He kissed her in the half light of the room, content that although some of the revelations about his past life and family had been traumatic, they did provide the insight necessary for their relationship to mature.

Next morning it was Natalie who woke first. Seeing Ballard slumbering, she kissed him on the neck, progressing to his ear and finally his lips.

Very slowly he began to stir. "I must be getting old. I thought *I* was the one ever alert, protecting *you* from the wolves at the door?"

"Crisis over, they poked their head in, howled and ran off – but I was ready for them."

He rolled out of bed. "Time for a quick shave before joining you in the shower, er, what I *meant* to say was, I'll have a quick shave *then* a shower."

Natalie chuckled as she raised both arms above her head in an extended yawn. "I'll leave either option to your discretion darling." Tossing her nightie at him she headed for the bathroom.

After breakfast Ballard suggested they head out to the farm to see the house he grew up in.

On the drive to the home property he pulled alongside the gum tree where his mother had died three years earlier. Reflecting he said, "We think she fell asleep at the wheel. Thank God she veered *off* the road and not into the path of an oncoming car with a family onboard." Natalie grasped his hand, her expression one of shared sorrow.

"I guess the only positive aspect was the fact it was instant. Mum was still fit and healthy and able to see out her last days on the farm where she'd lived ever since she was married."

"How old was she?"

"Eighty-one. Not bad for living alone and being self sufficient. She did her own cooking and washing and maintained the garden. She still drove all over the district and sang in the church choir. When we get there you'll see how big the garden is, well… was and what an effort that must have been. Dad died a few years earlier than Mum from a stroke, he was eighty-five."

Ballard looked embarrassed, a result of Natalie's enquiring expression. "Yep, they had Kathryn indecently late in life, almost caused a scandal in the district." He rested a forearm on the steering wheel. "Dad always said he wanted to be on the tractor when he died, charging through paddocks until he hit a tree. It turns out that's what Mum did. The thing is, both my parents died before they lost their physical or mental faculties. Ok, Dad was walking a bit slower, but that's all. Both were as sharp as ever, to the very end. This was what they would have wanted."

Ballard looked long and hard at the scarred tree then flicked into gear. Five minutes later they turned into the farm's gravel driveway entrance four-hundred metres from the house. He looked across at Natalie, a grim expression on his face. "The depressing aspect of coming here is seeing how overgrown the garden has become. When Mum looked after the place it had such life, that was the thing I remember most from my childhood." He pointed to where the circular lawn used to be, remembering the flower beds blazing with colour, presenting the house in a welcoming manner.

Natalie was in awe at the size of the gum trees bordering the grounds which covered over two hectares. Ballard proudly pointed to where the clay tennis court and the bowling green had once been. He described how the Bordertown residents would ride out in their buggies, or on horseback to enjoy a Sunday afternoon's entertainment. He lamented how it was now nothing more than a weed infested tangle. He also expressed distress for the house which was slowly crumbling, the massive sandstone walls falling victim to rising damp.

"When the estate was divided up after Mum died, my brother asked to keep the section of land with the house. Unfortunately he's never been able to stop its ever increasing deterioration, the money needed to fix it would be prohibitive. It's almost as though the house is being reclaimed by the land. I'm afraid it'll have to be bulldozed."

"Michael no! Surely not. All that history. It must break your heart because it's certainly breaking mine."

He shrugged. "It is, but it's also reality. I wouldn't show you inside even if I could. I don't want you to see it as it looks now. In my mind, it's as it was when I was young." Natalie shook her head, unable to hide her disappointment.

"Cheer up Nat. At least you can imagine how magnificent it must have been in its prime. The lounge room, now that was something I can tell you – a stained timber ceiling, imported English sofas and arm chairs, an upright piano and oil paintings on every wall. I've got photos of the room I can show you when we get back home."

"Yes please and *I'll* pretend it's still as it was."

He felt immense relief. "There's something else I want you to see, come with me and watch out for the snakes." No sooner had he uttered the words than Natalie clambered onto his back.

"Tell me you're joking!"

"Afraid not darling, this *is* a farm after all and it's summer."

She shuffled into a more comfortable position, her arms wrapping around his neck as her legs encircled his waist. Laughing he moved to a stand of mature bamboo. "Mum's dad used to send me here to cut off a piece he would fashion into a cigarette holder. Every year I'd have to fetch a new cutting for him. It's also where Brad and I would have sword fights with long pieces of bamboo. How we weren't blinded in the process

I don't know."

He turned and pointed to a depression in the ground approximately eight metres long and two metres wide. "It's mostly filled in now, but that's the swimming pool I dug when I was twelve…"

"You dug a swimming pool?"

"Yep. I slaved away over the Christmas holidays and finished it before I went back to school. Why you may ask?" He continued without seeking a reply. "Well, near the end of grade seven I jumped into the deep section of the school pool, showing off in front of my girlfriend and bloody near drowned. Despite the fact I'd never bothered to learn to swim, I couldn't help myself. After sucking in more water than the filtration system I was dragged out by the other kids and was so embarrassed I came home that afternoon and begged Mum to let me dig a pool. She thought I was mad and I remember overhearing her say to Dad that night she thought I couldn't possibly do it – so that *guaranteed* I would."

"But it's just dirt! It would've been muddy and…"

"Not only muddy… a green slime would form on the surface every few days which I'd skim off with a broom. It's a wonder I didn't die from swamp fever. The Labradors loved it though. But, I did teach myself to swim, along with Kathryn, despite her not being too keen on the green slick."

He pointed to one of the edges. "It was here that I learned all about persistence." Natalie tipped her head to one side, curious, her cheek near his. "While I was digging out the pool, a wasp landed on the edge and began rolling a ball out of the wet clay for its nest. As it took off I accidentally threw a shovel full of dirt alongside and it dropped the ball. Without hesitating and ignoring the ball it had just dropped, it set about rolling another one."

He paused. "This is the bit I'm *not* proud of – as it was about to take off again I flicked more soil at it and it dropped the second ball. You guessed it, without hesitating it started all over again as though it were the first. I did this ten times and the wasp didn't miss a beat. Finally I took pity on it and let it fly off with the ball, but I've never forgotten how determined it was, genetically locked into achieving what it set out to do.

"As odd as it may sound that taught me a very valuable lesson in life and one I've always remembered… never, never, *never* give up."

Natalie kissed the side of his neck. "That, my husband-to-be explains a lot and I mean a *lot*."

He playfully pinched her leg as he headed for the veranda, placing her gently onto the concrete landing. Leading her back to the front of the house he stopped alongside a Kurrajong tree near the lawn. "I used to sit in this tree as a kid and read." He walked over to the swing suspended from one of the branches and tested the ropes. "All good." He beckoned Natalie over and after she wriggled into position, he began pushing her as he had for his son many years before.

"Happy times Michael?"

"Very much so, but again I apologise for saying this, the very spot we're standing on has history." Natalie came to a halt, slipping off the swing.

Ballard shrugged, as though in resignation. "You wanted to know the full story about my past, well this is the uncut version." He pointed up to the branches.

"My Dad used to sit in this tree when *he* was a lad and down here," he indicated near the base, "well, that's where he had his stroke and died." Natalie moved to his side, clutching his hand.

His features darkened. "It gets worse Nat." He walked ten paces towards the house and pointed to a spot on the ground.

"It's somewhere about here where my grandfather was shot."

"My God, there's no end to this. How horrible."

He grimaced. "Why do you think I didn't bring you over here for a visit until you and I knew each other a whole lot better?"

"I admit I had wondered why I hadn't been invited over earlier, particularly as I had wanted to meet your brother and sister-in-law."

"Thankfully when Terry and Karen came to Melbourne last year you were able to meet up with them, so that gave me the excuse to delay this trip because I knew all the history would be confronting."

Natalie shook her head. "It's just a pity this trip clashed with them holidaying in Queensland."

Ballard nodded. "Unfortunately work got in the way of changing our holiday dates. Now, I hope my family history hasn't given you any second thoughts?"

She hugged him, her expression reassuring. "Are you kidding and miss out on all these stories?" She hesitated, looking guilty. "I'm sorry, I didn't mean to trivialise this, I…"

He encircled her waist. "I know *exactly* what you meant darling, I'm just glad you can see it for what it is, something a tad more challenging than the skeletons you would find in the average family closet."

Natalie muttered under her breath, a half smile on her face, "There's nothing average about you lot."

"Ok. Enough morbidity for one day and no more family surprises." He extended his hands towards her, palms outward as a peace offering.

Back in the car he sat looking at the house. "I think this'll be the last time I come out here."

"Michael, why?"

"No point darling."

She clasped his hand, remaining silent for several seconds. "You know you've replicated your parent's property with the farm back home, don't you?"

He looked at her perplexed.

"You've taken the house and grounds of your childhood and created an almost identical replica of it on the farm back in Gisborne, albeit bigger."

"No way!" He hesitated, his mouth open, questioning her statement before shaking his head. "On second thoughts, perhaps you're right. I've never realised that until now, very perceptive of you sweetheart. And to prove your point, the three Kurrajong trees at home came from seedpods off this tree."

Taking his hand, Natalie leaned across and kissed him. "So now you can be assured your childhood memories will live on forever."

Shaking his head again he started the motor and looked across at her, grinning. "Want to see where I used to ride my push bike to Sunday School?"

"Yes please."

During the next hour they drove the five kilometres to Mundulla, the town where his mother lived before she was married, viewing her family home. They walked around the country church where he attended Sunday School, then had tea and scones in the corner pub before heading back to Bordertown.

Back in their room they slumped onto the bed, each admitting the emotional rollercoaster throughout the day had been tiring but rewarding. Without planning to, they dozed off and slept for an hour. When Ballard woke it was with a sufficient jolt to stir Natalie.

"Everything alright darling?"

He blinked hard before answering. "I'm laying here alongside you, how could anything be wrong?"

For the remainder of the afternoon they visited several of Ballard's school friends to whom he proudly introduced Natalie, the ensuing conversations centering around old memories, with Natalie absorbing the stories like a sponge.

Back in the motel after the evening meal they lay on the bed looking at each other, a newfound understanding between them as a result of what Natalie had learned in the preceding thirty-six hours. She touched the tip of his nose with her forefinger, then pinched his cheek. "Many, many layers."

"What's that for?"

"For breaking your promise about no more morbidity, then showing me the house in Mundulla where that horrible man hung himself after drinking sulphuric acid. My God, what is it about this district that produces these horror stories?"

Ballard smiled wryly. "Makes you wonder what kind of werewolf I'm going to turn into later in life, doesn't it?"

"Don't joke, I'm serious! Nobody could make this stuff up."

Without warning she sat bolt upright. "Sandwiches."

"How on earth could you be hungry after the dinner we've just had?"

"No. I mean sandwiches for tomorrow on the drive back."

He kissed the back of her neck. "Don't worry sweetheart. We'll get something on the way." He knew his suggestion was a waste of breath and to confirm this, Natalie executed a prefect commando roll off the bed, slipping into her shoes. Sighing, he followed and minutes later they were walking hand in hand to the supermarket.

As they approached the store the Adelaide-Melbourne train thundered through the crossing, the warning bells clanged for nearly a minute after it had passed.

Once inside Natalie handed Ballard a shopping basket, setting about buying the necessary items to make the return trip to Melbourne an enjoyable and nourishing one. As the basket began to fill, Ballard tapped her on the shoulder. "Er, Nat, it's only four and a half hours on the road. There's enough food here to do the trip *and* provide for the guests coming to the BBQ."

"Don't worry, none of this will spoil and what we don't eat tomorrow we can put in the fridge."

He forced a serious expression. "You do realise we have to eat everything in the first nineteen kilometres?"

She stopped mid stride. "What on earth are you talking about Michael?"

"The Victorian border, we can't take food across. They have a checkpoint we have to drive through."

Disappointed Natalie said, "I can't believe it. I was *so* looking forward to making a picnic for us." Disheartened, she began taking items out of the basket, replacing them on the shelf. Ballard burst out laughing but didn't have to say anything for her to realise she had been made fun of.

She kicked him on the shin. "That's the sort of prank I'd expect you to play on Kathryn." She gave him her best coquettish pout. "But I'm to be your wife, how could you do such a..." Ballard halted her protest by kissing her, finishing with an exaggerated dip which had nearby customers gaping.

"Michael! We'll be run out of town for lewd behaviour."

"Let 'em try." With that he led the way to the checkout counter.

Returning to their room he helped Natalie prepare the sandwiches as best he could with the limited cutlery available. Fifteen minutes later the food was wrapped and stored in the mini fridge. Looking at each other they agreed it was time to catch up on their sleep in preparation for the return trip to Gisborne in the morning.

CHAPTER
34

Halfway into their return journey, they pulled up at the central park in Horsham. Natalie spread the picnic food on the only table in the shade. With his mouth stuffed to bursting point with wholemeal bread, chicken, avocado, lettuce and tomato, he gazed across at Natalie, the contented smile on his face systematically interrupted by the rhythmic movement of his jaw. "You were right. This *was* a good idea."

Natalie looked at Ballard reproachingly. "Try not to choke if at all possible darling."

The remainder of the trip was uneventful and included a short stop at Ararat and then home. Turning into the farm driveway, Natalie leaned over and kissed Ballard on the cheek. "Another faultless drive Jeeves."

"Why thank you m'lady. Consider yourself a very, very VIP passenger." Natalie activated the garage door and Ballard reversed in. After listening to the motor for several seconds he switched off the ignition.

As they carried their bags inside he called over his shoulder. "How about stowing this lot and heading to the sauna to ease our weary travellers' bones?"

"Sounds perfect. We don't make enough use of it and

afterwards I bags first session on the massage chair."

"Deal."

Minutes later they stepped inside the sauna and spread their towels on the wooden benches, feeling the soothing heat of the infrared rays on their bare skin. Ballard fiddled with the radio and after setting the temperature to 45 degrees, sat back taking Natalie in his arms.

"It's a tough life, but I guess we'll just have to take it on the chin." Natalie sighed, thoroughly content.

The timer in the sauna activated after thirty minutes and reluctantly they stepped out, heading for the shower. As soon as Natalie had towelled herself dry, she slipped into her dressing gown and strolled back to the sports room with Ballard. Lying back on the massage chair she selected her favourite routine before luxuriating in the gentle rhythm. Ballard propped on the end of the bench press and watched her as the chair eased away her tension. Fifteen minutes later they swapped places and it was Ballard's turn to feel the chair kneading him in all the right places. "Worth every penny."

"You can say that again my sweet."

"I said it was worth every... "She laughed.

Later, as they lay in bed Natalie looked up at the ceiling. "So, back to work for me in the morning and a sleep in for you. It doesn't seem fair."

"Oh, don't worry. I'll be thinking about you."

Natalie chuckled, then kissing him good night, turned over and fell asleep; Ballard followed soon after.

At 7 a.m. the alarm rudely disturbed Ballard's deep sleep. Squinting at the clock he realised his lifetime habit of 5 a.m. starts had already been eroded in the short time he had been away from work. Gently shaking Natalie, who continued to slumber as though the alarm had never sounded, he whispered in her ear, "I'll get your breakfast ready."

Stirring she mumbled, "No darling you relax, sleep in. I'll get up and slave away all day while you watch TV, then head home after work and start the cooking and washing, perhaps strip all the beds."

Ballard tickled her stomach. "You poor thing. Life can be so tough at times. I really feel for you."

She rolled over and kissed him. "Sounded pretty convincing huh, you have to admit."

"Never questioned you for a moment."

Natalie's hands began exploring his body. "Yep, no doubt about it, it's *not* a myth."

"Let's not start something I'll have to finish my sweet." Pouting she swung her feet over the edge of the bed before picking up her robe. Ballard followed, pulling on his shorts and T-shirt, still experiencing considerable pain across his ribs.

"See you in the kitchen sweetheart."

Thirty minutes later Natalie walked in dressed in a crisp tailored suit. Ballard glanced down at his own attire, feeling dishevelled by comparison. Natalie shrugged.

"Don't worry, when you put in half the effort I do, I'm the one feeling underdone."

"Yeah, right. Always underselling yourself. You know that's one of the traits I love about you."

All too soon he was standing at the front of the garage as Natalie's car headed up the driveway, the sensation of her lips a lingering memory. His goodbye wave was returned, confirming she had been looking at him in the rearview mirror; content, he headed inside.

Logging onto his emails he wound his way through the list and sent a number of invitations to guests he had accidentally overlooked in the first round, apologising for the late notice. He also responded to the caterers who had invoiced him for the food, plus supply of tables and chairs for the BBQ, confirming the delivery dates.

As he wound his way through his emails he noted one with the subject: 'They're back!' It was from John. In his usual blunt fashion, his partner had detailed that Parnell's wife and daughter were back from Italy.

As Ballard scanned the text he was surprised to read the Italian police had indeed located them. After numerous rounds of correspondence between the police in Italy and John, an agreement had been reached for Parnell's family to return on the understanding they would enter the witness protection program.

Ballard sat back and considered what this meant. He forwarded an email to John stating: 'Ring me.' Two minutes later his mobile sprang to life.

John came straight to the point. "We got 'em."

Ballard laughed. "You sound like Paul Bremmer announcing to the world he'd captured Saddam Hussein."

There was a slight pause. "Not quite the same thing, but I don't have to tell you how this may tie up some loose ends. And the good news is she *wants* to help us.

"Whether she can shed any light on the identity of Mario's hit-man and whether he was responsible for her daughter's accident, we're yet to find out. At the moment she's with the Witness Protection Unit and it may take some days before we can interview her and the daughter."

Ballard agreed. "It will also mean statements for the inquest brief can be finalised. I guess I have to take back my doubts about the Italians. How did they find her?"

"Believe it or not plain old fashioned elimination, or should I say relative elimination. The wife had family all over Italy – Jesus they must breed like rabbits over there. The police tracked them down and get this, the wife was planning on coming back anyway, mostly because the daughter really missed Australia.

"For her Italy was a foreign country and she hated everything about it, the food, the people, the language... gave her mother hell. Realising it wasn't going to work out the mother caved in."

"John, is there anything I can do?"

"No! You're on sick leave, remember? Delwyn made it crystal clear to everyone here that unless the world comes to an end, you're not to be involved. I'm taking a gamble talking to you now. If she caught me she'd skin me alive. She's bloody fierce when she wants to be."

Ballard hesitated, smiling. "But you told me you like strong women John, remember? Still all systems go with Sonia?" Ballard could have sworn he heard John swoon.

"You bet."

"Make sure you bring her along Sunday week. Any time from eleven."

"I'll be there." With a faint click he was gone.

Ballard finalised his list of emails and sat back, reflecting on the news he had just received. He looked at the time and considered it was too early to ring Kathryn and check on her progress, instead he sent her an email.

Stretching, he concluded he needed a quick work out in the gym as he had avoided any form of exercise while in Bordertown. Afterwards he began preparing his job list for the BBQ which was still ten days away. The work he had to complete amounted to no more than three days; he smiled to himself, recognising he was subconsciously formulating an excuse to return to the office to take a more hands on approach.

Working throughout the day his resolution to casually appear in the squad room progressed from a germ of an idea to a necessity. That night he told Natalie of his decision. While reluctant to agree, she understood he had made up his mind.

As she whispered her love for him, she reminded him not to overdo it, worried that he had not yet fully recovered from his beating.

Sleeping on his decision, he arrived refreshed for work at 9 a.m. the next morning.

CHAPTER
35

The first person he saw was Delwyn. She eyed him with extreme suspicion.

"So Parnell's wife and daughter lob in the country yesterday and you *happen* to call into work today, despite being on sick leave." She turned on her heel. "John! Has anyone seen John?" She disappeared into her office, her point made.

Ballard spotted John peeping cautiously from behind the lunch room door. Ballard walked up to him, grinning. "Very brave John."

Looking sheepish his partner emerged, heading for his desk. "Can you blame me – hell, she can be bloody ferocious."

Ballard followed, settling into his chair. "When are Parnell's wife and daughter being interviewed?"

Tipping his head back John exhaled slowly, his cheeks ballooning. "Yeah ... funny about that. I leaned on Witness Protection late last night. They promised we'd get a crack at them sometime this afternoon." He held up crossed fingers. "Here's hoping."

Ballard muttered his frustration. "Keep on top of them John, if they go to water we'll damn well lean all over *them*."

Ken, Susan and Bobby stepped out of the lift; surprised to

see Ballard they crowded over. Ballard placed a hand on Ken's shoulder while addressing Susan and Bobby. "You're all aware Parnell's wife and daughter are free to be interviewed some time today?" Everyone confirmed they were.

Ballard turned to Ken. "Guess what? You've got yourself a job. I want you and Bobby to interview the wife... Susan, you interview the daughter." John stared at Ballard, silently questioning the wisdom of his decision. Susan and Bobby's faces lit up; even Ken managed a half grin at the prospect of taking the lead role in such an important interview.

For the next fifteen minutes everyone discussed the points that needed to be addressed: whether the wife was aware of the eleven year threat to her husband and family, her possible knowledge of the hit-man's identity, along with any description she might have of the driver who had run down her daughter.

Next they covered the main issues Susan would explore with the young girl: did she have a description of the driver, was she too frightened to talk for fear of reprisal to herself or her parents.

Everyone wrote copious notes and Ballard could tell they were itching to prove themselves on the case. Ken went off muttering he was going to contact Witness Protection while Susan and Bobby put their heads together, planning for the interviews.

Ballard and John headed for Delwyn's office to give her an update.

Delwyn glared at John for several seconds before speaking. "I hear we have some interviews coming up... Any idea when?"

John responded. "Maybe today."

"And about bloody time!" Delwyn's sudden outburst emphasised the enormous pressure she was under.

Ballard responded. "Piece of cake Delwyn. We'll put our heads down and work through this." He attempted to look as laid-back as he could under the circumstances. "At least with the interviews over we can submit the Coroner's brief to get the inquest out of the way, once and for all. Perhaps beat the Christmas break."

Ken appeared at the door, knocking cautiously. Excusing himself to Delwyn he said, "I've arranged with Witness Protection, the interviews will be at their office. They have two rooms set up with video facilities. We'll head over there around 1.30." Nodding, he turned and left.

Delwyn looked across at Ballard, her expression leaving no doubt as to her unspoken question. John shuffled uncomfortably as Ballard replied. "Perfect opportunity for them to step up."

Delwyn responded positively. "I agree, it's time."

Standing, both detectives acknowledged Delwyn before leaving the room. Returning to their desks they were surprised to see Tim Robbin's sitting in Ballard's chair. He sprang to his feet despite Ballard's protest. Tim shook his hand as he peered into his face. "On the mend Michael. At least now you don't look like you've been hit by a bus."

Ballard touched where Parnell had repeatedly kicked him, thankful he was a rapid healer. "Perfect analogy Tim. *Exactly* what it felt like at the time. I still panic whenever I'm about to sneeze, my ribs hurt like hell."

Tim perched on the edge of the desk. "I hear Parnell's wife and daughter are back. "Who's doing the interviews?" Tim's innocent question brought a snort of disgust from John.

"Ken, Bobby and Susan."

Tim, pretending ignorance, threw a verbal hand grenade into the conversation. "Good choice. They have to run free some time, I can't imagine anyone better than Ken to get inside the wife's head. I almost feel sorry for her."

Ballard agreed. "So do I, plus Susan will be excellent with the daughter. She's great with kids. I've watched her with her partner's two daughters, she's a natural." John stood, humphing his displeasure before stomping towards the kitchen to make a cup of tea.

Tim chatted with Ballard for several minutes, confirming he would be attending the BBQ, then headed upstairs to the Serious Crime Task Force. When John returned his expression was concerned. "If the daughter *is* able to finger Mario's hit-man, how do we handle this?" Ballard looked hard at him.

John continued. "I know you've thought about it, the risk of dredging up a dangerous situation. At the moment the guy, whoever he is, thinks everything has died down. Even if the daughter does flush him out, all we have is a piddly hit-run… nothing more. We can't make the regular cash payments from Mario stick, unless he was stupid enough to bank them each time and that's unlikely. On top of that we'll never be able to prove he was the muscle lurking in the shadows, so the most he'll get is a year in the can for the hit-run, *if* we're lucky"

Ballard's brow furrowed and the look on his face bordered on anguish. "I know where you're heading on this John, that we should consider letting any ID from the daughter drop."

John glanced over his shoulder towards Delwyn's office. "Got it in one Mike. It's all very well being hairy chested about this, but the bastard will be back on the street in no time. Then you, Natalie and the kids will be sitting ducks while Parnell's wife and daughter are tucked away snug-as-a-bug in witness protection. You need to be very careful on this old son."

"I can assure you John it hasn't left my mind. The trouble is,

the decision whether or not to proceed isn't going to be mine."
John looked troubled as he took another mouthful of tea.

Ballard stood and waved at Ken, Bobby and Susan before
heading towards the kitchen. "Time for something to eat John."

While they were devouring their meals Ballard gave everyone
a condensed version of his trip to Bordertown. Throughout the
lunch Ken kept checking his watch. Bobby and Susan glanced at
each other, deciding they couldn't endure his nervous agitation
any longer. Standing, they gathered their food scraps.

"Time to go Ken. Best we get there a few minutes early."

The relief on Ken's face was immediate. He joined them at
the sink while they washed their utensils, then, collecting their
notes they headed out as a group, waving casually at Ballard and
John in the process. With a trace of mischief Ballard called, "Don't
leave any stone unturned Ken." Ken blinked, understanding the
seriousness of the task.

John leaned over and growled in Ballard's ear. "I hope you
bloody well know what you're doing."

Ballard took a long sip from his glass of water. "No doubt
in my mind John. They'll do a great job, trust me." John bit
savagely into his ham and lettuce sandwich, masticating the food
over and over before swallowing.

The next three hours were testing for both men, accustomed
to always being in charge. Leaving such important interviews to
less experienced detectives was a new but necessary experience.
Ballard shuffled through paperwork while John sat for the most
part sighing as though in physical pain.

As the hours dragged on each began to grate on the other's
nerves, finally agreeing they should separate to do their own
thing until the trio returned.

CHAPTER
36

The demeanor of the young detective's when they arrived back on the floor was mixed. The strain of obtaining the statement from Parnell's wife was etched on Ken's face; he looked thoroughly drained. Bobby was the complete opposite, all twitch and fidget, on a high, bursting to give his version of events. Susan, while pleased with herself, as usual kept her emotions in check.

Everyone stepped into the conference room and Ballard and John opened their day books to a blank page. Ballard took the lead. "Ok Ken, you and Bobby interviewed the wife, right?" This was confirmed with a nod. "What was her demeanour like?"

Ken surprised everyone by answering without staring at the ceiling or filling his lungs to bursting point. "Very detached. My guess is she's been under so much mental strain for the last six to eight weeks there's nothing left in the tank."

Bobby joined in. "Too right and I can tell you Ken was bloody fantastic. Got her onside straight away, she was eating out of his hand. I've learned heaps about how to conduct these types of interviews by watching him." Ken looked embarrassed, but remained silent.

John, showed impatience at what he considered irrelevant

veneration. "Did she know about the threat to her husband and family?"

Bobby deferred to Ken who answered. "She did, but only in the last few months. She told us that for some time she'd suspected there was something dark in her husband's past. When she found out he hadn't done anything criminal, that it was someone threatening her family, she was alarmed at the situation but relieved her husband wasn't a 'bad' guy.

John expressed his disgust. "I'm assuming she knows he tortured and killed Bivelaqua, kicked the shit out of Michael, as well as viciously belted Kathryn?"

"Yep, she's aware of all that *now* and is very distressed by it. Parnell told her before he did the deed on Bivelaqua that he was going to find out who the hit-man was, once and for all. Hearing this she panicked and took off overseas with her daughter. She saw the TV coverage of what happened at the factory and at Michael's farm while she was in Italy, said it was the most horrible experience of her life."

Ballard sat with his elbows propped on the table, the tips of his fingers, other than those encased in the protective cover, massaging his forehead. "Did she say whether she knew who the hit-man was and more to the point, does she know if Parnell got it out of Bivelaqua?"

This time Ken did fill his lungs before glancing up. "In my opinion I don't think she knows, but I can't be certain. She claims once she left Melbourne she never spoke to her husband again. What do you think Bobby?"

"I agree. I'm certain she's on the up and up. So we still don't know whether Parnell found out, irrelevant I guess now he's dead." He looked self consciously at Ballard who waved a dismissive hand.

"No point being coy about it Bobby. I did what I did. What about her husband's personality after his brother died in jail, anything mentioned on that front?"

Bobby nodded vigorously. "Yes, she said he changed overnight. Began drinking like a fish and just wasn't the same man she married. Put a huge strain on their relationship and was one of the factors in her deciding to go overseas with the daughter. I got the feeling she was planning to leave him even before the Bivelaqua issue came to a head."

Ken took the initiative, providing a brief summary of the interview. "Dina, er Mrs Parnell appears to be the innocent party in all this. She's mortified at her husband's actions, as well as terrified by the prospect there's still someone out there who may want to kill her and her daughter. We talked at length about witness protection and while she's very reluctant to vanish from the friends she and her daughter currently know, she understands why it's necessary."

Ballard looked up from his note taking. "Why didn't they stay in Italy?"

Bobby shook his head, bewildered. "Kids! The daughter went nuts over there and threatened to run away. The mother also realised that if the Italian police could find her, so to could the hit-man.

"Despite wanting to come back to Melbourne, Diana the daughter bitched about the restriction of entering witness protection. I'd hate to have to handle her case – it'd be a nightmare."

Ballard tapped his folder with his pen. "Do you think they'll stay in the program?"

Ken shrugged. "I know the mother will, she's terrified, but when the daughter gets a bit older, I wouldn't be surprised if she doesn't pack her bags."

Ballard and John exchanged looks, digesting the information.

Susan shuffled in her chair, drawing Ballard's attention. "Well Ms Deakin, how did you fare with the daughter?"

Susan shrugged in exasperation as she referred to her notes. "Diana Parnell, fifteen, going on thirty-five. Intelligent, spoilt to the point of being obnoxious. Has *never* heard the word no. The type of kid who by the age of three would have learned that by making a big enough scene, she could manipulate her parent's behaviour."

John snorted. "Come on Susan, tell us what you *really* think of her."

Ballard grinned at John before turning back to Susan. "What did she know about the threat to the family, before everything blew up?"

"Nothing by my reckoning. The parents kept her wrapped in cotton wool, she's an only child with a very unhealthy outlook on life." She shuddered. "God she was irritating, but despite all that I feel very sorry for her. I mean it's not her fault the world's falling apart around her."

Ballard sat upright in his chair, drawing a similar breath to Ken before asking the elephant-in-the-room question. "Did she see the driver who knocked her down?"

Susan hesitated, knowing the importance of her answer and the pain it would invoke. "Yes. Very clearly, it all happened near a pedestrian crossing and while it was night time, everything happened directly under street lights. According to her it unfolded in slow motion. She claims she had nightmares for weeks.

"As we thought, when she was first interviewed by police she clammed up because her dad warned her the guy might come back for revenge. The father never let on the real reason why she shouldn't describe the driver to the police."

John chose not to look at Ballard. "Has she been to the Identification Unit to develop an image of the guy for iFace?"

"Not yet, but I spoke with the Witness Protection chaps and that's on their agenda."

Ballard arched his back, attempting to relieve the tension in his neck.

"Anything else Susan, something that might throw light on the guy? Perhaps a conversation she might've overheard between her parents?"

"Sorry Michael. Nothing at all. She's a frightened young kid, angry that she's going to be separated from her school friends and will have to live this artificial existence for God knows how long."

Even John appeared sympathetic as to how unfair life was proving to be for the wife and daughter. "Hell of a price to pay for a threat that may never eventuate."

There was a polite tap on the conference room door and Delwyn's disembodied head appeared around the side. "Ok if I come in for an update?" Everyone waved her into the room.

Ken, Bobby and Susan gave a concise version of events and on completion Delwyn looked hard at Ballard. "Let's take this one step at a time Michael. At the moment Parnell's muscle isn't aware the mother and daughter have spoken with police. He may not know they've returned from Italy, perhaps he doesn't even know they went. Let's see what iFace brings up before we jump to conclusions."

Ballard appreciated the difficult decision she had to confront should the database flush out a suspect.

Snapping her folder shut Delwyn acknowledged the junior

detectives. "Fabulous work guys. Make sure everything goes into your statements and once the mother and daughter have signed them, get them to John so he can submit the inquest brief." Turning to her senior detectives she asked, "Will we beat Christmas?"

John answered. "I've a contact at the Coroners Court. I'll give the brief a hurry along so we *should* make it."

"Tremendous effort everyone." She looked across at Ballard and issued a direct order. "Go home Michael." Turning, she was gone.

Ballard addressed his three detectives before they left the room. "Delwyn beat me to it, well done all of you. Make sure you get those statements in as soon as possible." He looked across at John, inviting a response.

John shuffled uncomfortably. "Ok, so I had some doubts. I was…" his voice trailed away.

Ballard kept him on the hook. "Yes John?"

"I was… er, I was…" He screwed his eyes shut. "I was *wrong*."

"There now, that wasn't too hard was it?"

John answered by glaring at Ballard before stomping from the room. Everyone looked after him, grinning.

CHAPTER
37

Forty minutes later Ballard was sitting in the Chrysler heading back to the farm in peak hour traffic. His spirits were up, not concerned his average speed was less than thirty kilometres an hour.

He had left with Ken, Susan and Bobby promising they would finish their statements before going home; John threatening them with a fate worse than death if they didn't.

Pulling into the garage he sat for a moment reflecting on the day's activities and how the Parnell issue was coming to a close. He turned over in his mind John's warning regarding the hit-man and the spectre it cast over his life and that of Natalie and the children. The guilt of placing them in this situation chipped away at his previous high spirits.

Over the next three days he longed for Natalie's company and save for the evening phone calls, the days blurred into one. As a consequence he poured himself even harder into his chores which included mulching trees, mowing, weeding the island on the lake, cleaning windows and generally churning through his list of tasks with a purpose that even he admitted bordered on compulsive.

He knew the time would come when it was physically impossible to achieve what he was currently capable of and he recognised the frustration that would generate. As a consequence he enjoyed performing the current work that many would consider onerous.

Mid afternoon on the third day his mobile rang, it was John. "Mike, mate, want some good news about the inquest? I know this is short notice but my contact tells me the case can be slotted in the day after tomorrow, *if* we can rustle the witnesses together." He hesitated as though waiting for a response before continuing.

"The list is pretty basic… you, me, Tim Robbins and Gerald Matthews the pathologist. That's it. Kathryn's been spared, they only need her statement. Oh… Parnell's wife and daughter won't be required. Their statements were enough and under the circumstances the Coroner doesn't want them exposed. What does the quick turn around tell you old son?"

Ballard opened his mouth to respond but John pushed on. "They want this over lickety-split. Mate this will be done and dusted within the hour – thank Christ."

His voice took on a conspiratorial tone. "Now I've taken the liberty to ring around and Tim said he's free. I mentioned you and I wouldn't miss it for the world." He chortled at his own joke. "I rang Gerald and he said he can hold off on his scheduled autopsy for an hour or so. We can help him out by requesting his evidence be flicked to the head of the queue. Mate, we're good to go if you are. I said I'd ring back first thing in the morning, so what do you say?" This time he did wait for an answer.

Ballard's reply was brief. "Go for it."

John hung up, chuckling.

Ballard felt a weight lift from his shoulders as he called

Kathryn to relay the news she wouldn't have to attend. She was thrilled and jumbled her words saying so, punctuating how much she had been dreading the prospect of giving evidence. Her voice trembled as she thanked him over and over.

On a high, Ballard rang Natalie, telling her he would be at the town house by 6.30 the following evening. He gave a brief account of his conversation with John, deciding to limit the news until he arrived to speak with her in person.

Natalie avoided asking specific work related questions; instead they chatted about the wedding plans and possible honeymoon options before wishing each other goodnight.

Throughout the next day time couldn't go fast enough. After a stand-at-the-sink lunch Ballard worked for another three hours before calling a halt. Foregoing a workout in the gym, he chose instead a punishing session in the squash court. Chest heaving he headed for the shower and by 5 p.m. was dressed in an old but clean track suit.

He left a brief note for Vera before selecting a change of clothes for the morning, laying them on the back seat of the Chrysler. Plucking a rose from the bushes along the veranda he placed it on the console. Ten minutes later he was on the highway, heading towards Melbourne.

Ringing Natalie he informed her he was on the way before settling down to concentrate on the drive; the rumble of the motor music to his ears.

Pulling into Natalie's garage, Ballard hoped he had parked without her hearing his arrival. He picked up the rose before creeping to the door leading into the hallway. With infinite care he turned the handle, planning to surprise her in the kitchen or upstairs. Pulling the door partially open, he lifted his foot to step inside at the exact moment Natalie sprang out in front of him. Laughing, they collapsed into each other's arms.

"How on earth did you imagine you could bring that monster into the garage without the town house shaking?"

"I assume we *are* talking about the Chrysler?"

Natalie thumped him on the shoulder with an open hand. "Michael! Behave."

Ballard shrugged, conceding his humour was lame. "School boy stuff huh? Have I ever told you how I used to sneak up on Kathryn in the dark at the farm in Bordertown. She hated it, but I thought it was a hoot."

"Well *don't* do it to me."

Ballard kissed the tip of her nose. "Ok, a deal."

"Really?" The slight hesitation in his voice had her remaining sceptical.

Whipping the rose from behind his back he proffered it as a peace offering; an instant later the crush of her lips against his indicated her acceptance.

After dinner they sat together in the lounge. As Kayla and Josh were on school camp they had the town house to themselves. Ballard detailed the conversation he had with John and the fact the inquest was about to happen.

"It's great news Kathryn won't have to give evidence. As John said, her written statement was enough."

Tilting her head to one side Natalie commented, "What I don't understand is why there has to be an inquest at all. There's been an autopsy for the factory owner as well as Parnell. On top of that Parnell left a note confessing to the killing *and* he detailed to you what he did. There's a dozen police witnesses who can vouch you were acting in self defence while protecting Kathryn at the gorge – I mean what more can an inquest hope to…"

Ballard pressed a finger against her lips. "Public perceptions have a lot to do with it darling. Now, without getting too technical about inquests, it's mandatory under the Coroners Act that there be one if a person dies violently in police custody..."

"But Parnell *wasn't* in your custody. Quite the reverse."

Ballard agreed, acknowledging Natalie's frustration. "Tell me about it. However, despite that there were eight SOG police aiming high powered rifles at his head at the time. The public have a right to know formally that what happened was above board, not be limited to potentially distorted information via the media."

"Can anyone attend the hearing?"

Ballard confirmed they could. "Generally inquests *are* an open forum and it's doubtful a great deal of new evidence will come to light due to the press coverage. Thankfully Parnell's wife and daughter don't have to attend. Their statements are on the brief, but only to give background information regarding Parnell's state of mind.

"The fact that Bivelaqu had a stand-over man lurking in the wings ensures details about them won't be raised or made available to the public, especially as they'll be entering witness protection. To answer your question, I've a feeling the Coroner will play it safe and order a closed hearing, in case sensitive details *do* come to light. Eventually his written findings will be made public – minus any facts that might endanger anyone."

Natalie's natural thirst for knowledge came to the fore. "I've never been to an inquest, what actually happens?"

Ballard's features lightened as he recalled an event early in his career.

"What's so funny?" Natalie asked, intrigued.

"Promise you won't laugh when I tell you?"

"Cross my heart."

"Well, it was either the first or second year after I graduated from the Academy, I found myself on door duty at the Coroners Court. That means monitoring what happens in the public gallery, calling witnesses when directed, that sort of thing."

He chuckled, thinking back to the incident. "I can't recall the name of the deceased, but I remember being directed to call a particular witness, well you know my memory for names. I stepped outside the court and bellowed out the name three times as we were taught. When I returned I stated in my most commanding voice, 'No appearance your Honour.'"

Natalie nodded, despite being unsure where the story was heading.

"Well, all hell broke loose in the court; the deceased's relatives began sobbing uncontrollably while the Coroner looked at me as though I'd dropped in from another planet. I hadn't a clue what was going on.

"In a voice dripping with sarcasm he said, 'Constable, of course there's no appearance, the name you called out is the *deceased!*'"

A hoot of laughter escaped Natalie's lips before she could smother it with a hand. "How awful! What did you say?"

Ballard shrugged. "I couldn't say anything. I just stumbled outside again and called out the right name and didn't make eye contact with anyone for the rest of the inquest." Natalie attempted to keep her amusement in check.

Ballard's expression turned serious. "The Coroner's role is to identify the person or persons who've died, not an issue in Parnell's case, as well as determine *how* he died, including the cause and circumstances. In this instance the cause is self evident and the circumstances will be thrashed out during the inquest.

"The other thing about inquests is they're inquisitorial not adversarial. On top of that the Coroner doesn't attribute blame. If there's a criminal trial pending, that has to be finalised before the inquest. There's no criminal case here because the offender is dead, hence the reason I'm good to go tomorrow. It would've been earlier but we wanted statements from Parnell's wife and daughter's on the brief."

Natalie looked thoughtful as she absorbed the information. Sensing Ballard's preoccupation with the inquest in the morning she kissed him gently before leading him upstairs. Once in bed they embraced each other as though for the first time; then, with their passion sated, they lay curled in each other's arms, drifting off to sleep.

CHAPTER
38

At 9.30 the next morning John parked the police car in the reserved area of the Coroners Court. Ballard stepped out with a copy of the inquest brief sandwiched in his day book. John activated the vehicle's security before both men turned and headed towards the main entrance.

A car horn sounded twice behind them. Looking around they saw Tim scrambling from his vehicle one row back. Jogging up to them his face broke into a grin. "Glad I caught you both, thought it might be nice to walk in as a united front."

Ballard nodded in appreciation while John's expression showed his gratitude that Tim should think to support Ballard in such a way, despite his partner's repeated claims the inquest was just a formality. "Thanks Tim. Always a nice touch and can't hurt our cause. Thankfully Nashy's conducted a lot of our inquests in the past and knows how we operate." John was referring to James D Nash, a veteran Coroner with over thirty years experience and known nationally and internationally as a 'straight shooter'.

Walking up the steps they entered the building, heading over to reception. Showing their identification they signed the visitor's book, indicating they were required in court three. The receptionist, flashing pearl white teeth, pointed them in the general direction, not realising they had given evidence in that very court many times before.

Stepping inside they proceeded to the seats behind the legal representative's table. Police Sergeant Anthony Burton, a member of the Police Coronial Advisory Unit and known to all three officers, sat hunched at the table thumbing through the inquest brief.

His responsibilities were to oversee reportable deaths within Victoria in accordance with the Coroners Act; in addition he was required to provide information about all aspects of coronial investigations. He swivelled in his chair to face them.

"Good to see you guys, well the circumstances *could* be better, but don't let that worry you. This shouldn't take too long."

Ballard leaned forward, speaking in the lowered voice all court rooms engendered, a respect as old as the legal profession itself. "Gerald Matthews, the pathologist is giving evidence this morning Tony, are you able to bump him up to first spot? That way he can get back to some must-do autopsies on his plate?"

Without hesitating Anthony rose and walked over to the Registrar, whispering in his ear. Both men conferred before Anthony returned, giving Ballard a thumbs up. Five minutes later Gerald entered and sat down alongside them.

For the next fifteen minutes people filed into the courtroom; Ballard noted the majority were well known reporters. He looked across at Anthony who muttered under his breath, "Closed court as opposed to suppression order, five bucks." Ballard smiled tightly before sitting back, waiting.

Without warning the Registrar stood bolt upright. "Silence in the court, all rise. The Coroner, his Honour James D Nash is now presiding." Seconds later the Coroner entered the room. Everyone stood, bowing their heads in respect, another age old custom that John often joked would continue forever.

The Coroner, wearing a grey suit, white shirt and navy blue tie sat down with the gallery following. His hair as white as his shirt, he looked like a slimmer version of Colonel Sanders. He shuffled a number of papers into position then interlocking his fingers, rested his forearms on the table. Peering over his glasses he addressed everyone present.

"Good morning ladies and gentlemen. Thank you for attending." He hesitated as he looked about him. "The circumstances surrounding this inquest have been widely reported in the news. I note they're still generating interest by the fact so many of you here today are from the media.

"Unfortunately I have an immediate decision to make you won't like." Again he hesitated as he looked sternly at the attendees. "My dilemma is whether to invoke a suppression order or to request a closed session. The circumstances requiring me to consider these options are centred around the physical safety of a mother and her fifteen year old daughter.

"While I'm mindful of the fact inquests are attended by the public and the media for reasons of openness and fairness, if there's the slightest possibility of information being divulged that may jeopardise the safety of any individual or individuals, especially a child, I will always err on the side of caution."

Ballard noted the look of resignation on the faces of the press, their body language betraying their feelings as their shoulders slumped.

The Coroner continued. "As a consequence I'm directing this inquest to be conducted as a closed court, with only those persons who are required to give evidence to remain. My findings will be published in due course and made available on the usual public forums, however specific names and facts will be suppressed." He glanced at the Registrar who stood and requested the non relevant parties to leave.

Within minutes the only people remaining were the Coroner, the Registrar, Ballard, John, Tim, Gerald Matthews and Anthony Burton. The Coroner glanced around the room. "Well that's cleared out the non-essentials." Grinning, everyone acknowledged his decisive action.

Anthony stood and addressed the Coroner. "Your Honour, a small matter of scheduling. Mr Matthews the pathologist has a number of pressing autopsies, as such we respectfully ask that his evidence be listed first."

The Coroner waved an acknowledging hand. "Granted. I'm aware of Mr Matthews' workload and I can see no reason to detain him longer than necessary."

He picked up a file which Ballard assumed was Gerald's pathology report, perusing it momentarily. "I don't need to remind anyone here the purpose of an inquest is to identify the person who died and to determine the circumstances under which their death occurred. As always Mr Matthews' report is succinct but thorough. I note the deceased, Eric Edward Parnell has been identified by numerous sources, including dental records and DNA verification, therefore that requirement is resolved.

"Furthermore the physical cause of his death was massive head, chest and internal injuries, a result of falling approximately twenty-five metres onto a rock ledge with death almost certainly instantaneous."

He sat for a moment in deep thought. "Mr Matthews, because of the thoroughness of your report I wasn't going to call you to give evidence, however I've changed my mind. I've several questions I *would* like you to clarify." He turned to the Registrar. "Please swear Mr Matthews in."

Less than a minute later Gerald was sitting in the witness stand having given the oath. With his report read aloud to the court by the Registrar, Gerald sat looking expectantly at the Coroner.

"Mr Matthews the physical cause of death is obvious, however in my written findings I'd like to state with utmost certainty there were no extenuating circumstances that may have influenced Mr Parnell's actions preceding his death.

"Firstly, the shots fired by the Special Operations Group officers didn't strike Mr Parnell's body, is that correct?"

Gerald's reply was crisp. "Yes, your Honour."

The Coroner looked across at Tim as he made his next statement. "Mr Robbins you'll be giving evidence in a minute and can clarify this situation. I believe you waited until the very last moment to give the order to shoot and it was at that precise instant Mr Parnell slipped backwards, precipitating his fall onto the ledge?" Tim stated this was the case.

The Coroner turned back to Gerald. "The issue I want to be crystal clear on and will detail in my findings is whether there were underlying medical reasons for the deceased's earlier actions – no drugs in his bloodstream, no disease in his brain that could be identified via an autopsy, such as Paget's disease, meningitis, a brain tumor, past exposure to STDs or liver disease brought on by excessive alcohol consumption. Please don't consider this request for clarification as my telling you how to do your job Mr Matthews. Rather it is to refute possible public perception that the deceased's actions were influenced by *anything* outside his control."

Gerald shook his head. "Certainly not your Honour." He

looked at his audience before continuing. "It's a very valid point you raise. As a consequence I took specific care in assessing the toxicology and serology samples, noting in particular the general health of the brain tissue to identify any evidence of pre-existing conditions which may have impacted on or contributed to the deceased's mental capacity and subsequent actions."

He shrugged expansively. "There were none. The deceased did have alcohol in his blood and it would appear he'd been drinking significant amounts over a short period of time. By my estimate it was over the last three to six months due to what I determined to be mild, *recent* damage to his liver. Despite that, the deceased appeared to be in excellent health and had a muscular physique."

"In your expert opinion Mr Matthews was there anything to indicate the deceased's actions were beyond his cognitive control?"

"No, your Honour."

The Coroner sat digesting the information while everyone in the courtroom remained fascinated by the exchanges. Gerald sat patiently in the witness stand, confident of his ability to answer any question that may be directed to him.

Spurred into action the Coroner began to write copious notes during which he looked up, apologising to Gerald. "Please bear with me Mr Matthews. As I'm getting older I find I have to write down complex issues the moment I think of them, otherwise I risk them vanishing from my mind without a trace." Gerald's expression remained neutral, content to sit and wait.

The Coroner finished writing and looked up, stunning everyone by dismissing Gerald from the witness stand. "Thank you Mr Matthews, I compliment you on your thorough report and appreciate the effort you've put into your findings." He looked around the courtroom. "I don't need to remind you this is a high profile inquest and my findings will have a national and international audience, hence my need for specific verification. Mr Matthews you're excused from any further proceedings in this inquest. Thank you for your attendance."

Gerald stood and after bowing his head respectfully, strode from the room, winking at Ballard and John as he walked past. They smiled back, grateful for his contribution.

"Right Mr Robbins, you're next." The Coroner directed his gaze at Tim as he pointed to the witness stand. The Registrar administered the oath then read Tim's statement to the court.

Peering over the rim of his glasses the Coroner stared at Tim for several seconds. "Mr Robbins I won't pretend to understand the complexity of managing a siege situation, particularly where a police officer's sister is held hostage and the threat of an explosive device is present.

"That said I'm assuming it was unusual to allow the hostage's brother," he pointed towards Ballard, "into the house to attempt the rescue?"

Tim replied with confidence and without hesitation. "Yes, your Honour. In my fifteen years experience I can't remember this having ever been the case."

The Coroner paused, deep in thought. "Indeed. In your own words Mr Robbins, please detail why it was necessary to take this course of action as opposed to your team rescuing Ms Ballard."

It was clear from Tim's expression he had been expecting this question, fully appreciating how his answer would influence public perception regarding whether the police acted appropriately under the circumstances.

"At the time of the decision your Honour, we had limited

facts. What we *did* know was Ms Ballard was being held against her will and was not in a position to free herself – photos taken and forwarded by the deceased, Eric Parnell, confirmed this.

"We were also aware from a prior conversation Parnell had with Detective Inspector Ballard that he'd committed a recent murder. The photos showed he had an explosive device and was carrying a detonator to trigger it remotely. We also knew he'd threatened to activate the device unless Inspector Ballard attended the house alone, unarmed and within the hour.

"What we didn't know was whether the device or detonator were real. Standard police protocol in these circumstances is to proceed with the belief the threat is genuine and that Parnell would activate the bomb if his demands were not met. If Inspector Ballard hadn't been an experienced police officer, or wasn't trained in siege situations, we wouldn't have allowed him to attempt the rescue."

He hesitated long enough for the Coroner to squeeze in a question. "Under the circumstances Mr Robbins... and I don't envy the decision you had to make, did you consider it to be the lower risk option as opposed to your team attempting the rescue?"

"Yes, your Honour."

"Would you make the same decision again?"

"If Inspector Ballard was the person attempting the rescue, then yes. His familiarity of his own home and its surroundings, along with my understanding of his ability to act rationally under extreme pressure made this the logical decision, albeit a difficult one." Tim stared into the distance, as though reliving the moment. "The fact my men had no direct line of sight to Parnell inside the house made it an unavoidable decision."

The Coroner wrote feverishly for almost a minute. "Thank

you Mr Robbins. One last question, was the device able to be detonated."

Again Tim responded without hesitation. "Our experts believe it *could* have been. It did contain explosive material, however the activating mechanism and the detonator were damaged from the fall onto the rocks and as such there was no way of knowing definitively if it was wired correctly. There's no evidence to suggest it wasn't capable of being activated. By that I mean all the wiring and connections contained in the device were those necessary to produce an explosion, but they weren't intact when examined."

The Coroner looked thoughtful. "Thank you Mr Robbins, I realise the difficult decision you had to make. I also understand you left the command to fire at Mr Parnell until the very last second, literally. Again that must have been a stressful situation for you." The faintest of smiles appeared on his face. "Especially as your officers missed their target due to Mr Parnell slipping backwards at that precise moment." Tim's face remained expressionless, aware he was the subject of a light hearted dig.

The Coroner shuffled together his copy of Tim's statement before placing it to one side. "I find your actions throughout the siege appropriate and commendable. You may step down." A look of relief flickered across Tim's face as he headed back to his seat. Ballard nudged John, whispering, "Your turn and *keep your cool!*"

To everyone's surprise, especially John's, the Coroner looked directly at Ballard. "Mr Ballard, if you would be so kind as to take the witness stand." Moving promptly Ballard was sworn in by the Registrar; he sat motionless while his statement was read to the court.

"Mr Ballard, you were faced with a life and death decision

whether to allow the Special Operation Group rescue your sister, or risk your own life in an attempt to secure her safety. How did you come to the decision you made?"

Ballard had previously decided not to rehearse his answers, choosing instead to respond as spontaneously as he could. "Your Honour the decision was made for me. Eric Parnell had confessed to brutally murdering a factory owner several days prior. Further to that he stated to me I was to do *exactly* as he instructed or my sister would be killed. His demands meant I had to attend at my home in a specified time, alone and unarmed or my sister would die."

"Your decision meant you were prepared to risk your life attempting to save your sister?"

"Yes, your Honour."

"As obvious as this question may seem, at any time were you in a position to affect an arrest on Eric Parnell."

Ballard ran a hand over his face, the bruises not yet fading into his tan. "Unfortunately not your Honour. It was a rather one-sided affair until the very last second – the fact he had a weapon and an explosive device, plus a detonator, dramatically placed the odds in his favour."

"Finally, in your mind was there any course of action that could have been adopted that would have resulted in securing your sister's safety *and* capture Eric Parnell alive?"

"No, none that was evident to me under the circumstances."

Again the Coroner wrote furiously before looking up at Ballard. "An extremely courageous act for which I commend you. It was also a selfless act that I'm sure your sister will be eternally grateful for. Mr Ballard you are excused."

Ballard sat motionless, not believing that after such a build up the inquest was now over. He returned to his seat in a daze, realising the process had been as much a formality for the public as it was a fact finding necessity.

The Coroner looked expansively around the court as though it were brimming with witnesses and members of the public, instead of just the four police officers and the Registrar. "My written finding will be made available in due course, however as this is a closed hearing, I feel I'm able to verbalise my thoughts more openly than were it not. The death of any member of the public as a consequence of police actions always generates public attention, concern and scrutiny as it should.

"Be that as it may, in this instance the measures adopted by the police officers involved were exemplary and a testament to their training, their dedication to public service and their individual courage. One man's bravery clearly stands out and I only wish I had the strength of character Mr Ballard displayed on that fateful day.

"In conclusion, I find the death of Eric Edward Parnell to be the result of multiple injuries incurred from falling from a significant height onto a rock ledge in Jackson's Creek, Gisborne; the fall a direct outcome of his own reckless actions. This court is adjourned." The Registrar barked the order for everyone to rise. The Coroner stood and after bowing, left the court.

John turned to Ballard, shaking his hand vigorously. "Congratulations old son. Told you it'd be a piece of cake. No thanks to *my* evidence." Tim and Anthony Burton joined in, pumping Ballard's hand while the Registrar winked before leaving.

Ballard couldn't think of anything appropriate to say, continuing to look dazed as Tim and John led him from the court.

CHAPTER
39

Arriving back in the office Ballard and John gave Delwyn a concise version of the morning's events. Her face beaming with relief as she scrambled from behind her desk to wrap Ballard in a lingering hug. "Splendid news Michael. Life for you and Kathryn… and Natalie for that matter can return to normal." Ballard noted she refrained from mentioning Bivelaqua's hitman; as a consequence he chose not to spoil the moment.

As he and John were about to leave, Delwyn placed a hand on his shoulder. "*Now* will you stay on sick leave?" He opened his mouth to protest but she insisted. "That's a genuine request Michael. Oh, before I forget, I'll see you at the BBQ on Sunday." Mumbling his thanks he backed out of her office and headed over to his desk.

As he pulled out his chair he noticed John slide an A4 sheet of paper under a folder, the look on his face uncharacteristically innocent. Years of witnessing every nuance of his partner's psyche triggered immediate curiosity. He decided to test his suspicion.

"What's that?"

"What's what?" John's face remained deadpan.

Bingo! Ballard knew something was afoot. John looked at

him, shrugging before sighing in defeat. "Ok. It's the Face-fit Parnell's daughter came up with."

"And?"

"And you're supposed to be on sick leave."

Ballard leaned forward conspiratorially. "John, let *me* worry about my sick leave, ok? Now, *were there any matches*?"

"Three."

"Three!" Ballard registered surprise as he reached over and began studying the image, noting the square, cruel features.

"Yep. One guys been in goal for over six months, so we can rule him out. One's an ex-merchant banker on white collar fraud and physically Sonia could take him out with one arm tied behind her back."

Ballard waved the photo in his hand. "And this one – this is the winner at the Teddy Bear's picnic?"

"Correctamundo. Fits the bill whichever way you look at it. Priors for assault, although nothing recent. Built like a brick shithouse with one piece of evidence locking him in… a partial fingerprint."

Ballard inclined his head, confused. John continued. "Once we pulled this guy's record we ran his prints against the dozens we lifted from Bivelaqua's factory. Guess what, out popped a partial match.

"At the time of the murder none of the factory prints on their own were complete enough to link to any specific offender record. Face-fit pointed us to a record with attached prints which then enabled us to link one of the factory prints as a possible match. Not perfect, but it all adds to the circumstantial evidence we're gathering on this bugger."

Ballard joined the dots. "So the print proves he's been to Mario's factory and the daughter has pinged him for driving the car that bowled her over. From there it's a small leap of faith to say he's the hit-man."

"Couldn't have put it better myself." Both men slapped their hands together in a celebratory high five. John grimaced. "Damn Yank habit. When did we Aussies start doing that?" Ballard shrugged in defeat.

Still eyeing John with caution Ballard decided to push further. "There's more isn't there?"

John looked exasperated. "I guess this is the price I pay for working with you for so many years, we can't keep secrets. Well, you're right, the surveillance unit have begun tracking this guy, got his current address through VicRoads. Williams... Darrell Albert Williams, forty-two years old. Surveillance are building a places-frequented profile on him as we speak."

He shuffled amongst his papers and found what he was looking for, a hand written Information Field Report. "Apparently this guy drinks at the Tankerville Arms in Nicholson Street Fitzroy on Wednesdays and Fridays, regular as clockwork, usually between 6 and 11p.m. Lives up the road from the pub in a small renovated terrace house, less than a five minute walk away. Not clear *where* or *if* he works."

"Car?"

"Yep, but don't get your hopes up. Red Mazda coupe. Not the vehicle Parnell's daughter saw when she was run down."

"Married?"

"We don't think so."

"Kids?"

John's shrug matched his previous reply.

Ballard sat back, taking in the information. "What now?"

John continued to look uncomfortable, a result of having been sworn to secrecy yet torn between the direct order and his loyalty to Ballard. He shrugged again, obviously making a decision. "The fingerprint got us over the line for a warrant, so surveillance can go in and install a bug, perhaps even a camera."

Ballard responded. "So with today being Wednesday and him down at the pub where he can be kept under observation, well, knock me down with a feather – they could do it tonight."

"Not funny Mike." John looked anxious. "If Delwyn finds out I've told you this I'm in big trouble. Keeping you out of the investigation was for your own good. You... *we* can't be involved with this guy getting picked up. If we're in the mix when he's arrested and something goes pear shaped and he's injured or killed, then the public will automatically assume this is unfinished business from the gorge, that the force has rogue cops operating within its ranks."

Ballard conceded John's statement. "I know, I know, public perceptions can be a bitch. I'll control myself and not hook up on this one, *I give you my word*!" John's worried expression eased marginally, then immediately returned when he saw Delwyn glaring at him from her office door.

He punched Ballard on the arm, breaking into an extended forced laugh; through clenched teeth he hissed, "*Join in!*"

Ballard obliged. Not entirely convinced, Delwyn retreated back into her office as John wiped imaginary sweat from his brow. "Ok, that's it. I'm done."

Ballard stood and extended a hand. "Thank you John, for everything. Now, one last favour."

John grimaced, knowing what was about to be asked.

"When it's time to snap cuffs on this prick, give me a call beforehand. I'd like to be there – *in the background of course* – so I can look him in the eye."

John's pained expression intensified, but he nodded anyway.

"Doesn't change anything Mike. We still have stuff-all on him and there's no hope of any lengthy goal term."

Ballard packed his briefcase as he spoke. "Maybe not, but that's out of my hands I'll just have to deal with whatever risks float to the surface. Natalie understands this and we both accept we'll have to live with it. Such is life."

CHAPTER
40

Ballard eased the Chrysler through peak hour traffic on Toorak road as he voice activated Kathryn's mobile to give her the good news regarding the inquest. To his amazement she broke down sobbing, her tears slicing through him like a knife. Feeling inadequate he offered words of comfort as best he could.

"Don't worry, these are happy tears. I know that sounds ridiculous to someone like you, but it's true. Now go and hug Natalie." There was a brief silence. "Michael, I can't thank you enough for everything you've done."

Ballard forced his voice to be upbeat, despite the sting in his eyes. "Hang in there Sis. I'll be in touch."

Eager to pass on the morning's events he rang Natalie.

"Is this my future husband calling? How did everything go?"

"Nat I can't believe how quickly it finished, the Coroner really cut to the chase. The police force, I guess by default that means me, have no case to answer…"

"I should think not!"

He chuckled. "Settle down tiger."

"No I won't! You risked your life to save Kathryn. For the system to put you through all this scrutiny…"

"It goes with the territory."

Natalie drew a deep breath. "Sorry Michael, no, it's wonderful news. I'm so happy everything is now behind you, behind *us*. Does Kathryn know?"

Ballard gave a brief account of the conversation with his sister before indicating he would be there in ten minutes and was in a celebratory mood. Arriving at the town house he glanced at the console clock, noting it was 6 p.m. His mind wandered momentarily, contemplating whether the hit-man was walking along Nicholson Street to the Tankerville Arms at that very moment.

Natalie entered the garage and within seconds her lips and body pressed hard against his, interrupting his thoughts. "Perhaps a tad preoccupied with work are we darling?"

Ballard shook his head in mild exasperation at her ever accurate perceptions. Taking his briefcase he followed her inside, the inviting aroma of an oven baked smoked ham frittata tantilising his taste buds.

Thirty minutes later, having tucked into a second helping, he pushed the plate to one side before taking her hands in his. Hesitation flickered across her features as she observed the expression on his face. "What is it Michael?"

He held a finger against her lips. "Ssh darling, nothing's wrong. A work issue has come up that impacts both of us." Twenty minutes later Natalie knew as much about the hit-man and the current circumstances as he did. Despite it being a high priority police case, her implication meant his conscious was clear in divulging the information.

As always, while aware of the ramifications of the latest development, she was intrigued by the nuts and bolts of surveillance work. Ballard decided to add levity to the situation by describing a past event in which a drug trafficker's house was bugged by a surveillance officer but the installation went spectacularly wrong.

"Nat imagine this. The drug dealer leaves his house and isn't expected home for at least three hours. The surveillance chap crawls into the roof cavity to set up the equipment which included a camera and audio. While he's up there the guy returns unexpectedly and the copper has to stay in the ceiling all night"

Natalie's eyes opened wide. "No way!"

"True story. Obviously a support team was nearby, but they held off while the crook remained unaware of his hidden guest. The poor copper had to prop in the roof for over twelve hours not going to the loo, plus make sure he didn't sneeze amongst the dust or fall asleep. Next morning when the house was empty he was able to climb back down."

"The drug guy never suspected?"

"Nup. Blabbed his criminal activities to all his friends in the house for the next week. Finished up getting ten years."

"That's amazing Michael. As public we don't have a clue how the police risk their lives every day to protect us..." Her voice drifted away as she sat shaking her head in reflection.

After washing the dishes they sat down to watch the 8 p.m. news, Ballard placing an arm around Natalie's shoulder, drawing her closer. Ten minutes into the broadcast Ballard's mobile rang, it was John.

"Can't settle at the end of the working week?" Ballard was up-beat.

John's voice was serious. "I'm about to extend *both* our working weeks Mike."

Ballard's brow knitted. "How come?"

"Our surveillance chap went in just after 1730. For some reason Williams left for the pub early. Once inside the officer did what he had to do, not a big job as they decided to install audio only. Before leaving he poked his head in one of the rooms and guess what he saw on a pin-board?"

He didn't wait for an answer. "Photos and newspaper cuttings of the factory murder, your gorge where Parnell met his maker and some additional cuttings of you being interviewed after the event." He drew breath. "Now for the clincher, there were a series of long distance snaps – obviously taken with a telescopic lens of Parnell's wife and daughter out and about in the street. Must have been taken before they hot footed it to Italy."

Ballard felt a cold trickle down his spine. Natalie immediately sensed the change in his demeanour, clutching his free hand.

John continued, his voice all business. "Delwyn and Tim, hell everyone involved here has no doubt this is the dude we're after. Tim's sending in the SOGs as soon as the prick gets back from the pub – hopefully if he's got a skin-full it'll slow him down. Enquiries regarding previous pub visits indicate he'll be back around 2300, give or take half an hour."

His voice became conspiratorial. "I've been asked to sit off this guy's place until the SOGs take him down, then I'm to formally arrest him. I was supposed to bring one of the Serious Crime Task Force boys with me but... ah stuff-it, I figured what you've gone through over the past couple of weeks credits you with *some* latitude. I've drawn a car – want to tag along?"

Ballard didn't hesitate. "I'm in. Do you want me to swing by the office?"

"Nah. I'm about to head off, I'll toot outside Natalie's. See you in ten."

Although Natalie had pieced together most of what John had said, she still engaged Ballard in five minutes of rapid fire questioning. He explained that he and John wouldn't be in harm's way and would only perform the formal arrest after the SOG officers had the hit-man in custody. He gave her a reassuring hug.

She looked up at him. "Remember Michael, we have our wedding to attend and I want photographs with you at your handsome best."

He held up his left hand sporting the guard. "Even if I wanted to *and I don't,* I couldn't do anything. No, this time I'm just an observer – so is John for that matter." A car horn released him from further cross examination. Stepping outside with his arm encircling her waist, he kissed her goodbye before settling into the passenger seat.

Natalie leaned down and addressed John through the open window. "Take good care of him John and don't be heroes, either of you." Both men threw quick salutes.

Natalie had the final word. *"Please... I mean it!"*

CHAPTER
41

Thirty minutes later John parked the police car in a side street near the intersection with Nicholson, the vehicle positioned to allow William's terrace house on the opposite side of the road to be observed through the windscreen. The Tankerville Arms, also on the far side was a further four hundred metres towards the city. Dusk was setting and the street lights were becoming more prominent by the minute. The flow of vehicles in both directions was constant.

John anchored his elbows on the steering wheel as he scanned the terrace house with his binoculars. "No lights on." He glanced at his watch. "Nine-thirty. We'll be celebrating another birthday before this bastard gets back."

Ballard shuffled into a more comfortable position. "Whatever it takes old son." He leaned over to check the police radio. "Channel 22?" John nodded.

Both men sat in silence, willing time to fast-forward.

"How many stake-outs have we been involved in over the years?" John shook his head, not expecting an answer.

Ballard responded anyway. "More than I care to remember and they've all been bloody boring. Come to think of it, you've been the common denominator in most of them." John grunted, a half smile on his face.

Ballard massaged his temple with his right hand before asking, "What details has Tim given you about the raid?" He gestured for the binoculars.

"Not a lot. As soon as Williams gets back they'll wait for him to settle then go in. That way they can isolate any action from the street. The neighbours three houses either side have been evacuated."

"What about the rear?"

John nodded. "Bluestone lane, originally used for collecting household poo in the horse and cart days." He wrinkled his nose. "Can you imagine coming home and your wife asking, 'how many pans did you collect today dear? No accidents?'" He grinned at his own joke. "Thank Christ for modern sanitation." He grimaced at the mental image, then dragged himself back to the present. "The SOG will take up position some time earlier I should imagine to cover off the rear."

"Was the option raised to have our guys planted in the house to nab him when he comes in the front door?"

"Yeah, Tim floated it as a possibility but it was ruled out. Getting four or five SOG boys fully kitted up inside without being spotted by neighbours or a friend who might tip Williams off down at the pub was considered too risky. Hell, getting an *undercover* surveillance guy in there in broad daylight was a gamble in itself."

Ballard swept the binoculars along the street either side of the terrace house. "Good call. I guess Tim doesn't have any option other than to lob out the front with the van and pile the SOG lads out from there." He looked worried. "I've never liked raids in highly populated areas, but I can't think of any alternative."

"No sweat Mike, hell the manpower odds are stacked in our favour, try fifteen to one, not to mention we have the element of surprise. The end result's a foregone, trust me."

Despite John's confidence, Ballard's concerned look remained as he scanned the terrace house for the twentieth time. He noted the low wrought iron front fence and the narrow verandas on the ground and first floors. The upper veranda was accessible via two French doors leading from what was most likely a bedroom; iron lacework adorned the veranda posts which where spanned by wooden balustrades.

For the next hour they swapped stories along with the binoculars, the tension mounting as they sensed the time for the raid was fast approaching. Radio traffic was minimal other than Tim issuing limited instructions to his crew. At 11.15 John stiffened behind the wheel, the binoculars pressed hard against his eyes.

"*That's him*... Yep, Mike, that's him walking up the street!"

Tim's radio transmission to his men confirmed John's sighting.

Ballard snatched the binoculars from his partner, scanning the street to the right. "Bingo. Thank Christ he's on his own. That would've stuffed up Tim's operation."

Both men continued to watch Williams saunter along the street without a care in the world. John snorted. "The prick wouldn't be so cocky if he knew the shit that was about to drop on him." He hesitated before adding. "Jeez, look at the shoulders on the bastard. Even without binoculars I can see he's massive."

Williams walked up to his front gate, stopping as he reached into his trouser pocket. John wrestled back the binoculars, commencing a running commentary. "Keys out. Porch sensor light on. Opening the front door... hallway light on..." He hesitated. "Ok. He's inside. Now we wait."

Ballard looked to his left. "Not for long. The cavalry's just about to arrive."

John swung the binoculars. "You're right. The SOG van's mounting the footpath ... *damn!*"

"What?"

"The upstairs light's gone on. That means he'll have time to grab a weapon before our guys can bust in and get up there."

At least six officers disgorged from the van. With well rehearsed precision they used the handheld ram to break open the front door with one blow; an identical action was undoubtedly occurring at the rear. Officers poured inside while two remained on the footpath.

Ballard and John knew from experience there would be shouted commands for Williams to 'Get down! Get down!' Ballard made to snatch the binoculars but John resisted. "Can't see anything. They *must* have him by now – *Jesus Christ!*"

He stiffened in his seat as the French doors on the first floor burst open. Williams and a SOG officer tumbled onto the veranda, locked in mortal combat. Glass fragments sparkled in the street lights as they cascaded down into the front yard.

Both men slammed against the balustrade. Wood splintered as the railing gave way. They rolled off the veranda, dropping onto the garden beds below; Williams landing on top of the officer.

To Ballard and John's horror Williams struggled to his feet, the crook of his left arm encircling the SOG officer's throat. In his right hand he clutched a handgun, the barrel jammed hard against the policeman's head.

John groaned as though in pain. "This is turning to shit Mike!"

Ballard gripped his arm. "Tim will keep a cool head – hang in there John."

The two SOG officers in the street maintained their position, their rifles levelled at Williams. Tim appeared in the doorway. John's commentary resumed. "Tim's trying to calm things down. Bloody hell Williams is a big bastard. The poor copper he's throttling is out on his feet. No wonder with the prick lobbing on top of him."

Ballard finally wrestled the binoculars from John. "Williams is forcing the SOG guy onto the footpath – *no, he's dragging him into the street.*"

Cars began to brake violently with several failing to stop in time. The sound of multiple impacts could be heard despite the distance. A traffic jam of city bound cars resulted, growing with every second.

"He's going to hijack a car!" Ballard spat the words.

The prediction proved true. Williams dragged the officer up to the driver's door of a white Toyota. Ballard swung the binoculars. "Female driver – young – mid twenties, sole occupant. He's threatening her… she's climbing into the passenger seat."

Two shots rang out in quick succession. John grabbed the binoculars back, scanning furiously. "Can't see anyone hit. That'll be Williams warning everyone he means business."

With one massive shove the SOG officer was sent sprawling across the tram tracks. Williams squeezed behind the wheel while aiming the handgun at the driver's head.

John's knuckles whitened as he gripped the binoculars, attempting to make sense of what was happening. "She's paralysed with fear, couldn't get out of the car if she tried. Jesus Mike, this is bad – Christ knows what Tim can do. He can't shoot Williams, too risky, it's… it's bloody chaos over there."

Without warning the Toyota lurched forward, swinging hard right across the tram tracks in a screeching U turn. Traffic outbound from the city braked savagely. Cars crashing into each other as the Toyota accelerated along Nicholson Street, passing within metres of where Ballard and John were parked.

John fired the motor, slamming the police car into gear.

Ballard snatched the radio mike. "Tim, Mike here. We have the vehicle in sight." He looked across at John as he spoke. "We'll keep a safe distance and give location updates so you can scramble response units."

Tim's reply was calm and measured. "Received. Try not to be spotted. "

John accelerated along Nicholson Street to ensure he didn't lose the Toyota. Crossing over Johnston Street the traffic lights remained green and both vehicles sped through. Approaching the Alexandra Parade intersection the Toyota swung onto the tram tracks to avoid the stationary cars. Turning right it accelerated hard; John did the same, maintaining a safe distance. Ballard relayed the change in direction over the radio.

At the Brunswick Street intersection the Toyota once again passed to the right of the cars waiting for a green light, speeding recklessly onto Queens Parade. John followed, weaving between irate drivers crossing in front of him, some of them tooting furiously, all mouthing obscenities. He struggled to keep the Toyota in sight.

Ballard peered through the windscreen. "Is he onto us?"

"I don't think so. The stupid bastard just may think he's getting away."

No sooner had John uttered the words than the Toyota's brake lights flashed hard-on, the car skidding to the side of the road. Seconds later the young girl tumbled from the vehicle, scrambling towards the footpath. The Toyota's brake lights extinguished as it accelerated forward.

"Shit, I hope she's ok." John's words were heavy with concern. The girl tripped on the gutter in her haste to escape, somehow remaining upright. "Thank Christ. Do we stop?"

Ballard considered the options. "No! Keep after him. I'll radio the girl's position to Tim"

John's stabbed the accelerator to the floor. "Let's sort this prick out."

The Toyota was only fifty metres ahead with John approaching fast. Ballard glanced at his partner, knowing what he was about to do.

John called out. "Watch out for the airbags."

The impact as John rear ended the Toyota jolted both men hard against their seatbelts. Somehow the airbags didn't deploy. At the same time a shot rang out, the Toyota's rear window shattering.

"*The bastard's shooting at us.*" John's voice was thick with anger. He swung the police car to the right, accelerating alongside the Toyota before skillfully nudging the vehicle's right rear quarter panel. The Toyota skidded hard across the tram tracks, launching itself up and over the yellow concrete safety barrier.

Cork screwing through the air the car crashed heavily onto its roof before skidding into the path of a city bound tram. Striking the rear of the Toyota the tram screeched to a halt, passengers lurching forward while others fell off their seats, disappearing from view. The Toyota spun several times on its roof before coming to rest.

Petrol began pouring onto the road. "Jesus Mike, that's all we need, our crook being toasted in front of dozens of witnesses." Wrenching the police car onto the tram tracks, both men bolted back, ripping open the driver's door.

Grabbing an arm each they pulled Williams from the car, part carrying, part dragging him away from the vehicle, shouting at bystanders to get back.

Without warning Williams yanked an arm free and spun around, throwing a savage punch at Ballard who ducked deftly. John stepped forward, kneeing him brutally in the groin. Williams slumped to the ground, writhing in agony.

"Ungrateful shithead!" John's face distorted into a snarl.

Spontaneous applause erupted from the crowd, along with cries of "Good on ya mate." John snapped a handcuff onto William's left wrist, fastening the other cuff to the tram stop's metal safety rail.

Ballard clapped his partner on the shoulder. "Good to see you haven't lost any of your subtlety John."

Williams continued to moan, doubled over in pain. John grinned from ear to ear. "He won't forget today in a – *shit!*"

Both men dropped instinctively into a crouch as a muffled explosion and a hot blast of scorched air struck their faces, a consequence of the Toyota's petrol tank exploding. The crowd that had gathered scrambled backwards, some falling over each other in their haste. Even Williams halted his protest, gaping as the flames shot into the night sky while black, acrid smoke billowing from the smouldering wreck.

Ballard headed for the police car, calling over his shoulder. "I'll radio Tim while you check our spectators to make sure no one's injured."

"On it." John rechecked Williams' handcuffs before jogging over to the crowd who were gawking at the action unfolding before them.

Ballard opened the police vehicle's passenger door, reaching inside for the mike. Propping an elbow against the roof he stared along the tram tracks as he requested ambulance and fire brigade assistance. He then gave Tim a concise version of what had taken place with Williams.

"Tim, we'll need police units to manage the traffic here, it's bloody pandemonium. There's going to be nose to tails all over the place with motorists goofing off as they drive past. Also we need towing services to get the girl's car off the tracks once the firies put it out."

Signing off he approached the tram that had pulled up behind him, flashing his identification as he informed the startled driver of the circumstances. Looking back he saw John doing the same for the tram drivers who had stopped their vehicles on the far side of the crash site.

Within minutes two divisional vans arrived, lights flashing, positioning themselves strategically before the officers tumbled out to apply order to the traffic chaos.

Out of nowhere Tim appeared with a number of SOG officers. To Ballard's amusement two officers handcuffed William's hands behind his back before releasing the handcuff attached to the safety rail. They led him over to one of the divisional vans, both officers climbing in the back with him. Ballard gave Tim a wry smile. "Good move to play it safe. The bastard's as strong as an ox."

Tim didn't look happy. "Tell me about it. That's what caused all this shit in the first place. We had him on his knees in the bedroom upstairs, then when we went to handcuff him he hooked his arm around one of my guy's legs and dropped him on his backside… *while still kneeling.*"

Tim shook his head, struggling to comprehend Williams' strength. "From nowhere the bastard pulls out an automatic. My man jumps him and within seconds they're through the doors and over the balcony."

The honk of a fire truck caused both men to turn. They watched as it weaved through the traffic before positioning near the Toyota that was now a blackened ruin. Several firemen smothered the car with foam before approaching a uniform officer to advise him there was no risk of the vehicle reigniting.

Tim pointed towards John who was in deep discussion with a group of bystanders. "Jesus! Is he doing what I *think* he's doing?"

Ballard peered hard, not able to believe his eyes. "Bloody hell… yep, he is, *he's signing autographs.*" Ballard gave a shrill whistle and gestured abruptly at John who left his fans and strolled back to the police car.

A sheepish grin stretched across his face. "Thought I'd foster a little PR while I was at it… can't hurt."

Ballard pointed to a television van that had pulled up on the far side of the road. A cameraman was clambering up the ladder at the rear of the vehicle to raise himself above the crowd, his shoulder camera pointing their way. "I think Delwyn may have something to say about that if she spots you on TV handing out signatures."

John grimaced, muttering as much to himself as Ballard. "She's going to be pissed with all this isn't she?" Everyone nodded.

Two tow trucks arrived, one maneuvered onto the tracks, backing up to what remained of the Toyota. John scratched his head. "Jesus, the lady who owns that thing isn't going to be happy. Thank Christ she didn't have a kid in the back." All three detectives contemplated how the situation could have been tragically worse.

For the next ten minutes Tim coordinated his men before

returning. "This is going to hit the media big time, it's not every day you have a Lethal Weapon chase on the streets of Melbourne." He shrugged. "ESD's going to be involved, but as you didn't fire any shots it shouldn't be more than a formality. Major Collision will also want in. Despite that there's no point in you guys hanging around, I'll sort the squads out when they arrive. We can tackle the interviews and paperwork in the morning. I'll oversee here then head back to the office as soon as I'm done." He held out a hand. "Thanks again. You saved us all from what could have been a very embarrassing situation." He looked directly at John. "Perhaps a little spectacular mate, but effective nonetheless."

John uttered a moan not dissimilar to Williams when he was writhing in pain. "God, can you imagine the explaining we'll have to do when we see Delwyn?"

Ballard put an arm around his shoulders as he led him towards the police car, winking back at Tim as he said, "Don't worry, I'll tell her it was my idea."

"Yeah, as if she's going to believe that."

John leaned down to inspect the damage to the front quarter panel, declaring the car safe to drive. With care and assisted by police officers halting the traffic, he eased the vehicle off the tram tracks and headed for Punt Road.

Pulling into Natalie's driveway Ballard checked out his partner. "Are you ok to drive home? You're welcome to crash here."

John shook his head. "No thanks, the drive home will clear my head." He turned suddenly to face Ballard. "*Jeez we had some fun tonight didn't we? No wonder we love our job. We're sure going to miss it!*"

Ballard new exactly what he meant. "It's still not our time

John... well not yet anyway."

The front lights of the town house lit up and Natalie appeared in her dressing gown. She rushed over to the passenger window. "Are you both ok?" She pointed to the damage on the car.

John looked sheepish. "Everything's fine Natalie. I ran into a rubbish bin."

"Don't give me that! I saw you both on TV with WW3 erupting around you."

Ballard got out and hugged her. "All in a day's work Nat."

She leaned down to speak to John. "Do you want to stay here the night? It's no trouble."

John thanked her but shook his head. Ballard and Natalie stood with their arms around each other as John reversed the car out, waving briefly as he drove off.

For the next hour Ballard explained in detail what had happened. Natalie sat alongside him, rubbing his arm and shoulder to reassure herself he was physically unharmed. "You and John live for these moments don't you?"

Ballard opened his mouth to challenge the statement but thought better of it. "I can't deny we've had our excitement over the years. Just before you came outside John commented that leaving the job would be tough for both of us."

Natalie nodded; without expressing her thoughts she sat contemplating the prospect of Ballard no longer employed in a job that was a major part of his life. She decided that problem would require many conversations and considerable understanding on her part, but thankfully, not just yet.

After a hot drink and some chocolate biscuits, Ballard headed upstairs for a quick shower. Ten minutes later he was snuggled up against Natalie's warm back, feeling his adrenalin rush subsiding. In no time he dropped off to sleep without a care in the world.

CHAPTER
42

Ballard drove into his parking bay at 7.30 a.m. the next morning. As he activated the alarm he saw John approaching. "Well if it isn't the action hero. How did you sleep?"

"Actually I went over to Sonia's and she grilled me for what seemed like hours."

"Yeah, same thing with Natalie."

"I guess not being there makes it hard for them... they worry about us."

"Nice feeling isn't it?"

"You bet."

Ballard stared at his partner. "So you just happened to be in the car park when I arrived?"

John pretended to look puzzled. "I don't follow."

"It wouldn't have anything to do with you not wanting to brief Delwyn on your own in case she chews your ear off?"

"Who me?"

"Yes you who runs towards danger but goes to water when a strong woman takes you to task." An exaggerated shrug was John's response.

Stepping onto the floor they received a rock star reception with everyone wanting an account of the events.

"Michael! John! In my office, *now!*" Everyone spun around to see Delwyn standing commandingly outside her door, hands on hips.

Walking towards her John muttered from the corner of his mouth. "*Now* do you see why I waited for you?"

Once inside Delwyn slammed the door before twisting the slimline blinds shut. Turning towards them she smiled, following it with a wink. "Was that bossy enough?"

John's mouth dropped open and Ballard threw back his head, laughing out loud. "Well it certainly got everyone's attention, so yes I'd say it was."

Delwyn perched on the edge of her desk. "I'm never going to change the antics of you two, but I *do* need to keep my other detectives observing *some* basic rules." Both men looked at each other, not sure how to respond.

"That was meant to be rhetorical gents. Now, considering the chaos you caused last night there's a degree of fallout, but as I explained to the Deputy, you did save a young girl from who-knows-what fate, not to mention catch a crook that needed to be taken off the streets." She ran her fingers through her steel grey hair.

"Ethical Standards wants a quick chat but they've already told me it's a formality." Addressing Ballard she appeared frustrated. "Tell me Mike, what *do* I have to do to get you to stay on sick leave? If something had happened to you at the arrest I'd have copped it in the neck for having a detective on active duty who should have been recuperating."

Ballard looked serious. "I take your point Delwyn. I promise I'll put in my reports then I'm out of here… I need to because

I still have a lot to do at the farm before the BBQ on Sunday."

Delwyn's voice dripped with sarcasm. "Silly me. Here I was hoping you'd go on sick leave because you actually needed to mend your mind and body – what was I thinking?"

Everyone grinned, although in John's case hesitantly, still unable to fathom when Delwyn was and wasn't being serious. Both men stood and Delwyn gave them a brief hug. "Thank God you're both ok. Stay that way."

Opening her door she raised her voice, ensuring she was heard throughout the floor. "And let that be a lesson you can't go around terrorising the public – *do you understand?*" Both men joined in the charade, looking suitably chastised as they left her office, Delwyn slamming the door behind them.

Three hours later, reports completed and after a brief discussion with Ethical Standards, Ballard began his rounds of the office, promising that once he got to the farm he *would* remain on sick leave.

CHAPTER
43

Friday arrived along with the BBQ furniture. Ballard drove the Chrysler out of the garage and parked it on the concrete apron, ensuring its cover was in place to shield the paintwork from the sun. He chuckled to himself knowing what Natalie's first comment would be when she arrived that evening with the children.

He enjoyed having Kayla and Josh stay as they regarded the farm more like a resort, albeit minus a pool, a fact they often reminded him of. At any point in time they could be in the gym, the sauna or outside playing basketball, tennis or squash; while at the farm they forgot they were city kids and immersed themselves in country life.

Ballard swept the garage and began setting up the tables and chairs, followed by the serving bench. Over each of the tables he spread a blue cloth. A smaller table was positioned to one side for the tea, coffee and assorted accoutrements. Polystyrene boxes to hold ice for the drinks were positioned along the walls, together with plastic lined bins for empty bottles and rubbish. After that he set out the glasses on each table, checking they were clean and chip free.

He stood back and felt pleasure as the room took on the look and feel of a party, complemented by the double brick interior to give guests a warm inviting feeling. Tools and other items normally found in garages were locked in the adjacent store room, leaving the area free of clutter. He thanked his foresight in building the garage two metres wider than the standard, thereby accommodating up to forty guests with ease.

His final task was to position tennis racquets, basket balls, croquet and lawn bowls in the corner of the veranda for those guests who were sports inclined. In addition, he placed twenty golf balls in a plastic bucket alongside several golf irons and clubs, plus a golf mat for enthusiasts who may wish to try their hand at the golf net located amongst the trees to the side of the house.

Just after 7 p.m. Natalie parked her car alongside the Chrysler and Josh and Kayla tumbled out to greet Ballard. Taking their bags they headed inside, knowing from previous visits which bedrooms were theirs.

Natalie kissed Ballard and commented on how splendid the garage looked. "I hope you've taken photos. It looks amazing. Why didn't you wait, I could have helped?"

His eyebrows rose. "I distinctly remember you saying some days back that you'd be slaving away at work while I luxuriated up here in the country."

She smiled, inclining her head to one side. "I do remember saying words to that effect... but that was ages ago." She chuckled as she began collecting desserts she had prepared from the boot of her car. Ballard helped carry them inside.

He reflected on her not making mention of the car cover, thinking perhaps she was beginning to accept his more idiosyncratic ways.

For the remainder of the evening, other than during dinner, Josh and Kayla could be heard but only occasionally seen as they rushed between the sports room and the squash court. Natalie and Ballard sat on a veranda seat chatting about her work, their children, Kathryn's operation and the expected guests for the BBQ.

By 10.30 p.m. everyone was in bed with the silence of the farm wrapping them in a secure cocoon of peace, order and tranquility.

The next morning the remaining chores were tackled and by mid afternoon everything was complete. Ballard checked the on-line weather forecast and was pleased to see it would be sunny and mild, with a south westerly breeze. "Just what the doctor ordered," he commented to no-one in particular.

As a treat he piled everyone into the Chrysler and drove them to Sunbury for a movie, followed by dinner. Returning home everyone agreed to be up by 7 a.m. Ballard stated he would buy the ice for the drinks in the morning while Natalie and the children sorted nibbles for the tables. With the plan agreed upon they went to bed, satisfied all was in readiness.

Bronwyn, the caterer's Maitre d', arrived Sunday morning just before 11. Everyone helped carry the precooked lamb and beef into the kitchen, along with the salads, baked jacket potatoes, plus an assortment of steamed green vegetables and dinner rolls.

Ballard's mouth watered. "Bronwyn, just before you got here we took a vote and decided to cancel the BBQ and just pig out ourselves for the next week or so."

She glanced at him, uncertain as to whether he was joking.

Natalie stepped in. "Ignore him Bronwyn. Is there anything else we can do to help?"

"No thanks Natalie, carrying in the food was all that I needed. You've no idea how many places just let me lug everything in on my own."

Ballard thanked her. "We'll be outside with the guests, call us if you want anything. Josh and Kayla will help you take the food out when you're ready." Everyone shuffled outside and sat on the veranda seats waiting for the first arrivals.

The guests knew to park their cars on the nature strip at the top of the driveway as Ballard had included this request in their invitation.

Kayla called out, "There's Emma and Tricia." She ran with Josh to greet them and as the four approached, Tricia waved at her mother and Ballard.

"Hello Mum, hi Michael, I've bought a lemon slice for later."

Emma, not to be outdone said, "Greetings Michael, I've brought myself." She smirked. "Just joking, I've some wine here… a red and a white." Ballard gave them both a kiss.

Tricia, looking somewhat guilty confessed, "I really haven't been avoiding you Michael, it's just that after I got back from South Australia every time I visited Mum you were up here at the farm."

Ballard put his arm around her shoulder. "You're forgiven." Turning to Emma he said, "So what's your excuse?"

"I've taken on a second job to save up for my overseas trip."

"Another one?"

Emma held her palms uppermost, mimicking a set of scales. "So you can see my dilemma." She raised and lowered each hand in turn. "Visit Mum… work to save money… visit Mum… save more money… guess what I decided?"

Ballard's eyebrows rose. "Passports up to date?" Everyone laughed. Both girls took their gifts inside as guests began to arrive in numbers.

Among the first were several Special Operations members who had attended at the gorge on the day. They were led down the driveway by Tim Robbins. Ballard smiled to himself as he observed how rank still reigned supreme, even when the police officers were off duty. Tim held out his hand. "Good to see you Michael, especially under more pleasant circumstances." Ballard introduced Natalie and her children and after handshakes all round the men stepped into the garage to put their drinks on ice.

The next to arrive was Kathryn and two of her girlfriends. Everyone hugged before Ballard took her aside. "Sis, I'm proud of you. Stay as long as you feel comfortable. We'll understand."

"I can't believe it – I'm fine. The psychologist was right. With my friends and the guests, this really is the best way to beat this thing. I know I'll be strong."

"I've no doubt. Go knock 'em dead." Ballard mentally kicked himself for his poor choice of words.

From then on introductions became chaotic. Delwyn arrived at the same time as John and Sonia. As this was Delwyn's first visit, Natalie took her aside and offered a private tour of the house; Delwyn accepted enthusiastically. John appeared sheepish, self conscious that Sonia looked so young and stunning. He escorted her inside.

Bronwyn came up to Ballard, whispering that she was ready to take the food from the kitchen to the serving table. All four children volunteered and Ballard thanked them as he continued frenetic introductions, including a number of neighbours, one being someone he thought wouldn't attend.

As he was drawing breath, a heavy hand clapped him on the back and looking around he saw his neighbour, Alan Dempsy and his wife Helen. Ballard shook Alan's hand then kissed Helen. "Many thanks for keeping the place under control and overseeing the repairs, all completed to perfection." Alan flashed a satisfied grin.

Out of the corner of his eye, Ballard saw a car heading down the driveway, it was Natalie's parents, Robert and Barbara arriving in their Bentley. They were the only guests afforded the privilege of parking under the shade of the pergola and Ballard had no qualms making the concession, given the cost of their vehicle. He drooled at the sleek black lines and admitted to himself this was the one car he would gladly swap the Chrysler for. He shook Robert's hand and kissed Barbara before they were whisked away by Natalie.

Susan and her partner Will arrived just ahead of Bobby and his wife Sharon; Ken and his wife Kathy followed minutes later. As they had all been to the farm before they knew the routine and went into the garage to mingle. A number of guests asked for a tour of the house so Josh and Kayla did the honours. One of the last guests to arrive was Peter Donaldson, an old work colleague of Ballard's and someone who had been in his squad at the Academy all those years ago. He was now a superintendent and Officer In Charge of the Serious Crime Task Force, or as he secretly preferred to call them, the 'Armed Robbers'; like Ballard and John he was 'old school'.

By 12.30 the guests were mingling in the garage and Ballard encouraged everyone to take a plate and line up for the food which Bronwyn served with flair as their personal requests came flooding in. The noise generated indicated no one was short on conversation or laughter, their enjoyment echoing throughout the garage.

Ballard sought out Peter and they had a five minute conversation down memory lane. Peter confirmed retirement was a mental battle he too was grappling with and like Ballard, he knew it was a double-edged sword. Ballard refrained from mentioning that Peter's detectives would have conducted interviews on Bivelaqua's hit-man, deciding it was a social event after all.

Mingling, Ballard attempted to spend time with everyone and after two hours, often crossing over with Natalie who was doing the same, he was satisfied he had achieved everything expected of a host.

After lunch everyone gravitated to those areas of the house and grounds that suited their personality. Bobby proved popular on the tennis court, teaching anyone who cared to join in the finer points of forehand volleys. Ken entertained a larger group with his knowledge of lawn bowls and croquet while John gave free golf lessons at the driving net. Emma and Tricia enchanted two of the SOG members who were attentive to their every word. Kathryn had Tim Robbins paying her his undivided attention, while Josh and Kayla continued to conduct endless tours throughout the house and grounds.

Ballard took Natalie aside, whispering in her ear, "At this rate we could sneak off and no one would even notice."

"We could, but let's have dessert first." They began calling the guests back to the garage and Bronwyn commenced serving the assortment of sweets which included pavlovas, cheesecake, apple pie and ice cream. As these were devoured, tea and coffee was served and the conversations grew steadily louder.

Suddenly two mobile phones rang out, followed by a third. The crowd roared light-hearted disapproval. Embarrassed, Delwyn, John and Tim rose from their tables and headed for the veranda.

Minutes later John reappeared looking ashen. He gestured for Ballard to join him. Once outside, Ballard placed a hand on his shoulder. "What is it John? You look like you've seen a ghost."

Delwyn and Tim approached looking equally distressed as John replied, "The shit's really hit the fan Mike. Just over two hours ago Note Printing Australia in Craigieburn was knocked over by a bunch of crooks armed with automatic weapons, more than a hundred million ripped-off. One of the guards is dead and there's an unconfirmed report that the two choppers involved in the robbery have crashed near King Lake, one of the pilots riddled with bullets and burnt beyond recognition."

"Christ!" Ballard's legs weakened as he slumped onto the veranda seat. "Any coppers hurt?"

"Shot at but no-one hit..."

At the same moment Natalie appeared, her worried expression deepening as she approached the group.

"Michael, what's wrong?"

He looked up, his features grim.

"There's a gang of cold-blooded killers out there we need to hunt down... starting now."

Acknowledgements

Four key characters in this novel are based heavily on work colleagues who I have the utmost respect for and whose friendship I value highly. For Ken Sproat, Bobby Dzodzadinov and Susan Dodd I have taken the liberty of using their christian names in the book. Due to the fact that Glenys Reid is a 'force to be reckoned with', I whimped out and invented Delwyn Peters instead, however, I ensured the character of her pseudonym was every bit as fiesty as the lady herself. All four characters will feature in subsequent books.

Natalie for obvious reasons, figures prominently in this book and I had to look no further than my wife Leanne to find the inspiration not only for Natalie's physical attributes, but those of her character as well. As an added bonus, Leanne has proven to be absolutely vital as my unofficial editor and without her insightful suggestions, this book would be a poor version of what it is today. It should also be noted that Natalie's four children are based on Leanne's and they will play even larger roles in future books.

Another central character is John, who is loosely based on someone I worked with when I was a policeman patrolling the streets of St Kilda many decades ago. You know who you are John, so thank you for taking me under your wing way back then when I was just a raw recruit.

Peter Donelly, a former boss of mine, who read 'Payback' in one of its very early drafts, made the understated comment that the manuscript required 'a very heavy edit'. This was his subtle but thoroughly accurate assessment that it was a long way from being in a publishable state. He then referred me to a text that looked at writing from a holistic perspective and which gave me valuable insight into the craft of writing. I am resigned to the fact that I will need to continually hone my skills regarding this craft, but I am getting there Pete. Unknown to him, he will feature heavily in subsequent novels in a senior role that I am certain he will enjoy.

One of the first readers of this manuscript was Andrew Grimes, himself an author, who told me to 'tighten up the text and get rid of all those 'ly' words'. Now, whenever I write an 'ly' word, I feel as guilty as though I had just robbed a bank... but I do keep them to a minimum. Thank you Andrew.

Dillys, a friend who I often meet on the train when I'm travelling between Melbourne and Gisborne, also provided valuable input, she is a very sophisticated lady who knows her grammar. Nearly all her suggestions were included and although she doesn't know it yet, I will be employing her talents to review book number two and three and...

One of Leanne's closest school friends is Diane Howden, an avid reader who Leanne holds in high regard as 'extremely intelligent'. Not to let an opportunity pass me by, I provided

Diane with a draft of the manuscript and true to Leanne's word, Diane took an axe to the text, but for the better. Again I will be employing her skills and advice for future manuscripts.

My son's father-in-law, Don Wyer (who looks and sounds like Sean Connery and hails from the mother country) heavily edited the manuscript and in the nicest possible way suggested my dialogue was stilted and didn't ring true. I feel that is an area I still need to work on, but his suggestions at least helped me on my journey towards creating realistic dialogue that enters the reader's consciousness effortlessly. He also told me in no uncertain manner that the cricket term 'The Ashes', DID NOT originate at Rupertswood, so I quickly got my facts straight before I continued with the manuscript.

Last and by no means least, I must thank my agent Mark Zocchi and his wife Julie (who happens to be my editor), for reading my underdone manuscript, but believing it could be bashed into shape with a lot of work. Without their show of faith, I would be just another writer wondering when my big break into the world of fiction would arrive. I would also like to thank their 'typesetter extraordinaire' Wanissa Somsuphanqsri who went above and beyond in allowing me to make last minute edits, despite the typesetting having been locked down and signed off.

Looking back on all this I am beginning to wonder who DID write this book; but all I know is, it wouldn't have come to fruition without everyone's valued contribution.

Finally, a big thank you to you the reader, whoever you are, for choosing this book and emersing yourself in a world that most people thankfully never have to experience.

'PAYBACK'
WHEN DUTY CALLS

Harvey Cleggett

ISBN 9781922175250   Qty

RRP   AU$24.99   .....

Postage within Australia   AU$5.00   .....

TOTAL★ $_____

★ All prices include GST

Name:..

Address: ....

....

Phone:..

Email: ....

Payment: ❑ Money Order ❑ Cheque ❑ MasterCard ❑Visa

Cardholders Name:...

Credit Card Number: ....

Signature:...

Expiry Date: ....

Allow 7 days for delivery.

Payment to: Marzocco Consultancy (ABN 14 067 257 390)
PO Box 12544
A'Beckett Street, Melbourne, 8006
Victoria, Australia
admin@brolgapublishing.com.au

Be Published

Publish through a successful publisher.
Brolga Publishing is represented through:
• **National** book trade distribution, including sales,
marketing & distribution through **Macmillan Australia.**
• **International** book trade distribution to
    • The United Kingdom
    • North America
    • Sales representation in South East Asia
• **Worldwide e-Book distribution**

For details and inquiries, contact:
Brolga Publishing Pty Ltd
PO Box 12544
A'Beckett St VIC 8006

Phone: 0414 608 494
admin@brolgapublishing.com.au
markzocchi@brolgapublishing.com.au
ABN: 46 063 962 443
(Email for a catalogue request)